INTO THE DARK DIMENSION

Doctor Strange dropped back down to the ground, barely managing to stay on his feet – just as Spider-Man stepped up before him. T'Challa and Okoye stood behind him, their eyes glowing green.

"Like the lady said," Spider-Man said, "Dormammu wants a word."

"Dormammu," Strange hissed, "deserves so much more than words."

He watched in dread as his attackers fanned out before him, preparing to strike. The Black Panther, fierce and unyielding. Spider-Man, his blank eye-lenses eerie, unblinking. And Okoye, who now held a spear clasped firmly in her hand – face twisted in rage, the tattoo on her scalp marred by bruises and chemical burns.

All powerful, all fearsome. And all completely, persistently, under Dormammu's spell.

I underestimated him, Strange thought. His grip on this world, this universe, is just too strong. Even a Sorcerer Supreme, like myself, is no match for that.

MARVEL CRISIS PROTOCOL

Target: Kree by Stuart Moore
Shadow Avengers by Carrie Harris

MARVEL
CRISIS PROTOCOL

INTO THE DARK DIMENSION

STUART MOORE

ACONYTE

FOR MARVEL PUBLISHING

VP Production & Special Projects: Jeff Youngquist
Associate Editor, Special Projects: Sarah Singer
Manager, Licensed Publishing: Jeremy West
VP, Licensed Publishing: Sven Larsen
SVP Print, Sales & Marketing: David Gabriel
Editor in Chief: C B Cebulski

MARVEL

© 2023 MARVEL

First published by Aconyte Books in 2023
ISBN 978 1 83908 197 2
Ebook ISBN 978 1 83908 198 9

Distributed in North America by Simon & Schuster Inc, New York, USA
Printed in the United States of America
9 8 7 6 5 4 3 2 1

ACONYTE BOOKS

An imprint of Asmodee Entertainment Ltd
Mercury House, Shipstones Business Centre
North Gate, Nottingham NG7 7FN, UK
aconytebooks.com // twitter.com/aconytebooks

*This one's for Stan, and hell, the rest of you
Earth-humans too. As he used to say,
it just isn't a party without you.*

PROLOGUE

GOTTA GET A MESSAGE TO YOU

"Is he in there?" Peter Quill asked. "I can't tell."

Quill, the outlaw hero called Star-Lord, pressed his face against the thick glass, peering into the darkened tank. Black liquid swirled and bubbled before his eyes. He frowned, backed away, and scratched his head with the barrel of his element gun.

"I don't know," Gamora replied. "It's the same thing here."

Quill turned to look. Gamora, the deadliest woman in the galaxy, stood a few feet away, across the weathered stone floor of the large open chamber. She tapped her sword against a human-sized tube, one of a hundred or more stacked up in six horizontal rows along the wall of the arena-sized room. Like the large tank looming before Quill, the smaller tubes were filled with a black, utterly opaque substance. High-tech machinery lined the base of the tubes, in contrast to the ancient gray stone of the floor and walls.

"Rocket?" Quill turned toward a freestanding comm-unications array in the center of the room. "How's it comin', buddy?"

"Slow," the raccoonoid grumbled. His nimble fingers unhooked an access plate from the array, and he crouched down to peer into a mass of exposed circuitry.

Gamora took a step toward him. "I thought you said this was an unshielded Omni-Wave communicator," she said.

"Unshielded, yeah – the only one in the city without a flarkin' force field around it. But it's still got some firewalls I gotta get–" A shower of sparks burst forth from the comm panel. "Oww!"

Quill grimaced, shaking his head. Like most of the Guardians' plans, this one was going south in a hurry. It had *seemed* like a good idea to sneak into the chamber of the Kree Supreme Intelligence, decoying his guards away in order to send a message to Earth. For that matter, it had seemed like a good idea to come to Hala, ruling world of the Kree Imperium, to investigate whether the aforementioned Supreme Intelligence had been taken over and corrupted by the unseen menace that threatened the entire known universe.

Lots of things, Quill reflected, seem like good ideas. For a little while.

"Time's running out, boys and girls," he said, checking his chronometer. "The Kree guards'll be here soon."

Across the room, Drax the Destroyer leaned his massive head against an even more massive door leading to the corridor beyond. "I hear something," he said.

"I bet it's Ronan," Rocket grumbled. "It's always Ronan."

"Great." Quill jabbed a thumb behind him at the dark tank. "And we don't even know if the Supreme Intelligence is in there or not. His, whatever, nutrient fluid, has gone all dark and squishy. And nobody's seen him in public for months."

"Same with these guys," Gamora said, gesturing at the rows of tubes piled high along the wall. "They're supposed to contain dormant Kree, the slave-subjects that feed power and mind-energy to Supremor."

"To who?" Rocket asked.

"Supremor." Quill sighed. "You know, the Supreme Intelligence."

"He's called Supremor *and* the Supreme Intelligence?"

"I guess." Quill shrugged. "So what?"

"It's just a little on the nose, is all." Rocket straightened up, pressed a few controls on the comm panel. "It's like me calling myself Rocket, Rocko, and Rocket Rabinowitz."

"Hey, *Rabinowitz*." Gamora turned to advance on the raccoonoid, her sword drawn. "How about a little less color commentary and more Omni-Wave action?"

"Almost there." More sparks. "Ah, flark!"

"I most definitely hear something," Drax said.

The room fell silent – and then Quill heard it, too. A distant thumping, the footsteps of a dozen or more armored, heavy-booted soldiers.

"Ronan," Rocket said, his voice partly muffled by the laser torch he held clenched in his teeth. "I'm tellin' you, it's him."

"Maybe we shouldn't have trusted the kid," Quill said sadly.

Marvel Crisis Protocol

"Halla-ar can pull it off," Gamora snapped. "He's one of them, remember?"

"He's a Blue Kree," Rocket agreed. "But he's only, what? Sixteen?"

"Halla-ar is motivated," Drax pointed out. "Our enemy destroyed his homeworld."

Quill grimaced. The Guardians of the Galaxy had been present at the destruction of Praeterus, the late home planet of their new recruit. They'd failed to prevent that catastrophe, a failure that weighed on all of them.

"Yeah, but…" Rocket shrugged. "I know I asked for a distraction, but can you really just walk into a recruiting office and pretend to enlist in the Accusers?"

"Groot is with him," Gamora said.

"In that case, allow me to rephrase the question. Can you walk into a recruiting office and pretend to become an Accuser *with a giant walkin' plant lumbering along next to you?!*"

"Lumber." Drax laughed. "That is wordplay!"

"Groot is disguised as the kid's … what? Cotati pet?" Gamora shook her head. "It's a Kree thing."

"Halla-ar can pull it off," Quill said. "He told me he always wanted to be an Accuser. He used to stay up late pretending to Accuse, Accusing his parents in private, Accusing his stuffed animals of all kinds of stuff."

"He Accused me once," Drax said. "I found him quite convincing."

"He's been studying to join the Kree military since before he could walk," Quill continued. "He was pretty excited to see the place, right? He knows the layout of the city, the different military ranks, the whole deal. He got us in here, didn't he?"

The others looked at him, nodding reluctantly. But Quill had that familiar, awkward feeling that he was trying to talk himself into something. Even Gamora, who'd been training Halla-ar ever since he'd joined up with them on Earth, didn't look convinced.

The footsteps clomped louder. "Now or never, Rocko," Drax said.

"Boy, am I gonna be sorry I started *that*…" Rocket stepped back from the comm console just as it lit up with a bleep, indicator lights turning green. "Got it!"

Quill sucked in a breath and stepped up to the machine. The console stood alone in the center of the huge room, a mass of screens and controls labelled in the language of the Kree – which Quill, of course, could not read. On the far side of the room, Drax braced his thick body against the door.

"How, uh…" Quill helplessly gestured at the console, with its array of winking lights. "How does it know who to send the message to?"

"Just tell it who." A note of impatience crept into Rocket's voice. "It ain't the dumbest thing in this room."

"I'm gonna let that one pass." Quill paused, huffing in short breaths like a runner prepping for a marathon. "OK. OK. Just tell it…"

He stood for a moment, conscious of Rocket's beady eyes on him. He could hear the humming of the machinery, the distant thumping of the approaching footsteps. It's all down to you, he told himself. You are the leader of this intrepid team. You're Star-Lord. You can do this.

"Just do it!" Gamora exclaimed.

"OK, OK, doing it." He puffed out his chest, making an effort to enunciate. "This is a message from Star-Lord and the Guardians of the Galaxy, to…" He paused, winced, and turned to Gamora. "Who's this for again?"

"TONY STARK!" Rocket and Gamora yelled, in unison.

"Right, right." He squared his shoulders, raised his chin. "A message for Tony Stark of Earth. We've penetrated the *I'm sorry I'm still having a little trouble with all of this!"*

In a moment, Gamora had him down on his knees, her sword at his throat. "Do you want me to do it?"

He fought back a smile. At least once a day, usually three or four times, he found himself on his knees with Gamora's sword at his throat. Anyone else would have been terrified, but Quill found it… stimulating. Besides, she'd never *actually* slit his throat – not yet, anyway. She'd never even broken the skin. Well, once or twice.

"I just…" He raised both hands in surrender, rising slowly to his feet. "I can't seem to wrap my mind around the whole interdimensional invasion thing."

Rocket threw up his disturbingly human-like hands. "Which part exactly is your ape mind having trouble with?"

"I dunno. It's just so… big."

"Peter." Gamora lowered the sword and grabbed him by the lapels, pulling his face close to hers. "You saw the Kree guards, right? When we entered the building?"

"S-sure."

"You saw their green, glowing eyes? The sign of his mind control?"

"Yeah."

"You hear them outside? Coming closer, their boots skidding to a halt right outside that door?"

"I, yeah, I think so."

"You know we're out of options? That the Kree have impounded our ship, left us stranded on a conquered world? You know that Hala, that this whole Empire, is now lost to our enemy?"

"That's a grim way to approach the... Yeah! Yes, yes, I know!"

"Then *send the message!*"

She released his shirt, practically flinging him away toward the Omni-Wave console. He stumbled, turned, and straightened his tunic – just as a fresh shower of sparks erupted from the console.

"Flark!" Rocket exclaimed, running toward the console. He practically leapt on top of it, fingers flashing across the controls. "OK, OK, I got it. Go, Quill, go, before this thing–"

He was cut off by a loud thumping at the door. Drax flexed his enormous muscles and pressed his entire weight against it.

"I can hold them off for five minutes." The thumping grew louder. "Perhaps four."

The sound of Gamora's sword behind Quill, hissing through the air, spurred him to action. He faced the console, which was smoking slightly but no longer emitting sparks, and began to speak.

"This is Peter Quill, aka Star-Lord of the Guardians of the Galaxy, sending an urgent message to Tony Stark. On, you know, the planet Earth. Hope you get this, wherever you are... golf course, board meeting, maybe some private island for rich people..."

"A-*hem*," Gamora hissed.

"Right. So, you gotta listen. We're sending this from the heart of the Kree Empire, and you would not believe what's going down. The Empire has *fallen*, without a shot being fired. We had no idea... we didn't realize how deep the power of..."

He paused, closing his eyes for a moment. He still wasn't sure he could comprehend the idea of an interdimensional demon-lord conquering entire universes. But the name of that demon-lord, the concrete reality of him, sent shivers up Quill's half-human spine.

"…the power of *Dormammu* had reached."

A barrage of hammer-blows cut through the air.

"They're using some sort of battering ram," Drax said. "Do not worry, I can… Whoa. Slipped a little there."

"Like I said," Quill continued, "the Empire is completely compromised. This entire sector of space, a thousand parsecs square…"

"Cubed, actually," Rocket muttered.

"Square, cube, whatever! It's all gone, all under the Big D's control. And he's already taken over the Shi'ar Galaxy… which means he's gonna set his sights on Earth next." Quill paused, taking a deep breath. "Stark, you and I haven't always agreed on much. I guess things look different from a money bin full of coins, a mattress stuffed with thousand-dollar bills. But you're in grave danger, man. Beware. *Beware Dormammu.*"

He stepped back, casting a quick glance at the door before turning to Gamora. "I think that went OK. Right?"

"Sure," she said. "Except your voice went a little squeaky when you said 'grave danger.'"

"*Squeaky?*"

"Hmm," Drax said. "Perhaps *three* minutes–"

The door flew inward, sending him flying across the room. Quill barely had time to lunge out of the way before the Destroyer's massive body slammed straight into the Omni-Wave communicator. The device exploded in a paroxysm of fire and sparks, shattering into a thousand pieces. Quill dropped to a crouch and instinctively lowered his goggles, shielding his eyes from the glass and metal fragments.

"Oh," Rocket said. "Ahh, flark."

"Yeah," Gamora said.

The two of them pulled Quill to his feet. He waved away the smoke, staring over the still-flaming stump of the Omni-Wave device toward the far side of the room, and sucked in a breath.

"Good news, Rocket," Drax said, hauling himself back up off the floor. "It is not Ronan!"

Quill stared at him in disbelief. "You call this *good* news?"

Just inside the door, which lay flattened on the stone floor, stood an entire phalanx of Kree – a dozen of them, maybe more, imposing and powerful in their deep emerald hoods and uniforms. The three leaders held hammer-like Cosmi-Rods, the primary weapon of the Accusers.

"Hey, uh…" Quill spread his arms and plastered his most charming grin on his face. "Good to see you guys! We, uh, we just wandered in here by mistake…"

"Just a mistake!" Gamora agreed. "But once we were here, we got kind of worried about…" She turned and gestured at the dark tank behind them, still roiling with black liquid.

"…about poor old, uh, Rabinowitz back there…"

"Supremor!" Quill interrupted. He wished Gamora and Rocket would leave this to him. A homicidal assassin and a near-feral rodent weren't much help when he was trying to con an enemy.

The Accusers stood watching. They barely moved. Quill wasn't sure they were breathing.

"So anyway," he continued, "stupid old us, huh? Just stumbling in here. I'm sure you've heard how stupid the Guardians of the Galaxy are."

"We are practically morons," Drax agreed. He pulled himself

to his feet, brushing away shards of glass and tamping out a small fire on his leg.

"So, yeah." Quill grinned again, forcing himself to look the first Accuser right in his blank, tattoo-adorned eyes. "Hail the Empire, right? Hail Supremor?"

The Accusers tilted their heads up slowly, fists clenched tight around their weapons. Their eyes glowed green, pulsing with the inhuman light of the enemy. They moved as one being, which – in a very real sense – they were, now.

"Flark," Gamora cursed. "They're compromised, too."

"Yeah." Rocket frowned. "Hey, what are they lookin' at?"

Quill whirled, staring in surprise as tiny lights winked on, all around the edge of the gigantic tank. Within, the blank liquid swirled and began to clear, revealing a fearsome, glowing face as tall as a house and nearly twice as wide.

A face whose green, blazing eyes mirrored those of the Accusers who stood on the other side of the room, staring at him. With Quill and the Guardians right in the middle.

"Peter," Gamora said, motioning to the side of the room. He looked over, to see the rows of tanks lit up as well… each one with a distinct humanoid figure inside it, eyes glowing the exact same color as the rest of the Kree's.

"Quill," Drax said, his eyes scanning the room as if he were trying to complete a jigsaw puzzle. "Is this what you call 'Game over'?"

"Maybe not," Quill hissed, keeping his voice low. "They haven't caught all of us yet…"

As if in answer, the line of Accusers parted, swinging open like a gate. A lanky blue youth with bright blue skin walked into the room, his movements stiff and awkward.

"Halla-ar," Gamora said. "Oh no."

Halla-ar, the Blue Kree, turned to look at her for a moment. No sign of recognition showed in his face. He crossed over stiffly to join the line of Accusers, their eyes pulsing green in unison.

And then Quill's worst fear came to horrific, hope-crushing life. A thick vine snaked its way into the chamber, transforming into an exaggerated leg as it stepped over the fallen door. The Accusers moved aside, eyes flashing in excitement as the plant-man set roots down on the floor and grew to his full height.

"I AM *NOT* GROOT," Groot said.

"OK..." Quill turned to meet Drax's stare. "This is bad. But it's *still* not game over–"

"How about now?" a deep female voice said.

A shining figure hovered in the doorway, several feet above the heads of the Accusers. Lean and muscular, clad in bright red and blue, with short blonde hair and fists that glowed with pure photonic power. Quill swallowed. He knew that voice, that face, and – most important – he knew the planet-crushing power of those fists.

Carol Danvers. Captain Marvel.

Along with the Accusers, Groot, and Halla-ar, Captain Marvel formed an impenetrable wall of power blocking the Guardians' escape. Carol's eyes glowed green – and then she spoke again, in a voice that was more than words. The Accusers' voices rose in unison, along with the muffled sounds of the slaves in the tanks and the rich, commanding voice of the Supreme Intelligence. Halla-ar and Groot joined in as well.

"ALL HAIL DORMAMMU."

"*Now* it's game over," Quill shrugged.

The Accusers moved swiftly, efficiently. In less than a minute they disarmed the Guardians and clapped them in unbreakable plastanium chains. Rocket seemed subdued, dejected. Even Drax didn't try to put up a fight.

Captain Marvel eyed the room coldly from above as the Accusers marched them toward the door. Groot watched silently. Halla-ar fell in stiffly next to his teammates, his eyes glowing in perfect submission to his new master.

"Halla-ar." Gamora grimaced. "I failed you."

"Don't be sad," the boy replied. "Soon you'll be with the Master, too."

As they crossed the room, Quill flashed a glance at the smoking mass of machinery that had been the Omni-Wave communicator. "Well," he said in a low voice to Rocket, "at least we got the warning out."

"Maybe," the raccoonoid muttered.

"What? What do you mean?"

"I *think* I managed to hit the SEND button, but…" Rocket shrugged, chains clanking on his shoulders. "It's hard to tell with this Kree tech."

Quill clenched his fists. "All this and you don't even know if we managed to warn Earth?"

"You distracted me! With all that stopping and starting and mind-wrapping and the banging on the door and…" Rocket trailed off and looked down sadly, shuffling along with a short chain between his hind legs.

"Keep moving," Captain Marvel said.

Quill cast a nervous glance up at her glowing form. The emerald eyes of Supremor followed them as they trudged out of the room in utter defeat, toward an inevitable future as slaves of Dormammu. A future the whole universe might now share, very soon.

"You're right," Rocket said, hanging his head. "I blew it."

"We all did." Stretching his chain to the limit, Quill patted the raccoonoid gently on the shoulder. "We're morons, remember?"

He meant well. But when he saw the look on Rocket's face, he realized it wasn't as soothing a sentiment as he'd intended it to be.

SIX MONTHS LATER

PART ONE

PLANET DORMAMMU

ONE

As Kamala Khan walked into the gym, the bottom seemed to drop out of her stomach. She staggered toward the bleachers and nearly tripped but managed to grab hold of a thick pole holding up a basketball hoop.

She shook her head, struggling to clear it. Nothing in the room seemed odd or out of place. Kids trudged into the gym for the assembly, taking their places in clumps along the tiered bleachers. Ms Norris, the physics teacher, rolled her wheelchair back and forth along the floor, directing the newcomers. At the far end of the bleachers, a couple of girls passed a basketball, hurriedly finishing up a pickup game.

And yet something was very, very wrong. Kamala's head ached and her guts roiled, sloshing and churning with every step. Something deep inside her seemed upset, alarmed, nearly panicked by…

…by what? A schoolwide assembly?

Her backpack felt heavier than before, too. All at once it hummed, and she remembered the strange object she'd stuffed inside it this morning. She couldn't remember why she'd done that. But somehow, the pulsing sensation steadied her, calming her stomach.

As she resumed her trek toward the bleachers, Zoe Zimmer intercepted her. Kamala almost crashed into the girl.

"Easy, Kam!" Zoe said, blue eyes flashing under meticulously styled blonde hair. "You OK? You look a little rough."

"Just dizzy." Kamala gave her a weak smile. "You're full of juice this morning."

"Energy drink." Zoe held up a green bottle. "Hey, you know what this assembly's about? They called it less than an hour ago."

Kamala shrugged, wishing Zoe would find someone else to chat with. Zoe could be a lot to take at the best of times, and this didn't feel like the best of times. It felt like one of those times when she wished she were back home in bed.

"Oh! Hey!" Zoe leaned in even closer. "I'm going to the Tribute Booth down by the pizza place, after school. Want to come?"

Kamala shook her head. "I'm not due yet."

"You don't have to wait. You can contribute early if you want… the Master appreciates it."

"Maybe. I'll let you know. I might have to take care of some… you know." She lowered her voice, looking around as kids filed past. "Ms Marvel stuff."

Surprise crossed Zoe's face. "You're still doing that?"

Kamala turned away, strangely disturbed by the question. *Am I still doing that?* She wondered. Distracted, she stepped up onto the first level of the bleachers, and nearly pitched forward on her face. Zoe's strong hands caught her just in time.

"Whoa! Careful." Zoe eased her back down onto the floor. A couple of jocks edged past them, snickering at the reeling, dizzy girl.

"I'm all right," Kamala said, waving her away and standing. "I'm all right!"

Zoe smiled. "You know what you need?"

She reached into a large purse and pulled out another green bottle. As Kamala leaned out and grasped it, the churning sensation in her gut returned, stronger than ever. She stared at the bottle, blinking at the words on the label:

OSDRINK
The *Only* Energy Drink
With Real Dormamine!

"This stuff is amazing," Zoe continued. "I drink it all the time. I haven't had an anxiety attack in... wow! You know, I can't even remember!"

Kamala frowned at the bottle, tuning out Zoe's continued praise for the wonders of Osdrink. The green liquid seemed to glow through the glass, casting an eerie light on Kamala's hand.

Once again, her backpack pulsed and hummed.

"Hey Kam! Zoe!" Bruno Carrelli bounded up next to them, gesturing at the bleachers. "We better sit down, right? It's getting crowded."

"Uh, Bruno?" Zoe said.

Zoe mimed wiping at her mouth. Kamala frowned, then looked over at Bruno. His chin was wet with a liquid that seemed to glow green... the same green as the drink she held in her hand.

"Oh!" Bruno pulled out a tissue and wiped the liquid away. "Sorry. Water fountain's acting up again."

"Bruno," Zoe said, laughing. "You are such a dork."

"Is that... water?" Kamala asked.

Both her friends looked at her as if she were insane.

Bruno turned, without answering, and climbed the bleachers, dodging groups of laughing kids. Zoe raised an eyebrow at Kamala, then followed him. Kamala frowned, then trudged after them.

She stared at the glowing bottle in her hand, so distracted that she almost bumped into Nakia Bahadir, her best friend. Nakia gave her a little frown, followed by a worried look. As Zoe and Bruno settled down next to Nakia, Bruno patted the empty bleacher seat next to him.

Suddenly Kamala couldn't stand being with them. She had to get away.

"I, uh…" She forced a smile onto her face. "I think I'm gonna sit in the back."

"Oh." Nakia frowned again, then started to rise.

"By myself."

Before her friends could protest, Kamala started climbing again. The last of the kids filled in the spaces on the bleachers, a sea of fourteen through eighteen year-olds. She wove her way around them all, moving higher until she reached the tallest kid in the school: Hyam Eisgruber. She settled down in the back row, directly behind him.

Hyam turned, giving her a sympathetic look through his thick glasses. "Can you see? Want me to move?"

She flashed him a quick smile. "I'm fine," she said.

As Hyam turned away again, she placed the Osdrink down on the bleacher and shrugged off her backpack. The humming had stopped, but somehow she could feel the presence of the artifact inside the pack. She unzipped the flap and pulled it out, keeping both it and herself hidden behind her tall classmate.

The Eye of Vouk stared up at her, a bubble of liquid the size of a softball, contained within a delicate lattice of tarnished gold. The disturbingly human-like pupil within the bubble blinked and shifted, centering slowly as it focused on her face.

Her stomach flipped again in response.

Again, Kamala struggled to clear her head. She'd kept the Eye hidden for months, somehow knowing that her friends, her parents, and teachers – that none of them would approve of it. Something had made her pack it in her bag today, but she didn't know what.

Frowning, she realized there was something else she didn't know: where the Eye had come from in the first place! She turned from its relentless gaze, trying to remember. She could almost see a housing project, an alien boy with... blue skin? She was wearing her costume... on some sort of a job as Ms Marvel...

With a shock, she realized: I can't remember the last time I was Ms Marvel, either.

The sharp voice of Ms Norris cut through the air. "All right, settle down!" the science teacher called up from the floor below. "Since Principal Stanton seems to have better things to do on a Thursday afternoon, I'll be presenting our special guest for this assembly."

Kamala pushed the Eye back down, into the backpack. She left the flap open, allowing the Eye's glow to seep out, but she moved the backpack carefully onto her lap, keeping it hidden from view.

When, she wondered, *had* she last changed into her costume, gone into action as Ms Marvel...? Her schoolwork kept her so busy, these days. And all this work for the Master...

"First, though," Ms Norris continued, "let's all rise and recite the Pledge."

A murmur of excitement ran through the massed students. Kamala felt it too as she started to rise to her feet. Then, frowning, she sat back down, hidden against the back wall of the gym by four hundred standing kids.

"I pledge allegiance to the flag," the voices chanted, "and to the Dominion for which it stands..."

Maybe, Kamala thought, I'm just distracted by school. She had a geography test coming up, a tough one. She could never remember which country was New Dark Dimension and which was the Subjugated State of Latveria...

"...one nation, under Dormammu, indivisible..."

She took a swig of Osdrink and turned toward the wall. Pennants from the school's entire history hung there, each of them adorned with a triumphant face bathed in flames. *Dormammu High*, they read. *Dormammu Leads Us to Victory. Go Dormammu Demons!*

"...with freedom from troubling thoughts for all..."

I'm preoccupied with college too, she realized. That's a decision I'm gonna have to make. Although, really, where else was there to go but Dormammu U?

"...amen."

The students erupted into cheers. They raised their fists in the air, pumping and screaming. Dormam-MU, they cried. Dormam-MU. DORMMAMU!

A spike seemed to pierce Kamala's gut. She doubled up in the back row of the bleachers, grimacing in pain. What's happening to me? she wondered. Everything's fine, everything is normal. It's just the pledge, for Dormammu's sake. We recite it three times a day!

"All right," Ms Norris called, "settle down. I said settle down!"

Reluctantly, the crowd began to shift and sink back down

onto the bleachers. A clump of jocks were the last ones standing, a few rows in front of Kamala. They pumped their fists in the air and settled down with a final "Dormammu, *yeah*!"

"I get it!" Ms Norris said, laughing in a way that Kamala found disquieting. "I love the Master, too. But right now, like I said, we've got a very special guest for you. This is a real treat, a first for Dormammu High."

More cheering, more fist-pumping. More cries of "Dormam-MU!"

In Kamala's lap, the Eye pulsed. She glanced down to see it staring up at her. It seemed to be calling to her, issuing a cryptic warning: *Get ready.*

"Here, straight from his performance at the Hell's Kitchen Dormammu Appreciation Society... a master of misdirection, prestidigitation, and of course an expert on Dormammu himself..."

Kamala shrank back against the wall. Without thinking, she gulped down another mouthful of Osdrink.

"...Doctor *Stephen Strange*!"

She coughed, almost spat the drink back up. Stephen Strange – she'd heard that name before. But where?

Hyam raised his fist and cheered. Kamala crouched low and peered around him, watching as a tall man in lavish red and blue robes strode out onto the gym floor. The man's goatee was neatly trimmed. He smiled easily, slate-gray eyes scanning the rows of bleachers. Side to side, bottom to top...

Kamala ducked down quickly, out of sight, just before those eyes could make contact. The churning in her stomach became a whirlpool, no, a tidal wave. Something inside her screamed: No. Not him. Not Doctor Strange!

What did it mean? Was he some threat to the school, or to

her personally? Or… it was almost unthinkable… was he an enemy of Dormammu?

"Good afternoon," the man said in a deep, sonorous voice. "I'm here to tell you about– "

"DORMAMMU!" yelled a kid in the front row. Several others laughed.

For a moment, a concerned look crossed the robed man's face. Then he smiled. "Yes, of course!" he replied. "But first…"

He closed his eyes, furrowing his brow, and began to rise up into the air. One inch, two, then four. He stopped at that level, nodding in acknowledgment as a chorus of ooohs and aaahs filled the gym.

"…who wants to see a trick?"

As he spoke the words, Doctor Strange pulled out a deck of cards and fanned them in one hand. The smile on his face made him look like a performer, a common stage magician. But at his throat, a strange amulet glowed a rich, soft golden color.

Kamala shrank lower, keeping Hyam's tall body between her and the floating man. She felt sick, nauseous. She reached for the Osdrink, almost knocking the bottle off the bleacher with her shaking hand.

"Ms Marvel?" the man said.

Kamala jolted upright. She shrank back against the wall, not daring to look at the floating man. Somehow, she knew: if I look, I'll be lost. I will lose everything I have.

I will betray Dormammu!

"I sense that you are here," the man continued. "Don't worry, I haven't uncovered your true identity. Your secrets are your own. All I know is that you are in this room."

She looked around, frantically seeking an escape route – and noticed something odd. Hyam's fist was still raised, held rigid and unmoving in the air. To her right, a group of girls were frozen in mid-laughter. One of them pointed a stiff finger down at the gym floor, where Ms Norris sat very still in her wheelchair.

"I have cast a spell of suspension on this assemblage," Strange said, "so that we may speak. No one in this room can hear me, nor will they remember these proceedings. Only you are protected... by the Eye of Vouk, which you carry on your person." He paused. "That is how I tracked you here."

She darted a sharp glance down at the Eye, still resting in the bag on her lap. It was glowing again, pulsing in time with the man's words. Its deep gold hue matched the amulet on the man's neck.

She stole a glance at Doctor Strange. He stood upright in the air, his eyes closed. True to his word, he was not searching for her. The amulet pulsed at his throat. Now she could make out an eye within that glow, a twin – or cousin – to the talisman she carried in her bag.

"Your mind has been... compromised," he said, "along with eight billion minds around the globe. You do not remember this, but you and I fought to prevent this atrocity from coming to pass. We failed."

She looked around, desperate. She had to escape. Her arms and legs began to grow, to elongate, her powers manifesting subconsciously. No, she thought, don't do that – he'll find you for sure! She retracted her limbs and pressed herself back against the wall, hugging her legs and drawing herself up into a ball.

All around her, kids sat silently. As still as statues.

"Dormammu lives within you," Stephen Strange continued. "You must reject him, purge yourself of his evil. I can lend you strength... even now, my Eye of Agamotto feeds strength into your own mystic orb. But I cannot free your mind, your spirit. You must accomplish this on your own.

"Look upon the Eye. Return its gaze, and allow it to see you freely, without fear."

She looked down at the Eye, blazing in her bag. She reached out a hand to it–

–and all at once, her stomach erupted in fire. Something inside me, she thought. Burning, blazing, rebelling at the thought of contact…

It's the drink, she realized. The dormamine! The glowing green liquid that carried a hint of Dormammu in its every atom. Every drop of bottled poison – and not just bottled. There was dormamine, now, in every lake, every sea, every reservoir on Earth.

That poison, the product of Oscorp's unholy alliance with Dormammu, lived in her stomach as well. And now she could feel it rebelling, panicking, responding to a threat to its existence in the only way it knew how: by hurting her, stimulating her pain centers. Punishing her for daring to resist its Master.

"I know your strength, Ms Marvel," Strange said. "Your indomitable will has saved countless lives, including my own. I hope, today, it will be enough to save yourself."

The pain grew stronger. Her guts felt like they were burning to cinders, flaring and flaming to ash. She gritted her teeth, let out a muffled scream, and reached down with both hands to grab hold of the Eye.

Pain became agony, a thousand raw wounds seemed to rip open all at once inside her. She could feel the liquid, the Osdrink, fleeing her cells, sweating out of her pores, leaking from her tear ducts. She juggled the Eye onto one arm and wiped away green liquid from her brow, her eyes, her neck.

Then, all at once, she felt a terrible moment of doubt.

No, she thought, no no no! I can't do this. I don't *want* to do this. Let me stay here, in Dormammu High, cheering for the Dormammu Demons, filling out my applications to Dormammu U. Let me live and die in the peace, the calm, the unthinking warmth of Dormammu!

She picked up the bottle of Osdrink, raised it to her lips, upended it–

–and spat it out again.

Ugh, she thought. That stuff tastes like poison!

The bottle slipped from her fingers. It bounced against the bleacher seat, then rolled down one level and shattered on impact. Hyam Eisgruber blinked, dazed, and turned to stare down at the sharp broken glass, the green liquid spreading across the seat next to him.

With a shock, Kamala realized: I'm free. The influence of Dormammu… it's gone.

I'm myself again!

Slowly, one by one, the other students began to move. Hyam scurried to one side, casting an annoyed look up at Kamala. She shrugged helplessly and handed him a couple of tissues to mop up the spill. A few rows further down, Zoe and Nakia seemed to be comforting a frantic, confused Bruno.

And down on the gym floor, Ms Norris looked puzzled. She wheeled around in a circle, searching for something. It took Kamala a moment to realize what that something was.

Doctor Strange. He was gone.

Gone, but not forgotten – not anymore. Now she remembered the meetings at his house, the battles against the advance scouts that Dormammu had sent through dimensional portals to sow chaos, to soften up the Earth for an invasion. She recalled the frustration, the despair she'd felt as their enemy gained ground, slowly but steadily, no matter how hard Strange and his allies worked to repel him. And most of all…

She remembered the Shadow Avengers.

The Eye glowed bright, humming louder than ever. She looked down at it with a wry smile and said, "Yeah, I get it." She zipped up the bag and rose to her feet, slipping down the side of the bleachers and out of the gym as fast as she could. Zoe and the rest of her friends were too preoccupied to notice, and Ms Norris was busy trying to comfort several hundred dizzy, confused students.

In the girls' room, Kamala grabbed a pile of paper towels and locked herself in an empty stall. After she'd wiped the rest of the dormamine off her skin, she changed into her Ms Marvel costume. It seemed to lend her strength, like a talk with a close friend who'd been away for a while. It felt right.

The Eye led her outside. Hot afternoon sun baked the tar of the school parking lot, making her throat itch. She found herself craving an Osdrink, the cooling sensation of that familiar liquid… No, she told herself. No! Never again!

She followed the pulsing, throbbing Eye around a corner of the building to a shadowed grove of trees. Doctor Strange hovered in midair, eyes closed, his legs crossed in lotus position. His hands rose and fell in a regular rhythm, fanning that deck of playing cards back and forth through the open air.

The Eye of Agamotto glowed at his throat as she approached, and she felt her own Eye pulse in response from within her backpack. "Well, Doc," she said, "that was fun. Also, more than a little sweaty."

He opened his eyes. He seemed preoccupied, confused, and for a moment she wondered if she'd offended him somehow.

Then he smiled. "It's good to see you, Ms Marvel."

"It's good to be seen. I mean, to see *myself* again. Sorry, I'm still a little disoriented."

He uncrossed his legs slowly, like a yoga master, and lowered himself to the ground, clapping one hand expertly across the deck of cards. There's something different about him, she thought. Strange had always carried the weight of being Sorcerer Supreme, of protecting our reality from threats no one else could even see. But now…

"I can only imagine the, well, burden you've been under," she continued. "Has the entire world really been taken over?"

He looked off in the distance. "Not just this world."

"Right, I meant this universe."

"Not just this universe, either."

"Oh." Her eyes went wide. "Oh. *All* the universes?"

"Every one." He blinked, as if struggling to focus on the girl before him. "All the realities, all parallel worlds, now under the crushing thrall of Dormammu."

Wow, she thought. *That's* a conversation-killer.

"We're uh, gonna take care of that, though," she said finally. "Right? I bet you've got a whole brownstone full of heroes all freed, angry, and ready to kick some interdimensional butt."

"Actually…" He gestured at her. "Well. They say the journey of a thousand miles begins…"

"…with a single Shadow Avenger," she whispered.

He nodded.

"Doc, I'm gonna have to sit down for a minute."

She lowered herself shakily to the root of a tree, leaning back against its thick trunk. The task before them… it was almost too big to imagine. The two of them, two Earth people, against an all-powerful god with an endless army of mind-controlled slaves? It wasn't just ridiculous. It wasn't just impossible. It was *inconceivable*. She couldn't even visualize it in her mind.

"Ms Marvel?"

She looked up to see him holding up the playing cards. Raising an eyebrow, he plucked a single card out of the deck and handed it to her. Unlike the others, it had no numbers on it, no jack, queen, or ace. Its surface was dark, reflective.

"Your Kimoyo card," he said. "Do you remember?"

She nodded, reaching up to take the card. It felt warm to the touch. The Shadow Avengers had used these cards, created by the advanced science of Wakanda, to stay in contact during their missions. She turned it in her hand, watching her reflection shift and vanish, only to reappear as the afternoon sun struck the shiny surface.

"I don't know if I can do this, Doc," she said. "Just breaking Dormammu's conditioning... it almost killed me. I feel like a sheet that got hung out to dry."

"I sympathize. But I need you." He paused. "And I'm sorry to say... what you just went through?"

Something in his tone made her look up again. His face was hard, heavy with the weight of the world. But his eyes pleaded with her, begged for help.

"That was the easy part," he said.

TWO

"Verifying identity," said the smooth, female computer voice. "T'Challa, son of T'Chaka. Ruler of Dormammu sub-state Wakanda. Are you prepared to give Tribute?"

T'Challa stood very still, glancing in mild discomfort at the winking light on the white plastic wall before him. The Tribute Booths in America were cramped and humid, much smaller and less luxurious than their Wakandan counterparts. He felt vaguely claustrophobic.

"I am," he said.

"Your signed acceptance of the Terms of Tribute is on file. If this is still valid, say 'I accept' now."

"I accept."

"Then let's begin."

Hidden machinery, laced into the walls around him, began to hum. T'Challa closed his eyes and tipped his head back, willing the Panther helmet to rise and cover his face. He always preferred to give Tribute in his full uniform. It felt like a sign of respect.

The hum became a whine, then a vibration that seemed to shake the Booth. T'Challa felt energy surge through him, reaching deep inside to tap the power of the Black Panther. That power mingled with the dormamine in his lungs, his organs, his very skin – bubbling, simmering, rising, and flaring forth from every pore of his body.

He let out a laugh of pure joy.

Sensors in the walls glowed softly, absorbing the energy, channeling it through some unknown process into a force that could be transmitted across the realms, to the Dark Dimension where the Master lived. Shuri, T'Challa's sister, had tried to explain the science behind it all. Something to do with basic human energy, a common bond that all citizens of Dormammu-Earth shared – enhanced, in his case, by the herbs that had granted him his powers.

It was beyond him. All he knew was that it felt glorious.

The energy built, flowing through him like a song. How wonderful, he thought. How gratifying to contribute, to give freely of oneself. To be a part of something higher, something greater than the life of one man.

The power peaked, spiking through his frontal cortex. It felt cool and comforting, yet hot like a flame that warms but does not burn. As always, there was a moment of hollowness as the wave receded. A letdown, a tiny sorrow, as the majesty of Dormammu disappeared and the cold hard world seeped back in.

"T'Challa, son of T'Chaka," the voice said. "Thank you for your Tribute."

He nodded.

"Your receipt has been emailed to the address on file. Would you like to witness the Transmission?"

"I would," he said.

"Then go from this place, knowing that the Master is with you."

He reached for the door handle. It turned halfway, then stalled with an irritating click. He grasped it with both hands and managed to open the door. As he walked outside, he caught a glimpse of the Oscorp logo on the upper corner of the door. Shoddy engineering, he thought. Not for the first time, he missed the elegant architecture and careful craftsmanship of his native Wakanda.

Then the bright sun flared into his eyes.

"There he is!"

T'Challa adjusted his helmet lenses to filter out the sun. Ahead of him, at the edge of Madison Square Park, a dozen or more reporters stood holding out phones, microphones, and recording devices. General Okoye, his personal guard, stood between him and the throng, holding them back with an eight-foot-long spear held sideways like a crowd-control barrier.

"My king," Okoye said, not bothering to keep the irritation out of her voice. "Have you completed your errand?"

"Almost."

He held out a hand. Sighing, she shifted her spear to one hand, pulled a large green bottle from her bag, and flung it at him. A heavy axe hung from a holster on her belt, and he hoped she wouldn't try to use *that* on the crowd!

He caught the bottle, the impact stinging his palm. She didn't have to throw it so hard, he thought. But he kept the thought to himself.

He held up a hand to the crowd, motioning them to silence. They took a step back into the edge of the park, where curious joggers emerged from tree-lined paths.

T'Challa turned back to face the row of Tribute Booths. Larger than old-style telephone booths but smaller than garden sheds, they stood in a row between Broadway and the park, silent sentinels to the greatness of Dormammu. The booth he'd just exited let out a slight glow, humming louder and louder.

A flame flared up from the top of the Booth, blood-orange and wild. It resembled the visage of the Master himself, as seen on countless websites and in magazine articles. Like most citizens of Earth, T'Challa had never seen Dormammu in person. But that flame, like the Booths and the wondrous substance dormamine, was proof of the Master's steady, eternal presence.

The crowd let out a gasp as the fire flared up, rising high into the sky. It flashed against a cloud, climbing higher and higher, then vanished in the light of the sun.

"King T'Challa!" a reporter called. "That was the brightest Transmission I've ever seen."

Inside his mask, T'Challa smiled.

"Got time for a few questions?" the man continued.

"He does not," Okoye said, thrusting her spear toward the line of reporters.

T'Challa hesitated, turning to gaze out across 23rd Street. He was already late for his interview with the *Daily Dormammu*, the city's leading newspaper. Its offices stood just across the street, diagonally adjacent to the park. He could make out the illuminated letters spelling out the paper's name, across the roof of the blocky building, rising up over the line of Tribute Booths.

The reporters muttered, snapping pictures and holding out their phones. Okoye pushed her spear sideways at them, forcing them back with the blunt side of the weapon.

T'Challa came to a decision. He twisted the top off the Osdrink bottle in one swift motion and downed half the contents. As its Panther-etched glass indicated, the bottle had been manufactured in Wakanda. The dormamine tasted rich and thick, sliding down his throat without a trace of the bitterness he'd experienced in Norman Osborn's mass-produced swill.

Then he lowered his helmet, willing it to retract into the necklace at his throat, and turned to face the assembled reporters. The hot wind felt good on his face, reminding him of his homeland.

"Your people love the Black Panther," he said, grinning. "How could I refuse your request?"

He could almost feel Okoye rolling her eyes. As the reporters all spoke at once, the Dora Milaje guard opened her mouth and growled. "One at a time," she said. "One at a time!"

"Your highness!" a dark-haired woman called, holding out a wireless microphone. "Marika Gore, *Dormammu Star-Ledger*. Why are you in New York City?"

"My sister is consulting with Oscorp," he replied. He smiled at the bottle in his hand. "Norman's chemists are good, but Wakandan science is better."

"Mister Panther! Deron Seely, *Dormammu Record-Traveller*." A tall Black man held out his phone. "How do you find the Tribute Booths here in America?"

"They are … serviceable," he replied. "But of course, comfort is not a priority in this matter. We must all pay Tribute to the Master, as frequently as possible."

Murmurs of agreement in the group. Even Okoye turned toward him, her expression solemn, and nodded.

"T'Challa! Kit Laserson, *Dormammu Science Monitor*–"

T'Challa cut the newcomer off with a wave of his hand. "I'm afraid I must be going now," he said. "I've promised an interview to a Mister Leeds of your rival news organization, in that impressive office across the street. If I give all my best stories to you fine people, he'll be understandably peeved…"

A beeping noise cut through the air, interrupting his train of thought. He glanced down at the Kimoyo bracelet on his wrist, but no – that wasn't the source. Frowning, he reached into a hidden pocket on his belt and pulled out a dark, wafer-slim card.

As it beeped again, he stared at it in confusion. *I've seen this before,* he thought. *My people built it – Shuri herself supervised the engineering. Why can't I remember what it is?*

Okoye moved swiftly to his side, peering at the card. "My king?" she said. "What is it?"

As they watched, two words appeared on the card's surface, shining in incandescent letters:

LOOK UP

T'Challa tore his eyes away from the card. The reporters had backed away, staring and pointing upward. A few of them had crouched down, aiming phones and cameras up at the sky.

Okoye raised her spear.

T'Challa motioned her away, willing his helmet to cover his face. Above and before him, hovering over the trees and paths of the park, floated a man in red and blue. His hands swooped gracefully through the air, conjuring images of light.

"T'Challa," the man said in a deep, penetrating voice.

"Do I…" T'Challa moved closer, ignoring a hiss of warning from Okoye. "Do I know you?"

The reporters fanned out around the edge of the park, phones recording video of the strange encounter. T'Challa stood fierce and ready before the line of Tribute Booths, watching with panther-eyes as the man wafted downward. A talisman of some sort popped free from a fixture on his throat, rising in the air past his face…

…to form a glowing third eye in the middle of his forehead.

T'Challa felt frozen, immobilized. He tried to turn toward the Booths, to reassure himself of the unbreakable majesty of Dormammu. But all he could do was stare into that Eye, the all-seeing talisman wielded by this strange, powerful sorcerer.

"No," Doctor Strange said. "You don't know me. Not anymore…"

The Eye blazed brighter, piercing the walls around the Panther's captive soul.

"…but let's see if we can fix that."

THREE

Ms Marvel tensed, shielding her masked face from the hot wind. Behind her, twenty-foot-high letters rose up from the edge of the skyscraper's roof, spelling out the words DAILY DORMAMMU.

Here, Doctor Strange had said, she would find the person she was looking for. And as usual, Strange was right. She could already hear the newcomer, climbing up the opposite side of the roof…

"Hey!" she called. "Come on up, OK?"

A red-gloved hand appeared on the opposite side of the roof, gripping the stone lip to haul itself up from the outside wall. Another hand appeared, both of them covered in a familiar webbing pattern. With a silent flip, the Amazing Spider-Man vaulted up onto the roof, leaping half the distance to Ms Marvel in less than a second.

He stood still, his expression hidden behind that web-patterned mask. Eye-lenses staring, blank-white, in her direction.

She hesitated, unsure how to begin. *Hey man, want to get un-brainwashed?* Or maybe, *Missed a few Shadow Avengers meetings, huh?* Or should she ease into things, with a friendly *Hail Dormammu?*

"You?" he said, pointing a shaky finger at her. "You're the big danger?"

She frowned. "Danger?"

"My... my Spider-Sense." He shook his head seemingly confused, disoriented. "It drew me up here. Went off like crazy... a planetary-scale, extinction-level alert."

"Oh – oh yeah! The Spider-Sense thing." She smiled, in a way she hoped was disarming. "That was Doctor Strange. He cast a spell... called it the Summons of Bahayan."

"What? Doctor who?"

"No, Doctor Strange."

"Are you... are you being funny?" Spider-Man took a step forward, stumbling a bit. "Because I'm kind of an expert on funny, and I don't understand a word you're saying."

She frowned. His movements seemed stiff, uncoordinated. The effects of the dormamine, no doubt, compounded by whatever the Tribute Booths did to keep Dormammu's subjects docile.

That was me, she realized. I was like that, too. Just a few hours ago, before Doctor Strange "deprogrammed" me.

He lurched toward her. She tensed in response. Drugged or not, Spider-Man was one of the strongest humans on Earth. She had to proceed carefully.

"Do you remember me? From the meetings at the Doc's house?" She watched him closely. "I always liked working with you. You were the only one that never talked down to me."

He studied her, then looked up at the sky. "I'm... not sure."

This is hard, she realized. I can't see his face, so I can't tell if I'm getting through to him. "This is gonna sound crazy," she continued, "but you're… well, you're not yourself. Nobody is. There's this extradimensional demon called Dormammu–"

"Dormammu," he echoed, his voice almost robotic.

"Yeah. He's changed all our memories, made us think this is the way things always were. That the whole human race loves him, that we give him Tribute and turn over all the profits from our companies to him, and feed him energy that he can use to conquer and subjugate other dimensions.

"But that's *not* the way it always was. And the memories, the remnants of what used to be, are still there in your mind, someplace. I need you to look deep, way down inside, and see if you can *what in the world are you looking at?*"

He looked past her, reaching out to point a finger at the base of the sign. In the center, between the giant words DAILY and DORMAMMU, stood a tall wooden icon in the shape of a musical instrument.

"Why is there a horn here?" Spider-Man asked, cocking his head. "I never noticed it before."

"It's a bugle," Ms Marvel replied. "That's what I'm talking about. This used to be called…"

"…the *Daily Bugle*," he murmured.

"That's right." Keeping her eyes on him, she shrugged off her backpack, letting it drop to the tar surface of the roof. "And you and me… we were in the Shadow Avengers together. Remember? Spooky brownstone, endless meetings, faltering attempts to save the world? Forensic-level debates about the relative benefits of different snack foods?"

He stood perfectly still, staring at the carved bugle.

"I know what you're going through," she continued. "I've been there. I know what it's like to… get lost."

"Lost?" His voice was barely audible.

Despair washed over her. If it was this hard to deprogram one Dormammu subject – and a friend, even! – then how could she and Doctor Strange ever hope to liberate the entire world? Let alone the universe?

Let alone *all the universes?*

Stop it! she told herself. There's no time for despair – all you can do is keep trying.

She crouched down to open the backpack, keeping a close eye on the red-and-blue figure before her. "Yeah," she said, "lost. So lost you aren't even yourself… just a wraith, adrift among the voices." She reached into the pack and pulled out the Eye of Vouk. "But this got me out of…"

She barely had time to register the mistake she'd made. In an instant, Spider-Man leapt toward her, his hands outstretched. A barrage of webbing shot forth from his palms, ensnaring the Eye in its sticky grip. With a flick of his wrist, the talisman flew out of her hands, whipping through the air to vanish over the edge of the roof.

She reacted swiftly, her embiggening power kicking in by pure instinct. She lurched to one side, her legs stretching out to three times their normal length. Spider-Man couldn't change course in time – he tumbled right past the space where she'd stood a moment ago.

But he didn't stay off-balance for long. He landed on his side, rolled into a crouch, and whirled to face her.

"You," Spider-Man snarled, "are an enemy of Dormammu."

Crap, she thought. I pushed it too far. I challenged him, and the dormamine inside him – the part of him that *is* Dormammu – responded with a vengeance–

Before she could even complete the thought, he was airborne again. She flinched backward, toward the edge of the roof, and stumbled over the wooden bugle-icon in the center of the newspaper sign. Then his strong arms grabbed her around the waist, and they tumbled together, through the air, twenty stories above the city street.

Doctor Strange hovered in the air over Broadway. He barely noticed the swiftly flowing traffic, the few stragglers hurrying out of the Tribute Booths at the edge of the park. He didn't even register the mob of reporters and civilians, aiming cameras and speaking excitedly into their phones.

All his will and concentration was focused through the Eye of Agamotto on his forehead. Its beam linked him, like a laser, to T'Challa, who stood before the Tribute Booths with fists clenched, his proud face hidden behind the mask of the Black Panther.

Sweat broke out on Strange's brow. He dipped lower, dangerously close to a speeding truck. This was difficult – more difficult, he realized, than it had been with Ms Marvel. All he'd given her was a nudge, and she'd done the hard work of deprogramming herself. T'Challa, on the other hand, was resisting him.

"Your will is strong," he said.

"Foe of Dormammu!" the Panther cried, shaking a fist in the air. "You will soon learn how strong."

A city bus honked; Strange tucked his legs up to avoid it as it sped by. Hovering, he realized, took up too much of his concentration. He swerved over toward the trees, lowering himself down beside a small stone monument at the park's entrance.

He touched down lightly – and did a double-take at the sight of the monument. It depicted a figure in frilly nineteenth-century garb, seated majestically on a simple but elegant chair. Its face – its entire head – was obscured by a column of flame, carved in marble.

Dormammu. Of course.

Strange stood in a corner of the park, which spread out in a rectangle beyond the monument. Trees grew to various heights, most of them in full bloom, obscuring his view of the farther seating areas. Plenty of places for a disciple of Dormammu to hide. Or, he thought grimly, a lone mystic on the run.

He whirled to face the Panther – who was already on the move, advancing like his jungle namesake. Good, Strange thought, willing the Eye to blaze brighter. Come closer. Let the Eye inside… let it cleanse your –

A mystic sense warned him just in time. He ducked, avoiding the sharp blade of an axe to his skull. But the weapon's blunt end caught him on the back of the neck, a heavy blow that knocked him off his feet. He dropped, wincing in pain, and rolled on the hard stone at the base of the monument.

As his concentration faltered, the Eye blinked and went dark. Dimly he registered a few reporters moving closer, cameras still aimed to capture the incident.

He looked up, vision blurred, to see the Panther's guard striding toward him with that axe raised for another blow. Okoye, he remembered, that was her name – she'd attended a few Shadow Avengers meetings at his house, in T'Challa's company. Strange remembered her from an unfortunate kitchen incident involving a toaster oven and a very sharp spear.

He rolled aside, barely missing another two-handed blow from her axe. The blade buried itself in the ground, cracking a pavement square in half. He rose to a sitting position, then began to back up into the park as she advanced again, now swinging a long dagger in the air.

He raised both hands, mystic energy crackling feebly at his fingertips. Blast it, he thought, I need time to concentrate and conserve my power! But there was no time. Okoye was too fast, too skilled a fighter. He stumbled to his feet, casting his awareness out around him.

The reporters had scattered, peering out from behind trees. He was too dazed to levitate, and Okoye was rapidly closing in on him with T'Challa right behind. Doctor Strange had confidence in his own skills, but he knew he couldn't match a pair of Wakandan fighters in hand-to-hand combat. If either of them got hold of him, the fight would be over quickly.

In desperation he raised both arms, whispered three words in a long-dead Chaldean language, and cast a Random Karma spell. The results were unpredictable, but maybe they could buy him a little time…

"Come here, funny man," Okoye snarled, reaching out both hands toward his neck. "The Master would like a word–"

A bizarre, irregular-shaped lump, about the size of a basketball, hurtled down out of the sky and struck her on the back of the head. Okoye let out a cry and fell to the ground.

Strange barely had time to jump out of the way, his cloak lifting him a few inches off the ground. Hmm, he thought. Random Karma spells aren't usually *that* random!

"Okoye!" the Panther cried.

"What is it?" Okoye cried. "Get it off me!" The object, whatever it was, had affixed itself to her shaved scalp. It seemed to be coated in some sort of sticky substance, covering a glowing core.

The Eye of Vouk! But what was it doing here? Had Ms

Marvel lost it? Or had it fled from her on its own, seeking help?

The Panther reached Okoye and stopped short. He glared briefly at Strange, then whipped out a vial. He crouched down and took hold of his general's head.

"Hold still," T'Challa said. Flipping open the vial, he squeezed out one drop at a time onto Okoye's tattooed scalp. The sticky substance began to dissolve.

Strange paused, thoughts whirling. The Eye of Vouk couldn't be allowed to fall into the hands of Dormammu, but a direct physical assault on Okoye and the Panther, at this juncture, would be suicide. The Eye would have to wait. Hopefully, the mesmerized Wakandans wouldn't even recognize its power.

He spun around and took off at a run, into the park.

The narrow paths wound through a maze of trees. Time, Strange thought again – I need time! He levitated briefly up in the air, then dropped down in a thick grove of trees. Perhaps he could lose his pursuers there.

As his feet pounded down the path, Doctor Strange became aware of the fatigue in his body. In normal times, it was not the way of the Sorcerer Supreme to run and jump, throw force bolts, engage in physical combat with mortal enemies. His path, his responsibilities, were wider in scope. Strange had been known to spend days in contemplation, unmoving, casting his consciousness far beyond himself; monitoring the threats from outside this universe, the etheric flows of nearby dimensional planes.

Dormammu's conquest had changed all that. Strange felt as if he'd been running, nonstop, for the past six months. His legs ached. Sweat leaked from his brow. And he could already hear the footsteps of his Wakandan pursuers, just out of sight on the curving path behind him.

I'm tired, he realized. Tired on a bone-deep, human, very *un-magical* level. He recalled the day of Dormammu's victory, the terrible moment when Wong had walked into his study with green-glowing, mesmerized eyes. It had taken all Strange's strength to subdue his former ally and flee from his own house.

He hadn't gone back. His home, his Sanctum Sanctorum, was now lost. He'd barely managed to grab a few artifacts and precious talismans, before abandoning it to the enemy.

He ducked down, almost losing his footing, as a pair of red-and-blue figures hurtled through the air above him. He caught a quick glimpse of Ms Marvel, falling, her embiggened limbs flailing in all directions as she struggled to free herself from the grip of a second plummeting figure…

… Spider-Man.

Well, Strange thought, at least she found him!

"C'mon, Spidey!" Ms Marvel cried, stretching her body in all directions. Spider-Man held on tight, but she managed to twist in midair so that, when they struck a thick tree, his body took the brunt of the impact. The tree toppled and fell. The two figures lost momentum and tumbled to the ground.

Branches rained through the air. Through the hail of bark and wood, Strange caught sight of T'Challa and Okoye, gaining on him again. He turned, wafted up over the stump where the tree had been…

…and found himself facing an open-air burger stand, with a gravel seating area spread out before it. The tree had landed right in the middle of the tables. Most of the diners were already on their feet, scrambling toward the park exits.

Over by the food counter, Spider-Man and Ms Marvel lay on the gravel, dazed and moaning. The counter had been abandoned, apparently in a hurry. A few unwrapped hamburgers sat on trays, unattended, in the serving window, beneath a tin sign reading BIG D BURGERS.

Strange settled to the ground, watching as the last of the patrons fled the area, scattering straws and paper plates in their wake. All but one man – a large Black man in a hoodie and shades, wearing thick headphones. He sat calmly at his table, sipping from an extra-large soda cup.

"*Cage?*" Doctor Strange called.

Luke Cage showed no sign that he had heard. He just lifted a foil packet, staring through those shades at the biggest cheeseburger Strange had ever seen. Then he leaned forward and took a bite.

Strange frowned. Luke Cage was a powerful and determined hero, a valued member of the Shadow Avengers. But Strange hadn't seen him since the world turned upside-down. If he was working with Dormammu now...

"Doc! Look out!"

Ms Marvel's cry came a moment too late. A barrage of webbing closed in on Strange; he turned to see Spider-Man firing off both web-shooters in his direction. He flung himself up into the air, struggling as the webbing wrapped around him. But it was no use. His Cloak of Levitation clung tight, binding him like a straitjacket.

He dropped back down to the ground, barely managing to stay on his feet – just as Spider-Man stepped up before him. T'Challa and Okoye stood behind him, their eyes glowing green.

"Like the lady said," Spider-Man said, "Dormammu wants a word."

"Dormammu," Strange hissed, "deserves so much more than words."

He watched in dread as his attackers fanned out before him, preparing to strike. The Black Panther, fierce and unyielding. Spider-Man, his blank eye-lenses eerie, unblinking. And Okoye, who now held a spear clasped firmly in her hand – face twisted in rage, the tattoo on her scalp marred by bruises and chemical burns.

All powerful, all fearsome. And all completely, persistently, under Dormammu's spell.

I underestimated him, Strange thought. His grip on this world, this universe, is just too strong. Even a Sorcerer Supreme, like myself, is no match for that.

I need help, he thought, struggling against the webbing that held him tight. I need more power! At least Okoye and the Panther seemed to have forgotten about the Eye. Now that Ms Marvel had arrived, it would return to her, sooner or later, on its own–

A sudden motion caught his eye. He whirled to see Luke Cage, a few tables away, staring at him through those opaque sunglasses. But the moment Strange made eye contact, Cage turned away and resumed shoveling french fries into his mouth.

Then the gloved fist of Spider-Man cracked against his cheek like a block of granite. Pain lanced through Strange, shattering his consciousness into a thousand shards. Dazed, he dropped to his knees and let out a long, pent-up cry of agony and frustration.

Stars swirled before him. He saw worlds, whole realms, shattered and burned to ash. He saw heroes – Avengers, Defenders, a rainbow of former comrades in bright-colored costumes – all marching in lockstep to Dormammu's will.

He saw Clea, his silver-haired ex-wife, walling herself away in a pocket dimension. A place where she could plan, where she could be safe. Where she might, just possibly, escape death at the hands of Dormammu – her own uncle.

And he saw Wong. Wong, he thought, I'm so sorry. I failed you… I failed them all. But I *will* make this right, even if it costs my very life.

Stephen Strange staggered to his feet, struggling against the sticky web binding him. Marshaling all his strength, he muttered a spell of liberation, dissolving the webbing to atoms. Then, the Eye of Agamotto shining bright on his forehead, he raised both arms, summoned dark magic, and prepared to rejoin the battle.

FOUR

A mystic cage ballooned out from Doctor Strange's fingertips, the bars glowing with power. When it was large enough, he flung it at his enemies. The Panther and his general stepped back. Spider-Man stood his ground, firing off both web-shooters, but the webbing passed right through the cage, which closed over the super hero, holding him tight.

Only for now, Ms Marvel thought, watching the action from behind the Big D Burgers stand. But Spider-Man and the others wouldn't stop. The power, the will of Dormammu, would keep fueling them until they defeated their foes, or until they died.

She touched her side, wincing at a bruised rib. She'd managed to crawl to safety, seeking a brief rest to regain her strength. But soon she'd have to rejoin the battle. Doctor Strange could wield some pretty amazing magic, but even he couldn't last against Spider-Man, that kick-butt Wakandan warrior woman, and...

"Little one," a deep voice said.

She turned sharply, looking up. The Black Panther had crept up behind her, silent as his namesake, and crouched in a tree above the back of the burger stand. His eyes glowed a deep, eerie green.

"Hey," Ms Marvel said hesitantly. "Uh, nice day to give Tribute? Maybe?"

The Panther tensed and leaped.

She took off running before he could reach the ground. She stretched her legs out to three times their normal length, making long strides across the park. That gave her a head start – but the Panther was fast, wild, lithe. She could hear his breathing close behind.

She skirted around Spider-Man battling Strange, noting that Spidey had broken free of the cage. Hopefully Doctor Strange could hold him off for a while. The Terrigen Mist had given Kamala increased strength along with her other powers, but she didn't welcome the idea of going hand-to-hand with Spider-Man – her closest friend during their Shadow Avengers days.

And on the outskirts of the dining area, Luke Cage still sat alone at a table. He seemed fully focused on his meal. What was *that* about? Cage had been an imposing but friendly figure in the Shadow Avengers meetings, but what was he doing here? Had Dormammu robbed him of everything but... well, his love of burgers?

Never mind that, she scolded herself – right now you've got an Wakandan king to worry about! As the Panther gained on her, she leaped over a thick, fallen tree trunk – the same tree that she and Spider-Man had slammed into on their way down to earth. She crouched down, reached out, and tore off two thick branches. With a grunt, she flung them at the Panther.

He stopped short, hands on hips. The branches bounced off him with a metallic *twang*. He didn't move a muscle or notice the attack.

Vibranium, she remembered. The Panther's uniform was

laced with that rare metal, mined from the vast reserves in his home country. According to the articles she'd read, it could absorb any impact.

"Let's test that," she said.

She bent down, ignoring the pain in her side, and forced both her hands under the fallen tree. It weighed several hundred pounds; its trunk lay across the entire seating area. She strained, struggled, but it wouldn't budge. It must weigh hundreds of pounds, she realized.

She willed herself to grow – eight feet tall, nine, then ten. Slowly she lifted the trunk, hoisting it high above her head. Her legs wobbled, her back aching under the strain.

When she reached twelve feet in height, she threw the tree at the Black Panther.

It struck him in the chest – and this time, he staggered back a little. His uniform glowed, energy crackling across its surface. He dropped to his knees, leaned backward, and allowed the tree trunk to roll down off his body. Then, agile as his namesake, he leaped forward over it–

–just as a blast of energy burst forth from his chest, in the exact spot where the tree trunk had made contact.

If Kamala had had time to think, she'd have remembered: the Black Panther's uniform incorporated advanced Wakandan technology. The vibranium mesh woven into it allowed it to absorb the kinetic energy of any attack and return it in the form of deadly energy bolts. She'd learned that months ago, while fighting at his side.

Unfortunately, she had no time for that. All she could do was let out a loud *"uff!"* as the energy knocked her off her feet, sending her crashing into the trees. She shrank frantically down to normal size, trying to stay out of sight.

She caught a quick glimpse of Doctor Strange, down on his knees behind a mystic shield, barely managing to hold back the advancing Spider-Man. And Cage – Cage was popping fries into his mouth one at time, pausing only to wipe the ketchup off his lips–

A thick cord caught Ms Marvel around the neck, pulling her backward into the trees. Some sort of vine, she realized, cutting off her wind. She whirled in panic to see the Panther's aide – Okoye, that was her name – staring at her with fiery green eyes.

Ms Marvel struggled, clutching at the vine. Concentrating, she willed her body to become paper-thin and slipped free, ducking down to the ground. But before she could regain her footing, Okoye kicked her viciously in the stomach. She dropped to the ground, dazed.

When she looked up, Okoye and the Black Panther both stood above her, staring blankly with those Dormammu-ized eyes. Ms Marvel gasped, holding up a hand, but no sound came out.

"We are victorious," the Panther said. "Good work, General Okoye."

Okoye turned to him and smiled. Together they crossed their arms over their chests and shouted:

"DORMAMMU FOREVER!"

When the battle cry rang out, Luke Cage whipped off his sunglasses. He shot to his feet, slammed his metal chair to the ground, and shoveled the last chunk of burger (with Gruyère, his favorite) into his mouth. Before he'd finished swallowing, he was halfway across the seating area, pulling back his fist to strike.

Okoye barely saw the blow coming. She flew back against a tree trunk, losing her grip on the vine-weapon, which fell limp to the ground. Cage leaned down, reaching out a hand to help Ms Marvel up.

"Go, kid," he said. "Get out of here."

She coughed, nodded in gratitude, and stumbled into the trees. Cage spun around–

–just as the Black Panther's gloved fist slammed into his chin. The vibranium in the fabric let out a metallic clang. Cage felt the blow, scraping like nails across his face. But his unbreakable skin protected him from harm.

"Hail Dormammu!" the Panther cried.

"Hail this," Cage said, aiming a fierce uppercut at the Panther's face. Cage had trained with the Panther, he knew the crazy things that Wakandan armor could do. At the time, he'd never thought they'd wind up on opposite sides of a war for the Earth itself.

T'Challa leaped aside, lightning fast. Cage's fist grazed his cheek, barely making contact. Cage stood his ground while T'Challa leaned forward like a boxer, fists blurring as he peppered Cage with a series of jabs.

Cage just smiled.

"I can do this all day, chief," he said.

"Oh yeah? How 'bout this?"

He turned – too slow! – to see Spider-Man reaching out for him. Spidey grabbed Cage by the legs and torso, hoisting him into the air. Cage growled and twisted, reaching out for the wall-crawler. Another former teammate, he thought grimly. The strongest one, too–

Spider-Man flung him into the air, straight across the seating area. Cage locked eyes briefly with Doctor Strange, who watched the battle from the edge of the tree line. Then he saw the tree looming straight ahead.

Cage twisted in midair, managing to strike the tree with his shoulder instead of his face. He grunted, went limp, and dropped to the ground. In an instant he was back on his feet, brushing leaves off his torn hoodie, and started back across the ground toward his foes.

"That hurt," he admitted, his thick legs stomping toward Spider-Man and Black Panther. "But you can't break me. Nothing can break me."

Spider-Man's huge bug-eyes glowed bright green. The Panther's lenses glowed in response, a moment later.

"The Master can," they said in unison.

Cage landed the next blow, a brutal karate chop to Spider-Man's larynx. The web-slinger gasped and clutched at his throat. But the claws of the Panther managed to slice into Cage's hoodie, shredding it to ribbons.

And then Okoye leaped onto his back, holding up a tiny weapon glistening with vibranium. Grinning, she brought it down onto Cage's exposed chest.

Pain filled his body as a thousand volts shot through him. He lashed out wildly, reaching for Okoye, but T'Challa blocked his arms, holding him at bay. Out of the corner of his eye, he could see Spider-Man reaching for him with those web-shooters... about to fire off a burst of that irritating sticky homemade goo.

Cage grimaced. He hadn't been bragging; he could hold off a super-powered attack all day. But nothing he could do would stop his opponents from coming back, either. Stalemate–

"Mister Cage!" Ms Marvel's voice cut through the air. "Duck!"

He did. The Panther and Spider-Man looked up and around, distracted for one crucial moment–

–as a powerful beam of mystic energy sliced through the air, just a few feet above the ground. The Panther and Spider-Man stiffened and froze, caught in the etheric glow. Their eyes pulsed green, then white, and then green again.

Cage flattened down against the ground, keeping his body below the raging flow of mystical power. Scraping his back against the gravel, he inched away from his paralyzed enemies. When he got clear of the energy flow, he sprang to his feet and surveyed the scene.

Doctor Strange stood at the edge of the dining area, braced against a trash dumpster. The Eye on his forehead glowed bright, projecting its power in a thick beam through the air, across the fallen tables. That beam held Spider-Man and the Black Panther in its grip, suspending them, motionless, in a halo of energy.

And on the far side of the clearing, Ms Marvel sat on the lip of the abandoned Big D Burgers window. She held up that weird talisman of hers – the Eye of Vouk, Cage remembered. A beam from its mystic pupil lanced out, meeting the matching power of Dr Strange's amulet in the middle of the clearing. Feeding on it, amplifying it, increasing its intensity… with the two Dormammu-possessed heroes caught in the crossfire.

Spider-Man let out a strangled cry and collapsed to the ground.

The Panther watched him, eyes still glowing green – but less brightly now. "Dormam…" he gasped, "Dormammu Forev…"

A deep orange glow shimmered up from his uniform, spreading out to cover his body. It was the same color, Cage realized, as the Transmission energy from one of those blasted

Tribute Booths. The energy mingled with the beams from the twin Eyes, swirling and roiling in some sort of mad dance.

As the Panther felt to the ground, a flame like the power of Dormammu himself rose from his body – and Spider-Man's, too. A howl of rage filled the air, like the helpless cry of a furious god.

"Enough!" Doctor Strange called.

The Eye on his forehead winked shut. Across the clearing, Ms Marvel lowered her talisman, cutting off its beam as well.

Cage watched, leery, as the last of the Dormammu-flame vanished into the sky. Spider-Man and T'Challa lay moaning, twitching, on the ground.

"Mister Cage," Ms Marvel said, approaching him cautiously. "You're, uh, with us? You're *not* Team Dormammu?"

"Hey girl," he said, giving her a wide grin. "What you think?"

"How'd you get free? Did Doctor Strange already talk to you?"

"Nah." He shrugged. "Just couldn't get with that Dormammu crap."

She smiled in return. "So… why did you wait so long? Why didn't you jump in sooner?"

"Had to figure out who was on which side." He grimaced. "Been a lonely few months. A man gets suspicious."

He gestured for her to follow him. Together they walked to the center of the seating area, where Doctor Strange was helping Spider-Man and the Panther to their feet.

"Doctor," T'Challa said, "my pride and my intellect tell me to thank you. My skull is less pleased with the proceedings."

"I second that royal headache," Spider-Man said. "But… wow. It's nice to be myself again."

Doctor Strange nodded at each of them in turn. He seemed very tired.

"Lucas," he said, holding out a hand to shake Cage's hand. "I wish I'd known."

"I tried to call." Cage shrugged. "Your phone was disconnected."

"I'm, ah, currently homeless."

"But this is good, right?" Ms Marvel asked. "The Shadow Avengers, back together? Watch out, Dormammu! Right?"

A moment of awkward silence. A few civilians had crept back into the park, looking around cautiously. Cage shot one of them, a young kid, a glare, and the kid stared back with glowing eyes.

"We shouldn't stay here," Strange warned. "Dormammu doesn't see everything instantly through each of his slaves. But the more people we're around…"

"My general, Okoye, has already fled," the Panther noted. "If the 'Master' does not know what has occurred here, he will learn it from her."

Strange frowned. "Unfortunately, as I said, my house is no longer a viable meeting spot."

"Well, we can't go to my apartment," Spider-Man said. "I've got a roommate, and I'm pretty sure he's got a hotline to the Big D, too."

"Same with my parents." Ms Marvel rolled her eyes. "Not that anybody *ever* comes out to Jersey City."

"I know a place," Cage said. "Doc, you should come with me first. Everybody else, meet us there in a couple hours."

He rattled off the address, and they all shook hands. To his surprise, Cage felt an immense wave of relief. He'd always been a loner and used to looking out for himself. But he had to admit: it was damn nice not to be the only sane person in Manhattan anymore.

"Three hours," he said. "No sooner. And keep off the radar till then."

He turned his back on them and started walking across the seating area, toward the lunch counter. "Lucas?" Doctor Strange called. "Where are you going?"

"Just gonna grab one more burger." He turned with an apologetic smile. "Sorry. You guys want?"

FIVE

T'Challa and Spider-Man both had business to attend to, so Ms Marvel found herself navigating the streets of Manhattan alone. There wasn't time to go home, and in any case, she wasn't ready to deal with her Dormammu-ized friends and family. The thought of her parents staring at her with glowing green eyes sent a chill up her back.

As she walked up and down the avenues, edging slowly west, she grew more and more anxious. Street signs, buildings, even sidewalk vendors – everything blared out the dominance of the so-called Master. Dormammu Keys & Hardware. Barnes & Dormammu Books. Dormammu Drip Coffee. Dormammu Bath & Beyond. Dormammu Says: Recycle! She tried not to imagine what was going on inside Dormammu's Comedy Shack.

Even worse: every person she passed carried a spark of Dormammu inside them. She found herself crossing the street to avoid people, looking away when they turned toward her. When a woman brushed past her, Kamala let out a yelp, as if Dormammu were a virus she could catch through casual contact.

And her mood didn't improve as she approached the meeting site. She had a bad feeling when she'd recognized the address, and it wasn't a place she wanted to see again. It was a place where very bad things had happened, where people had died, where Dormammu's agents had infiltrated Earth, early in the invasion. Why would Luke Cage want to meet *there*?

Stop obsessing! she told herself. Pretty soon, you'll know.

Night was falling, painting the city blood-red, by the time she reached Tenth Avenue on the west side of the Meatpacking District. Half a block away from the Hudson River, a broken neon sign hung above a one-time subway entrance. The sign was dark and shattered, pieces of it dangling loose from the concrete roof of the overhang. Kamala couldn't remember whether it had ever spelled out anything intelligible, but it sure looked like gibberish now.

She descended the steps into darkness, turning right by memory. A plain wooden door, open slightly, came into view. She could hear grunting from behind it.

"Mister Cage?" she called, pushing open the door.

The pub looked pretty much the way she remembered it. Short wooden bar, bare shelves, dust and cobwebs everywhere. Most of the furniture had been cleared out and only one small, high table remained, with stools crowded around it.

And right next to the door, Luke Cage stood bracing a custom-fitted piece of drywall up against the wall directly beneath the street. Paint and plaster surrounded him, along with cans of bolts, assorted cleaning products, and a portable sander. He wore denim overalls covered with spatters of white paint.

Ms Marvel tried to stifle a laugh. "I *heard* this was a fashion district now."

"Ha ha," Cage growled. "Little help, maybe?"

She shrugged off her backpack and hurried over to his side, growing her body to twice its normal size, which, as always, increased her strength as well. She reached out to brace the huge sheet of drywall. Cage looked at her, raising an eyebrow to ask *You got it?* She nodded and he released the sheet. He turned away, considered the range of equipment on the floor, and picked up a drill.

"You, uh…" She hesitated. "You know this was one of Dormammu's power centers, right?"

"I bought the place, remember?" He held up the drill, activating it with a loud whizzing noise. "Doc did me a favor and 'deconsecrated' it months ago."

"Yeah, but that was before the invasion."

"That's why I asked him to come with me. Give the place a sort of 'booster shot', make sure it's still hidden from prying mystic eyes."

He picked up a handful of large bolts, turned to the wall, and jabbed one into the drywall with his bare fist. Ms Marvel jumped, startled. He didn't even turn – just held up the drill and screwed the bolt expertly into place.

"Can't go back to my wife and kid," he continued. "They're still corrupted. And I been runnin' out of safehouses – Dormammu's spies are everywhere."

"I know," she said. "This whole town feels haunted."

"We needed a meeting place, and Doc agreed this might work." Cage moved down the wall, jabbing and drilling a new bolt every foot or so. "Turns out he's been keeping an eye on the place… he even crashed here a few nights, while he's been among the unhoused. I saw the bedroll in the back, but I thought it was just kids." He stepped back. "You can let go now."

She backed away slowly. The wall stayed in place.

"It ain't pretty," Cage said, assessing his handiwork. "Needs some cleanup, a good sanding, couple coats of paint. But it's a start."

"It's not like this place was ever known for its décor." She looked around, shrinking her body back down to its normal size. "Where is Doctor Strange, anyway?"

"In the bathroom."

"The bathroom?" Spider-Man said, creeping in through the outside door. "He does that? Somehow, I never pictured it."

Cage frowned at him. "*Why* would you picture that?"

"Fair point." Spider-Man stepped into the room, turning to Ms Marvel. "Hey, kid. How you holding up?"

"Oh, I'm good." She tried to smile. "Other than feeling like everyone in the world wants me dead, I mean."

"Yeah. I should be used to that! But this is different." He paused, scratching his head. "I just watched my aunt give Tribute. Creepy, but at least she's safe for now."

"We all have relatives in Dormammu's power," the Black Panther said. Ms Marvel jumped at his voice. She hadn't heard him enter the room.

"Your highness," Spider-Man said, turning to greet him. "I take it that means we won't be expecting any help from the nation of Wakanda?"

T'Challa retracted his helmet, revealing the grim expression on his dark face. "I have spent the past three hours ridding my uniform of any technology they might use to track me," he said. "My people fell to the invader as thoroughly as everyone else on Earth. They are entirely compromised."

"Just folks, huh?" Cage asked, a sad smile on his face. "Like the rest of us."

"Well." T'Challa returned the smile. "Not quite like you."

"Yeah, Cage," Spider-Man said. "Did you really free *yourself* from Dormammu's influence? How'd you pull that off?"

"Took a while, but…" Cage shrugged. "I been fightin' authority figures my whole life."

"Can we sit down?" Ms Marvel asked, suddenly weary. "I've been on my feet for hours."

They crowded around the high table, perching on the battered stools. Only four seats, Kamala noticed. Not even enough for a full Shadow Avengers meeting.

Spider-Man didn't join them right away. He vaulted over the bar and started peering at the nearly empty shelves. "I was gonna suggest a toast," he said, pulling open a small refrigerator. "But any potables in this place are probably *way* past their sell date."

Ms Marvel's stool clinked against something on the floor. She looked down, stretched out her arm to triple length, and scooped the object up. It was an old, dusty bottle reading *Kapitansky Dzhin.*

"What's this?" she said, holding it up.

"Left over from the previous owner," Cage replied, startling her as he yanked the bottle out of her hands. "That stuff's poison, girl. Even if you were old enough, I wouldn't let you near it."

"I didn't want to *drink* it," she muttered. "I was just curious."

"What the *devil?*" the Black Panther cried.

Before Kamala realized what was happening, T'Challa leaped to his feet and strode rapidly toward the bar. Spider-Man looked up in surprise as the Panther reached across the bar and slapped something out of the wall-crawler's hand.

A bottle landed on the wooden floor with a splash, shattering on impact. Bright green liquid seeped into the floorboards. With a shock, Kamala recognized the label on the broken bottle.

"Osdrink," she whispered.

Spider-Man stood staring at the bottle which had just been in his hand. "I was about to drink that," he said, the horror audible in his voice. "It was in the fridge. I just… I didn't even think."

Cage rose to his feet and moved toward a mop propped up in the corner of the room. "Habit," he said. "It's a killer."

"Indeed," a somber voice cut in. "The influence of Dormammu runs deep in us all."

The temperature in the bar seemed to drop instantly. Ms Marvel turned, along with the others, to see Doctor Strange looming in a small doorway leading to the back of the building. He gazed past them, crackling with magical energy, his expression grim and distracted.

"Doc!" Spider-Man called. "Everything come out all right back there?"

Kamala lowered her head to the table, groaning. She felt that deep, unique brand of embarrassment that one feels for a truly stupid older brother.

Doctor Strange made no reply. His eyes swept the table, unblinking. He seemed to barely register the presence of Kamala and the others. Then he noticed the spilled liquid on the floor.

"I got this," Cage said, holding up the mop.

"Actually," Strange replied, "if I may?"

Cage shrugged and backed away. Levitating slightly, Strange hovered past them until he stood over the stained section of floor. He stopped, turning to look almost straight down. At his throat, the Eye of Agamotto flared bright.

A beam shot out from the Eye, casting a blinding glow on the floor. When it faded, all trace of the dormamine was gone.

"Is, uh…" Cage hesitated. "Is the place secure?"

"Now it is," Strange replied. "I also took the liberty of securing a few artifacts that I had hidden, elsewhere in the city."

Again he stared past the bar and the other four Shadow Avengers. His gaze seemed to penetrate into other, distant realms.

Once again Kamala was struck by the enormity of the task at hand. Doctor Strange, alone among them, had the mystic power to bear witness to the full scope of Dormammu's atrocities, across the infinite dimensional planes. It would take every bit of courage, every ounce of strength in all their bodies, to defeat this ubiquitous, almost inconceivable enemy.

"You, uh, want a seat, Doc?" Cage gestured at the table. "I'll stand."

Strange blinked. "Thank you."

He moved shakily to the table and perched on a stool. Spider-Man and the Black Panther took their seats, and Ms Marvel leaned forward to join them. She felt vaguely awkward.

"This isn't quite like… old times," she said.

"It is like no times I have ever known," the Panther replied.

Another awkward moment. Doctor Strange's lips moved silently, his eyes flicking back and forth.

"Doctor?" Ms Marvel asked. "Are you OK?"

He jumped, almost visibly. Then he turned to her and, surprisingly, he smiled.

"Yes," he said. "Thank you for asking, Ms Marvel."

She smiled back. "Thank *you* for not calling me 'kid'."

"I am distracted," Strange admitted. "But I'm also very glad you're all here."

"Where else we gonna go?" Spider-Man shrugged. "I've had enough Dormammu Pizza to last a lifetime."

"You know…" Doctor Strange paused, frowning. "I spent so many months dreading this moment. I went without sleep, barely eating, making what scant preparations I could… desperately fearful of Dormammu's plans coming to fruition. And now…"

"Now here we are," Cage rumbled.

"Here we are," Strange agreed. "It's a living nightmare that has engulfed the world. But for myself – much as I hate to admit it – it's almost a relief." He sighed. "No more dread, no more waiting for the other shoe to drop. Now there is only action."

"That's what I'm talking about!" Cage slammed a fist on the table, startling the others. "How 'bout we start by stepping up the deprogramming?"

"Yeah," Spider-Man said. "Maybe we can recruit more heroes to the cause. Like Scott Lang, or Reed Richards? Never thought I'd say it, but I'd even love to see the Hulk's terrifying face again."

"For that matter," Ms Marvel said, "can't Doctor Strange deprogram everybody? Expel that dormamine stuff from everyone on Earth, free the whole planet?"

One look at the sorcerer's face told her the answer.

"I cannot," Doctor Strange said. "There simply isn't time."

They all stared, waiting for him to continue.

"My power is limited," he explained. "Under normal circumstances, I could draw upon the resources in my home to magnify those magics. But with my innate abilities and the few artifacts I was able to take with me, I fear I could only liberate one or two people at a time from the influence of Dormammu."

"And we are sitting on a bullseye," the Panther said grimly.

Strange nodded. "Dormammu's attention is spread thin," he explained, "layered across a thousand, thousand realms. That's the only reason he hasn't found us already but he will. We must move swiftly, decisively, and ruthlessly. Repelling Dormammu from Earth is no longer enough; we have to destroy him, or at least weaken him beyond all possible recovery."

"That's all?" Ms Marvel grimaced. "I thought this was going to be hard!"

"What about Osborn?" Cage offered. "Oscorp is the biggest manufacturer of that soft-drink poison. They build and operate the Tribute Booths, too."

"A public-private partnership," Spider-Man said. "Sounds like old Norman."

"He could be a weak link," Cage continued.

"My sister is working with Norman Osborn now," T'Challa said. "That makes him far less 'weak' than before."

"It's much too risky," Doctor Strange declared. "Even if we could get past his defenses, Osborn might alert the 'Master' himself. And then…"

"…then there'd be no shadows left for the Shadow Avengers to hide in," Ms Marvel whispered.

She looked down, gloomy, as the group fell silent. Slowly, she became aware of a faint smile tickling the corners of Doctor Strange's mouth.

"You've got a plan," she said.

He nodded. "A perilous one."

"What other kind is there?" Spider-Man asked.

"As I have said," Strange began, "one Sorcerer Supreme is not powerful enough to repel Dormammu from this plane. I require assistance."

"What? Who? Oh!" Spider-Man leapt up. "I know who you're talking about."

"We all know, dingus." Ms Marvel rolled her eyes. "Doctor Voodoo, right?"

"Yes," Strange said. "He is not merely Earth's other Sorcerer Supreme; he is an expert on possession in all its forms. If we hope to free Earth's population from Dormammu's mental grip, his particular skills would be invaluable."

"Doctor Voodoo..." Ms Marvel furrowed her brow, struggling to remember. "Sorry – everything from the Before-Time is still fuzzy. Dormammu sort of yanked Voodoo off the Earth, didn't he? After the big throwdown with the World-Breaker?"

"Not precisely," Strange replied. "He snatched away Voodoo's brother Daniel, who exists only in spirit form, and flung him away like a twig in the wind. Knowing that my fellow sorcerer would give anything to find his brother – would search forever, if necessary, through the veils that separate our various realms."

"Umm..." Spider-Man raised his hand, like a student in class. "Didn't you say there were a thousand thousand realms to choose from?"

"Well..." Strange smiled gently. "That was a figure of speech."

"Oh," Spider-Man said. "Whew!"

"There are actually *billions upon billions* of individual dimensional planes. Billions of billions of billions, in fact. Multiplied by several billion more–"

"I get it," Spidey said, slumping back down on his stool. "Lot of planes."

"So how you gonna find the man, Doc?" Cage asked. "They got neighborhood watch in the Dark Dimension?"

"No. But I have something better."

As Strange spoke, the Eye of Agamotto began to glow softly at his throat.

"Doctor Voodoo and I share the mantle of Sorcerer Supreme," he continued. "As such, we have a rare affinity for each other... a partly shared consciousness. I feel him constantly in a corner of my mind, almost like a part of myself."

"That's how you know he's still alive?" Ms Marvel asked.

"Yes." Strange closed his eyes, breathing evenly as the eye pulsed. "And I believe I can track him. I was preparing to do so six months ago, before..."

"D-Day," Cage nodded.

"Again, without the magical implements in my home, I lacked the ability to traverse the dimensional paths. However..." Strange stood up. "Would you all follow me, please?"

He led the way to a small door leading deeper into the building. A broken sign reading OYEES ONLY hung loose by one corner.

"Ms Marvel," Strange said, "it's best you bring your bag along."

She nodded, ran to the front wall, and picked up her backpack. Then she followed Strange, Spider-Man, and the Panther into a dark hallway behind the bar. Cage went last, looking behind as he walked, alert for danger.

The passageway was narrow, walls covered with cracked plaster. A ceiling panel hung loose to reveal open wiring. Doctor Strange raised one glowing hand, atomizing a cobweb with a spark of magic.

"Lucas asked me to check the building for signs of mystical incursion," he explained. "But while I was renewing the wards I'd placed before, I discovered something we'd all forgotten."

"Oh," Cage said, eyes going wide. "The portal."

"A dimensional portal," Strange confirmed, "created by Dormammu himself, to bring one of his agents here. A warrior woman who, if I recall correctly, gave you a pretty tough time, Lucas."

"She was all right," Cage replied. "Pretty sharp fighter, too."

"Are, uh…" Ms Marvel frowned, running a hand along the layer of dust lining the dark wall. "Are you saying we're gonna travel through a *Dormammu portal*?"

"The portal itself has been dormant for months," Strange replied, "as have the others scattered around the world. I doubt Dormammu even recalls their existence. I believe I can reactivate this one and redirect it for our own purposes."

"If we're gonna go friendly neighborhood dimension hopping," Spider-Man said, "maybe we can keep an eye out for Eddie Brock. Dormammu sent him someplace else too, and I don't have some magic soul-link to tell me whether he's alive or dead."

"I am aware of Brock's fate," Strange said, leading them past a door marked STOREROOM. "Dormammu banished him to the depths of the Dark Dimension itself."

"Oh. *Oh.*" Spider-Man paused. "The Big D's home realm?"

"The same," Strange replied. "I owe Venom a debt. We all do. But I can't risk taking this team so close to the center of Dormammu's power – not yet. We must find Doctor Voodoo first."

"At least Eddie's alive," Spider-Man said. "He is still alive, right?"

"He lives. But I cannot speak to his mental state."

Eddie Brock, Venom, had sacrificed himself in an earlier skirmish, to save the Earth – and the Shadow Avengers, too.

Venom was a complicated case. Ms Marvel found him terrifying, and over the course of his career, he'd spent more time as a villain than as a hero. But in the end, against Dormammu, he'd done the right thing.

As she remembered the events, Kamala realized this was another memory that had been suppressed, squelched by dormamine and the effect of the Tribute Booths. Now the Shadow Avengers all remembered Venom's tragic fate... and from the way Spider-Man had reacted, the memory weighed heaviest on him.

Maybe, she thought darkly, some things had been *easier to bear* under Dormammu. She remembered a pre-Dormammu history class back in school, a discussion of totalitarian dictatorships over the centuries. That was the lure of an authoritarian government: it gave its citizens permission not to think about disturbing things. The leader – the Master, in this case – did all their thinking for them.

And all they gave up was their freedom.

Doctor Strange stopped at a small door. It creaked as he pushed it open. A rancid odor wafted out.

"Again with the bathroom?" Spider-Man asked.

Kamala winced at the smell. The room was small, barely larger than a closet, with boxes piled up on the right side and a battered sink on the left with a few open shelves above it. Most of the space was taken up by a toilet, which stood before the far wall. A small blacked-in window, high on that wall, hid the room from whatever backyard space lay above.

"Rat droppings," Cage said, indicating the space before the toilet. "I ain't had time to clean up back here yet."

"This, uh, this is where the portal is?" Ms Marvel asked.

"I did not choose the portal's location," Strange replied,

frowning, "nor do I currently have the resources to move it. Unfortunately."

"I'm, uh, really not too sure about this." Spider-Man took a step back. "Can I take the subway instead? Other dimensions have public transport, right?"

Strange gestured for the others to step back, crowding together in the cramped hallway. He spread his arms wide, his elbows forming sharp ninety-degree angles. His fingers were a blur of motion, filling the small bathroom with blinding light.

As the light faded, Ms Marvel stared into the bathroom. In the open space before the toilet, a rip in space glowed with mystic fire, strobing from blue to red and back again. The "rip" stretched vertically almost up to the ceiling, energy flaring up from it like living flames. She leaned forward, but it was impossible to see through to the other side.

"It resembles Dormammu's portals," the Panther observed. "But it bears your colors, Doctor Strange."

"The journey will be long, and quite dangerous." Strange touched the amulet at his throat; it glowed brighter now. "But I can sense the one we seek. The Eye will lead us to him."

"So we just… step through that?" Spider-Man asked.

"Yes," Strange replied.

"Into the, uh, toilet?"

"You will not fall into the toilet, Spider-Man." A look of annoyance crept onto the sorcerer's face. "This I swear, by the Hoary Hosts of Hoggoth itself."

"I trust you, Doc." Spider-Man peered around the portal, staring through those blank lenses at the toilet beyond. "But it's a big leap of faith."

"Perhaps this will help."

Doctor Strange stepped into the small room, raising his hands again. They flared yellow this time, covering the group in an aura that remained, even after the glow on his fingertips had faded.

"A spell of protection," he explained. "It will protect you all, for a time at least, from any adverse environmental conditions we may encounter."

"Enough talk," Cage said, pushing his way to the front of the group. "If it'll help me save Jessica and Dani, I'm down with this program. Let's get moving."

Doctor Strange opened his mouth – but before he could speak, Cage crouched down and, flexing his thick-muscled legs, jumped through the portal. In an instant, he was gone.

"No splash," Spider-Man observed, crouching down to leap. "That's a good sign."

Ms Marvel barely saw Spider-Man jump, the movement was so fast. Then he too was gone, passed through the portal to some unknown dimensional plane.

"T'Challa?" Strange said. "You've been quiet. I know you have duties here… if you need to skip this journey, we'll make do without you."

"My first duty is to Wakanda," the Panther replied. "Right now, I am a man without a country, and I find I cannot live that way. If this is the best path to freeing my people from the tyrant's yoke…"

"I believe it is," Strange said.

T'Challa gave him a solemn nod. With a touch of the beads at his throat, he raised the mask of the Panther up to cover his face. Then he followed the others, passing through the fiery portal.

"Well, I can't jump like that," Ms Marvel said, stretching her legs to twice their normal length. "But I've got a pretty good stride when I–"

"No," Doctor Strange said, holding up a hand to block her path. "Not you."

"What?" She clenched her fists, frustration rising in her gut. "We've been through this, Doctor. I'm not just a kid – I can take care of myself. I've proven myself, haven't I?"

"That is not the problem." He gestured at the bag on her back. "Would you produce the Eye of Vouk, please?"

Frowning, she lowered the bag, shrinking herself back to her normal proportions. When she pulled out the Eye, it began to glow, swiveling by itself to face Doctor Strange's own shining amulet.

"The Eyes are now locked together," he explained. "Yours must remain here on Earth, to serve as a mystic… anchor, I suppose. A homing beacon, to allow the rest of us to find our way back to this realm."

"Oh." She fished into her pocket and pulled out her Kimoyo card. "I can't just call you with this?"

"Not where we're going."

She looked down sadly. He took a step forward, gazing down at her with a kind look.

"I trust you completely, Ms Marvel," he said. "Both your fighting skills and your noble spirit. But right now, I need you to stay here and provide the rest of us with a lifeline." He smiled. "Besides, even in Dormammu's twisted domain, you have to go to school."

She gave him a hesitant look. "Do I really?"

"To do otherwise would risk drawing… the wrong kind of attention." He paused, clearly troubled. "As it is, you will have to be constantly vigilant. I doubt Dormammu will send his minions after you, but the possibility exists."

She looked away, frowning. "What do you need me to do?"

"I have placed protective wards around this entire block." He turned to face the glowing portal. "The Eye must remain here, in this room. You need only check up on it from time to time. Keep it safe until we return."

"Which is… when?"

He paused and looked at her. He said nothing, but the grave look on his face spoke volumes.

"And if you don't…" she trailed off.

"Then you must live your life as best you can," he said solemnly. "And never stop fighting to free those you love."

For a moment, his eyes locked onto hers. Once again, she saw the burden he carried, and something else. He knows, she thought, that by leaving me here, he's leaving me in a terribly dangerous position. But he has no choice.

And neither do I.

Then his cloak swirled, whipping him up into the air. With a burst of mystic power, he shot away, flying straight through the portal–

–which flared bright, blinding her. She shook her head, holding up a hand to shield her eyes. By the time her vision cleared, the portal, too, was gone.

"And then there was one," she said to herself. Then, glancing sadly down at the Eye in her hands: "Or two, I guess."

She studied the room, searching for a place to leave the Eye. When she turned right to examine the boxes, it swiveled within its metal frame, "staring" to the left. Slowly she pivoted to the left, and it turned right in response. When she dropped to a crouch, it looked up.

It's staring at the portal, she realized. I can't see the gateway anymore, but *it* can. Like Doctor Strange said, it's sending out a beacon to guide him and the others home.

Stepping gingerly around the rat droppings, she tiptoed into the bathroom and placed the Eye on a shelf above the small sink. Once again it turned, its pupil aiming straight at the area above the toilet, where the Shadow Avengers had embarked on their deadly, possibly fatal quest.

Leaving Kamala alone. Not just in a stinky bathroom, she thought. Not just in a dirty bar on the edge of Manhattan Island.

She was alone in the *world*. A world that had fallen, horribly and completely, to the will of a monstrous conqueror – whose full power she couldn't even guess at.

She stood perfectly still in the dark hallway, thinking of those she loved. Her mother and father, their eyes shining with that terrible, alien energy. Her friends – Zoe and Bruno and Nakia, sitting together in the bleachers reciting the Pledge to Dormammu. And her other friends, too – the young heroes she'd fought with as the Champions. Miles and Sam and Nadia and all the others.

All gone, all lost to her. Lost to Dormammu.

Slowly, she curled her fingers into a fist. Let the despair in her gut turn to raw, unstoppable resolve.

"Never stop fighting," she whispered.

Then Kamala Khan – the last free person on Earth – turned to walk back out into the world and resume the fight.

PART TWO

BIG TECH

SIX

Tony Stark squirmed, flailed, thrashed his arms and legs. Panic flooded his mind, pure and primal and all-consuming. He seemed to be swimming in some sort of thick liquid, a hazy viscous sea surrounding him in all directions. There was no beginning to it, no end – just Tony, the void, and a raging fear that threatened to devour him whole.

Where, he wondered, is the land? Where's my safe harbor?

Where is my *armor*?

He couldn't remember anything – how he'd gotten here, what had happened to his life as a billionaire industrialist and an Avenger. His fortune, his home, his gadgets, his friends… everything was gone. Snuffed out, vanished, as if it had never been.

He spied a light up ahead, a deep orange glow burning through the haze. He kicked off, swimming toward the source. As he drew closer, the glow resolved into a rising dark flame, rippling through the miasmic liquid.

He kicked harder, eyes widening with hunger.

He stopped just before the flame, holding his hands out to

feel its warmth. The fire lived within the wet haze, consuming it for fuel while remaining untouched by it. A soft voice called to him, promising warmth in the cold; shelter within the sea; dreamless sleep in a world of anxiety and fear.

Tony reached out and embraced the flame with both arms. It glowed warm against him, penetrating his hands without burning his skin. He nuzzled up against it, willing the fear to recede. Hoping, desperately, that this entity, this warm sweet flame, could banish the crippling anxiety that plagued him.

For a moment, it worked. He pulled back and saw vague features in the flame: a pair of searching eyes, a softly smiling mouth. He closed his eyes, smiling back.

Then he felt the intruder.

He opened his eyes, whirling to look behind him. A red-and-gold ball of shining metal bubbled in the haze, drifting toward him. It gleamed bright, its surface unnaturally sharp and clear through the thick substance surrounding it.

Tony felt a stab of fear. Even from here, he could feel the bitter cold emanating from the newcomer. It threatened him, he knew, threatened his newfound peace and contentment. It was icy, polished, inhuman. It was *wrong*.

He turned back to the flame, hugging it tighter. But something had changed. Now he could smell something, an acrid tang emanating from the living flame – from his guardian, the warm one that protected him from the cold, manmade metal of the red-and-gold sphere.

Words sounded in his mind, a memory from long ago:

You must recall his evil… the stench of his presence.

Someone had said that to him – but who? It was a warning, a premonition of sorts…

A part of it is with you. Part of it will always be with you.

Who? Whose words were these? A doctor, he remembered that much. A doctor with an odd name…

The sphere moved very close, close enough to reach out and touch. Its surface was carved into segments, like a soccer ball, forming a mosaic of red and gold.

Are you happy? it asked.

The fire surged, searing his skin. He released the flame, crying out in pain and confusion. Why? he thought. Why have you turned on me, my Master? Have I offended you?

The flame made no reply. Its half-glimpsed facial features stared at him, lips curled down in displeasure.

Tony floated, lost in time and space. Before him loomed the flame, the warmth that made life bearable. Behind him floated something cold, artificial. Something without comfort, something that struggled every day to go on, to forge its own path in a world without meaning.

He hated that thing, the red-and-gold ball that dogged his path. He wanted nothing to do with it. But deep inside, so deep he couldn't even articulate the thought, a part of him knew:

That thing is *me*. The true me.

The sphere quivered, vibrating with power. Once again, it spoke:

Are you–

Tony shot up in bed, gripping the sheets in terror. He sucked in short breaths, blinking as he struggled to orient himself. He reached up and wiped the sweat from his brow.

Then he saw her: Pepper Potts. Standing rigid before his bed. Staring down at him with unblinking blue eyes.

"Pep," he said. "This is a surprise." He blinked, sat up fuller. "A good one!"

She said nothing.

He frowned, looked around. This was definitely his room: enormous round bed, Elizabethan armchairs, lush throw rugs over polished oak floors. Across the room, one door led to a large private bathroom, while a second – slightly ajar – revealed a walk-in closet filled with Armani suits.

The dream was over; he was definitely awake now. So why was Pepper standing like a zombie?

For that matter, why was she here at all? She'd left him, months ago, pleading for time to think. He'd nodded in acceptance, though a part of him felt withered, half dead. They'd been through this dance before, separated and broken up, and always they'd managed to find each other again. Yet somehow, this time felt different. The whole world seemed on the edge of... something.

And ever since that time, he couldn't stop thinking: why does she always leave? Why do I drive her away? Why can't I be *better*? He'd tried to escape into his company, into the pure joy of manufacturing weapons for Dormammu. But even that hadn't been enough.

"Pepper?" He swung to his feet, reaching for a discarded pair of pants. She still didn't move.

"Don't take this wrong, but..." He frowned, buttoning his pants. "You look like a roommate that's thinking about killing me in my sleep. I mean, you're not carrying a knife, but it *looks* like you are."

His head throbbed; his throat felt dry. Too many martinis, he thought, at the opening of the new Stark/Dormammu branch office last night. He reached for a S/D-branded water bottle on the night table. The green liquid flowed down his throat, cool and soothing.

"Pepper, for the Master's sake, what's this about?" He stood up, moving to face her directly. "Are you back? Or is this some kind of mind game? Not that I don't deserve it, that's not what I'm..."

He trailed off, lost for words.

Her unnaturally clear eyes still didn't blink. But she met his gaze and said:

"Are you happy?"

"Wh-what?"

He stumbled back, away from her, half-falling onto the edge of the bed. She stepped forward, eyes still fixed on his. He outweighed her by half, but somehow she terrified him.

"Are you happy?" she repeated. "Is this the world you dreamed of?"

To his shock, she reached out, lightning-quick, and snatched the water bottle out of his hand. "This," she said, pointing at the Stark/Dormammu logo. "Is this the company you worked so hard to build? The legacy of your father, the financial empire you saw through so many difficult times?"

"I... What?"

"You used to be your own man. Your own person." Her voice was even, clear; it seemed to cut right through his brain. "Remember when you turned Stark Enterprises around? When you made the decision not to build weapons anymore, despite the financial risk?"

He looked away, his head spinning. Weapons? Had he done that? Had he really made such a bold move, out of... what? Principle?

"Remember," she continued, "when you stopped drinking?"

He squeezed his eyes shut, remembering the flame. The warm presence of the Master, of Dormammu, that made life bearable.

That presence, that entity – it relieved him of responsibility, absolved him of all decision-making. It gave him inner peace…

"Are you happy?" Pepper said again.

"Stop *saying* tha–"

She grabbed his cheeks with both hands and pulled his head close, leaning down to glare at him. Her grip was firm, strong, unbreakable. It felt like iron.

"Are you *happy*," she said, articulating each word carefully, "living under the thumb of an extradimensional tyrant?"

Shock lanced through him. He squirmed, struggled in her grip. What, he wondered, is she saying? No one speaks like that about the Master! No one even *thinks* that way about–

"Doing *his* bidding?" she continued. "Churning out his interdimensional weapons, his tools of conquest? Serving his agenda, his will, his monstrous dominion…"

"Stop," he said. "You can't…"

But inside, a part of him stirred. A part that was cold and metal – and, at its core, a product of his own humanity. Like the machinery he'd used, many times, to keep himself alive.

"Surrendering your mind," she said, "your will. Doing his bidding without thought or question…"

He thrashed in her grip, but she held firm. He felt like he was back in the miasma again, flailing, searching for a lifeline.

A lifeline, he knew, that she was offering him. Right now.

"Living in thrall," she said. "Your life, your very existence, devoted to carrying out his will. *Just like everyone else–*"

"NO!"

Just like that, his mind was clear. The invader was gone; the green liquid held no power over him. He wrenched free of Pepper's grip and spat out a small mouthful, onto the thousand-dollar rug.

"That's gonna leave a stain," he muttered.

Before him, "Pepper" flickered and faded. She dissolved briefly into static and vanished. In her place, an egg-shaped metallic object floated a few feet off the floor. It was roughly four feet high and completely featureless, except for a pair of tiny, whisper-quiet jets on its underside.

"Oh!" Tony said. Then, disappointment creeping into his voice: "Oh, yeah. You."

"Are you happy?" the object asked. Its voice was flat now, filtered and metallic.

"Shut up."

The object went silent.

Tony shot to his feet, studying the shiny, blank-faced thing. "The EgoMech," he said, speaking aloud to focus his thoughts. "I remember now... I built you. In kind of a hurry." He let out a dry laugh. "It shows. You look ridiculous, you know that?"

The object – the EgoMech – bobbed once in the air, but said nothing.

He began to pace around the room, running a hand nervously through his thick hair. Memories flooded back, incidents that had been blurred and suppressed before. Now they crowded his mind, overloading his senses.

More than a year ago, Tony had become aware of the threat posed by Dormammu. The destruction of the planet Praeterus, the battle with the World-Breaker Hulk, the threat of the supernaturally charged criminal The Hood... all of it added up to a scouting campaign. A series of assaults designed to soften up this world, this dimensional plane, for an invasion.

So Tony drew up a grand plan: a network of pandimensional screens to be deployed in near-Earth orbit. Together, they'd provide an early warning system and, hopefully, a defense against the invader.

Then the message arrived. It was faint, garbled, and typically incoherent for Peter Quill – Tony had never had much patience with the self-styled Star-Lord. But there was no mistaking the urgency of it:

"…*Empire is completely compromised… entire sector of space… set his sights on Earth next…*"

Suddenly, Tony had known, there was no time. Dormammu wasn't just coming – he was already here. He'd crossed over from his own Dark Dimension, conquering the Kree Empire as a first salvo. If he hadn't taken Earth yet, it was only a matter of time. Weeks, maybe days. Perhaps only hours.

No time for a defense screen; no time to perfect the engineering, or to construct the hundreds of satellites the plan would require. No time, either, to convince the governments of the world of a threat that they couldn't see, couldn't even conceive of.

Sitting alone in his workshop, six months ago, Tony had realized: there probably isn't even time to save *myself*.

So he'd cobbled together a failsafe. The EgoMech: a custom-built robot designed to analyze the brainwaves of a human subject and respond accordingly. Once it had a read on its subject, it would craft a holographic image of the person most likely to influence them. Then it would challenge the subject, peppering them with questions, with probing comments. A series of challenges, designed to force the target to confront the reality of life under Dormammu and, ultimately, to reject that life.

He'd designed and constructed the thing in one marathon seventy-two-hour session. Blearily, he loaded the Avengers database into it, then customized its programming. The Mech, he knew, had next-gen A.I. capabilities built in, but it had no real-world experience. In time it could use deep-learning techniques to gain insight into human – and superhuman – psychology. But for now, he had to give it a head start.

So, tense and wide-eyed, he'd told it about his own weaknesses. His father issues, his struggles with alcohol. The guilt he still felt over the years Stark Enterprises had spent manufacturing munitions.

And, of course, he told it about Pepper. All the ups and downs, the fierce love and crushing heartache they'd shared over the years.

The EgoMech had listened, humming softly. Bobbing gently in the air, just as it was doing right now.

After that, the memories grew hazy. He remembered giving it a code phrase, a trigger to activate its program. But then… the world went crazy. He recalled a full-scale alert, a mad dash out to the penthouse terrace. Portals opening everywhere in the sky: hundreds, thousands of them. Too many to stop, too many even to count. Each of them blazing with green fire, showering the city with deadly mystic power. Letting loose the evil of the Dark Dimension to drop like a shroud over the streets, over all the land.

The next thing he remembered was standing proudly outside the main offices of Stark Tower, supervising the addition of the word DORMAMMU to the façade.

Dormammu took me, he realized now, before I could activate the Mech. What was the trigger? Two words… a simple phrase I programmed it to respond to…

"'Safe harbor,'" he said aloud. "I said it in my sleep, a few minutes ago, purely by chance. And you responded."

The Mech bobbed a little more vigorously. It remained silent, but Tony had the strange feeling it felt proud of itself.

"Don't get cocky," he said. "You're basically an overgrown mirror neuron with a mean streak."

The bobbing settled down a little.

"You're an act of desperation," he continued. "A crisis protocol. A Hail Mary pass that only made it halfway across the... aaahh, I'm sorry." He reached out and patted the thing's smooth metal surface. "I didn't mean it, little guy."

I've lost six months, he realized. Six months of retooling the factories, gearing up to produce weapons he'd once sworn never to manufacture again. Dormammu's grip on several neighboring dimensions was not as firm as his control of Earth; these weapons, the products of the new Stark-Dormammu, were intended to quash rebellions, to nullify any resistance to the "Master," wherever in the Multiverse it might crop up.

A crushing weight descended on him, heavier than any armor he'd ever worn. Here he stood, in his lush penthouse bedroom, surrounded by the trappings of his wealth. The wealth that had been redirected toward the iron fist, the utter unquestioning rule of Dormammu.

He remembered the warm glow of submission, the comforting bliss of no-thought. Along with that memory came the taste of bourbon, from the party the night before. How easy it would be to slip back into that life... to lose himself, abandon all principles and responsibilities, to sink back into the soft green flame...

A part of it is still with you. Part of it will always be with you.

And what was the alternative? What could any lone person do, against a world? Against a *universe*?

Part of it is still with you. Doctor Voodoo had said that, he remembered. A fellow Avenger, another comrade lost.

He shook his head to clear it. He couldn't abandon Voodoo, or the rest of them. And while Tony Stark might be just one man, that man held control of a personal fortune…a dozen holding companies… a penthouse apartment in one of the largest cities in the world…

…and a couple dozen armored suits, waiting in charging bays a few floors above.

He could still feel it – that thing, the shard of Dormammu's essence. A tiny flame, an intruder, a little cancer deep inside him. I can live with it, he thought. I have to live with it. Just as I've learned to live with so many other things, so many flaws I can never fully banish.

"You, EgoBoy," he said, turning toward the Mech. "Display Avengers database. Slideshow format."

A hologram, in the shape of a computer screen, flickered to life in front of the EgoMech. It showed a posed photo of Captain America in full uniform, accompanied by a datafile of specifications: age, height, place of birth, etc. Tony swiped sideways, and Cap's photo was replaced by Natasha Romanov, the Black Widow. The next swipe brought up Thor, then the Scarlet Witch.

Slowly Tony nodded. Maybe, he thought, one lone person couldn't defeat Dormammu. But an Avenger was never truly alone.

"Friday," he called to the air. "You online?"

"Yes sir," the A.I. replied, its female voice carried over hidden speakers. "And a happy Dormammu morning to you."

"Yeah, we'll have to work on that." Tony rummaged in a dresser drawer, pulled out a screwdriver. "I can have you thinking straight in about twenty minutes."

"As you say, boss. Hail Dormammu."

He rolled his eyes.

Holograms continued to slide across the front of the EgoMech. Black Panther. The Vision. The Beast, Wonder Man, Moondragon...

"Are you happy?" the EgoMech asked, startling him.

"I don't need happy," Tony snapped. "I just need a purpose. And now I've got one."

He would do it, he resolved. One by one, he would drive Dormammu from their minds, expel the toxic fluids from their bodies. Tony and his teammates had successfully fought off space armadas, incursions from the far future, even the legendary threat of Galactus. No tyrant, no invader could stand for long against the assembled might of his team.

If all went well, the Avengers would be back in business in a matter of days.

SEVEN

"Note to self: all has *not* gone well.

"Sent out pings to all active and recent Avengers… and fell flat on my tin face. Couldn't even locate Thor, T'Challa, or Spider-Man. Utterly failed to convince Cap, Natasha, Logan, and the others I *did* find, of the error of their Dormammu-ized ways.

"Which is how I find myself, on this fine spring morning, somewhere in this glorious borough called the Bronx, engaged in pitched battle with… ahhh, let's not get ahead of ourselves…"

Two blocks west of Grand Concourse, three blocks north of the Cross-Bronx Expressway, a one-story building with a flat roof stood on a quiet street corner. A dark crimson flame raged atop that roof, as wide as five bonfires and several times as high, behind a wide sign reading: Order of the Golden Dormammu.

Something odd about that name, Tony thought – aside from the ubiquitous Dormammu reference, of course. He'd traced the Order's ownership, just far enough to learn it was a branch of the Young Men's Dormammu Association (YMDA). But he hadn't had time to probe further, and he had to be careful about setting off alarms during his investigations. Dormammu's eyes were quite literally everywhere.

Now he stood on the roof next door, five stories above the Order, clad in his full Iron Man armor. He'd switched to stealth mode, so the armor was busy bending light rays around his body to conceal him from any distant eyes. If someone were to land on the roof, they'd be able to see him, but that wasn't likely – not with that unnatural flame burning on the adjacent roof, stretching ashy tongues toward the sky.

The flame was unnerving, but it wasn't the reason he'd come here. Further below, on the sidewalk, a fateful confrontation was taking place.

At least, he hoped it would be fateful.

"Zoom in, Friday," he subvocalized. "Let me see what's happening down there."

"Yes sir," the A.I replied. "And may Dormammu be with you today."

"Really? Still?"

"Apologies, boss. Just a few vocal tics I haven't purged from my system yet."

The scene below zoomed, blurred, and came into focus on his helmet's internal display. A pale young woman, dressed in white, stood before the entrance to the Order building. She glowed with an inner radiance, a power that could not be contained.

"That's Dagger," Friday said. "Real name: Tandy Bowen. Possessed of radiant-light powers, based in something called the Lightforce–"

"I know who she is," Tony muttered. "She's the reason I'm here. Well, half the reason. Crank up the audio, will you?"

Dagger's delicate voice filled Tony's ear. "...don't understand, Ty," she said. "What are you saying?"

"I'm saying," a deep bass voice replied, "that maybe all of this is... wrong."

Tony panned over to the speaker: a hooded man with a dark face barely visible within the depths of his jet-black cloak. That cloak seemed to spread out to cover the sidewalk like a shroud, swallowing all light, even on this bright, sunny morning. Passersby skirted carefully around him, glancing nervously at that all-encompassing darkness.

"And that is Cloak," Friday said, "longtime partner to Dagger. His Darkforce allows him to teleport and–"

"That isn't Cloak!" Tony snapped. "You know who it is. What it is, I mean."

"Of course, boss. It's the EgoMech, projecting an *image* of Cloak." The A.I. sounded confused. "Apologies again. I still seem to be experiencing–"

"–a mild Dormammu hangover," Tony finished. "My fault, not yours. We'll deal with that later, OK?"

He shook his head, turning his attention back to the street. Dagger – Tandy – was pointing at the sign on the front of the building, specifically at the word Dormammu.

"...remember why we joined the Order?" Dagger gestured at a couple of ragged-looking teenagers, watching as they walked into the building. "To give kids a chance – kids who were lost and living on the street. To provide them with a safe place to learn martial arts, to channel their anger and confusion into something positive."

"You mean..." Cloak – the EgoMech – paused, cocking its head. "...into Dormammu?"

"Well, of course!" Dagger turned to him, staring into his

blank, pupil-less eyes. "Remember how we used to be? When we were homeless? Nobody helped us out – *nobody*. We can make things better for other people. Maybe these kids can grow up in peace, knowing that the Master is always looking out for them." She paused, and Tony thought he saw a tear in her eye. "A peace we never knew."

Once more, Tony felt that shiver of doubt. Was Dormammu's influence really an unalloyed evil? Was it possible that the so-called "Master's" dominance actually brought *peace* to some of his subjects?

And did he have the right to deprive a troubled young woman of that peace?

"The EgoMech," Friday observed, "seems to be operating with a bit of a lag."

"It's not programmed for her," Tony whispered. "I only had time to input the Avengers' profiles into it, and Dagger's never been an Avenger. It doesn't know her powers or her psych profile, so it's just scanning on the fly, picking up cues, and responding the best it can." He grimaced. "Like a bad improv comic."

Down on the sidewalk, the EgoMech seemed to come to a decision. It moved forward, spreading its holographic cape out, almost engulfing Dagger in its depths.

"You have so much light inside you," it said. "I've depended on it, relied on it to keep me sane, for longer than I can remember."

She nodded, staring at him. "I know."

"But now… that light has dimmed."

"What? No." She shook her head quickly. "No, you don't understand. I've found myself. I'm more at peace than ever before."

"You're *not* yourself. You're deluded." The EgoMech gestured up at the raging Dormammu flame, rising from the building above. "You've allowed your light to be perverted. Used as a weapon, a tool to hurt and lash out and control–"

"NO!"

Dagger raised both hands, fingertips glowing with power, and took a half step back. White-hot knives of light shot forth, slamming straight into the holographic image of Cloak. They struck "him" full-on in the chest, lifting him off the ground and flinging him through the air.

"Oh, Squeaky," Tony hissed. "You overplayed your hand."

Cloak's figure slammed into a streetlamp with an incongruous clanging noise. For a moment the hologram fritzed, revealing the slender egg-shape of the EgoMech beneath the illusion. Then the Mech's circuitry stabilized, and the image solidified again, just as "Cloak" slumped down to the sidewalk.

Dagger advanced on him, both hands glowing. People scurried away, avoiding her. Even in Dormammu World, ordinary New Yorkers knew better than to get in the way of a super-hero battle.

"You think you know me," she hissed. "Ever since we were fifteen, you thought you knew what's good for me. Well, we're not kids anymore, Ty. And maybe I know some things you don't." She paused, the light on her hands fading slightly. "The Master has enemies, you know. They're everywhere."

"Ha!" Tony snorted to himself. "I *wish* they were everywhere."

"Something's happened to you," Dagger continued, stopping to stand over the image of her fallen partner. "Something has turned you against Dormammu. But we'll heal you. Get you back to normal…"

Tony turned down the audio. "Well, that was a bust," he said.

"The appeal to ego doesn't seem to work on everyone," Friday noted.

"That's the whole trouble," he agreed, turning his attention away from the street. "I designed that gizmo to work on myself, and nobody else in the world—"

"—has as big an ego?"

He paused, trying to decide whether to be offended.

"You know," he said finally, "I think my ego is actually big enough to *admit* that I… Wait a sec…"

A dark space-warp forming on the sidewalk, at the far end of the block, caught his attention. As he watched, Cloak – the *real* Cloak – stepped out of the warp and walked toward the Order building. People shrank back to avoid him, just as they'd shied away from his holographic double.

Dagger hadn't noticed her partner's approach yet; she reached a hand out to the fallen EgoMech, whose hologram was still intact. "I think you should give Tribute," she said. "When was the last time…"

The EgoMech inched away, not saying anything. It seemed to be having trouble figuring out how to respond.

"I'm calling this one," Tony said. "Friday, deactivate the EgoMech. Let's get it out of there before our girl starts seeing double."

"As you say, boss. But—"

"Let me finish. We'll wait till Cloak is alone, then try again. Maybe an image of *her* will work on *him*, instead of—"

"Boss—"

Tony never heard the end of Friday's interjection. He caught a brief glimpse of silver gauntlets, then a red tunic with a patterned gold stripe, flashing through the air. Something hard and wooden caught him straight in the chest, knocking the breath out of him. Dazed, he flew backward through the air–

–and struck a chimney full-on, cracking it in half. Bricks rained down around the flailing armored man, clanging off his metal shell as he slumped to the roof.

Shang-Chi, son of Zheng Zu, landed easily, twirling his long wooden staff in the air. He lowered himself to a defensive crouch, eyeing the man he'd just flung halfway across the building's roof. The enemy's face was hidden behind that segmented helmet, eyes glowing like a demon's. But Shang-Chi could tell the battle wasn't over yet.

As the armored creature rose to his feet, Shang-Chi cast a quick glance beyond the broken chimney. The Master's Flame flickered against the sky, rising up from the Order building next door. Its dark fire seemed to fuel his own resolve, granting him strength.

"Shang-Chi!" the metal man said, his voice filtered through that demonic helmet. "Oh. Oh, yeah. The Order of the Golden Dawn."

"Golden *Dormammu*," Shang-Chi replied. "Do I know you, demon?"

"We've met." The demon took a halting, clanking step toward him. "Don't you remember?"

Shang-Chi raised the staff, narrowing his eyes. The metal man *did* seem familiar, somehow. But like many of his memories, this one seemed distant, unimportant. The important parts of his past all revolved around Dormammu... the Master his father had trained him to follow. The deity from which all martial arts disciplines, ultimately, drew their strength.

"This … Order." The metal man gestured at the flame. "You're using it to recruit children?"

"Lost children," Shang-Chi said. "They must be returned to the way of Dormammu."

"There's that name again," the metal man replied. "Look, I know you. I know how strong your will is."

A hiss escaped Shang-Chi's lips. Something about this man infuriated him – the cold rasping voice, the unnatural hum of his movements. Even worse, though, the armored man threatened the inner peace he'd fought so hard to achieve. The peace of Dormammu.

Kill him, the flame seemed to whisper. *Kill him and be at peace again.*

"C'mon, Shang-Chi." The metal man spread his arms. "Repeat after me: 'I'm my own person. I don't need some pyrofaced dictator to tuck me in at night.'"

"The word 'I'," Shang-Chi snarled, "no longer exists."

And then, like a leaf in the wind, he leapt toward the enemy, foot outstretched for a flying kick. At the last instant he whirled in midair and struck out with the staff instead, jabbing it hard against the enemy's midsection. The staff chipped slightly; the impact flung Shang-Chi away. But the enemy doubled over in pain.

"Not … bad," the metal man gasped, "for a mind-controlled–"

"No one *controls* me," Shang-Chi replied. "The fire of Dormammu lends me strength, which in turn sharpens my focus. As you have just seen."

The enemy let out a long, metallic sigh. "Whatever."

Then he raised one gleaming glove and fired off a ray-beam from his palm. Shang-Chi's instincts kicked in fast. He leaped up and tucked his legs underneath him. The beam sizzled below, missing him entirely.

"You are Dormammu's enemy," he said, pivoting to perform a somersault in midair. "Therefore, you are my enemy."

Once again, he attacked, brandishing his staff before him. But this time, the enemy was ready. The metal man took to the air in a burst of jet power and let out a barrage of quick blasts, forcing Shang-Chi to twist in midair to avoid them. Too late, he saw the trap: that second metal hand, curled into a fist, swinging straight toward him.

He flipped, evading the worst of the blow. But the fist caught him on his side, flinging him back behind his enemy. He grabbed on to the stump of the chimney, just in time to keep himself from tumbling off the edge of the roof.

"Look," the metal man said, lowering itself back down. "I really don't want to fight you. This is more of a recruitment sort of deal."

Shang-Chi ducked behind the chimney, considering his situation. The demon stood beyond that pile of bricks, still at full strength. Its weapons were built into that armor; it could not be disarmed by any of his usual techniques.

But he could feel the flame at his back, granting him strength. The power surged within him. He felt it like a drug, like a living electrical current. He stood quickly, wielding the staff before him–

A white-hot beam flashed from the metal man's chest, slicing into the upraised staff. Shang-Chi flinched, his hands singed, as the beam cracked the staff in half. The pieces clattered to the roof.

"I can do this all day!" the enemy said. "Come on, buddy. Deep down, there's a part of you that knows this is wrong."

Shang-Chi studied his enemy. The man – the demon – outpowered him, and it could apparently fly as well. It outweighed him, too, by a factor of three or four. That gave it an advantage in close combat…

"Hey, I know this is selfish, but I could use a win here." The metal man laughed. "Help a brother out?"

…but Shang-Chi had a hidden ally, a secret weapon. The enemy, he realized, had made a fatal mistake. It believed that Shang-Chi's will could be turned against the Master, could be persuaded to rebel against his influence. In fact, the opposite was true. The bond with Dormammu served to *strengthen* a martial arts master's resolve, not weaken it.

The flame burned hot on his back, infusing his body with the power of a god. *Use me,* it said. *I am your strength. I am your weapon!*

"Last chance." The demon's metallic palms glowed with power. "Let me help you. Let me free your mind."

Shang-Chi smiled.

"'To express yourself in freedom,'" he said, "'you must die to everything in yesterday.'"

The demon cocked its head. "Shakespeare?"

"Bruce Lee."

With a sudden flex of his leg muscles, Shang-Chi rose up into the air, twisted backward, and leapt off the roof.

EIGHT

Shang-Chi caught a quick glimpse of blue sky, the hot orb of the sun glaring down. Then, as he pinwheeled in the air, the street came briefly into view. People stood in groups on the sidewalk, in the street, stopping their cars to watch. Pointing fingers up at him, at the battle raging five stories above their heads.

Then he plunged into the flame. It engulfed him, pure and hot and cleansing, blotting out the world. It raged, but it did not burn. Even his injured hand ached less than before.

He looked down and saw the roof of the Order building, three stories below. The building was only a single story high, lower than the surrounding structures. The fire flared up from a complex of braziers arrayed along the front half of the Order's roof. Shang-Chi spread his arms, drinking in its warmth. He spun in midair, looked up…

…and saw his enemy flying toward him, in pursuit. Golden armor gleaming in the hot sun.

That's it, he thought. Follow me down–

–into the fire.

The metal man screamed as the first tongues of flame licked

at its shell. Jets flared at its feet, and it turned, jerkily, to soar up and away.

"It burns!" Shang-Chi cried in triumph. "The flame burns *you*. But not me."

He stretched out both arms, bent his knees, and landed easily on the Order's roof. All around him, the braziers blazed, the flame of Dormammu erupting toward the heavens above.

Shang-Chi whirled around, seeking his enemy. He peered through the flame, but its raging fury obscured the enemy from view. Had the demon fled? Had it finally recognized the futility of its quest, the unstoppable power of Dormammu?

A barrage of ray-beams flashed past. Shang-Chi lunged and ducked, avoiding them. The demon, he realized, hovered outside the range of the flame, firing blind with its hand-mounted ray-weapons. It could not see him, but it hoped to get lucky with a random shot.

He leaped up as a pair of beams passed low, narrowly missing one of the braziers. He was safe here; his armored foe would not enter the flame region. But a lucky shot might cause considerable damage... possibly even cripple the flame of Dormammu.

That could not be allowed to happen.

He crept to the edge of the flame, between two red-hot braziers. There, beyond the fire, he could make out the outline of his enemy, hovering above. A monstrous, inhuman threat; a bulky metal monster silhouetted against the sun.

Behind him, a clamor rose from the street. More bystanders had noticed the battle above; no doubt some of Shang-Chi's own student-warriors had grown curious as well. But the fire shielded him, and his opponent, from view. The enemy waited in the sky above the roof, hidden from prying eyes.

That was good. Shang-Chi preferred it that way.

Tensing his legs, he leapt up through the fire. As before, it licked at him but did not burn. Dormammu was still with him. Dormammu was always with him.

As he cleared the fire, he twisted in midair and kicked out with every ounce of strength in his body. His boot struck the enemy in its chestplate, raising a shower of sparks. The demon let out a metallic yelp and tumbled backward through the air, jets flaring.

But the enemy recovered quickly. It lumbered around, turning to face its opponent, swiping out with both of those gleaming crimson arms. Shang-Chi shrank back in time, the wind from the demon's fist whistling past his nose.

By the time the demon turned again, Shang-Chi was out of range, his legs spread for a landing on the roof below. Behind him, the fire burned hot and steady; ahead lay bare roofing with nothing but a single, sealed trap door interrupting its black tar surface. Higher buildings surrounded them on three sides, forming a sort of makeshift arena.

"No spectators, demon," Shang-Chi hissed. "No acolytes. Just you and I, and the power of–"

"I know, I know! Dormammu."

The demon landed before him with an impact that shook the roof. It started toward him, eyes glowing white, clanking forward with one heavy footstep after another.

Shang-Chi danced back, staying out of its range. The demon was strong; he could not out-shoot it, outrun it, or overpower it. And at close quarters, one good blow from those metal fists would knock him right out of the game.

But Shang-Chi had been trained to analyze an opponent's fighting style, to locate and exploit the weak point of any enemy.

As the battle had raged, he'd found that weak spot: as powerful as the demon was, it did not seem to want to harm its enemy.

That gave Shang-Chi the advantage.

The demon reached out, ray-blasts flashing. Shang-Chi ducked low, then lunged to one side. He grabbed hold of the demon's arm and wrenched it sideways, sending the creature tumbling. Its chestplate, he noticed, was smoking; he'd managed to damage it slightly in his first assault.

The metal man staggered, lost its balance, then jetted a few inches up into the air. Shang-Chi danced backward, raising both arms to shield his face. By the time the creature turned to look down, Shang-Chi was halfway across the roof, headed toward the wall of the higher building at the back of the roof.

"Look!" the demon called, pausing in midair. "I don't want to hurt you."

"I know!" Shang-Chi cried triumphantly.

"Why can't you see?" Even filtered through that helmet, the voice sounded desperate now. "Why can't any of you see what's happening? Am I really the only sane human left in the *WHAT ARE YOU–*"

Shang-Chi jumped twenty feet straight up, crying out. The demon let out a surprised noise as Shang-Chi tackled it, wrapping both arms around his enemy's thick metal torso.

"Brazilian jiu-jitsu," he explained. "It's all about maintaining the proper distance from your opponent."

"You–" The demon twisted, flailing in midair, but Shang-Chi held on tight. "You call this distance?"

"I said *proper* distance."

Maintaining his grip, Shang-Chi waited for his moment. The enemy squirmed and rocked in the air, but at close quarters, it couldn't get the right angle for a physical blow. The weapons in its hands glowed, bursting with power, but did not fire.

Shang-Chi felt a surge of triumph. His gamble had paid off. At this range, the enemy would not risk blowing his head off.

At last, in desperation, the demon fired off its boot jets. With split-second timing, Shang-Chi reached out and shoved its metal helmet downward. Jets flared, sending the two combatants soaring down toward the roof. Again Shang-Chi twisted in midair, legs kicking upward to level out their shared descent.

He barely had time to release the demon before its back struck the roof, metal grinding and sparking against the black tar. Shang-Chi raised his arms and rode the man down like a surfer, rejoicing at the cries of pain as the demon skidded along the roof.

Shang-Chi leapt free as the demon's helmet struck the back wall, denting the brick with a ringing clang. He landed in a crouch atop his enemy, staring down into those blank glowing eyes. His own eyes flared green, filled with the raging power of Dormammu.

He paused for an instant to catch his breath. The enemy's struggles had raised bruises all along his chest and stomach; he'd be feeling those for days. But there was no time to think of that now. He pushed away the pain and reached down, pinning the demon's arms to the roof.

The creature struggled, hidden mechanisms whining in protest. But smoke still wisped up from its chestplate. Its power had been diminished.

"I could blast you to pieces!" it cried.

"But you won't."

The demon flailed one way, then the other. Shang-Chi shifted his weight, blocking its every attempt to rise. Even injured, the creature was strong than he. But by jabbing and pressing the proper points on its armor, he was able to keep it from throwing him off.

"No," the demon said, its voice rising in fear. "No no no no NO!"

"That armor is your anchor," Shang-Chi replied. "It weighs you down, both physically and spiritually."

"You think that's never *occurred* to me before?"

"It will be your doom–"

"SHANG-CHI!"

The voice, coming from behind, shot through him like ice. He sat up straight, spine rigid, almost losing his grip on the metal man.

"No," Shang-Chi said, not turning around to look. "No, it cannot be."

The demon slumped, the glow in its eye-sockets fading. Had it lost consciousness? He couldn't tell – but there was no taking chances. He jabbed a sharp karate blow against its neck, exactly where its carotid artery should be underneath all that metal. It let out a strangled cry and went silent, its head swiveling to the side.

"Shang-Chi," the voice repeated. "You will face me when I speak to you."

Taking a chance, Shang-Chi loosened his hold on the metal man. It didn't move. He released its shoulders and rose to his feet, turning in dread to greet the newcomer.

Zheng Zu, father of Shang-Chi, stood on the roof, his figure bathed in the glow of Dormammu's flame. Deep orange robes draped his tall, regal form, framing an aged face dominated by sharp, glaring eyes. Sunlight gleamed off his segmented, three-pointed helmet, the symbol of his leadership in the Order.

"No," Shang-Chi said. "No, you can't be here."

"So this is what my son has come to?" Zheng Zu stepped toward him, gesturing at the fallen demon. "Brawling in the service of an extradimensional dictator?"

Shang-Chi glanced back at the demon, but it lay still. He blinked, frowning, struggling to process his father's words.

"I don't understand," he said. "You taught me all I know… You trained me to take your place as leader of the Order. All in… in the service of Dormammu."

"Dormammu?" The old man practically spat the word. "I serve no one."

"That's… That's not true." Shang-Chi's mind spun. "You used to say we were one mind, one chi. You, I, and the Master."

Zheng Zu shook his head. "My son," he growled. "Always a disappointment."

"No!" Shang-Chi gestured wide. "You taught me, trained me, and I learned at your feet. We built this place, together, and then you…"

He trailed off, suddenly confused.

"Then what?" The old man took a step closer. "What happened?"

"You… you died." Shang-Chi shook his head. "You can't be–"

"How?" The old man seemed to stare into Shang-Chi's soul. "How did I die?"

"I…"

Memories collided in his mind. Part of him remembered a glorious funeral, the assembled disciples of Dormammu honoring the death of one of the Master's greatest champions. The funeral pyre rising into a black sky, glorious with the flame of Dormammu.

But another part of him… Shang-Chi flinched, shying away from the memory. It was horrible… too horrible to relive…

He remembered his father dying, an evil broken man, crouched down like a dog to lick up the mystic blood he hoped would extend his life.

Shang-Chi blinked, staring up at the figure before him. Which father – which Zheng Zu – was this? The proud servant of Dormammu, or the twisted psychopath who'd tried to bring the world to its knees?

"Are you content to follow your father's path?" the old man asked. "Are you secure in the righteousness of your journey?"

"I... I don't..."

"Are you *happy*?"

The words pierced him like a blade. He shook his head, feeling his thoughts begin to come into focus. The black cloud began to part; memories swirled together, coalescing, revealing the truth beneath the lies.

"No," he said. "No, Father, I am not."

"Continue," Zheng Zu ordered him. "You have found your escape tunnel, but you have not yet glimpsed the sunlight. What did you–"

Shang-Chi watched, frowning, as his father's figure flickered, like an old-style TV signal picked up from too far away. Zheng Zu shook his head, wavered, and vanished...

...revealing a featureless oval machine hovering just above the surface of the roof. It gleamed silver, almost blinding in the bright sunlight.

"Father?" Shang-Chi stepped forward, anxiety crowding all other thoughts from his mind. "What–"

Before he could reach the machine, it exploded. Shang-Chi flinched, holding his hands up against the searing burst of white light. He stumbled and fell into a crouch.

Bright spots danced before his eyes. His mind was a

whirlpool of confusion. All clarity had fled. All the truths he'd felt approaching vanished into mist. He looked up, baffled, to see the silver machine reduced to a heap of jagged metal on the surface of the roof. Some sort of central computer unit sparked and burned; a thin flickering light stabbed up out of it, projecting a dim, three-dimensional image of his father's grim face.

And behind that face, Dagger stood, light-blades dancing on her fingertips. She reached out and fired off one final burst into the computer. The hologram vanished, taking with it the last trace of Shang-Chi's father.

"Light-Child," Shang-Chi said, rising to greet her. "My sister in… in…"

"In Dormammu," she replied, smiling.

"This… thing…" He crouched down to examine the smoking, sparking machine. "It was not my father."

"I knew right away." Dagger's bright eyes glowed green. "The Master showed me."

"Not a living being at all." Anger grew within Shang-Chi, rage at the deception. "Just another cold, inhuman construct. Anti-Dormammu… anti-life."

She nodded, resting a hand on his shoulder.

Shang-Chi turned away, fists clenched. His doubts, his conflicted memories – all that had fled now, replaced by red-hot purpose. His fury left no room for questions. Once again he lived, whole and secure, in the emerald glow of the Master.

A large figure emerged through the flame of Dormammu, stepping heavily onto the black tar of the roof. It was Dagger's partner, the Dark-Child: Cloak. His cape swirled like a living thing, obscuring all but his green-glowing eyes.

Light-Child and Dark, Shang-Chi reflected. In every possible way, they were opposites… except for those eyes. The Eyes of Dormammu.

"We've got to destroy it." Dagger pointed at the broken machine on the roof. "Tyrone?"

Cloak stopped in response, spreading his arms wide. A great yawning blackness gaped within him, where once his body had been. That blackness, that void, was as dark as a starless night and hungrier than a forest wolf.

Shang-Chi smiled a hard tight smile. He crouched down, flexing powerful arm muscles, and took hold of the broken machine. One jagged edge cut into his hand, drawing blood. But he managed to heft it into the air, shifting carefully to avoid losing any of its pieces, and fling it across the roof.

Cloak stepped forward, dropping to one knee. The machine flew into his body, into the void, jarring him and forcing him backward. Then the hungry thing, the Darkforce within him, took hold of its prey and began to feed.

Cloak smiled. Inch by inch, little by little, the hunks of metal began to vanish inside him.

A blur of red and gold swooped overhead, arcing down to land before the fire. Shang-Chi ducked down, dropping to a defensive crouch. But by the time he could get his bearings–

–the metal demon stood behind Cloak, one thick gleaming arm clamped around the Dark-Child's throat.

"Sorry, kid," the demon rasped. "I know you're not in control of yourself. But I can't let you gulp down this particular snack."

Shang-Chi tensed, starting forward. Dagger sprinted up beside him, light-knives gleaming in her hands. But before they'd moved more than a few feet, the demon fired off a barrage of ray-beams from its free hand. The beams seared into the roof, melting the tar at their feet.

"Stay back!" the demon called. "I'm talking to your buddy here. He's about to *ingest* something that belongs to me."

Shang-Chi peered at them. The Dark-Child struggled in the demon's grip but could not break free. Shards of the broken robot, linked by frayed cords, still protruded from the front of his dark cloak.

"Knock it off, OK?" The demon sounded frustrated, almost desperate. "The EgoMech hasn't won any science fair awards so far, but I still need it."

The machine seeped further into Cloak's void. One inch, then another…

"Spit it out, kid." The demon's arm tightened on Cloak's throat. "I said SPIT IT OUT!"

With a strangled gasp, Cloak collapsed forward. The machine – the EgoMech – shot out of his body. It clattered to the roof, landing in a heap of broken metal.

"Ty!" Dagger cried. She started forward, eyes on fire, her light-daggers piercing the air. Shang-Chi moved to follow–

–but the metal man was too fast. It ducked low, avoiding the barrage of light-weapons, and scooped up the pieces of its broken machine.

"You can't win, demon," Shang-Chi hissed. "Once more my path is clear."

The demon whirled to face them, boot jets flaring. "The path of Dormammu?"

"Yes. Whose glory I was proud to share with my beloved father."

"Beloved…" The demon lowered its head in despair. "You know what? Maybe this *is* over. For now, anyway."

The demon jetted straight up into the sky, pausing to study Shang-Chi for a frozen moment. Then it veered sideways, boots flaring, and vanished into the gathering clouds.

No, Shang-Chi thought, watching the enemy's jet trails dissolve into mist. It's not over, demon. You'll pay for what you did today. For attacking my stronghold… threatening my friends… impersonating my beloved father. And most of all…

…for making me doubt Dormammu.

Cloak approached, leaning against Dagger's smaller form. The attack had weakened him, but he seemed uninjured.

"It's gone?" Dagger asked, her eyes searching the sky.

"Escaped," Shang-Chi replied, "but defeated. We have won a victory today."

Dagger stumbled under her partner's weight; Shang-Chi reached out a hand to steady them. He realized he was smiling. These two, his brother and sister in Dormammu – they not only supported each other, but gave each other strength. Every day, by their support and their example, they lent some of that strength to him as well.

"Come," he said, "let's go. There are children depending on us."

He stepped forward, wiping a trace of blood from his hand. The Light-Child and Dark-Child drew up beside him and together they strode, unafraid, into the column of flame.

NINE

The EgoMech hung in the air above the null-grav stage, vibrating in a way that struck Tony as almost *nervous*. Its component parts had been split apart, making it look like a schematic diagram linked by frayed wires and conduit tubing. Its outer shell was no longer a gleaming, unbroken arc of metal. Now it was pocked with dents, dirt, and a few clumps of melted tar from the Order's roof.

"Are you," the Mech rasped, trying to speak. "Are you ha ha hap–"

"Oh, stop," Tony said. "Now you don't just *look* ridiculous, you sound silly too."

He stood in his shirtsleeves, a soldering gun in one hand, tablet computer held loose in the other. He glanced behind him at a wallscreen covering almost a quarter of the multistory workshop. The screen displayed an actual schematic of the EgoMech, a plan that Tony himself had drawn up... well, it seemed like a lifetime ago. Hand-drawn circles showed the spots where the machine required re-welding and electronic repairs. There were an awful lot of circles.

Tony sighed. Another job that seemed endless, maybe even hopeless.

He cast his gaze up and around the dome-shaped laboratory, which filled three stories at the top of the Tower's penthouse. To his left, an open stairwell and a large freight elevator took up most of one wall. To the right: piles and piles of electronic equipment. Catwalks stretched around the walls of the dome, providing elevated vantage points for those times when he needed a change of perspective. And straight ahead, beyond the null-g stage, three rows of Iron Man suits had been mounted in cases along the back wall.

He'd designed every corner of this space himself, furnishing it with all the equipment he needed for cutting-edge research – and for Iron Man's work, too. And yet, even before Dormammu's arrival, he'd found himself dreading to come up here, because this huge area had originally been planned as the core of his and Pepper's penthouse apartment. A loft living space, a private screening room, a state-of-the-art marble-furnished kitchen. The place where they'd spend the rest of their lives together.

And how long after she left, he reflected, did it take me to turn it into a high-tech playpen? A week? Two?

"Maybe that's *why* you left," he whispered.

He looked at the rows of armor, arrayed along the upper wall. The early, dingy gray suits; the later, more flexible models. The Thumper heavy-construction unit, the radiation-proof "Jack" model. Mark 5, Mark 13, Mark 22 – that one had always been trouble. Silver Centurion, Peacemaker, Hammerhead, Igor…

"I can feel you judging me, guys," Tony said. "Knock it off, huh?"

"Are you ha?" the EgoMech repeated. "You don't sound ha ha *happy*–"

"Congratulations, you said a word," Tony snapped. "Now let's try something useful, huh? Are your video files intact?"

"V-v-video files," it replied. "Intact."

"Good. Display the Shang-Chi battle again, please."

The machine vibrated more quickly, semi-detached pieces shaking in the space above the stage. A metallic whine filled the air.

"D-d-dis," it said. "Display."

"Yes! Display!"

The EgoMech shook and shuddered. An exposed lens – the core of the holographic imaging system – flashed once and went dark.

As the machine subsided, Tony's tablet let out a harsh bleep. He held it up, noting the alert on its screen: EGOMECH STATUS: HOLO EMITTER INOPERATIVE.

He turned back to the Mech, which hung still in midair. It looked sad, defeated. He felt a sudden pang of sympathy.

"Just throw the footage up on the big screen," he said. "Two-D will be fine. And, uh, I'm sorry I barked at you."

He set the soldering iron down on a workbench, then turned toward the wallscreen. This should be fun, he thought – like a TikTok video of my most recent failure. But what the hell. We learn from our mistakes, right?

Tony watched, frowning, as the screen replayed every frame of his battle on the Order roof. Shang-Chi's initial ambush; the fall into that bizarre flame that only burned non-followers of Dormammu. The dance on the roof, the appearance of the EgoMech in the guise of Shang-Chi's father, and finally the entrance of Cloak and Dagger.

"You were in a million pieces, but you kept recording?" Tony nodded at the Mech. "Respect."

His eyes scanned the screen, studying every frame – searching for a weak point, any detail he might have missed at the time. He winced as he watched himself, in full Iron Man armor, scoop up the damaged pieces of the EgoMech and turn to face his opponent.

"Once more," Shang-Chi said, fists clenched, "my path is clear."

"The path of Dormammu?" screen-Tony asked.

"Yes. Whose glory I was proud to share with my beloved father."

"Pause playback," Tony said.

The image froze. He paced in front of it, staring at the strangely serene image of the martial-arts master, three times life-size on the big screen.

"We goofed," he said.

"Goo goo goofed?" the EgoMech replied.

"Oh, I can't talk to you," Tony said. "Friday, you back online yet?"

"Yes sir," said the female voice, filling the room. "I have just completed an extensive diagnostic purging protocol."

"Wonderful. Aces. I assume all traces of Dormammu are out of your, and I use this term quite literally, system?"

"I believe so, boss." Friday paused. "Though I suppose if they weren't, I wouldn't tell you."

"That's both logically rigorous and a tad disturbing. Never mind, I gotta trust somebody." He stroked his beard, thinking. "So. Dormammu. His mind control is… well, it's different from any kind we've encountered before, am I right?"

"I suppose–"

"That was rhetorical. Just listen." He frowned, remembering. "When I was under the influence, I just… I didn't want to be a super hero anymore. I didn't want anything, really." He paused. "Dagger's a different story. She's got the same demons driving her as always, so she's pursuing the same mission as she did in her former life: helping kids get off the street."

"And into the service of Dormammu," Friday said.

"Well, social services ain't what they used to be." Tony turned to look back up at the screen. "And then there's the Avengers... and finally, Shang-Chi. Friday, tell me: What's the common thread here? What do we all share, once Dormammu gets his chemical crap into our brains?"

"A depressingly familiar human submission to authority?"

"Insulting to my entire species, but I'll allow it. Not what I was thinking of, though." Once again, he paused. "Altered memories."

"Ah, yes."

"I thought... I really believed that I had *always* manufactured weapons – guns, bombs, armored attack vehicles – for that interdimensional conqueror. I had no concept that my life had ever been lived another way." He gestured up at the screen. "We saw that with Shang-Chi, too. His whole life has been defined by his rebellion against his father. Yet in Dormammu World..."

"...they were allies," Friday finished.

"Yup." He shook his head. "We tried to appeal to Shang-Chi's strength of will, the spirit that makes him the warrior he is. But that was a mistake. That exact quality, channeled by the 'Master', might just make him the most devoted, loyal follower Dormammu has."

"So so sorry," the EgoMech offered.

"Not your fault, Squeaky," Tony said. "Free thinking is tough on everyone. Only upside is, well, that it's real."

He pulled up a folding chair and turned it to face the

EgoMech. The bot hung suspended in midair, waiting for him to repair it. Just like the world, he thought. Eight billion people, all waiting for the only free mind on Earth to break *their* minds out of their gilded cage.

Silence hung over the laboratory, thick and oppressive. The words of Shang-Chi echoed in his mind:

Your armor is your anchor.

It will be your doom…

"Not your fault," he repeated, his voice low and raspy. "Nobody's fault but mine."

"Boss," Friday said, "you're being a little hard on yours–"

"Not now, Friday." He lowered his head to his hands. "I can't do it. It's too big. I can fix anything, but I cannot see how to fix this."

He searched his mind for allies, running down a mental list of the most powerful beings on Earth. T'Challa and Spider-Man seemed to have disappeared. The Sentry wasn't answering calls. The EgoMech had already tried and failed to deprogram Cap, Wolverine, and She-Hulk. Tony himself had taken a shot at Black Widow, with results that could charitably be called *discouraging*.

Carol Danvers – Captain Marvel – hadn't been heard from either. Probably deep out in space, ruling some hapless planet in the Master's name. Tony had sent messages to the other active Avengers, too, asking in neutral tones whether they'd be willing to talk with him. No luck so far.

Thor, he thought, would a perfect target for the EgoMech – no one on this plane of existence thought more of himself. But the thunder god was probably off on Asgard, constructing who knew what sort of Norse temples to Dormammu.

Targets for the EgoMech. Something in that phrase lit a spark in Tony's mind, planting the seed of an idea. But the idea wouldn't come. Experience had taught him he had to wait, to distract himself, while his subconscious did its work.

"Boss," Friday said, "should I play your messages? A few calls came in while you were practicing kung fu in the Bronx."

"Why not," Tony said. "I haven't had enough rejection today."

A low voice came up. "Tony? Tony who?"

"That's Clint Barton," Friday explained. "Hawkeye–"

"I know, I know," Tony said.

"Listen," Hawkeye's voice said, "whoever you are, quit calling here. I've got important Dormammu stuff to do." The line went dead.

"Important Dormammu stuff." Tony sighed. "Sure. Have fun with that."

He turned, despairing, to study the image of Shang-Chi, still frozen on the wallscreen. What had the martial arts master said, there at the end? *My path is clear.*

That's the problem, he thought darkly. Everyone's path is clear now. Except mine.

Another message clicked on, a high male voice filling the air. Tony recognized the speaker as Scott Lang, Ant-Man.

"Tony! I mean, Mister Stark. This is an honor. I, uh…" A pause. "I'd love to get together, but I've got some research I have to finish for the Master. You know how it is. Anyway, thanks for thinking of me!"

Tony cast his eyes up past the EgoMech, scanning the suits of armor arrayed along the wall. Maybe, he thought, maybe Shang-Chi was right. Maybe Iron Man is a dead weight, an anchor. A useless relic; a lump of slag in a world on fire…

"Tony?"

He shot upright at the voice.

"That's–" Friday began.

"I know!" he said. "Ms Marvel."

"Tony, Mister Stark, it's, yeah, it's me." She paused. "I appreciate you reaching out. I'm fine, I want you to know that I'm… uh, I'm myself, if you know what I mean."

Her voice. It was worried, unsure, but sharp as a blade. Instantly he knew: she's free. Ms Marvel was *not* under Dormammu's influence.

"But I don't know if… I mean, I don't think we should meet." Her voice quavered slightly. "I've got a lot going on, a lot of responsibilities. And, well, I'm not really sure who I can trust."

Tony's mind whirled. Someone else is free. She's just a kid, barely a junior Avenger. But it means I'm not the only one. I'm not alone!

"So let's not… like, please don't call me again," the voice continued. "But I'm fine. I'm OK. Right, bye then."

She's free, he thought again. I have to find her, have to talk to her.

Almost on instinct, he reached out a hand, mentally summoning his armor. Components flew through the air from the corners of the workshop, clicking together as they converged on his body. How do I locate her? he thought. I don't know Ms Marvel's true identity. No one does…

"Friday," he called. "Was there a caller ID on that message?"

"Sure was, boss. Landline – a commercial establishment, here in Manhattan. I can pinpoint the exact location."

"Hallelujah! Feed it to my GPS." His helmet snapped together, forming the last piece of the Iron Man armor. He started to snap it closed, then turned back to the helpless EgoMech. "Soon, Squeaky," he told it. "I promise."

It made no reply.

Tony jetted up into the air, veering toward the staircase. "Good hunting, boss," Friday told him. "And happy Dormammu."

He stopped short in alarm, just before the freight elevator. "Happy *what?*"

"Just kidding!" Friday said hastily. "Too soon?"

Tony muttered a string of curses.

"*Way* too soon," he said.

TEN

Over the past two weeks, Kamala had washed down the bar, polishing it until it shined. She'd dusted the shelves, swept the hallway, and scrubbed the floors clean. She'd run a mop across the ceiling, gathering up an impressive collection of cobwebs. She'd laid down rodent traps and even cleaned the bathroom, working carefully around the Eye of Vouk as she dropped sponge after sponge full of rat droppings into a trash bag.

Basically, she'd been spending as much time here as she could. Why? Because the rest of her life was a living nightmare. School, in particular. All day she sat in that classroom, pretending she belonged – that she was just like the other kids, the zombies who sat there through lesson after ridiculous lesson. Dormammu Philosophy, Dormammu Lit, Dormammu Through History. Dormammu Math.

Dormammu Math was the worst of all. It didn't make the slightest bit of sense.

So every day she bolted at the sound of the bell and jumped on the PATH train to Manhattan. Today had been a half-day, so she'd been sprung early. The relief was overwhelming.

But the stress of living in Dormammu World was getting to her. She lived in constant fear of being discovered, of being followed to the bar – her only sanctuary. In a fit of paranoia, she'd bought a painting of Dormammu himself from a street vendor and hung it over the bartender's station. Just to make the place look like a normal, Master-friendly establishment, in case some loyal subject wandered in.

With a sinking feeling, she realized it was getting late; if she didn't get home soon, her parents would start calling. So she gave the bar top another once-over and cleaned the sink behind it. Then she started down the dark, narrow corridor in the back of the establishment, to perform her one vital duty.

She pushed open the door to the cramped bathroom, noting with pride that the room no longer smelled like sewage. The Eye of Vouk still sat, undisturbed, on its shelf above the sink. She adjusted it, making sure it was stable. The Eye's pupil swiveled within its mount, staying focused on that one crucial spot above the toilet.

The spot where the Shadow Avengers had vanished.

"You guys have been gone a long time," she whispered. "Wherever you are, I hope you're safe."

Her cell phone buzzed, startling her. A text from Ammi, asking when she'd be home. She sent a quick, barely civil reply, then trudged back out to the bar.

Halfway down the corridor, she froze.

Footsteps – coming from the bar area, up ahead. Heavy, possibly metallic. Her heart raced in alarm. Was this it? Had Dormammu's forces finally tracked her down? Maybe they'd followed her here, or seen through her admittedly listless performance at school?

She shrugged off her outer clothing, changing quickly into

Ms Marvel. Lately she'd worn the costume everywhere. More paranoia, she'd thought, but now she wasn't sure. Was it really paranoia if the dangers were real?

She crept down the hall, activating her powers by instinct. Her body grew larger, arms and legs elongating, until she had to duck to avoid the ceiling. If someone out there wanted a fight, she'd be ready. At last she reached the door and pushed it open... slowly...

...only to see Iron Man in full armor, leaning against the bar like an impatient customer.

"Hey kid," he said, his voice filtered through his helmet.

She stepped into the room, studying him. His face was hidden; his armor, as always, looked like it could crush anyone or anything that got in its way.

"What are you doing here?" she asked.

"Traced your call," he said.

She clenched her fists, frustrated. Stupid, she thought. She hadn't wanted to call him on her cell, but in avoiding that, she'd made another mistake! Dormammu World was really getting to her.

He turned sharply and took a step forward. She stepped back, edging around the side of the room. She grew a few more inches and clenched her enlarged fists. Her fight-or-flight reflex was running wild; she felt trapped, cornered, every nerve exposed and raw.

"Stay back!" she warned.

"Hey, hey, whoa." His faceplate snapped open, revealing the worn, tired face of Tony Stark. "It's me, kid. See? It's me."

"Yeah?" she asked. "You you, or Dormammu you?"

"Me me!" He paused. "Though as a wise woman once said: I suppose if I wasn't me, I probably wouldn't admit–"

"I told you not to come find me." She circled around the edge of the room, keeping away from him. "I can't trust you. I can't trust anyone."

"*You* can't trust *me*?" He pointed at his face. "I'm right here, kid. This is me, Tony Stark. I'm the one that should be suspicious... I don't even know your real name." He gestured up at the painting, hanging over the bar. "Nice portrait, by the way."

They stood in silence for a moment. Hot air hung heavy in the bar; the one thing Kamala hadn't had time to fix was the air conditioning.

"You know..." He ran a metal-clad finger along the surface of the bar. "I think this is the cleanest tavern I've ever seen. And I've been in quite a few."

"If you're looking for an Osdrink, you're in the wrong place," she muttered.

"Ms Marvel..." He stared at her. "Why are you here?"

"This is my bar."

"You're fifteen and you own a bar?"

"I don't own it! My friend Luke Cage does."

"You know *Cage*?" He blinked. "What is going on?"

He *seemed* sincere – and desperate, too. She wanted so much to trust him, to believe in what he was saying. To know that there was someone else like her in the world who'd managed to throw off the shackles of Dormammu.

But she couldn't. She couldn't take that chance, not with the lives of Doctor Strange and the Shadow Avengers hanging in the balance. If just *one* of Dormammu's agents should learn about the portal... if Tony was only *pretending* to be himself, to inform on her to the so-called Master...

"On the way over," he said, "I detected some powerful energies surrounding this place."

She grimaced. Doctor Strange's wards of protection, she knew. But she couldn't explain that either.

"They don't quite match up with the Dormammu readings I've taken," he continued, "but they're magical in nature. You know anything about that?"

She cast a quick glance at the door leading to the back.

"Kid – Ms Marvel – ahhh, I wish I knew your name!" He collapsed onto a bar stool, hanging his head. "We've been through a lot, haven't we? The Praeterus business? The whole Civil War thing – the second one, I mean?"

She felt a stab of guilt. "Yeah," she said. "We have."

"So why won't you help me?" He stared at her, his eyes sunken and unnerving. "I am out of options, out of ideas. On the way over here, I was even thinking about trying to recruit some villains to help out." He let out a harsh laugh. "You know if Galactus is available? Venom, maybe?"

"You won't find Venom," she said softly.

"What?"

"Dormammu took him." She turned away. "He's trapped in the Dark Dimension."

"See, that, right there! How do you know that?"

She slammed an oversized fist against the wall. *Just leave, Tony!* she thought. *I can't answer your questions. Why won't you leave?*

"You keep looking at that door," he said, rising to his feet. "Where's it lead? Some hidden lair or something?"

He took a step toward the door, the one that led to the back hallway. She darted over to intercept him.

"What's back there?" he continued. "You got a pot burning on the stove?"

"You can't," she said, blocking his way. "I can't let you go back there."

"Why? Are you working for Dormammu?"

"Are *you?*"

He took another step. "I could force my way through."

Concentrating, she grew even larger. Her body stretched out to cover the door; she raised both fists, the size of boulders, directly in front of his glowing chestplate.

"You could try," she said.

Her heart beat like a hammer. Tony Stark stood before her, in full armor, repulsors charged and ready to fire. If he wanted to, he could blast this building to rubble. She'd seen his weapons in action, seen him topple far larger structures without breaking a sweat.

But she couldn't let him pass. No matter what, she could not risk anything happening to the Eye of Vouk. That was the Shadow Avengers' lifeline, the only hope they had of ever finding their way home again.

"You're *not* an agent of Dormammu," he said. She could hear the frustration in his voice. "I know you're not! So *what are you hiding?*"

"Just trust me," she said. "Please. For a little while."

He stared at her, sweat shining on his brow. Then he stepped back, tilted his head, and let out a scream of frustration.

Kamala flinched. Her enormous fists quivered. But she didn't move from the doorway.

He took one last look at her, and his expression nearly broke her heart. Betrayal, desperation, loneliness. Hopelessness.

She knew those emotions, all too well. She'd been living them, nonstop, for the past two weeks.

Before she could say anything, he slammed his helmet down over his face. Then he turned on his heel and, with a few quick clanking strides, marched out of the bar.

Kamala stood still for several seconds, listening as his heavy footsteps vanished up the steps. Only then, she realized she'd been holding her breath. She let it out all at once, her limbs shrinking as she slumped down to the floor.

"I'm sorry," she whispered. "I'm sorry, Tony."

In her pocket, her phone buzzed again. She didn't even look at it; she didn't have to. Ammi again.

She crept back into the hallway, changed into her civilian clothes, and strode out past the bar. In the front doorway, she paused to look back, her mouth set in a grim line. Then she marched back to the bar, climbed up on top of it, and pulled down the portrait of Dormammu. With a grunt, she cracked it in half and tossed it in the big trash can behind the bar.

That made her feel a little better.

ELEVEN

"Update: all is *still* not going well. In fact, all continues to not go well in a spectacularly consistent fashion.

"The Avengers are a dead end. Everyone that I've been able to locate, with the exception of Ms Marvel, remains under Dormammu's influence. The Ms Marvel situation, bee tee double-you, I find utterly baffling. But I can't focus on that now; it's a problem for another day.

"Moving forward: the EgoMech, we have now proven, cannot help with my fellow heroes. The machine was designed for my own personality, and it doesn't work on people with, let's just delicately say, a less highly developed regard for self. Given time, I could reprogram it, but I have no time. Dormammu's eyes are everywhere; my current activities could attract his attention at any moment.

"Fortunately, that seed of an idea I had percolating in my brain seems to have blossomed. It's crazy, dangerous, and almost guaranteed to blow up in my face. As an added bonus, it involves dealing with some of the most unpleasant personalities on Earth.

"But they're *impressive* personalities. They're movers, shakers – people who've pulled off audacious, near-impossible feats. And I think the EgoMech, in its current form, might be able to snap them back to their senses.

"After I finish these repairs, anyway. Oh, Squeaky, every inch of you needs soldering. You are *literally* a hot mess, you know that?"

Two days after his unsuccessful meeting with Ms Marvel, Tony paused inside the freight elevator, steeling himself for the confrontation ahead. He closed his eyes and let out a long, deep breath.

If this works, he thought, then I'm about to pull off the greatest gamble of my life. If not, well, I guess we all better get used to Osdrink cocktails.

The door creaked open and he stepped out into the workshop. It looked much the way it had before – holographic stage in the center, giant wallscreen to the right. Rows of armor still hung on the walls, staring down at him as he entered. But the floor was strewn with extra equipment: portable analyzers, robotic arm-helpers, petabyte hard drives salvaged from labs elsewhere in the tower. A heavy plastic containment box, its back panel open to reveal exposed wires.

The sum total, he thought grimly, of six months' work in the service of Dormammu.

Tiberius Stone, a lean man with dark wavy hair, looked up from a repulsor flow degausser. He wore jeans and short sleeves under a casual but expensive jacket, and glasses that were much thinner, Tony knew, than his prescription would normally require.

"I'm surprised, T," Stone said, a smirk tickling at his lips. "In the old days, you never would have let me get a look at this tech. You going open source on us?"

"What can I say, Ty?" Tony started across the room. "Consider it a gesture of faith."

"Faith? Or desperation?"

Tony didn't answer. He knew from experience that rising to Stone's bait could lead to hours of pointless sparring.

"This is quite the assemblage of kit," Stone continued, holding a Tribute Booth trigger mechanism up to the light. "Looks like you made out pretty well under the 'Master.'"

"Maybe. I'm sleeping better now, though."

Smirking openly, Ty dropped the mechanism onto a pile of circuits. "Money don't matter 2night, huh?"

"Ty, you can ride me, needle me, belittle my dress sense if you must. But please, please, I beg you…" He sighed. "Stop quoting Prince."

Stone smiled and picked up another piece of equipment.

"And quit picking through my stuff!" Tony snapped.

Stone had a mock-innocent look on his face. "Isn't that why you invited me? Or did I imagine that keycard that suddenly appeared outside my door?"

Tony turned away, fists clenched. Ever since they were kids, Ty had known exactly how to rile Tony – which nerve to press at any given moment. The stakes had risen, of course, after Stone murdered his own parents (maybe) and tried to kill Tony (for sure). But in a lot of ways, their relationship hadn't changed.

A low chanting rose from the other side of the room. Tony whirled around and started off around the stage, through the obstacle course of equipment.

"This ought to be fun," Stone said, following close behind.

Tony walked past the wallscreen and around a human-sized server bank, where he saw… a yoga mat. A yoga mat with a late middle-aged man sitting on it, hands laid flat over his crossed knees, eyes closed. He wore sweatpants and a hoodie, and he muttered something in a language Tony didn't recognize.

"Hammer?" Tony asked, astonished.

Justin Hammer didn't answer, didn't even open his eyes. He held up one stiff hand in acknowledgment, then continued chanting.

Tony found himself, uncharacteristically, at a loss for words. Had Hammer actually brought a *yoga mat* to this meeting?

"If this dude was running *my* company," Ty said, shaking his head, "I'd call for a no-confidence vote from the board."

Suddenly Tony's big gamble didn't look like such a good bet. He scanned the room, peering around the piles of equipment. "Just the two of you?"

"More like one and a half," Ty shot back, gesturing down at Hammer.

Tony frowned. He had deprogrammed and recruited *three* men, invited them all to this meeting. But one of them – the riskiest one, the loosest of the three loose cannons – hadn't even bothered to show. The odds of this scheme working grew worse and worse. He could almost taste those Osdrink cocktails.

"Let's, uh, get started," he said. "Hammer, can I have your attention? Hammer? JUSTIN!"

Hammer's eyes snapped open. For a moment, a murderous look crossed his face. Then he blinked, muttered "Namaste", and smiled. "Of course, Anthony," he said, his voice butter-smooth. "So good to see you."

Tony grimaced, turned away, and walked to the wallscreen. Hammer and Stone just watched him, unmoving. Tony gestured for them to follow, waiting while Hammer climbed stiffly to his feet.

"OK," Tony said, activating the screen with his phone. "You know what we're up against. Dormammu controls... well..."

A world map appeared on the screen. Its surface glowed red, with the darkest spots in Asia and the northeastern United States.

"...everyone," Tony said.

"That's just a population map," Stone said, crossing his arms.

"I'm trying to make a point." Holding up his phone, Tony projected a laser beam up at the blood-red New York area. "See those four yellow dots?"

"No," Stone replied.

"Nope," Tony agreed. "You can't, can you? How about now?"

The image zoomed in. New York grew, expanding until the island of Manhattan filled the screen. Then it zoomed in further, the green outline of Central Park becoming visible within the sea of red.

"I still don't see the bloody dots!" Ty said.

"Patience, boy," Hammer said, laying a hand on Stone's shoulder. "'If you wait by the river, the bodies of your enemies will float by.'"

"Get away from me with your Sun Tzu stoner crap," Ty snapped.

"Ty is right," Tony said, "again. The dots are still not visible... because out of the eight billion people on Earth, and several million in the New York metropolitan area..."

The image continued to zoom in, resolving into a block-by-block schematic of an area in upper Midtown. Four yellow dots appeared, finally, clustered together in the spot where Stark Tower – this very building – stood.

"...we are the only four free people on this planet."

"Tony," Ty said through gritted teeth, "I could never match you at higher math. But I'm pretty sure I only see three people in this room."

"The fourth one – he must be coming. He's nearby." Tony shook his head. "The point is, we're the planet's only hope."

Actually, there were *five* free people. But Tony wasn't about to tell Stone and Hammer about Ms Marvel. He didn't trust them that much.

"Well," Ty snorted, "you sure think a lot of yourself. But then, that's nothing new." He turned to gesture at the wall, at the rows of Iron Man suits gazing down on the room. "What I don't understand is, why not call your super friends to help you? Why us?" He smirked again, pointing both fingers at his own chest. "Did you just miss your old buddy?"

"Actually, *old buddy…* " Tony faced Stone directly. "You want to know the truth?"

"Always." Stone's eyes bored into his. "Nothing else hurts quite so much."

"The truth is, the super hero community has pretty much let me down."

Tony felt a sudden pang of sadness. He hadn't realized, until this moment, quite how hard that series of rejections had hurt. Especially Ms Marvel…

"What about those aliens you had on a pilot work program?" Stone asked. "The ones you were paying undocumented-immigrant wages to, so you could treat them like crap?"

"That's not… First off, those conditions were *not* my doing, and I corrected them the first chance I got," Tony said, trying to keep the defensiveness out of his voice. "Second, I thought of that – I wondered if the Kree might be more resistant to Dormammu's mind control. Turns out they're not. When I approached my workers' liaison, she tried to drag me out to a Tribute Booth."

"No luck with super heroes," Hammer said, a thoughtful look on his face, "and no luck with aliens."

"That's … basically right …"

"So you turned to your *third* peer group."

Tony paused, his head spinning. What in the world was going on with Hammer? Stone had made one attempt on Tony's life, but Hammer had been a thorn in his side for most of his career. The industrialist had tried to take over Tony's company more times than either of them could count; he'd even framed Iron Man for murder. Now he stood, smiling that weird smile, like some cut-rate ad for antidepressants.

"Ah," Ty said, "I'm beginning to get it."

"I needed people like … like me," Tony admitted. "You know, techies. Industry leaders. Tycoons, geniuses … visionaries …"

"… rich people," Hammer said.

"Well," Tony began, "well, yeah! Men who understand the world, who know what they want and just go for it. See, I had this deprogramming machine. It didn't work on most people, but it worked on both of *you*. Why? Because you're egomaniacs."

Ty frowned, and for a moment Tony thought he would take offense. Then Ty turned toward Hammer, and they both shrugged.

"Fair point," Hammer said.

"Egomaniacs." Stone stared at Tony. "Like yourself."

Tony paused, then – inevitably – shrugged in turn.

"I don't like being, well, *demoted* to the level of ordinary people," he admitted. "Especially by an interdimensional conqueror. And I don't think you two do, either."

"What I *think* is that I should be insulted," Stone mused.

"Not by the ego thing, but because you're comparing me to yourself. On the other hand, you seem to be complimenting my strength of will."

"I am," Tony said. "That is absolutely what I'm doing."

"On the *other* other hand, you manipulated me."

"In order to free you from Dormammu's influence!"

"Yeah. About that." Stone stepped forward, right in Tony's face. "Do you know how your stupid robot recruited me? What form it took, in order to shock me to my senses?"

"I…" Tony shrugged. "I think it was an accountant? I've reviewed the video, but not in detail."

Stone stared at him for a moment, then paced away. He glanced down at the containment box, the one Tony had carried up on the freight elevator, then lowered himself to perch on it, using it as a stool.

"When Dormammu moved in," Stone began, "I was on the verge of something. I'd been toiling away as head of R&D at Alchemax for three years. Bit of a comedown for me, T. As you know, I used to own a media empire. But I bided my time, put in the work…"

"…tried to disrupt the entire world economic system…" Tony said.

"Like I said, I did the work." Stone flashed him a cold smile. "And I was *this close* to assuming control of the entire company – when everything changed."

Tony nodded, struggling to remember. The period of Dormammu's ascension was still hazy in his mind. "The contracts," he said. "A whole category of defense and weaponry deals… they suddenly shifted from Alchemax to Stark/Dormammu."

"Right. Other projects were moved to Osborn," Ty affirmed.

"In the blink of an eye, Alchemax was ruined. And me along with it."

Tony shook his head. "I didn't know that, Ty. But I don't know how bad I can really bring myself to feel for–"

"I'm not finished." Ty glared at him. "Sure, you made billions while I fell on my face. That's nothing new, it's been happening all our lives. But it isn't my point."

Tony cocked his head, confused.

"Your robot... the EgoMech... it appeared as my personal financial manager."

"A good financial manager!" Hammer nodded. "They're like family. *Better* than family."

"Well, this one gave me a pretty good shock." Ty turned away, but not before Tony got a glimpse of the pain on his face. "This particular *family member* hanged himself three months ago. After I, and the other eight Alchemax execs he worked with, lost our virtual shirts."

"Oh." Tony blinked. "I... I didn't..."

"Your little *robot*," Ty snarled, "showed me the face of a dead man."

"I'm sorry, Ty." Tony blinked. "I didn't know that would happen–"

The wallscreen exploded in a shower of glass.

Tony raised one arm, sending out a quick mental command. Faster than the eye could follow, five metal fingers and a palm gauntlet flew through the air to fasten onto his hand. He flipped his palm outward, sending out a wide-beam repulsor ray to atomize the glass fragments flying toward his face.

At least, he thought, six months under Dormammu haven't dulled my instincts!

Stone let out a cry and leaped back, vaulting over a pile

of computer components. Hammer frowned, took a step backward, and calmly adopted a downward-dog yoga position.

Shards of glass clinked to the floor, smoke billowing out from the shattered wallscreen. A gleaming tentacle, coiled and deadly, thrust its way through the opening, grabbing hold of the jagged rim of the screen. The tentacle yanked, pulling three more tentacles through along with it.

A thick-bodied man in goggles followed, carried aloft by the four metal "arms" fastened to his torso. He paused, waved aside the smoke with a sweep of his tentacles, and turned to smile at Tony.

"I apologize for my tardiness," Doctor Octopus said. "Shall we begin?"

TWELVE

Tony stepped forward, the single repulsor still glowing on his palm. The room had been a mess before, but now it looked like a tornado had blown through it. Chunks of the wallscreen lay scattered among the piles of equipment; one of them had cleaved a hard drive in half. Shards of glass had gotten caught in the holostage, floating and glittering in the null-g field.

Doctor Octopus bobbed, unnervingly, on those four arms, which remained in constant motion. But he made no further aggressive moves.

"This?" Stone stepped out from behind a large server. "*This* is our fourth member?"

Ock just smiled. "Otto Octavius," he said, executing an elaborate bow with all four of his tentacles. One of them passed disturbingly close to Stone's head.

"B-minus for the apology, Otto," Tony said. He gestured at the broken screen. "By the way, you're paying for that."

"Take it out of my fee," Ock replied, still smirking. "Which, I assure you, will be considerable."

"I sent you a keycard, man! To the front door! Didn't you get it?"

Ock looked around; he seemed bored. "I dropped it."

"You can build a nuclear reactor with those mandibles, but you can't hang onto a *keycard?*"

Ock just shrugged. Which, with all those arms, added up to quite a shrug. One tentacle brushed against a console, raising sparks.

"Tony," Stone said, ducking, "what kind of hologram did you use to recruit this psycho?"

"Actually," Tony said, "it took an image of the entire Sinister Six to deprogram Otto."

"My will is quite formidable," Ock said.

"Burned out all the EgoMech's circuits – trashed it for good, this time." Tony shook his head sadly. "Poor Squeaky. Rest in pieces, pal."

Stone circled around Ock, keeping his distance. "This man is a wanted felon," he said. "His crimes are extremely public, and well documented."

"We don't all try to kill people in the shadows, boy," Ock growled. "Some of us prefer the direct approach."

"First off, Otto, Ty isn't a boy," Tony said. "Lot of Botox in that face… Never mind, that is *so* not the point. Holy Colonizers of Rigel, what the devil are *you* doing?"

To his right, Hammer stood upright and rigid. The older man's hands were clasped together above his head; one foot was bent and raised, like a stork standing in shallow water.

"Vrksasana," Hammer replied calmly. "Good for the spine. You should try it."

Stone backed away, staring at each of the others in turn. He looked like a warden who'd been trapped in the asylum.

"Tony," he said slowly, "I can work with you. I know you, I know what you're capable of. If I had to, I could probably take you out. Cut your throat, kill you in your sleep or something…"

"Um," Tony said. "Good?"

"But these two?" Stone shook his head. "I just don't see it."

"OK, just listen for a… Doc, can you stop bobbing around like that? It's, like, super distracting."

Ock let out a short laugh. He lowered himself a foot closer to the floor, then resumed bobbing around.

Tony sighed. "Ty," he said, "Otto here is right. He's direct – direct as in *practical*. He's a practical engineer."

"Om mani padme," Hammer murmured, nodding.

"You're an R&D genius, Ty," Tony continued. "Hammer is… well, I'm not sure quite what he is right now, but his skills are big picture. That's all good – I can barely keep up with you guys in those areas. But none of it translates directly to *building* stuff." He gestured at Ock's metal arms. "Look at those mandibles! Microcircuit-laced, mentally controlled, with the tensile strength of titanium alloy. Could *you* have constructed them?"

"Given time," Stone said. "And with the proper assistance."

"Or partners," Tony countered. "The proper partners."

Stone glared at him, then up at Ock.

"He's not even rich," Ty grumbled.

"You'd be surprised how much I've stashed away over the years," Ock replied. *"Boy."*

Stone looked away. Hammer stood completely still, his eyes closed. He held one elevated foot in his hand, the other hand raised toward the ceiling.

Ock murmured something that sounded vaguely conciliatory, and dropped down another six inches. "I should add," he said, "that I have no more love for Dormammu than anyone else in this room."

"OK." Tony stepped into the center of the group. "OK, this is good. We're all on the same page, and I really do think our skills complement each other. But we need to lay down a couple of ground rules. First off: let's keep radio silence for the duration. No contact whatsoever with the outside world. Copacetic?"

Stone shrugged. The others looked away, bored.

"Then there's the biggie." Tony took a breath. "The elephant, the super-powered pachyderm in the room."

Stone and Ock frowned at him, waiting.

"If we're going to work together," he continued, "*no trying to kill me*. All right?"

Ock glanced at Stone. The younger man looked back, raising an eyebrow.

"This shouldn't be a hard question," Tony added. He turned to face Stone directly, also raising an eyebrow.

"Oh, I was kidding before, T," Stone said. "I can't see how killing you would be to my advantage. Right now, anyway."

"Anthony?"

"Whoa!" Tony almost jumped as Hammer laid a hand on his shoulder. "Uh, Justin! Yoga's made you pretty stealthy."

"Thank you." Hammer's face, unnervingly close to Tony's, burst into a beatific smile. "It's part of my self-improvement plan."

"OK…"

"About this killing business," Hammer continued. "Allow me to relate a story."

"Do I have a ch… no no, that's rude of me. Please go ahead."

Hammer stepped back, raising a hand to his chin. He looked as if he were about to begin a TED Talk. Stone and Ock moved closer, frowning.

"Twelve months ago," Hammer began, "before the world…

changed... I found myself in a most vexing situation. Hammer Industries had fallen on difficult times. A series of human resources debacles had reduced morale to an all-time low, causing an exodus of talent from the company." He looked down, shook his head. "I confess that many of these HR problems stemmed from my own actions with regard to my employees."

"*Quelle surprise,*" Stone murmured.

"Fortunately... and in keeping with my lifelong flexibility and my philosophy of futurism... I was able to right that ship," Hammer continued. "I took a temporary step down from my responsibilities, a move I recall as almost completely voluntary on my part. In a frenzy of self-improvement, I enlisted a battery of the finest therapists, spiritual gurus, and pharmacologists in the service of one single, all-important goal: altering my outlook on life.

"And I succeeded." Hammer smiled. "By the time this little Dormammu scuffle began, I was a new man."

"Scuffle?" Stone said. "He conquered the world!"

"Yes," Hammer said, "and me along with it. But now..."

He turned to face Tony and clapped both hands on Tony's shoulders. This time Tony actually jumped.

"...Anthony Stark, my longtime foe and rival, has freed me from bondage, wrested the interdimensional monkey from my back." He smiled an unnerving smile. "And I owe you, Tony. I am in your debt."

"It's, uh – I mean, let's not make too big a–"

"I mean it, old boy. World conquerors come and go, but men like us strive on, performing great works beyond the reach of ordinary mortals. Sure, I've sabotaged you in the past... discredited you, even tried to murder you in cold blood. But the *new* me, the reborn, sensitive Hammer you see before you – he understands the special bond we share."

Tony could feel sweat breaking out on his brow. He considered ordering an Iron Man suit to blast a hole in the wall, just to end this conversation.

"I'm trying to say…" Hammer took a step closer. "Anything you need, Tony Stark. Anything. I'm at your service."

Then the worst thing of all happened. Worse than Tony's failures with the Avengers, worse than his time under Dormammu's mental yoke. Worse, even, than the moment when Pepper had walked out of his life.

Justin Hammer hugged him.

Ock's metal arms vibrated in disbelief.

Stone shook his head at Hammer. "I think I liked him better under Dormammu."

Hammer hung on, pressing his thin frame against Tony's body. "Uh," Tony said, raising his arms for a half-hearted return hug. "That's, uh. I, uh, appreciate. It. Can we, uh? Can we not, now?"

Hammer didn't move. Tony began to fear that the hug would last forever – until one of Doc Ock's tentacles slammed into the floor, startling everyone.

"Thank you," Tony said, disengaging himself from the still-smiling Hammer. Then he noticed the shattered floor tiles. "You're paying for that, too."

"Enough of this!" Ock said, elevating himself on his tentacles. "What is the plan? What would you have us build in this untidy playpen of a workshop?"

"If it involves an assault on the Osdrink production facilities," Hammer said, "I doubt our old friend Norman will make things easy for you."

"Too slow," Tony agreed. "And yeah, probably too well

guarded as well. I hear he's moved most of that operation to Hydra Island, out in the Pacific. Even the location is classified."

"In that case…" Stone crossed to the containment box, the one with the exposed wires. "You've been staring at this particular component ever since you walked in. I assume it has something to do with your plan."

"It does." Tony walked over and crouched down next to the box. It was about the size of a large bread maker, with circuit boards hanging loose from its open back flap. "This is–"

"I know what it is," Stone interrupted. "It's part of your magnificent tech, the gear you spent six months developing for the 'Master.'" He crouched down to peer at the device. "Amplifies Tribute energies, doesn't it?"

"Yes. In conjunction with a larger complex of machinery, it magnifies those energies on an exponential level." Tony stood up, hissing in a breath. "We're going to adapt it to a different purpose."

"Adapt it." Hammer ran his hands along the box, taking in its contours. "To what parameters?"

"Well, for one thing, it's gonna have to be a lot bigger," Tony said. "After all, we're talking about an assault on the Dark Dimension."

The room erupted in voices.

"Bigger? How much bigger?"

"Dark Dimension?"

"What are we supposed to trap in this thing, anyway?"

"Is it a weapon?"

"Hold up. We're talking *Dormammu*'s Dark Dimension?"

"Yes!" Tony said, sweeping a hand through the air to silence them. "We have to take the battle to Dormammu, to his home realm. It's our only hope of stopping him."

The room went silent. Ock swiveled one tentacle in a wide arc, using its pincer to gently scratch his own head.

"Anthony," Hammer said, his face grave, "I can see the possibilities here. It should be a simple matter to construct a larger version of this containment box, and to convert the energy inputs."

"Says the man who's not doing the converting," Stone grumbled.

"Or the constructing," Ock added.

"All that said," Hammer continued, "exactly what sort of carnivorous feline are we attempting to grab by the tail here? What kind of weapon could possibly work in Dormammu's seat of power?"

Tony nodded solemnly. "That," he said, "is exactly the right question."

"So what's the answer?" Ock demanded.

Tony crossed over to a work table, eyeing a sealed suitcase sitting among a pile of blueprints and work tools. He allowed himself a smile, feeling an unfamiliar emotion wash over him. With a jolt, he realized what it was: hope.

"I'll tell you tomorrow," he said, "after I consult our fifth partner."

Then he picked up the suitcase, turned on his heel, and strode back into the freight elevator.

As the doors slid shut, he closed his eyes in relief. Maybe, he thought, this plan could actually work. These people had been his enemies in the past, and all of them had performed acts ranging from amoral chaos to outright evil. But they were also men who had built financial empires, constructed vast works. Stone and Hammer and, yes, even Doctor Octopus: they all knew how to get things done.

Maybe, he thought, I should have done this a long time ago.

It took half an hour for him to realize that Ock had *not* promised not to kill him.

THIRTEEN

The freight elevator carried him to a second-floor loading dock, where an eighteen-wheeler was disgorging a fresh supply of water-cooler jugs filled with bright green Osdrink. Tony grimaced, flipped a quick wave at the dock foreman – who wore overalls and a cap with the Stark/Dormammu logo on it – and scurried over to the passenger elevator as quickly as he could.

That elevator terminated three levels down, at a deserted sub-basement corridor. Tony strode down the hallway, shifting his briefcase from hand to hand, footsteps echoing in the near dark. With each step, he wondered: Is Dormammu watching me? Right now?

At the end of the corridor stood a thick wooden door. It had been installed by bootleggers a hundred years ago and refitted, more recently, with handprint and retinal scanners. As he passed through into an even darker passageway, the door swung shut behind him.

A bare stone staircase with no railing spiraled down into utter blackness. Vaguely, Tony recalled shutting off power to these levels in order to divert more resources to the company's

Dormammu research. As he descended, winding around the cramped space, the air grew stale and foul.

Halfway down he stopped, snapped open the suitcase, and donned his Iron Man armor. He gasped in relief as a flood of fresh air hissed into his helmet. He activated his chestbeam at low power, shining the light ahead and down to show the way.

The staircase ended at a dirt floor. Another door – cast iron, this time – barred the way forward. This one had no high-tech sensors attached, just a big rusty keyhole. It took him several minutes to locate the iron key in his civilian clothes, which he'd stuffed into the suitcase. When he inserted it into the keyhole, the key jammed for a second. Then the door clicked open.

And Tony stepped into the Iron Vault.

The room was utterly dark – the electricity had been cut off down here, too. "Emergency reboot," he said aloud. "Restore power to this level."

"Complying," a voice replied. "Minimal power only available."

Dim red lights winked on around the domed chamber, revealing bare stone walls. A row of thick metal doors, roughly twice the size of morgue drawers, were embedded in the walls at eye level, with a dark video screen in the center. A simple worktable stood in the middle of the room, along with a single folding chair.

Tony took a deep breath, hissing in the filtered air. Every one of those drawers, every piece of equipment hidden in these walls, posed a danger to life on Earth. Bombs, explosives, bizarre extraterrestrial weapons – even a key component of the Large Hadron Collider. He'd stashed them all down here, deep beneath the streets of Manhattan, where only he even knew they existed.

If Dormammu *is* watching, he thought grimly, then I've already lost the game.

"Authorization Stark Omega," he said. "Open Drawer Five." Another deep breath. "Show me the Stane Solvent."

The machinery hummed briefly. Then a single drawer clicked open and began to extrude its contents. Tony stood patiently, waiting as a hidden panel slid open in the ceiling and a Waldo-style grabber arm swung down into the room. The arm took hold of the object in the drawer, lifted it up, and deposited it on the table.

Tony stared down at the object: a thick transparent tube with metal seals on either end. Dark blue liquid, thick and roiling, filled most of the tube.

"*Heeeeeey*, Tony."

He jumped. The video screen had flashed to life, revealing the smiling face of Obadiah Stane. The one-time industrial tycoon wore a dark, expensive suit; his bald head was perfectly smooth.

"Crap," Tony said aloud, "I forgot about this part–"

"If you're viewing this," the Stane image continued, "then I guess I'm dead. Which means you won our little rivalry, Tone." He paused. "Can I call you Tone? We were never close. I always sort of regretted that… is that weird?"

"No weirder than talking to a ghost," Tony muttered.

But inside his metal gauntlets, his hands were shaking. Stane had been Tony's most hated rival, the man who'd come closer than anyone else to destroying the Stark legacy. He'd taken full control of the original Stark Enterprises, forcing Tony to rebuild from scratch. Then, in his Iron Monger suit, Stane had almost killed Tony personally.

Tony glanced down at the transparent tube. He'd only

seen it once before, and that time he'd cut off the video after a single recorded sentence. He considered doing that again, but decided against it. In order to defeat Dormammu, he'd need every ally he could get. That included villains… world-destroying weapons…

… and a dead man. A man who'd almost broken him years ago, at the worst time of his life.

"Anyway." The image on the screen gestured forward, almost as if it could actually see the table. "This, in case you're wondering, is the modern miracle I call the Stane Solvent. Upon contact with another substance, it breaks down molecular bonds at a frightening rate. In early tests, we found it could *decorporealize* almost any form of matter. And it spreads – oh boy, does it spread! We lost half a lab building, a good deal of sewer substructure, and most of a prototype Iron Monger suit before my techs managed to corral the stuff inside this adamantium-laced holding container."

Stane leaned forward. A flurry of expressions crossed his face; Tony couldn't sort them all out.

"I know what you think of me," Stane continued, "and I won't argue the point. I've done a lot of things that, well, won't exactly get me through the pearly gates. But I've got my limits, and this stuff is *way* past them." He looked aside and took a deep breath. "The Stane Solvent is the deadliest substance on Earth. Let loose again, it would keep dissolving and dissolving things until, well, the entire planet was gone. Except, I guess, for a few floating scraps of adamantium and, maybe, vibranium. Maybe.

"No one can know about this stuff, Tone. I mean *no one*. If somebody less responsible than myself were to try and duplicate the process… well, it hardly bears thinking about. Five of my scientists worked on the project, and while I don't like to brag, I've made sure they all met with unfortunate accidents."

Tony shook his head in despair. Stane, he thought, you monster. If you weren't dead, I'd strangle you with my metal hands.

But the man wasn't wrong about the Solvent.

"You're my greatest rival," Stane said. "I always thought of us as, well, two of a kind. Maybe that's why I despise you so deeply."

"Back at you!" Tony spat.

"So hear me now." A terrible smile crossed Stane's face. "In the event of my death, all data regarding the Stane Solvent is to be passed to you, along with the only existing sample. This is my last jab, the final blow in our years-long sparring match. From beyond the grave, I hereby…"

The figure erupted in a terrible, wheezing sort of laughter. Inside his armor, Tony cringed, waiting for the ordeal to end.

"…I hereby burden you with a power that could destroy the Earth."

Tony looked down at the thick blue liquid, sloshing inside its adamantium tube. The words echoed inside his mind: *a power that could destroy the Earth.*

"Use it wisely, Tone." Another short burst of laughter. "Knowing you, I figure that's 50/50."

The screen went black.

Tony reached out, willing his arm servos to pinpoint control, and lifted the tube as gently as he could. Stane's revenge had been fierce, his aim true. The Solvent was indeed a terrible burden, a deadly weapon that had to be hidden at all costs. In the days before the coming of Dormammu, Tony had worried constantly that some enemy – or even a well-meaning friend, like Nick Fury – might stumble upon the substance and use it for their own ends.

But now – in the world *after* Dormammu – it might be his only hope.

He tilted the tube to one side, watching in almost hypnotic fascination as the deep blue gel flowed slowly from one end to the other. Even his Iron Man suit, the state-of-the-art armor he'd constructed and honed over the years, offered no protection against the Solvent. He could almost feel its power, sense its barely contained fury, calling to him: *Let me out. Let me out! Let me be your weapon… your savior.*

And then something else stirred inside him. The memory of Dormammu, the warm mewling thing. The horror he could never forget, the cancer that must be expelled – from himself, and from the rest of the world as well.

Forever.

With a clang, he braced the tube against his shoulder. Then, almost reverently, he turned to begin the long walk back up into the light.

PART THREE

MINDLESS

FOURTEEN

On the seventy-first day, Jericho Drumm allowed himself to go mad.

He'd begun his search in the near realms, the closest ones to Earth. His brother Daniel was unlikely to be in one of those; that would be too easy. But with a billion dimensional planes to search through, he had to start somewhere. So he kept a tight grip on the Staff of Legba, allowing the wooden staff to guide him through the veils, from one strange world to another. One was an endless expanse of sand; another smelled of cinnamon and teemed with floating, balloon-like creatures. Still another world reeked of charred metal, smoke rising from the devastated pits of its cities.

And every single realm, from the most barren to the ones that practically burst with life, bore the bitter scars of Dormammu's invasion.

He found no sign of Daniel in the near realms, so he widened his search. The Staff flung him through thicker veils, to stranger worlds. A thousand barren realms, some so terrifying he could barely remember them afterward.

Thus passed the first twelve days.

(They weren't really *days*. Jericho had no idea how much time actually passed around him, or even whether time had any meaning here. But he thought of the journey in terms of days. That kept him sane – for a while.)

He began to tire; his hands trembled on the Staff. But he carried on. He had to find Daniel – his brother, his twin, his guiding light since childhood. Daniel, who had been corrupted by Dormammu, then flung into some otherworldly realm as punishment for his defiance.

Daniel, who – along with Jericho himself – formed the Sorcerer Supreme called Doctor Voodoo.

On the twenty-sixth day, Jericho found himself on a world of jagged craters swirling with sickly-sweet, violet gases. He dropped to his knees, mind whirling, and for a moment he succumbed to despair. He considered giving up, letting go of the Staff and allowing himself to be lost in the chaos between the realms.

Then he saw it – just a glimpse, in the corner of his eye. The Mindless One. The lackey of Dormammu that had dogged his steps, every moment of this journey. Its thick granite body crouched just beyond the dimensional veil, faceless maw glowing fiery red as it slowly turned in his direction.

He had to keep moving. To find Daniel, yes. But also because, if ever he stopped to rest, the Mindless One would find and destroy him. That had been Dormammu's plan, all along: to lure Jericho off Earth, where – separated from his source of power – he could be killed.

He had seen the trap opening before him, even admired the cold logic of it. But there was no avoiding it. He could not allow his brother to suffer for his – for Jericho's – sake. Daniel had endured too much already, both in life and in his long, lonely afterlife.

Jericho thrust the Staff out before him and lurched forward, into the next world.

The realms grew even more bizarre. One was made entirely of soap bubbles; another assaulted his ears with all the music ever written. Another seemed composed entirely of rage, a hideous beat that echoed the relentless, all-consuming power of Dormammu. With a tremendous effort Jericho gripped the Staff tight, forced the anger from his mind, and swept through yet another veil.

Eventually, yes, he went mad. He never knew how long *that* lasted, either. He forged through world after world: a subatomic atom, a sky of ticking clocks, a poison jungle. But he no longer knew whether anything he saw was real.

He found himself walking on a beach, hot sun on his bare back. He turned to look, and beside him walked a boy, about twelve years old. A boy like himself, with dark skin and bare feet. A boy *exactly* like himself.

Daniel. His twin.

Daniel grinned, reached out, and punched Jericho on the shoulder. Jericho laughed. Somehow they were back in Haiti, at the time of their shared childhood. Before Jericho had moved to America and become a psychologist. Before Daniel died; before his restless spirit had joined with Jericho's to form Doctor Voodoo.

Joy surged through Jericho. He'd found him – found Daniel! He reached out a hand to touch his brother…

…a hand that passed through fading mist, as the boy dissolved into the air.

Jericho blinked, squeezed his eyes shut. When he looked up,

the beach was gone. He lay in a cold metal coffin on a world of coffins. A necropolis left behind by a race that had chosen death, rather than living under the yoke of Dormammu.

The beach, he realized, had not been a realm, but a memory. The fantasy of an exhausted sorcerer, a wish-dream of things that had been. A dead end of the mind.

He sat up in his coffin. Spires of fallen buildings lay toppled all around, charred blacker than black. A squat, flat-topped silo stood nearby, a hint of a faded radiation symbol visible on its cracked concrete wall.

This world, he realized, was utterly dead, devoid of even the simplest animal life. Nothing lived here, not anymore. Certainly not Daniel.

Jericho raised his hands to his head and wept. This chase, he thought, is hopeless. My whole life has been a waste of time. I cannot find Daniel, cannot save my brother. Cannot even save myself.

From deep within, the phrase rose to his mind: *Dormammu is despair.*

And then, with that thought, an epiphany. Dormammu, he realized, did not lure me here merely to finish me off. He did it because he needed to remove me from the playing field. Dormammu's conquest of the realms, his planned dominion over all that lived – it was only possible if the Sorcerers Supreme of Earth could be wrenched apart, weakened, and disposed of separately.

I am important, he thought. I alone, in some manner I do not yet fully comprehend, may prove the key to this monster's defeat.

I matter!

Strength flowed through Jericho's frame. He stood – and

reeled, immediately dizzy. The knowledge of his role in this cosmic game had lent him new resolve, urged him forward. But his body, his mystic powers, were still depleted. The days between realms – or was it years? – had taken a toll.

No matter. He had to forge on. He reached into his belt and pulled out a small drawstring bag, sniffing it quickly. The herbs inside had lost most of their potency during his long journey; this spell had little chance of succeeding. But a houngan, he reminded himself, is much more than his tools. His will power is what sets him apart.

He snapped a hair free from his head, opened the bag a tiny bit, and pushed the hair inside. Then he gripped the Staff in his other hand and raised it high. Ignoring the stench in the air, the overwhelming despair radiating from all the realms. Ignoring, even, the looming Mindless One, gazing at him with eyeless eyes, somewhere just beyond the gray-black sky.

"Papa Legba," he chanted, closing his eyes, "open the gates for me. Open, open, open the gates. Open the gates for me to pass!"

Images shimmered before him. A dozen realms; a hundred, a thousand. Dark and light, warm and frigid, pink-smelling dreams and foul snapping nightmares. In one of them, his brother waited, afraid and alone…

"Daniel." He almost choked on the poison air. "Daniel, I can feel you. Speak to me now! Guide me to you, that I might atone for the part I've played in your terrible fate."

Nothing.

"Daniel!" he cried.

Then – so quietly he feared, at first, that it was just another memory–

Brother, a voice said. *Please.*

Jericho's eyes widened. He waved the Staff back and forth in the air, searching the realms.

Please find me, Daniel continued. *Save me!*

The realms stretched and shimmered, wavering in and out of view. "I hear you," Jericho said. "I feel you, brother. So near…"

The images fanned to all sides, like a flower's petals blooming wide. And in the center: a single, violet-gray realm. Wispy figures, thin and wavering, filled that world. They shuffled back and forth, passing through and around each other, barely acknowledging each other's presence.

A shiver ran through Jericho. He nearly dropped the Staff of Legba. He dreaded this realm more than any other. But he had no choice.

Brother?

"I'm coming!" he cried, and ran through the portal.

As he touched the first of the ghostly figures, a profound *hunger* came over him. He felt a chill to the core of his bones, as if all life had been sucked from his body. The human-shade didn't look at him, didn't react in any way. It just moved on and was lost in the miasmic haze, in an endless gray mass of a million others like it.

In the Realm of the Dead.

Jericho held up the staff, willing it to find Daniel. Of course, he thought – of course Dormammu would hide his brother here! Daniel, after all, was one of the dead himself. Here, he was just one of a trillion fallen souls, the dead and gone of a billion worlds.

"Daniel?" he called – and then, in the telepathic language of the dead: *Daniel?* The Staff glowed weakly, its power nearly depleted. But Daniel was close. Jericho could feel him…

Brother!

As Jericho watched, astonished, the shades parted – and his brother stumbled toward him, arms spread, reaching for salvation.

Jericho tensed, bracing for the cold sensation of a dead soul. But Daniel's arms felt solid, his body warm and real. Jericho stumbled, startled, and let out an embarrassed laugh.

Here in this place, he realized, Daniel *was* real. A ghost who had defied death; a shade who had lived on Earth, well past his appointed time. A very special, rare spirit.

They fell together to their knees, laughing and crying. For a moment, Jericho forgot the horde of souls massing around them; forgot even the looming menace of the Mindless One. Nothing was real except his brother, his friend, the other half of himself.

Doctor Voodoo was whole once more.

I found you, Jericho gasped. *I knew… not all the realms could keep us apart.*

Thank Papa, Daniel sighed. *I have waited – how long has it been?* He blinked, tears forming in his spectral eyes. *I nearly lost myself.*

I can only imagine. Jericho held on tight to his brother. *The Realm of the Dead is not meant for our kind!*

What?

Daniel pulled away, staring at his brother in surprise.

Realm of the Dead? Daniel continued. *What are you talking about?*

Jericho blinked, looked around. The ghostly shades shimmered, milled around…

…and evaporated into the air.

He shot to his feet, alarmed. A white void surrounded him,

glaring and empty and utterly, unimaginably terrifying. The dead had vanished without a trace, as if they'd never been.

Which they hadn't, he whispered.

Daniel stood up, staring at him. *You saw something?*

Yes, Jericho replied. *A ploy, an illusion. Another trick…*

… by Dormammu, Daniel finished.

He ran me through a maze, Jericho said. *Led me through a thousand realms, forced me to expend my power… to deplete my magical reserves, until now…*

He held up the Staff. It glowed once, then went dark.

… now I have nothing left.

You mean… Fear filled Daniel's eyes. *You mean we're both trapped here?*

Jericho couldn't bring himself to answer. In desperation he cast his gaze all around, past his brother and up into the air. For a moment he caught a glimpse of the Mindless One, its face glowing fury-red. Then it turned away from him and shimmered into nothingness.

He knows, Jericho thought. Dormammu has called off his assassin, his attack dog. He knows I'm no longer a threat to his dominion.

He no longer even needs me dead.

Oh, brother. Daniel dropped to his knees and began to sob. *Oh, I am so sorry.*

It's not your fault, Jericho replied.

But it is. I allowed myself to be seduced by Dormammu… I used our shared body in his service. I brought you into this!

Dormammu had always planned to conquer Earth's realm, Jericho replied, forcing a smile onto his face. *I would have been "brought into it" one way or another.*

But he has used me against you again! And now you must share my lonely fate. Daniel looked away, off into the void. Oh, brother, I am sorry. I am so sorry...

Jericho stood, stoic, as his brother repeated the phrase over and over again. Eventually, it lost all meaning. Just a string of thought-syllables, echoing in the void:

I'm sorry. I'm so sorry...

He never knew how long they stood there: the dead man and the depleted sorcerer. The houngan who had made bad choices, and the brother who had risked everything to find him. The helpless pawn and the captured knight.

The two sides of Doctor Voodoo.

There was nothing to do, no further path to walk. Dormammu had sealed the portal, trapping them in this vacant, antiseptic pocket realm. The Staff of Legba's radiance dimmed, faded, and gradually went out.

He threw it down, to the ground that wasn't ground in this realm with no boundaries. Without the Staff's power – without the link to Earth, to the source of his mystic power – Jericho was helpless. Useless.

And yet...

Over time... and again, he never knew *how much* time... he began to feel something. A spark, a light. A link to a something beyond Dormammu, something that might even be a new beginning...

Brother, Daniel cried, pointing. *Look!*

Jericho whirled to see the Staff – glowing, rising up into the air. It pulsed with power, with renewed energy. It pivoted in midair, coming to rest in a horizontal position.

It's pointing, Jericho realized. It sees something...

At the tip of the staff, a hole began to appear in the not-air.

Light shone through from the other side, pure and golden and wonderfully, gloriously familiar. Jericho felt his heart soar; he knew, even now, what that light meant.

What? Daniel asked, moving to his side. *Who is it?*

Slowly, like an old-style film reel burning away, the hole shimmered and widened. The light focused, dimmed, and resolved into the unmistakable form of the Eye of Agamotto. Doctor Strange thrust his head forward, the eye shining on his furrowed, sweat-drenched forehead.

Jericho sagged in relief. He felt his knees buckle, barely managed to right himself before he fell.

As the portal expanded, other figures came into view. The Black Panther, coiled and muscular in his vibranium-laced uniform. Luke Cage, fists clenched, eyes wide in alarm. And a smaller man, leaping up behind them...

"What a trip," Spider-Man said, shaking his masked head. "Expedia is *not* getting a good review for that one."

Are... are we... Daniel turned to his brother, eyes wide. *Does this mean that we're...*

Yes. Jericho smiled and reached forward for Strange, helping his fellow Sorcerer Supreme through the portal. *We are rescued.*

Strange smiled weakly, touching the Eye with one finger. "Spider-Man is... not wrong," he said. "That was quite the voyage."

They all gathered together, exchanging quick pleasantries. The portal remained open behind them, glowing with power.

"We got to get back, right?" Cage asked. "I mean, assuming we can..."

"Yes." Strange closed his eyes, and the Eye pulsed bright on his brow. "The journey back will be taxing, too. But our link to Ms Marvel remains strong."

"Doctor Voodoo," the Panther said. "Do you require assistance?"

Jericho exchanged a smile with Daniel. Then the two of them turned to T'Challa and spoke in unison: "No thank you. We're fine."

Strange nodded and turned back to the portal. As they moved to follow him, Daniel added in a soft whisper:

"We *are* fine. Now."

FIFTEEN

Tony had a sinking feeling before he entered the workshop, and it didn't get any better when he saw what was going on inside. So startled, he almost dropped the Stane Solvent – which would have been a *very* bad idea.

To his right, Doc Ock had all four metal arms braced on the floor, his body lifted up so he could work on… a heaping, sparking pile of metal and circuitry. Ock's human arms flashed back and forth, welding and wiring and hammering. Tony shuddered to think what all *that* was about.

Beyond Ock, past the now-repaired wallscreen, Justin Hammer paced back and forth in a bathrobe and slippers. At first, Tony thought he was talking to himself. Then he noticed the tiny wireless earbuds in Hammer's ears.

Ock's suspicious building spree and Hammer's unauthorized phone call would have been more than enough to ruin Tony's day. But what he saw to his left, beside the main construction stage, was far, far worse.

Tiberius Stone knelt in a pile of broken glass, meticulously disassembling a silver-and-red suit of Iron Man armor.

"Ty!" Tony cried, sprinting over to him. "What the hell?"

"Tony!" Stone blinked, mock-innocent. "Good morning. Sleeping late, were we?"

"More like not sleeping at all …" Tony pointed at the armor. "Would you step away from that, please?"

"Sure! Just one… sec…"

With a wrenching noise, Stone yanked the head loose from the armor. It was an old model, bulkier than recent suits. Tony glanced up, grimacing, at the wall where the armor had stood, next to a dozen other models. The glass of its compartment had been shattered.

Stone held up the helmet, peering intently at it. "Alas, poor Anthony," he intoned. "Forced to call on his hated childhood rival for help…"

Tony shifted the Stane Solvent behind his back and, with his free hand, snatched the helmet away from Stone. "How did that happen?" he asked, pointing up at the broken glass case.

Stone shrugged and cast a glance over at Octopus. The doctor grinned, waved a tentacle in the air, and said, "I get clumsy."

"I noticed." Tony gestured at the wallscreen, which boasted a brand-new glass display. "Good thing I keep spares of everything."

He'd been up all night, planning and plotting and assembling the equipment strewn across the room. And yes, he'd had to replace the big screen, that had eaten up the last hour he might've used for a nap. Thanks, Doc, he thought.

He crossed over to Octopus, tossing the armor-helmet up and down in his free hand. "And what are you *doing*? Building a robotic butler to serve me poison tea?"

Octopus paused, glaring at Tony through his thick goggles. "Actually," he said, "I am very close to curing cancer here."

Tony looked down at the pile of components. A long cathode-ray tube flickered red and orange, sparking erratically.

"OK, OK." Ock shrugged. "Death ray."

Hammer chose that moment to stroll by, head raised high as he spoke imperiously to the air. "Yes, yes," he said, "see that it's done. All right? That's good. Are you happy, my dear? I want all my employees to be happy! All right. Yes, yes. Blessings."

"Listen," Tony said to him, "I think it's time we got started on–"

Hammer held up a finger, then jerked his head away. "Yes?" he said. "Roxxon? Oh, that's unfortunate. Please have Dario call me directly? Thank you, dear. Blessings."

"Justin." Tony frowned at Hammer's robe; there seemed to be nothing under it. "I thought we agreed–"

"He won't listen," Stone said, approaching. "Mister Hammer's got a *financial empire* to run."

"What? What if they *won't*… " Hammer's eyes narrowed. "Listen, I have enough trouble keeping *Norman bloody Osborn* from turning this company into a *parking lot*. You tell Mister *Agger* that if I don't hear back from him in *twelve hours* his little *holding company* will be *fish food* for the *sharks*, and every member of his *family* will know *eternal agony* in the *fires of Dormammu's flame*, along with anyone who's ever *seen* or *heard* his *thrice-cursed name*…"

He trailed off, noticing Tony's and Stone's eyes on him.

"Oh, lovely!" Hammer continued, breaking out in a smile. "Just pass on the message, dear. Blessings!" He reached up and clicked off his earbuds.

"I, uh, I don't know where to begin," Tony said. "First off, Justin, we said no communications for the duration."

Hammer turned slowly to face him. In those steely eyes,

Tony saw the ruthless corporate magnate who'd tried, so many times, to bury him.

"*You* said," Hammer rasped.

"What are you up to?" Tony stared him down. "Are you working with…" He trailed off, letting the thought hang in the air.

Hammer sighed, closed his eyes. He raised his hands to a prayer position, then spread them wide in a showy gesture. He exhaled loudly, then turned back to face Tony.

"If you must know," Hammer said, "I was instructing my people to reorder my holdings. To move my business, as much as possible without risk of detection, *away* from Dormammu and his lackeys."

"Oh." Tony paused. "Oh, that's good, then."

"Perhaps you should do the same," Hammer replied, a bit condescendingly.

"Well, maybe. After we—"

"I could give you some pointers."

"Do it, Tony." Stone smirked. "Why don't you just give him your passwords?"

"Enough!" Tony tossed the Iron Man head on the floor, pausing for dramatic effect as it made a loud *clank*. "Can we get started, please?"

Reluctantly, the group assembled around him. Hammer approached first, smiling; Tony couldn't tell whether or not he was on another phone call. Ock's nascent death ray let out a loud sizzling noise and shorted out. He swore, raised a tentacle, and smashed the thing to scrap with a single blow.

Stone snorted briefly at the disassembled suit of armor at his feet. He paused to give it a gratuitous kick in the crotch, then moved to join the others.

This group, Tony knew, was trouble. Hammer and Stone

were erratic sociopaths; Ock was a full-blown super villain. It was hard to conceive of them pulling off the dangerous, radical, insane plan he'd spent all night working out in his mind.

But right now, they were all he had.

"The suspense is killing me, T," Stone said, miming a sarcastic yawn.

Keeping the solvent hidden behind his back, Tony turned to the screen and pressed a button on his phone. The giant display lit up to show a dark, blobby humanoid figure with gaping jaws and a coiled, protruding tongue. Its entire body seemed to be made of some sort of viscous, oil-slick substance.

"Remember this guy?" Tony asked.

Hammer's eyebrow went up. "Venom," he said, a glint in his eye.

Ock shook his head. "That psychopath," he growled.

"Venom," Tony affirmed. "AKA Eddie Brock, a former reporter now merged with a symbiotic alien organism."

"Spider-Man's enemy, right?" Stone asked.

"*Frenemy*, more like," Ock spat back. "Brock once helped the web-slinger foil one of my Master Planner schemes. He's not loyal to anyone."

"Well, Dormammu agrees with you," Tony said. "In one of his early, unsuccessful attempts to conquer the Earth, the Big D was deceived by Brock. As revenge, Dormammu exiled him to the Dark Dimension."

"Ha!" Ock said. "Good riddance."

"The Dark Dimension," Hammer mused, "Dormammu's home domain. Tell me, Anthony – how is it you know so much about dear Mister Brock?"

Tony hesitated, thinking again of Ms Marvel. She'd trusted him with this information, but he still couldn't tell this group about her.

"I have connections," he said.

"So this is why you want to go to the Dark Dimension?" Stone stared at him. "To find some erratic human-parasite combo that might be able to help us?"

"Oh, I'm not the one that's going to find him," Tony replied. "They are."

The image onscreen wavered. The roiling, slippery limbs of Venom multiplied, expanded, becoming a dozen, then a hundred shifting symbiotes. All coiled around each other, all raging, with teeth bared and lizard-tongues whipping in all directions.

"Other symbiotes," Tony continued. "Dozens of them. Like Venom – the same species. But lacking the moral constraints of his human host."

"That's not encouraging," Stone said.

Hammer frowned. "Are there that many symbiotes on Earth?"

"Not currently," Tony said. "We'll have to lure them here. That's what the accumulation chamber is for."

"The containment box," Stone said. "The one you showed us yesterday."

"It was designed to accumulate and magnify Tribute energy," Tony replied. "Your job is to build a larger model, and adapt it to attract–"

"–lethally hostile aliens?"

"Hey, you're making it sound like a *bad* idea."

Tony smiled, in a way he hoped was disarming. Judging from the looks on the others' faces, it wasn't.

"So let's say we build this giant roach motel," Stone said, "and fill it full of creatures that, if the *tiniest little thing goes wrong,* will slice us to pieces and munch our brains like popcorn. Then what?"

"The symbiotes have a link," Tony said. "They can sense each other, share emotions. I'm hoping they can track their, uh, 'brother' through the realms, providing us with a path to the Dark Dimension."

"Dimensional travel requires a portal of some kind," Hammer said. "Last I checked, Stark/Dormammu did not have that sort of mystic research arm. At least, not since Doctor Voodoo left your employ."

Tony raised an eyebrow. "You *have* done your homework on me."

Hammer just smiled.

"Your information, unfortunately, is correct," Tony continued. "No portal. I'm working on it, though."

Doctor Octopus slammed a pair of tentacles down, cracking the sheet-metal floor. When Tony looked up in surprise, Ock was hovering above on those maniacal arms, glaring down at him.

"Otto." Tony folded his arms, telling himself: *Pretend you're in a staff meeting with an unhappy employee.* "What's on your mind?"

"The whole plan is useless," Ock snapped. "I can construct an accumulator, and I assume the teen wonder over there can figure out how to lure the symbiotes to it. And let's say you somehow, miraculously, manage to shift them into the Dark Dimension. What are they supposed to do there? What in the world could possibly hurt Dormammu?"

"Tony's been hiding something behind his back," Stone said. "I assume that's the answer."

Ahh, Ty! Tony thought. You ruined my big reveal. Always upstaging me – just like when we were kids!

Reluctantly, he held out the tube full of blue gel. The others leaned in to look.

"This solvent," he said, "can decorporealize any matter.

Released in the Dark Dimension, it should spread instantly, scattering anything it touches to atoms."

"Including Dormammu." Hammer eyed Tony. "Perhaps my homework wasn't as thorough as I thought."

"You said 'should spread', T," Stone observed. "That sounds a little shaky."

Octopus peered at the tube, cocking his head at different angles. His tentacles snapped and hovered in the air, as if they were itching to touch the substance.

"*Will* this kill Dormammu?" he asked.

"I don't know," Tony admitted. "I don't really know what the 'Master' is even made of. But the Stane Solvent should disperse his essence, hopefully to the point where it'd take him an extremely long time to pull himself together."

"This was developed by Obadiah Stane?" Hammer watched as Tony slowly lowered the tube to the floor. "Ah! The fifth partner!"

Stone made a show of clearing his throat. Then he held up a hand and began counting on his fingers:

"Containment field to gather the symbiotes. Symbiotes to find Dormammu's realm. *Something* for a portal – we'll circle back to that. Bomb to destroy, or at least 'decorporealize', Dormammu." He pointed his last remaining finger at Tony. "Seems to me there's still a missing link in this plan."

"Control," Hammer said, making the word sound like a threat. "Somehow the symbiotes must be directed – kept in line."

"Yes," Ock agreed. "It's not like we can just stuff them into a net and fling them into the Dark Dimension."

"You are shrewd," Tony said. "All three of you. Maybe you actually can pull this off."

"Gee thanks, T," Stone said, his voice dripping with hatred.

Tony didn't rise to the bait. He turned to the screen and

pulled up another image: a schematic of a man's body. As he ran a finger down his phone screen, an aura appeared around the body, radiating from a thin harness slung over the figure's shoulders and chest.

"Some sort of transparent polymer bodysuit," Ock observed, cautiously touching the aura along the figure's back. "And this is… a control harness? To direct the symbiotes by remote control?"

"Not exactly."

Tony hissed in a breath and gestured at the image. As it continued to morph, a stylized version of one of the symbiotes sprouted on the man's chest. Another popped up around his neck, and then a third, wrapped around his leg.

"Someone has to physically host the symbiotes," Tony said.

The group watched in silence as one symbiote after another appeared, covering the figure on the screen. Soon his entire body, including the bodysuit, was lost beneath an oily, shifting pile of symbiote flesh.

"One symbiote nearly drove Eddie Brock mad," Stone said. "Spider-Man, too. And you want someone to bond with a *hundred* of them?"

"Two hundred, if we can get that many." Grimacing, Tony gestured at the screen. "The bodysuit will prevent them from fully merging with the host."

"But the host will have to *share consciousness* with them," Hammer said. "Otherwise, the merger will be useless. That many savage, hungry alien minds linked with a single human being…"

"Who'd be dumb enough to volunteer for that job?" Stone asked, holding up both hands. "Not me, I'll tell you that."

"I, ermmm, I have considerable fiduciary duties," Hammer said. "To my firm, I mean."

Ock just let out a snort and turned away.

"I figured, guys. Don't sweat it." Tony sucked in a breath, staring at the image on the screen. "I can't ask anyone else to do this."

And there it was. The core of the plan, the task Tony had been trying not to dwell on. The obligation, the dark duty, that was his and his alone.

"Anthony." Once again, disquietingly, Hammer laid a hand on his shoulder. "Even if you manage to maintain control enough to direct the symbiotes... even if your sanity can prevail under the assault of those slavering, inhuman minds..."

"I'll never make it home again," Tony said. "I'll be lost in the Dark Dimension, atomized in the explosion of the Stane Solvent bomb."

They stood together in silence for a moment. Octopus lowered his body to the floor, tapping one tentacle nervously against the wall.

"Unless...?" Tony prompted.

They all stared blankly at him.

"Unless you can build enough protection into the suit to give me time to escape the explosion!" He raised his arms, appealing to them. "Work with me, people?"

"Ah," Hammer said.

"We can, umm, try to do that," Octopus said.

Tony swallowed, his mouth suddenly dry.

"So." He pulled up a bullet list on the screen. "First, build the accumulator to gather the symbiotes. Otto, that's probably up your alley. Then we'll need the suit; Ty, you and Ock should probably work together on that. Hammer can start work on the bomb."

"Actually," Hammer said, "I may have a prototype that could

be adapted for the suit. It's the same tech I once used to take remote control of your armor... remember that?"

"I do," Tony said, struggling to keep his voice even.

"It's already keyed to your bio-signature," Hammer added. Then, eyeing the Stane Solvent at Tony's feet: "I do like bombs, however."

"T," Stone said, stepping forward. "Do you really think we can pull this off?"

"This crew? Probably not."

The words were out of Tony's mouth before he realized it. In the awkward silence that followed, he could almost feel their eyes like angry lasers, burning into him.

I really am tired, he thought. Blast it, Stark, motivate them. Motivate them!

"But, uh, you can try!" he said. "All the schematics are in the files I've shared with you; equipment should be in this room, or in the storeroom on level five. You've all got access." He turned and started toward the stairwell. "Good luck."

"What?" Stone called. "Wait a minute. What do you mean, *we* can try? Where the hell are you going?"

"I've got a job to do, as Iron Man. Another recruiting job." He paused, allowed himself a smile. "The sixth partner, I guess."

Those six laser eyes followed him as he started down the stairs. As usual, Stone got in the last word:

"Have fun. *Boss*."

SIXTEEN

Oscorp headquarters loomed dead ahead, twin triangular spires rising up from its summit like bat ears. Grim leather-clad guards patrolled the courtyard below, whispering into shoulder mikes as they prowled the bushes and benches of an otherwise unremarkable industrial park.

Tony Stark ignored them, soaring high above, toward the summit. His armor's stealth circuits bent light and scrambled radar, making him undetectable by normal means. He hadn't been sure this would work; "normal" and Osborn didn't usually go together. But so far, the guards hadn't noticed him.

Which was good. After drawing up plans all night, adding up figures and running down specs until his eyes fogged over, Tony had concluded that his plan was just barely workable. But he'd also concluded that the combined efforts of Hammer, Stone, and Octopus – and, he admitted, himself – would not be enough to pull it off. There were just too many holes in the plan.

So he'd set out alone to recruit the only person who could help. Norman Osborn: ruthless tycoon, veteran super villain, and prime representative of the creature that had conquered the Earth. He'd avoided this option earlier, for fear that Osborn would turn straight to Dormammu. But now he had no more options left.

Under other circumstances, Osborn would have been the perfect candidate for the EgoMech's deprogramming protocol. Norman's ego might just be the biggest on Earth. But thanks to Ock, the Mech had been reduced to a pile of smoldering scrap. Another plan down the chute, Tony thought grimly.

Which left only one hope: the human touch. He had to confront Osborn himself, man to businessman – magnate to magnate. With no guarantee that this would work, or even that he'd come out of it alive.

He scanned the sky; still no security, no attack from above. He shook his head, trying not to think about Ock and the others – the Big Tech Crew, as he thought of them. What were they doing, right now? He imagined them dressing up in his various Iron Man armors, staging battles for fun, instead of building the accumulator and the bomb. Maybe the "new Hammer" was practicing yoga in Tony's gauntlets and jet boots.

Had it been a mistake to leave them alone? No – even as the thought crossed his mind, he knew he'd had no choice. Pepper could have kept the Tech Crew in line; so could Kir-ra, the Kree woman who'd joined his staff last year. But right now, both of them were lost to him.

Once again, he felt very much alone.

As he drew near the twin spires, he scanned the rooftop between them. An outdoor space, like a balcony – but the surface was hazy, covered with some sort of energy screen. Not as sophisticated, he noted with pride, as his own stealth tech. But powerful enough to confuse his optical sensors.

The attack seemed to come out of nowhere. He caught a

quick glimpse, a flash of green and violet. Fiery jets on a bat-shaped glider; sharp ears atop a grinning emerald mask. He had just enough time to form the thought: *Green Goblin–*

–and then the figure swooped down, still moving too fast to see clearly, brandishing a metal staff. The blunt weapon swept through the air, striking his helmet with a fierce blow.

A deep ringing filled his ears, piercing his brain, scrambling his thoughts. Alerts flashed before his eyes. One of them read *Stealth Mode Disabled*. The ground wheeled past, city streets rushing by at dizzying speed.

Then his boot jets kicked in, automatic circuits steering him back into an upright position. The view shifted to open sky.

"Friday!" he cried, still falling through the air. "Was that–"

"Vibranium," she said.

"Since when…" He thrust his legs out, firing both jets to arrest his uncontrolled flight. "Since when does the Green Goblin use vibranium weapons?"

"Is that another rhetorical question, boss?"

He muted the A.I. with a mental command. The Goblin – Osborn – whirled around in midair, sheathing that vibranium staff in a back-mounted holster. He reached into a bag of tricks, prepping for another attack.

Or – Tony paused, startled – *was* this Osborn? This Goblin costume looked different, sleeker than the one Tony knew. The fabric was skintight, gleaming with a metallic sheen; more vibranium, he realized. The boots were tightly fitted, and the figure looked smaller, perhaps younger than the man he'd fought in the past. Some sort of wiring, too, glittered on the arms.

Could this be *Harry* Osborn? Norman's son had worn the Goblin costume before. But that didn't explain the new weaponry. Was Dormammu feeding power directly to Harry, or whoever was inside the suit?

Tony raised a hand and fired off a medium-strength repulsor beam. It struck the Goblin in the chest, just below that grinning mask. Energy sparked across the surface of the Goblin's purple vest, shimmering harmlessly off into the air. Yup – definitely vibranium. Tony jetted back, bracing himself for the next attack–

The Goblin spun in place on that batwing flier, shooting off a series of rapid-fire finger blasts. Particle beams filled the air, sizzling and burning the top layer of Tony's armor. He checked the readouts; the holes were sealing already – this was nothing the armor couldn't handle. But he knew that, like himself, the Goblin was just getting warmed up.

"Osborn!" he called, turning up his armor's speakers to full gain. "You in there?"

The figure did not answer. For just a moment, Tony caught a glimpse of the green glow of Dormammu's power, behind the Goblin's unnervingly wide eye-lenses.

"I just want to talk!" Tony said, venturing closer. "Like, you know. People?"

Down below, in the courtyard, the guards had stopped to look up at the combat. But their guns remained holstered, their radios silent. Somehow that made Tony uneasy. Whoever was directing this dance – Norman, or some automated security system – it had full faith in this Goblin to stop the armored intruder.

And the Goblin seemed in no hurry. Silently, it crouched down on slim, athletic legs – and leaped off its flier, into the open air. Freed from its rider, the tiny vehicle swooped around in a one-eighty-degree turn and fired its jets, blasting Tony point-blank with a shot of fire. Again, he flew back in the air, looking down in time to see the Goblin land gracefully back down on the flier, like a ballet dancer.

"Reality check, Friday," he said. "That was definitely *not* a Norman Osborn sort of move–"

Before he could finish the sentence, the Goblin was on him. A violet glove, gleaming with reinforced vibranium mesh, twisted Tony's armored hand behind his back, wrenching his shoulder out of its socket. He cried out in pain as alarm lights flashed past his helmet display.

He raised his knees and kicked out, forcing the Goblin away. As the figure flailed momentarily, he got a better look at the piping running up its arm. Three tiny tubes ran up each of the Goblin's arms and shoulders, vanishing into the figure's mask at the base of its neck. Tubes filled with bright green liquid, bubbling and flowing up the arms and into the Goblin's body.

"Osdrink!" Tony exclaimed, his eyes wide in horror.

"Looks like it," Friday said. "Possibly some sort of concentrated derivative."

Again the Goblin whirled, tossing a pair of pumpkin-shaped bombs into the air. Tony braced himself, but the bombs exploded before they reached him, filling the sky with thick black smoke. He switched his helmet view to radar, watching as a schematic of the Goblin's body and flier appeared before his eyes. He reached out and grabbed the figure's head… tugging, pulling hard, ignoring the Goblin's frantic motions…

The smoke cleared as he pulled the mask free. He was so surprised, he dropped the grinning mask, which fluttered away like a stray plastic bag.

As he'd guessed, the face beneath the Goblin mask was not Norman Osborn's. It belonged to a young woman, barely out of her teens, with dark skin and hair gathered in a tight bun. Her teeth were gritted, her eyes glassy-green with the mark of Dormammu. Tony had met her before… in Wakanda. What was her name…?

"Shuri?"

The woman looked at him in surprise. For a moment, the green hue in her eyes faded. They hovered together, less than twenty feet above the building's roof deck, but she made no further move to attack.

Then Tony gasped as he noticed: the Osdrink tubes stretched all the way over the top of her head, vanishing into tiny implants at the tip of her forehead. Whatever that stuff was – whatever its purpose – it was being injected straight into her frontal lobe.

"What – who did this?" he asked. "That's… definitely Wakandan tech…" A horrible thought came to him. "Did you do this to *yourself*?"

Shuri's lips twisted into a snarl. Green flared from her eyes, and she raised sparking fingers to attack again.

Tony didn't even think. Acting purely on instinct, he reached out and grabbed one of the tubes, yanking it free of her head port. Bright green liquid sprayed into the air.

Shuri cried out, Goblin-gloved hand scrabbling for the tube. She grabbed hold of it, pinching the end shut to stop the flow of Osdrink. With her other hand, she fired off a barrage of finger blasts straight in Tony's face.

Tony's lenses protected his eyes automatically, but the view flickered to static for a moment. When it cleared, the Shuri-Goblin had backed off in the air, eyeing him with wild green eyes. One of her hands held the liquid tube, while the other was clamped over the port in her forehead.

Tony felt a moment of sympathy. He remembered the warm

rotting feel of Dormammu in his mind, the terrible addictive quality of that presence. "I'm sorry…" he began.

"Why?" a man's voice said. "She wanted this."

Tony backed away, turning to study the newcomer. A large, muscular man in a well-tailored suit and tie, jetted up toward them from the balcony space below. He rode a batwing glider, larger than Shuri's but of a similar design.

"Norman!" Tony said. "Decided to fight your own battles?"

"When I do," Osborn replied, "you'll be the first to know."

He eased upward to meet Tony, glider bobbing gently in the air. If there was a single word to describe Osborn, it had to be *arrogant*. His demeanor, his very being, radiated superiority and confidence. Only the vial hanging from his neck, filled with a few drops of the glowing green Osdrink, showed that he acknowledged an authority above his own.

This isn't going to be easy, Tony realized. I'm not dealing with chronic failure Tiberius Stone or "new age" Justin Hammer, here. This is Dormammu's regent on Earth, and there's a reason the Big D chose him for the job.

"I assume you're here to discuss a merger?" Osborn began.

Inside his helmet, Tony blinked. "What?"

"You're tired of living in my shadow," Osborn said, a condescending smile creeping onto his face. "I can understand that. After all, the Master doesn't really need *two* megacorporations to serve his will on Earth." He laughed. "And we both know antitrust regulations are a thing of the past."

Tony hesitated. Osborn wasn't acting like one of Dormammu's mind-controlled puppets. He seemed… well, he seemed like exactly the same conceited plutocrat Tony had always known in the past.

"Stark," Osborn continued, "I understand your reticence –

it's not easy to acknowledge your inferiority to a business rival. But you *are* here to discuss our mutual work for Dormammu, aren't you?" He paused, raising a hand to his chin. "I could definitely make use of that Kree workforce you assembled…"

Tony cast a quick glance at Shuri. She sat balanced on her glider in midair, crouched down in a ball. She'd pulled out a small tool and was attempting to repair the severed Osdrink tube on her head.

Osborn moved closer, startling Tony, and dropped a few inches so his eyes stared straight into Tony's lenses.

"Remove your helmet," Osborn ordered. "I want to see your face."

This time, Tony didn't hesitate. With a mental command, his faceplate receded. Hot afternoon air washed across his cheeks as he found himself staring straight into Osborn's eyes.

Eyes – he suddenly noticed – that contained not a trace of green in them.

"You're not under Dormammu's control," he said.

"Nor are you," Osborn replied, raising an eyebrow.

Tony paused, processing this new information. If it's true, he thought… if Osborn really is following Dormammu of his own free will… then the job of converting him just got a hell of a lot tougher.

"OK," Osborn said, "then why are you here? If this is some old-fashioned hero-versus-villain pageant, I'll warn you I'm not feeling particularly nostalgic."

"You're not under…" Tony gestured at the vial hanging from Osborn's neck. "What about the Swarovski?"

"This? I like it." Osborn smiled, touching the vial. "It reminds me of my status. My position as partner to the most powerful being in the Multiverse."

"His prize pet, you mean."

"You can't bait me, Stark. I have nothing to fear and nothing to hide." Osborn spread his arms, indicating the city sprawled out below. "The world is mine now... as close as a mortal man can get, anyway."

Shuri edged closer, glaring at Tony. The severed tube hung loose from her arm – she'd given up on reattaching it – but the other five still fed Dormammu's poison into her brain.

"Could we move this meeting someplace, uh, solid?" Tony asked, eyeing her nervously. "Preferably somewhere I can stop watching my back?"

"I don't allow guests in my office anymore. Things tend to get broken." Osborn gestured down at the penthouse. "We'll talk on the terrace."

He turned and glided downward, not waiting for a reply. As Tony watched, Osborn's glider touched the privacy screen covering the balcony and continued on through...

...leaving Tony and Shuri alone in the sky. She seemed disoriented, confused. Her head jerked up and down, from the balcony to him and back again.

Tony eyed her, curious, then shrugged. "Goblins first," he said, and followed her down.

SEVENTEEN

Osborn stood to one side of the patio, next to a fully stocked bar. Smiling, he held up a bottle labelled *Champagne*. Like almost every other bottle on the bar, the liquid inside it glowed bright green.

"Drink?" Osborn asked.

"Pass," Tony said, touching down softly.

He paused to take in the simple open space dominated by a round metal table with four chairs. Assorted lawn furniture, some potted plants. It didn't look much like the lair of a super villain – except for the two reinforced steel doors on either side, leading to Norman's office and living quarters, respectively.

Shuri crouched over by the far door, rummaging inside a freestanding supply closet. Tony caught a glimpse of Goblin equipment: spare gliders, a row of slack, blank-eyed masks, and an assortment of Osdrink-related paraphernalia. She tossed her glider inside with a clatter, then selected a fresh length of tubing.

Above all three of them, the energy screen shimmered slightly. Keeping all our secrets safe, Tony thought. But from whom?

"I never touch the stuff either," Osborn said, setting the off-color "champagne" back down on the bar. He selected another bottle – the only one, Tony noticed, that was filled with clear water.

"Don't get high on your own supply," Tony replied. "Smart business."

"Always."

Osborn took a seat at the table, turning to gaze out over the metal railing. Watching him, Tony felt a surge of anger – fueled, he knew, by heat, exhaustion, and adrenaline from the battle with Shuri. He had to fight the urge to crack a metal glove across his host's smug face.

Shuri sat down across the terrace, perched on the edge of a chaise longue. She pulled out a tiny tool and started working, again, on her severed liquid tube. Tiny sparks danced on the tip of the tool.

"So," Tony said, turning back to Osborn. "You're recruiting help from Wakanda now?"

"The princess came to *me*," Osborn replied. "Of her own free will."

"You mean Dormammu's will."

"Is there a difference, these days?" Osborn shrugged. "Shuri is a brilliant scientist. She'd already managed to reverse-engineer the formula for my Osdrink – quite a feat, actually. She proposed a merging of our technologies: a Goblin suit laced with vibranium. The user would be supercharged by a concentrated Osdrink derivative."

"Ah." Tony touched his forehead, which still ached where the Goblin had struck him. "And I was the first test?"

"We didn't plan it that way, but…" Osborn smiled. "What did you think?"

"Could use some debugging." Tony frowned, watching her. "Is that stuff affecting her speech centers?"

"The direct feed is designed to amp up her motor control, quicken her reflexes. But yes, there seems to be problem with the Broca's Area, which controls language."

"That sounds like a pretty big glitch."

"Shuri will sort it out. She insisted on test-driving the suit herself." Osborn turned to gaze at her. "She is driven by a thirst for knowledge…" He jiggled the vial of Osdrink around his neck, "…among other things."

All at once, Osborn leaned over the table, fixing his eyes on Tony's. When he spoke again, his voice was hard.

"So," he said. "What's your pitch?"

Tony frowned. "Huh?"

"Come on! You came all this way." Osborn spread his arms. "Make me an offer."

"You… you want me to negotiate for your services?" Tony shook his head. "Against Dormammu?"

Osborn turned away, frowning. "You really are terrible at this, aren't you?"

Tony felt another flash of anger. He'd been rejected by the Avengers, stonewalled by Ms Marvel, forced to turn to a group of amoral sociopaths. And now this! Why, he thought.

"Doesn't anyone just want to help save the world?" he asked.

Osborn grimaced, still staring. "What," he repeated, "is your *pitch?*"

Then Tony realized: Osborn just opened the door. Maybe someone *can* help. Maybe someone will.

"What I need," he said, "is a dimensional portal."

"Ah." Osborn turned back to face him. "You've got a plan."

"Calling it a *plan* is the definition of wishful thinking,"

Tony replied, "but whatever I've got, it won't work without a doorway to the Dark Dimension." He leaned forward, a conspiratorial smile on his face. "Come on, Normie. You got a portal around here, right? For those special, intimate chats with the Big D?"

Osborn let out an amused noise.

"He wouldn't have to know it was *your* portal," Tony continued. "That'll be our little secret. One master of the universe to another."

Osborn took a long drink of clear water. He's enjoying this, Tony realized. Enjoying my discomfort, my pleading.

"Don't you have resources of your own?" Osborn asked. "A mystic in your back pocket, perhaps?"

"I can't find Doctor Strange," Tony admitted. "He seems to have vanished."

"Smart man."

"No portal? All right," Tony said, shifting tactics. "How 'bout a containment chamber, about *yay* high by *so* wide? Or maybe a giant-sized, pandimensional version of one of those nifty pumpkin grenades?"

He turned, startled, as Shuri approached the table, watching the two of them with sharp green eyes. She made no threatening moves, but her presence was enough to put his already frayed nerves on edge.

"Stark," Osborn said, "have you noticed that there are no churches to Dormammu?"

Tony blinked. "I hadn't thought about it."

"It's true. In the past, the Master has sought worship – but this time, his rule is purely secular." Osborn leaned across the table again, raising an eyebrow. "Do you know why that is?"

Tony nodded. "You," he said.

"Me." Osborn leaned back, lacing his hands together behind his head. "I convinced a godlike being, the unquestioned master of his home realm, to use *unbridled capitalism* as his primary tool in the conquest of Earth. After all, it's worked out well for me." He gestured at Tony. "You too, for that matter."

"I, uh. I suppose." He frowned. "The Tribute Booths have a sort of… religious flavor to them."

"I struggled with that," Osborn admitted. "I considered calling them Taxation Booths, but everyone hates taxes – you can't sell that to a population, even a thoroughly mesmerized one, as a positive thing. 'Investment' is the financial term, but that's too cold, too uninviting. So we settled on Tribute, but decided to promote them as self-care, as a therapeutic measure. And, of course, as a way of supporting a beloved, benevolent regime."

Tony's head was whirling. He felt like he was trapped in the world's worst marketing meeting.

"It turns out," Osborn continued, "that *faith* – the beliefs that ordinary people use to get through the day – can be applied to secular causes as well as religious ones. I'm even working on an interdimensional futures market for Osdrink. It's a challenge, but we've got the entire staff of Goldman-Dormammu running simulations right now."

"That's, um. Appalling?"

"The point is, Stark…" Osborn shook his head, a contemptuous smile on his face. "I've got everything, and I've got it on my terms. Why on Earth would I give all that up?"

Tony clenched a fist under the table.

"It could work for you, too," Osborn said. "All you have to do is put profits – the interests of your shareholders – above those petty, old-world ideals of yours. Like you used to, before you gave up manufacturing bombs."

Control yourself, Tony thought. Do not leap at him. Do not attack him. Do not wrap your metal hands around his slimy throat...

"What makes you think you're special?" Tony snapped.

"Well..." Osborn gestured at the penthouse, then down at the city below.

"To Dormammu, I mean! You don't mean anything to him – none of us do. He could squash you flat with one finger, and not even break a flaming nail."

Osborn didn't answer right away. He stood up, walked to the railing, and gazed out over the edge.

Shuri took a step closer. She's watching me, Tony realized – but with her own eyes, or Dormammu's? Is she getting ready to defend Osborn, in case I attack him?

"You're right," Osborn said, turning back toward Tony. "Dormammu doesn't care about any of us. But what does that matter? No one can stand against him, either."

"Someone's got to try!"

Osborn let out a little laugh.

"They have," he said softly. "Do you know the fate of Eddie Brock?"

Tony grimaced, remembering Ms Marvel's words: *You won't find Venom.*

He leaped to his feet, glaring, as Shuri took another step. "Call her off," he said to Osborn.

"I don't control Shuri," Osborn said coolly.

"You knew." Again, Tony felt the anger rise inside him. "You *knew* you were going to turn me down. So why see me at all?"

"Partly to test my new toys. Partly out of curiosity." Osborn smiled. "And if I'm honest, partly just to show off."

"And now what? You report back to the 'Master'?" Anger

turned to rage; suddenly he couldn't stand this a moment longer. "You gonna tell him my *plan?*"

He snapped his helmet down, glaring with bright-shining eyes. Without thinking, he lunged for Osborn – whose eyes went wide. Not in fear, but in astonishment.

"Really?" Osborn said.

Before Tony could reach the railing, Shuri lunged between them, blocking his path. She held up an arm to stop him, her eyes boring into his.

"Get away from me," Tony snarled, struggling to force his way past her. "Get…"

Then he noticed something. The broken tube had been reattached to Shuri's forehead; like the others, it shone with bright green Osdrink concentrate. But something looked different now. The fluid in the tubes, running along Shuri's arm… up over the top of her head…

…the fluid was flowing *backward* now. Not into her brain, but out of it.

He stared into her eyes, and she looked back. Then she nodded.

"Are we through, Stark?" Osborn asked, leaning casually against the railing. "I've got a ten o'clock."

Tony turned back to Shuri, his mind racing. There was no doubt in his mind: she'd broken Dormammu's conditioning. His arguments, which had bounced right off Osborn's hard skull, had gotten through to her.

"Come with me," he whispered.

She shook her head. "Not yet. Too weak…" She reached into a pocket of her costume. "Here."

She thrust a small object into his gloved hand. A hard round stone, like a large bead or small jewel. He closed his hand over it, hiding it immediately from view.

Osborn wasn't even paying attention. He was already walking away, toward his office, speaking in a low voice into his phone.

Shuri's arm trembled. Sweat glistened on her brow, glowing green as the Osdrink purged itself from her system. She leaned in close and, shaking, spoke two more words into his ear:

"Wakanda forever."

"I…" He nodded. "Thank you."

"Now go." She stepped back, gesturing up into the sky. "Go!"

Tony hesitated. Osborn paused at his office door to look back, and as their eyes locked one final time, Tony felt the contempt radiating from the so-called partner of Dormammu.

He took to the sky, clutching Shuri's gift, and didn't look back.

EIGHTEEN

In the southern hemisphere of the moon, deep within the Copernicus crater... between the brightly lit peaks of the Harbinger Mountains and the former landing sites of Apollos 12 and 14... something stirred.

The creature shook, quivered, and stared up. Dark rocky walls surrounded it, stretching up more than two miles to reveal the distant lights in the sky. The creature had been asleep for a long time – decades? Centuries? It had no way of knowing.

Now it was awake. And it felt a call, a summoning it could not resist. Its shapeless body stretched upward, protoplasm curling slowly into a sharp, hooked claw. A second claw took shape, and with a shiver and a groan, the creature began to climb the walls of its airless prison.

When it reached the top, it vaulted over the lip of the crater and paused. Gray sand all around, rocky cliffs... and one severed wheel, half-buried in the shifting regolith. The remains of a vehicle left behind by visitors, decades ago.

The creature stood for a moment in silence, its form oozing

and undulating in the solar wind. Its brain, scattered and decentralized throughout its ever-shifting body, ached with a longing it could not name. Something called to it, urging it onward – but where? Forward, miles away? Across the trackless gray sands?

No. Not forward.

Up.

High above, in the sharp clear sky, hung a large sphere swaddled in mist. Patches of green and blue showed through its distant cloud cover: glimpses of life, of water. This globe – this world – was the source of the call.

The creature formed sharp teeth, bared them at the sky, and *hissed.*

Then, like a salmon drawn helplessly upstream, it flexed new-formed muscles and leaped into the sky. Defying the moon's gravity, it shot out into open space, arrowing straight for the white-swathed planet. And with every mile, every moment that passed, the call grew stronger.

Soon it was plunging through the mists, through the thick veil of oxygen and nitrogen, caught by the pull of the larger world. Clouds gave way to open air, revealing a maze of tall structures crowded together on a narrow island. One of those structures, the creature knew, was the source of the summoning. One of the tallest, in fact, nestled amid the others, a large metal circle just beginning to iris open on its roof…

The creature felt a surge of panic. It had been trapped, held captive, before, and suddenly it knew this was what was about to happen. It struggled, squirmed, formed random appendages as it plummeted down through the air. But it was no use. The pull was too strong, the summoning too true.

With a grunt and a squish, the first symbiote shot through

the iris atop Stark Tower and was sucked into the accumulation chamber.

As the creature splattered down in a mass of protoplasm, Doctor Octopus looked upon his work and smiled. The newly built accumulation chamber dominated Stark's workshop, filling two-thirds of the domed, multileveled room. The chamber was shaped like a beaker, its narrow spout vanishing into the ceiling where it led to the exterior iris. Its walls were adamantium-reinforced plastiglass, two layers thick but transparent, revealing the captive symbiote within.

"Well," Justin Hammer said, coming up behind Octopus. "I'm sure *that* won't draw Dormammu's attention."

Ock waved him off, studying the symbiote. The creature had sprouted arms, claws, hands bristling with knives; it prowled and crawled, up and down the sides of the chamber, scurrying in circles around the plastiglass floor. When it caught sight of Octopus, the symbiote flattened its face against the side of the chamber, opened a maw gaping with deadly teeth, and hissed.

"*Hsss!*" Ock spat back.

His metal arms waved in the air, mirroring his jittery excitement, but Ock barely noticed. After so many years, the arms felt both like extensions of his own body and like weapons cocked and ready to fire. He'd been using them so long, sometimes he wasn't even aware of the mental commands he fired off at them.

"I don't believe it," Tiberius Stone said, keeping his distance. "I didn't think it would work."

"I knew the chamber would hold the creatures," Ock said, whirling to confront him. "But I'm a bit surprised that your summoning tech worked so fast." He grinned. "Or at all."

"Keep riding me, old man." Stone clenched his fists. "See what happens."

Ock raised all six arms in a mockery of the creature in the chamber. "*HSSSSSSS!*"

Stone shrank back, rattled. He stumbled over the torso of a large Iron Man suit – a big one, with hydraulic lifters in the shoulders – and swore softly.

Ock laughed. He wasn't used to operating as part of a team – his forays with the Sinister Six tended to end badly. He only knew one way of working with people: to dominate them. Fortunately, Stone was a bit of a physical coward. All Ock had to do was wave a metal arm in his direction, and the man shrank away.

Hammer was a different matter. He seemed calmer, more cautious than his reputation would indicate. The bathrobe and yoga mat had been a bit ridiculous; thankfully, he'd changed into a casual jacket and slacks. But he didn't scare easily, and Ock didn't like the way his eyes took in everything in the room.

Ock turned back to the symbiote. The creature had not yet accepted its captive state; it continued to prowl, testing the walls of its prison. He watched it with a growing, scientific fascination. *I was like that*, he thought, *not long ago. Toiling away on a Tribute Booth assembly line, working for the glory of Dormammu. A simpering, passive man, my metal arms – the engineering triumph of the modern age! – used for the pettiest of purposes: welding together metal boxes to feed the vampiric hunger of an interdimensional conqueror.*

Another person would have empathized with the trapped symbiote, felt for its plight. Not Otto Octavius. All he felt for it was contempt. The sight of it, trapped like a bug in a jar, filled him with rage.

Then again, a lot of things filled Ock with rage.

"One symbiote isn't going to do it," Stone said, turning to walk away. "The rest have to come from a much greater distance."

"I wonder if our *employer* gave that any thought," Ock mused.

"Tony's not my employer," Stone replied. "And believe me, there's a lot of things he doesn't think about."

"The symbiotes appear to travel faster than light," Hammer said. "I believe they can naturally sniff out space warps, or some such."

Ock followed Hammer around the narrow space between the wall and the edge of the accumulation chamber. A row of Iron Man suits lay strewn along the floor, pulled apart in various configurations – the group had "liberated" a few more of them, shortly after Stark's departure. Ock had to pick his way over the suits, his metal arms crunching against the floor.

"You and our boy wonder," he hissed, "seem more interested in dissecting Mister Stark's technology than in completing our work."

"I'm a multitasker," Hammer replied, pausing to pick up a silver-red gauntlet with wires sticking out of the stump.

Ock leapfrogged over him, coming to rest before the small null-grav stage. A thin metal harness hung in the air, resting on a holographic image of a man's shoulders and torso. Stone stood before the image, circling it, making notes on his phone with a tiny stylus.

"Harness should work," he said. "Tony's plans, hate to admit it, were solid."

Ock hovered in the air, shifting back and forth on his metal arms. "What about the bodysuit?"

"We're still fine-tuning the fabric," Hammer replied. "The weave is crucial... it must allow the symbiotes to interact with the wearer, but only a little at a time."

"It's not the fabric," Stone shot back. "I've cracked that one. Tony's crappy 3-D printer is just having trouble with the actual manufacturing."

"Not exactly a suit of armor, is it?" Hammer asked, running a playful finger along the harness. "Bit of a comedown for our dear old friend."

A movement caught their attention. The symbiote twitched within the chamber, following their progress, its single eye pressed against the double-thick glass. It's been watching us all this time, Ock realized.

"This is taking far too long," he snapped. "Have you even started on the bomb?"

Hammer and Stone exchanged grimaces. Hammer crooked his finger in an imperious gesture and edged past the harness-stage, moving further around the room.

Ock followed, his tentacles slamming even harder into the floor. Everything Stone and Hammer did made him angry. He considered lopping off both their heads with a single swipe of his arms, then finishing the job himself. But he knew that, alone, he'd never complete the suit before Dormammu found this lab.

And although he hated to admit it, nothing mattered more than vanquishing Dormammu.

On the far side of the accumulation chamber, a few armor components and welding tools lay on the floor, strewn about haphazardly. Past them, the tube containing the Stane Solvent sat with the area around it carefully cleared. No one wanted to trip over *that* thing by mistake.

Ock swept a metal arm across the floor. "I don't see any hint of a bomb casing," he hissed.

"Yeah…" Stone backed away from the deadly tentacle. "We're just starting on that. There are a lot of problems."

"The casing must be sturdy," Hammer said. "It's not enough that it holds in the Solvent. It must be strong enough to survive the interdimensional passage, as well."

"Assuming we can create a portal," Ock growled.

"And then there's the symbiotes," Stone said. He'd propped up an Iron Man suit and stood fiddling with it. "We've gotta make sure *they* don't set off the bomb. You wouldn't exactly hire those guys to move fine china – HEY!"

Stone stumbled backward as Ock's tentacle swooped down, snatching the Iron Man armor out of his hands. "What are you doing?" Stone demanded.

Ock didn't answer. Sneering, he lifted the armor into the air, raising a second tentacle to hold it in place. Then, with a third tentacle, he ripped the control circuit out of its chest. A shower of sparks erupted, filling the air like a comet as he tossed the circuit away.

Within the accumulation chamber, the symbiote watched as the reactor clattered to the floor, a safe distance away. The tiny power source flashed once, smoking, then went dark.

"You nearly overloaded the power circuit!" Ock cried.

"That's… That's Tony's fault," Stone said, clenching his fists. "His tech was always sloppy."

"And *you* are dangerously careless." Ock waved a pair of tentacles, metal claws clenching in anger. "Stop *tinkering* and focus on the task at hand!"

"Gentlemen." Hammer strode up between them, holding up a hand. "Might I point out that this display actually shows how well our skills complement each other? Otto's engineering skill, combined with young Tiberius's insatiable curiosity..." He smiled, that maddening smile that made Ock want to crush his skull. "Perhaps 'Sloppy Tony' knew what he was doing when he brought us together."

"Yeah?" Stone replied. "That what the Buddha tells you? Or Machiavelli, or bloody Ghandi or somebody?"

Ock ignored Stone, rising a few feet on his metal arms. He turned to confront Hammer, who stared coolly up at him.

"If Tony Stark has such confidence in our abilities," Ock said slowly, "then why isn't he here, working with us? Hmm?"

Hammer frowned, raising an eyebrow. Stone wore a puzzled look on his face.

"He's gone after Osborn, you fools!" Ock exclaimed. "We're not enough for him. He doesn't believe we can pull this off..." He paused, gesturing wide at the mess on the floor. "...and I'm not sure he's wrong."

"Yes," Hammer said, "that must be it." His eyes bored into Ock's. "Do you think he can actually recruit Osborn?"

"No," Ock spat. "He'll fail, as he's failed at every stage of this operation so far. Because he doesn't understand who Norman Osborn is, what drives the man." He shook his head, his tentacles waving in sympathy. "Stark is a fool."

Hammer grunted, turning to gaze across the wall of the room. A row of Iron Man suits, some of them still intact, stared down with blank, dark eyes.

Stone crouched down before the Stane Solvent, staring at it intensely. "Maybe..."

Something in his voice caught Ock's attention. "Yes?"

"Maybe we can solve two problems at once," Stone said.

Ock moved closer. "How?"

"What if we combine the bomb casing with the suit?"

"You mean…" Hammer crossed toward him. "Build the bomb right into the harness?"

Before Stone could reply, Ock reached down with a pair of tentacles and lifted the Stane Solvent off the floor. He paused briefly to deliberately shake the deadly tube in the air, enjoying the fear in Stone's eyes. Even Hammer seemed slightly alarmed, his eyes widening slightly.

Ock carried the Solvent back to the null-grav stage, where the half-built harness hung waiting. The others followed. The symbiote kept pace with them, following the group's every move.

Lowering the solvent carefully, Ock placed it at the base of the stage. "That's it," Stone said. "Incorporate the two designs together. Like a backpack."

They stood for a moment in silence, the three figures studying the hologram.

"It, ah, goes without saying," Hammer began, "that this will reduce the safety factor."

"Mmm," Stone said. "That's true."

Another moment of silence. The symbiote shifted within the chamber, as if it wanted a say in the decision.

"We can make the bomb detachable," Stone said. "That'll give him a slightly better chance."

"Very slight," Hammer said.

More silence.

"His chances were never *good*," Stone said.

"I have no issue with this," Ock said.

"Well." Hammer smiled, an oddly serene smile. "The fate of the Earth *is* at stake…"

A loud *thunk* interrupted him, shaking the room. All three

men whirled toward the accumulation chamber. Ock pressed his face to the plastiglass, bracing himself with a pair of tentacles. The symbiote had retreated to the center of the chamber, where it shifted and circled, keeping its distance from …

"Another symbiote," Ock said.

"No," Stone said. "Two more."

Thunk thunk thunk thunk THUNK.

Symbiotes poured into the chamber, squeezed like globs of dark jelly through the narrow spout at the top. They hissed and snarled, circling each other like rival predators. More creatures dropped down among them, filling the chamber with roiling black protoplasm.

Soon the chamber was a single mass of symbiote, swirling and surging in a symphony of inhuman hunger. Ock found he could no longer tell where one creature ended and the next one began. At the base of the chamber, machinery hummed and glowed, containment fields flaring to keep the creatures confined.

"Hmm!" Hammer's voice betrayed his surprise. "This might actually work."

"Only if we finish our tasks," Ock snapped.

The others nodded, turning their attention back to the harness. Ock joined them, realizing, somewhat to his surprise, that he was smiling. Tony Stark, he thought, this is what you get. For flying off on your all-important errand, for delegating the boring work to us. For insulting our abilities, insinuating that three genius-level intellects weren't enough for you. Did you think that would *motivate* us? Did you hope that your contempt would inspire us to show what we could do?

Actually, he realized, I suppose it worked. We'll show you, all right. We'll show you what we're capable of.

"Let's mount the bomb casing *here*," he said, pointing with one tentacle. "Right behind his heart."

NINETEEN

Kamala entered the bar, moving on autopilot. Her whole life felt that way now. Go to school, tune out lessons about Dormammu. Go home, tune out parents' talk about Dormammu. Get on the PATH train, ignore all the ads for Dormammu. Weave through the Dormammu-plagued streets of Manhattan until she reached the bar...

The moment she stepped inside, she smelled it. Something burning, rancid. Like rotten jelly that had been set on fire.

She dashed past the bar, panic rising, and flung open the door to the back hallway. By the time she reached the bathroom, the stench was overwhelming. She reached into her bag, pulled out the sash of her costume, and wrapped it around her head to cover her nose. She hoped she wouldn't need to change into the rest of the suit.

When she pushed the bathroom door open, her heart sank.

The Eye of Vouk was still there – what was left of it, anyway. Its metal frame was smashed to bits, black char-marks all along the surface. The Eye itself had been punctured, blown apart. The pupil floated, dark and glassy, in a shallow pool of liquid, dripping slowly down the shelf onto the tile floor.

"No," she whispered, reaching out a finger to the gelatinous liquid. It felt cold to the touch.

I've failed, she realized. It was *my* job to protect the Eye – my only job, the whole reason they left me here. And now Doctor Strange and the others are trapped, somewhere in the outer realms, with no way home.

Who, she wondered, had done this? Then, she laughed. She could think of nearly eight billion suspects, and that was if you only counted Earthers! It could even be… she didn't want to form the thought…

…Tony?

She looked around, suddenly paranoid. Whoever the attacker was, were they still *here?* In the bar, inside the building? Hastily she checked the hallway – nothing – then backed inside the bathroom. That seemed empty, too. Sink, toilet, shelving, cleaning brush in the corner…

A flash of light caught her eye, above the doorway. There, up near the ceiling: a small green oval, like a scar in the air. Growing smaller, fainter, as she watched.

A portal.

She reached for it, then hesitated and pulled her hand back. The next moment it was gone.

Then she realized: the place felt different. Less secure, less of a sanctuary. Doctor Strange's wards – his protective spells – had been pierced, violated. By the one entity, the one creature in all the realms that could squash a Sorcerer Supreme like a bug.

She turned back to the shattered Eye, a lump rising in her throat. Despite herself, the word rose to her lips.

"Dormammu," she whispered.

•••

Tony saw the crowds first, gathering like ants in the street below. He put on a burst of speed, eager to reach Stark Tower. His boot jets flared bright, propelling him through the late afternoon sky. A red sun hung low to the west, dropping slowly over the Hudson River.

The Tower came into view, along with the spectacle playing out above it. A steady stream of glistening symbiotes, plummeting down out of the sky. One by one they fell, squirming and growling in protest, drawn helplessly toward the opening in the building's roof.

He paused in midair, thinking: my god, they did it. Those idiots actually pulled it off!

He zoomed in with his armor's telescopic lenses, studying the people below. Their tiny hands pointed up in the air, moving excitedly each time a new symbiote appeared. Some of them held up phones, either to video the sight or to view it on other people's news feeds.

He turned back to the Tower, watching in fascination as the iris flashed open and closed, sealing shut behind as a new symbiote was delivered to the workshop below. How many had they collected? The crowd had been watching for a while... by now there must be dozens, maybe a hundred of the creatures bottled up inside the accumulator.

For the first time in a long while, he felt hope. Maybe this insane, dangerous plan would work after all. Maybe Dormammu's iron grip *could* be broken.

A murmur rose up from the street, far below. Tony looked down, smiling inside his helmet as he saw people pointing at him, too.

He wheeled in the air and gave them a big wave, forcing himself to enjoy the moment. He tried not to think about two things. First, his own chances of survival under this plan were still vanishingly slim. Second, and more immediately: the aerial dance of the symbiotes wasn't exactly a subtle display. Even the busiest interdimensional conqueror was bound to take notice, sooner or later.

Below, the people's muttering grew louder. Wait a minute, he thought. *Now* what are they pointing at…?

He flipped again in midair, searching the sky. There – beyond the Tower, high in the darkening sky – something was forming. A ring of green fire, sparking with unearthly energy. Growing, widening… five feet wide, then ten… twenty…

"A portal," he whispered.

"Big one," Friday added.

"Byproduct of the summoning?" he asked. "More symbiotes, maybe?"

"Not likely, boss."

He raced upward, firing both jets, and nearly collided with a falling symbiote. The creature swiped at him with a newly formed claw, raising sparks on his armor, then let out a squawk as it was sucked inside the Tower.

Inside the portal, a humanoid form appeared – twelve feet tall and nearly half as thick. Its body seemed to be carved from solid rock, misshapen limbs formed into a mockery of humanoid life. Its face was a single open wound, glowing with crimson power.

A Mindless One. An emissary, a servant of Dormammu. As Tony watched in horror, it turned to face downward, kicked off, and hurtled head-first toward the Tower, face beam flaring bright.

He wheeled back in the air and fired off both repulsor rays. Gigawatt-level energy flared from his hands, sizzling through the air – and bounced off the Mindless One's rocky hide. The creature didn't slow down, didn't even seem to notice the attack.

Tony paused, thinking furiously. In a few seconds, that thing would strike the Tower – and, at this speed, crash right through the roof to the workshop below. The workshop, he knew, that held the machinery currently drawing half the city's power to do its vital work. If the Mindless One managed to destroy that machinery, the entire plan would be ruined.

But that wasn't the worst of it.

A hundred-plus angry symbiotes would be unleashed, all at once, on the streets of Manhattan.

He called up a miniature rocket-launcher, which sprouted from his right elbow down to his hand. He fired off one mini-missile, then a second and a third.

The Mindless One barely noticed the first shot. The second missile ricocheted off its head. It reached out a meaty hand and deflected the third one, sending it sputtering off through the air.

Swearing, Tony called up a schematic on his armor's heads-up display. The Mindless One's trajectory hadn't changed a bit.

"Special Purpose Mode," he hissed. "Protocol: Guided Missile."

The armor swelled and grew around his body, servos and reinforced metal shielding snapping into place. State-of-the-art weapons systems locked together, transforming a sleek metallic super hero into an engine of pure destruction, four times the size of the man inside the shell.

Before the transformation was even finished, he whirled in midair and fired off all jets. "Intercept course," he said.

The armor responded instantly. He turned and plummeted

down at an angle, boots flaring like the sun. The Mindless One had a head start, but it couldn't fly – all it had was downward momentum. Tony poured on the speed, drawing closer… closer…

"Boss," Friday said in his ear, "this is gonna hurt."

"I know."

He watched in something close to terror as the creature drew closer. The roof was just below now, the iris lensing open to receive another symbiote. The Mindless One's face beam flared, preparing to blast the building wide open.

"On your left!" Tony yelled and lurched right.

He struck the Mindless One with the force of a freight train. The impact jarred him, sending alarm signals flaring all through his armor. Pain shot through his arm, up his shoulder, all the way to his neck.

"Again!" he cried.

The second strike rattled his teeth. Something went *snap*. Not something in the armor. Something inside him. Several ribs, he was sure, were broken.

But he'd finally gotten the creature's attention. It lurched sideways, its maw firing off crimson energy uncontrollably. The beams shot wide of the building – the creature skidded sideways, grabbed hold of the lip of the roof–

Tony tumbled away, dazed. Don't pass out, he told himself, don't pass out! He righted himself in midair, turned to look–

–and saw the Mindless One scrape down the side of the building, taking the outer wall with it in a deafening crunch of metal and stone. Huge chunks of wall, of heavy brick and granite, cracked free and began to fall to the street below.

"Oh, crap," Tony said. "Cancel Missile Mode!"

As the armor returned to its normal configuration, he

pivoted to face downward, firing off both repulsors in wide-angle beams. Agony shot through his right arm, the one that had struck the Mindless One. He screamed, but kept up the barrage until the severed bits of Stark Tower had been atomized.

He exhaled in relief. That would prevent any casualties on the ground, at least. But there were probably several hundred workers still at risk *inside* the building... including his "Big Tech" collaborators...

He turned, staring at the gaping hole the creature had torn in the side of the building. He could barely recognize the workshop. Half the display cases along the wall had been smashed, the Iron Man suits scattered in pieces across the floor. The small null-grav stage stood, empty, on the far side of the room.

The main event, of course, was the accumulator. It took up most of the room – and every inch of it was filled with the roiling, semi-liquid bodies of the symbiotes. Despite the urgency, Tony couldn't help taking a moment to admire the engineering. A row of machinery at the base of the device hummed with power, keeping the symbiotes bottled up tight. Maybe, he thought – with a pang of guilt – maybe I underestimated that loose-cannon crew, after all.

Ock and the others were nowhere to be seen. But the Mindless One had planted itself on the floor, just inside the hole in the wall, and was marching straight toward the accumulator. The symbiotes' prison was intact, but it wouldn't be for long.

Tony swooped in through the hole and charged the monster from behind. It whirled around, registering his presence for the first time, then turned to wrench the big screen off the workshop's wall. It hurled the screen at Tony, who barely managed to duck in time. As the wallscreen soared out the hole in the wall, Tony aimed a repulsor at it and reduced it to dust.

"Second TV in two days," he muttered.

The Mindless One's face opening flared again; left unstopped, it would blast the accumulation chamber wide open. Tony leaped and tackled the creature, sending both of them plummeting toward the floor. They struck with a jarring impact, sending a fresh round of agony lancing through Tony's *other* shoulder. Metal stabbed into his hand with a sickening crunch; a display before his eyes read LEFT GAUNTLET – REPULSOR DAMAGED.

As he rolled free of the creature, he caught a quick glimpse of Ty Stone peering out from behind the curve of the accumulation chamber. Stone glanced at Tony with wide eyes, shook his head, and took off for the stairway.

Running away, Tony thought bitterly. Good old Ty – hasn't changed a bit.

He checked his helmet's display. The armor had sustained serious damage; overall power was down to 34%, and that left repulsor was toast. A big red warning proclaimed SPECIAL PURPOSE MODES: INOPERATIVE.

The Mindless One hauled itself slowly, heavily, to its feet. Its head swiveled from side to side, face beam flashing faintly. But it made no sound.

They never speak, Tony thought; never think, never express any sign of individuality. The perfect servants of Dormammu. That's what we'll all be eventually, if he has his way.

Tony struggled to rise; his armor whined in protest. His side ached, ribs flaring with pain whenever he shifted position. He shook his left hand, relieved to find he hadn't broken anything there.

"Boss," Friday said, her voice wavering in and out, "give yourself a minute."

He grimaced, watching the Mindless One. It moved toward him for a second, wind whipping past it from the hole in the wall. Then it turned away and resumed its march on the accumulation chamber.

"I don't have a minute," Tony hissed.

The Mindless One stopped a few feet from the chamber. A hundred symbiote eyes watched from within, tracking the creature's every movement.

Tony rose to one knee, then fell back again. Pain stabbed through his broken ribs.

The fiery maw of the Mindless One flared, then faded again. It raised both fists, rearing back to smash them into the transparent accumulation chamber.

And as it did–

–for Tony Stark–

–time–

–seemed to slow down.

He was slipping into shock; he realized that. But as he watched the gigantic rocky fists swing slowly through the air, everything changed for him. He was still Anthony Stark, the Invincible Iron Man. Still one of the richest men in the world, still a genius inventor, a founding member of the Avengers. Still, as far as he knew, the only person on Earth who'd managed to anticipate Dormammu's rule and make the necessary arrangements to free himself.

But all at once he knew: *I've pushed things too far.*

He'd been cocky – lucky – all his life, and he'd let it go to his head. He'd gambled and won, then gambled again and again and again. He'd bought and sold companies, negotiated billion-dollar deals, amassed great wealth and lost it and built it back up again. He'd cheated death, restarted his dead heart and soared up into the air, laughing and blazing with power.

But the thing about gambling was, sooner or later, the house won. And in this game, the house was an interdimensional tyrant with a billion billion conquered mind-slaves. Even worse, though – Dormammu didn't *need* those billions. When faced with a threat from Tony and his partners, the "Master" had sent just one creature. The least of his minions, a monster not even capable of independent thought.

In less than one second, when those clasped stone fists connected with the plastiglass accumulation chamber, Tony's streak would come to an end. The game would be over.

And Dormammu? *He hadn't even bothered to make an appearance.*

Tony lifted an arm in protest and cried out as a fresh round of agony pierced his shoulder. No good, he thought. I can't... can't do it...

With a flash of metal and a howl of fury, Doctor Octopus hurtled down from the ceiling, all four tentacles whirling in the air. The metal appendages scraped and clanked as they encircled the Mindless One, yanking it sharply away from the accumulation chamber. In the air, above those deadly arms, Ock let out another cry and lurched toward the wall. The tentacles mirrored his movements, tugging the Mindless One along with them. The creature's fists flailed. It began to lose its balance.

"Destroy *my* work, will you?" Ock spat.

Ock leapt to the floor, less than two feet away from the gaping hole in the wall. He paused, his short-cropped hair whipped by the outside wind, and glared at the creature with a hatred that might have been aimed at the entire world.

Then he *pulled*. The Mindless One struggled, but those uncanny metal arms held it tight. The creature tottered, tipped, and crashed to the floor with an impact that shook the building.

Ock hovered over the creature, tentacles flashing menacingly. The Mindless One lay, quivering slightly, on the floor...

"Anthony?"

Tony, lying on the floor himself, looked around in shock. Justin Hammer stood above him, holding out some sort of bulky contraption. Hammer's piercing eyes flickered from Tony to the fallen Mindless One, across the room.

"Justin. Ow!" Tony winced, forcing himself to rise to a crouch. "You here to, uh, g-gloat at my fallen state?"

Hammer turned to stare back at him. Tony couldn't read the expression in those gray eyes. Alarm for sure, mixed with a familiar tinge of superiority. And yes, he was sure: a touch of sympathy as well.

"Actually, old man," Hammer said, "I'm here to give you this."

Tony's shoulder screamed in agony – again – as he reached out to accept Hammer's offering. He stood up shakily and raised his faceplate, staring at the device with his naked eyes.

"The harness," he said. "You got it built."

Hammer gave him a condescending smile. "That *was* the job."

Tony turned the harness over, examining it. Two metallic loops, with a transparent bodysuit cover rolled up at the top. And something else, too – something that hadn't been in the initial plans. Along the back, running crosswise... a large brace with a very familiar tube mounted inside it. A tube filled with thick blue liquid.

"The bomb!" Tony's eyes went wide. "You... attached it to the harness?"

Hammer grimaced. "Needs must as the devil drives."

"You can carve that on my tombstone."

Across the room, the Mindless One stirred. Ock flashed all four tentacles at it, keeping it at bay like a lion tamer in the ring.

"It was the only way," Hammer said, his voice grave.

The Mindless One struggled to its feet. It reared its head back in fury, or what passed for fury in that empty granite head. The open maw of its face flared with renewed power.

"*Om Vasudhare Svaha,* Anthony," Hammer said. "And good luck."

Then Hammer spun on his heel – surprisingly quickly, for a man his age – and sprinted for the exit.

"Back at you," Tony sighed, "you new-age fruitbat."

He hefted the harness in his hands. The harness that now, almost certainly, would mean his death. If the Dark Dimension itself didn't kill him, there'd be no escaping that bomb – not when it was strapped right onto his back!

One thing at a time, he reminded himself. Priority One: get out of this room alive.

He checked his armor: power was up to sixty-four percent. That should be enough to do – well, something. If he could keep from screaming in agony every time he moved…

Ock and the Mindless One circled each other, like boxers in a ring. But the monster kept advancing, pushing Ock dangerously close to the gap in the wall. Ock raised all four tentacles, waving them in a random pattern. The Mindless One whipped its head one way, then the other–

–and its face flared. Fiery energy seared the air; Ock ducked–

–but the raging beam made contact with two of his four tentacles, slicing the ends clean off.

Ock watched, mouth open in shock, as his metal claws

clattered to the floor. The stumps of the injured tentacles waved helplessly in the air.

The Mindless One began to advance on him again. One step after another, slow and steady. Each footstep like a mini earthquake, shaking the floor.

"Doc!" Tony called. "I'm coming…"

Ock turned in response. His eyes, behind those thick goggles, made contact with Tony's for a moment. Then he turned back to the approaching Mindless One.

And then, in a single graceful motion, Ock turned and leaped out of the building. The Mindless One let out another deadly blast, searing the air where Ock had been. But his tentacles had already propelled him down, out of sight.

The Mindless One stood watching, confused. "Friday," Tony said, subvocalizing to avoid drawing the creature's attention. "Did Ock just commit suicide?"

"No, boss," the A.I. replied. "He's climbing down the side of the building."

"I, uh, don't suppose he's doubling back? Taking the creature by surprise?"

"It really doesn't look that way." Friday paused. "He's moving pretty fast for a fellow with two broken 'arms.'"

Slowly the Mindless One turned, its faceless maw seeming to notice the accumulation chamber all over again. Within, the symbiotes watched and flowed, like some Greek chorus observing the ongoing drama.

Tony set the harness down gently on the floor, taking care not to disturb the bomb casing. Then he stepped forward, toward the chamber… and the Mindless One.

"And I alone am left to tell the tale," he whispered.

He dropped to a crouch, powering his remaining repulsor

to full. His body ached; his ribs sent stabbing pains through his side. But Octopus, that rage-fueled psychopath, had bought him a little time. Maybe, he thought – just maybe, it'll be enough –

It wasn't. He saw the back of the Mindless One's thick hand coming, just in time to twist away – preventing his injured side from taking the brunt of the blow. But the rock-hard fist struck him full-on in the stomach, knocking the breath out of him even through the armor's layers of nanoshock padding.

Then he was flying backward, skidding along the floor toward the symbiote chamber. With a shuddering impact, he crashed into the machinery at the base of the chamber.

Sparks flew. Alarms danced before his eyes. He shook his head, dazed.

"Chamber is holding, boss," Friday said in his ear. "But the summoning tech is trashed. Iris on the roof won't open, either."

"That's fine! We've got enough symbiotes," he snapped back. "And I've got a much bigger problem."

The Mindless One advanced toward him, face-maw glaring red-hot. Tony crouched low, waving out the little fires spreading across the base of the accumulation chamber. Pain stabbed at him from both sides of his stomach. Every muscle in his body screamed in protest. He braced against the back of the chamber…

…and noted, with alarm, that the bomb harness sat on the floor between him and the Mindless One. If Priority One was getting out of the room, Priority Two was keeping that bomb from going off. The Stane Solvent, let loose from its containment tube, could quite literally consume the planet.

Holy crap, he thought – I've demoted the symbiotes to Priority Three. Who came up with this insane plan, anyway?

He lunged forward, diving to grab hold of the harness. In one quick move, he snagged a shoulder strap and yanked the device toward his body. But as he did–

–the Mindless One flared bright, filling the room with red-hot fire.

Tony's faceplate dropped down automatically, protecting him – for the most part. But the raging, other-dimensional flame still seared his face, overheating his armor, setting off alarms in his helmet. For a moment he thought: Feels like a blast furnace in here. I'm being cooked alive!

Then the armor's coolant systems kicked in. The heat eased off on his torso and arms; his face was burned, but he couldn't tell how badly. That would have to wait.

He took quick stock of his surroundings. He stood backed up against the accumulation chamber; inside, the symbiotes flowed and danced in a symphony of teeth and claws. The harness lay at his feet, the bomb casing still intact. For now–

"Boss!" Friday yelled.

He lunged aside, barely in time to avoid another deadly blow. The Mindless One's fist slammed into the accumulation chamber, shaking the entire room. Tony crouched, looked up…

… and saw, to his horror, a thin crack in the outer layer of the chamber wall. The symbiotes swarmed and hissed around it, poking with an array of newly formed limbs.

Eyeing the Mindless One, he checked his readings. The armor's power was down to thirty-one percent. One repulsor was shot; several dozen relays had been shorted out by the creature's face beam. Most of the still-functioning circuits were trying to cool the armor down to a normal temp.

"Friday," Tony said, kicking the bomb harness behind him. "What have we got?"

"Not much," the A.I. replied.

The Mindless One turned toward him again.

Tony raised his right hand, willed the palm repulsor to full. It sputtered and winked out. A display flashed before his eyes: INSUFFICIENT POWER.

The Mindless One took another thundering step. Behind it, the wall gaped open, sun setting blood-red behind the helpless city below.

Tony sighed, closed his eyes. "House wins," he whispered.

Then, all at once, he remembered the bead. The strange object, the device that Shuri had thrust into his hand, seconds before he'd left Norman Osborn's penthouse complex.

What was it? Why had she given it to him? It was clearly Wakandan tech. Was it something she'd devised in her lab? Something she knew would work against Dormammu and his minions?

More immediately: where *was* it?

For a moment he panicked, then remembered a small compartment at his waist – he'd stashed the thing there. Keeping his eyes on the advancing Mindless One, he willed the compartment open, reached in, and pulled out the bead.

He held it up, examining it quickly, urgently. A layer of thin vibranium weave, across its surface, hummed slightly as he shifted the thing in his palm. It looked like Kimoyo technology, similar to the cards T'Challa had given the Avengers to keep in touch on missions. But what was it for? The Wakandans had always guarded their tech closely, even before the arrival of Dormammu.

It didn't look like a weapon. It had no trigger, no barrel, no opening for an energy discharge. It wasn't even warm.

The Mindless One paused, less than two feet away from

Tony. Its maw gaped crimson, energy building up to a furious discharge. If we're lucky, Tony thought grimly, that blast will *only* kill me and set loose the symbiotes. If we're unlucky, it'll set off the bomb!

He stared at the bead in frustration. "What *are* you?" he cried.

With a tiny ringing sound, the bead pulsed in his hand.

Then he remembered: *communication.* Kimoyo tech was all about communication – with people, machines... maybe even...

...Mindless Ones?

The creature raised both fists, preparing to strike. Trying not to flinch, Tony held up the bead in front of him and stared straight into that red-hot face-maw.

"Shoo," he said. "Go away."

The Mindless One paused, raising its head. It looked confused.

The bead let out another small peal.

"Go away," Tony repeated. *"Get out of here!"*

The Mindless One shot upright. The energy in its maw flared once, harmlessly, then faded away. All at once it turned, strode across the room to the gaping hole where the wall had been. It paused, staring out at the twilight cityscape.

Then, to Tony's astonishment, the creature flexed both massive legs and leaped up into the sky.

He took a step forward, still clutching the bead. Pain flared through his right leg – it must be broken, he realized. In all the chaos, he hadn't even noticed. He dropped to one knee, alarms flashing before his eyes.

"Boss," Friday said, "you've got internal bleeding."

"Not now."

He crawled to the edge of the room. A sheer drop lay before him, stone and plaster still crumbling off the hole in the wall. He forced himself to ignore the pain and looked up…

…just in time to see the Mindless One vanish into the flaring green portal hanging in the sky.

More alarms. They rang in his ears, echoing in his dazed brain. I did it, he thought. I got rid of the Mindless One, with a little help from a new friend. The chamber still held the symbiotes tight; a single crack in the outer wall wouldn't be enough for them to escape. And the Stane Solvent remained secure, held within its containment tube. The Earth would not be overrun by extraterrestrial monsters, or consumed by a deadly artificial substance.

But the planet's population still suffered under a conqueror's mental control. And in my current state, Tony realized bitterly, there's no way I can take my little vacay into the Dark Dimension.

He dropped to the floor, rolling slowly onto his back. Three ribs were definitely broken – maybe four. That leg was fractured in at least two places, and his stomach was wet with blood. His face ached too, seared by the creature's face beam.

He lay still, willing his faceplate to open. Night air swept across his face, soothing his burns. He stared up into the sky, watching as the emerald portal pulsed and glowed, expanded and contracted.

For just a moment, it flared bright. A column of fire appeared, crimson-hot and yellow, glaring features visible within its depths. Two arched, blazing eyes; a smiling, self-satisfied mouth.

Dormammu.

Those eyes seemed to stare straight through Tony,

penetrating all the way to his core. He remembered the dark flame within his mind, the terrible mewling thing. The piece of Dormammu that would never leave, that would live inside him forever.

"Go away," he gasped.

But he knew it was useless. The bead felt cold and dead in his hand; it had served its purpose. And Dormammu was no Mindless One, to be banished with some high-tech gadget.

The sky swirled before Tony's eyes. Dormammu smiled wider, just for a second, and then he vanished. The bead slipped from Tony's hand, rolling over the lip of the building into open air.

At last, consumed by pain and regret, he passed out.

PART FOUR

SHADOW AND IRON

TWENTY

In the time of Dormammu, the lights of Times Square shone dimly. A few tourists slumped their way through the night streets; taxis prowled, sullen and empty. Even the huge Broadway show signs seemed to fade into the background. *The Girl from Dormammu Country, Little Shop of Dormammu, Between River-side and Dormammu*. A small line for *Dormammu-lin Rouge*.

Amid this gloom, the Shadow Avengers returned to Earth.

Doctor Strange appeared first, blue-and-red robes barely visible within a corona of white light. His hands, pressed together in a prayer position, drew slowly apart, creating a rift in the air radiating out from the amulet at his neck.

"Hurry," he gasped, sweat breaking out on his brow.

With a tremendous effort, he raised his hands above his head. Luke Cage and the Black Panther leaped out of the rift, plummeting to the sidewalk below. T'Challa spread his legs and landed gracefully. Cage thundered down, his boots shattering the concrete of a pedestrian seating area, sending little tables scattering all around.

Spider-Man came next, tumbling end over end like a cannonball. For a moment, the transition between realms was too much for him. He panicked, reached out with both web-shooters, and fired wild. One webline wrapped around a lamppost, anchoring him as he swung around for a landing. The other…

…the other, he saw, had struck a very angry Luke Cage in the stomach. One of the big man's hands was now firmly stuck to his own shirt.

"Uh," Spider-Man said. "Sorry."

Cage said nothing, but the murderous look on his face spoke volumes. He tugged once at his shirt, then rolled his eyes and turned away.

A few bystanders stopped to stare at the newcomers, smiling pleasant, Dormammu-dulled smiles. "Nothing to see here," Spidey called after them. "Just a bunch of heroes that've been through some stuff you wouldn't believe."

The Panther retracted his mask, revealing sharp, haunted eyes. "New York City," he said, gazing around. "Doctor Strange… he did it."

"Looks like he's still doing it," Spider-Man said.

He gestured at Strange, who stood glowing in the middle of the seating area, surrounded by overturned metal tables. His arms were spread wide, energy flowing up and out of his body. As the others watched, a pair of figures appeared, ghostlike, within the radiance. Two men, both in robes… both poised within the rift…

As they leaped, the two men seemed drawn together, their forms passing into and through each other. Their forms intertwined, making it hard to see where one ended and the other began. By the time they landed on the pavement, they'd merged into one solid figure.

Doctor Voodoo. Dark robes, a ring of skulls around his waist.

The Staff of Legba, his strength and his guide, clasped firmly in both hands.

Doctor Strange blinked and let out a very un-Doctor-Strange-ish sort of gasp. As the mystic glow faded, his knees buckled under him. Spider-Man started toward him, but T'Challa got there first. The Panther caught Strange and lowered him gently to a public bench.

"I'm fine," Strange said, waving him off. "I'm… I'm just not sure what happened."

"I can barely remember any of it," Cage rumbled. "Were we in a red room? With stripes on the floor?"

"I seem to remember a blue police box," Spider-Man said.

"The memories are fading," T'Challa said. "Like visions from the heart-shaped herb."

"How long were we gone, anyway?" Spider-Man asked. "Feels like months! Hey, I should call my friend Carrie – she could write a whole novel about that trip."

Cage glared at him. "Maybe *after* we kick Dormammu's butt off this planet?"

"Oh, you and your whole priorities thing."

Cage didn't smile. I better lay off him, Spider-Man thought. He doesn't look too happy about the webbed-up hand. It's gonna be a while till that webbing dissolves!

Doctor Strange stood up, amulet glowing softly at his throat. "Doctor Voodoo," he said, approaching his fellow sorcerer. "You are one?"

"Yes," Voodoo replied, his voice seeming to echo in the night. "Upon our return to this realm, the essences of Jericho and Daniel Drumm have coalesced back into this form." He held up his staff, which glowed briefly. "And I can feel the power of my ancestors, hovering close to me once more."

"Good," Cage said, "'cause we're gonna need all the help we can get."

They assembled around a small metal table under a tree, pulling up folding chairs. Spider-Man perched on top of one, his legs balanced on the back, and paused, drawing in a deep breath of hot night air. Man, he thought, it's good to be back! There's no place like the city – Dormammu or not.

Voodoo settled into a chair directly across from Doctor Strange. "I owe you my thanks, Stephen," he said, "not just for finding me, but for guiding us home."

"I'm not sure how I accomplished that," Doctor Strange said, flashing a weak smile. "I heard a… a voice. Calling in my head… feeding me the mystic knowledge I needed."

"What matters is, you did it," Cage said. "When that trail from the Eye of Vouk winked out, I thought we'd never get back. Felt like this time I was trapped in Bay Ridge, with the trains out of service."

"Oh, man," Spider-Man said, "Ms Marvel! If something happened to the Eye…"

He whipped out his phone, waiting an agonizing moment while it located the cell network. Like a lot of things, phones didn't work as well as they used to, pre-Dormammu. Then, with trembling fingers, he called up Ms Marvel's number and thumbed the audio to speakerphone. He laid the phone down on the table and watched, along with the others, as the phone started to ring.

"Hello? Spider-Man?"

A chorus of relieved sighs around the table. "Yeah, it's me," Spider-Man said, grinning inside his mask. "It's us. We're all back."

"Oh g–" Ms Marvel replied, her voice partly obscured by static. "That's a relie – I was afraid–"

"Us too," Cage replied. "Glad you're OK."

"You're cutting in and out, though," Spider-Man said. "Where are you?"

"Subway, about to enter tunnel," she said. "Someth– – appened."

"Something…" Spider-Man stared at the phone. "What? What happened?"

"–ark Tower. On my way now–"

Doctor Strange rose to his feet. "Did she say Stark Tower?"

"She did," the Panther called.

Spider-Man looked up, startled. T'Challa had climbed the tree above them and sat crouched on a high branch, peering between the tall buildings nestled together to the north.

"Stark Tower has been damaged," T'Challa continued. "Some sort of smoke rising from the top."

"How can you see that?" Spider-Man asked. "I can't even make out the Tower from here."

A burst of static from the phone. He snatched it up, noting the display reading: CALL ENDED.

Strange and Voodoo exchanged glances. "Dormammu?" Voodoo asked.

"Almost certainly," Strange replied. "And before we've even managed to concoct a plan to stop him."

"I was gonna ask about that," Spider-Man said. "The whole plan business."

"It will not be easy," Voodoo said. "Even with the combined power of two Sorcerers Supreme. We are … Daniel, in particular, is struggling to re-adapt."

"Later for the plan," Cage said, tugging on his webbed-up arm in frustration. "Right now, get me to the Tower. You'd be surprised what I can do with one wing."

"That'll be gone in a half hour!" Spider-Man said, gesturing at the webbing. "Forty minutes, tops."

Doctor Strange raised his arms to summon a short-range teleportation portal. As the energy started to build, his eyes rolled back in his head and he slumped into his chair. The portal faded.

"I am clearly... not recovered from our journey," he said.

"I can get us there," Voodoo said, raising his staff. "But it will take me a few minutes to gather my mystic energies."

"In that case, I'll scout ahead," Spider-Man said. "This is my home turf – I'll just web my way up to Stark's crib first, and the rest of you can..."

He trailed off, noticing the grimace on Cage's face. With his free hand, Cage pointed across the street. Spider-Man looked over – and saw T'Challa already on the move, dodging cars as he made his way north, toward a thick cluster of skyscrapers.

"Ah," Spider-Man said. "In that case, I'll get to Stark Tower *second*. That's OK – I'm not the kind of guy that has to show off all the time! You know?"

Cage's look grew even more withering. Doctor Voodoo raised an eyebrow, and an amused look crossed Strange's exhausted face.

"Don't answer that," Spider-Man said, shooting out a webline to begin the trip uptown.

TWENTY-ONE

A crowd of sluggish people stood in front of Stark Tower, their faces glassy with the familiar Dormammu-stupor. Ms Marvel paused for a moment on the tree-lined plaza, peering upward. Dust and smoke wafted down from the top floors; part of the outer wall was missing. But she couldn't make out any details from the ground.

She grimaced, elbowed past the people, and pushed her way in through the front door.

A few emergency workers bustled around the lobby, where they'd set up a triage unit for injured employees. But no one even glanced at the girl in the brightly colored costume as she made her way to the emergency stairwell. Sometimes, she reflected, that Dormammu-stupor came in handy.

She took the steps ten at a time, extending her legs to quicken her pace. Even so, twenty stories up, she began to doubt the wisdom of this climb. But the elevators were out, and she had to get to the top fast. Scaling the outer wall was a nonstarter – it was at least forty, maybe fifty floors to the top. Even with her powers, she'd make a nasty splat if she fell off.

As her muscles grew sore, her anxiety grew. She'd just lived through four hours of utter despair, terrified that she'd doomed the Shadow Avengers to permanent exile in some unknown hell dimension. Thankfully, they were all right. That should have made her feel better–

–but what about Tony? He'd come to her for help, and she'd turned him down. Now someone had attacked his home, where he lived and worked. Was he injured? Dead, even?

If so, that would be her fault too.

On the thirtieth-floor landing she paused, dizzy. But there was no time to waste. She had to find out what was going on at the top of the building.

By the time she reached the workshop, her legs ached and her thoughts frenzied. She leaped up the last few steps, stumbled into the room – and nearly tumbled out into open air, through the hole that gaped open in the two-story wall. Whoa, she told herself. Take it easy!

She turned to study the room – and gasped. Most of the interior was filled with a giant, beaker-shaped terrarium of some kind, filled with… Venom stuff. Raging, shape-shifting symbiotes, like the one Eddie Brock shared consciousness with. They watched her with a hundred liquid eyes, surging and flowing in their tight prison.

She blinked, unable to comprehend the scene before her. Who would want to pen up a roomful of the most dangerous beings in the universe?

No emergency workers up here; clearly they hadn't reached this level yet. She cast her eyes along the floor – and noticed an Iron Man costume, torn to pieces. Leg over here, arm there, torso halfway across the room. Oh no, she thought. Tony – they've ripped him apart!

Then she saw part of another costume – an older, solid gray

one. And the bulky Hulk-Buster arms of yet another. Finally, she noticed the shattered display cases on the wall.

Stop it, she told herself. Stop panicking! There isn't even any blood…

Correction: there *was* blood. Just a little – a few droplets on the floor, spaced a foot or so apart. Leading around the corner of the symbiotes' prison unit, out of sight…

As she followed the trail, she heard a moan.

She rounded the corner and stopped in her tracks. At first, she couldn't quite register what she was looking at: some sort of man-shaped tub, lying face-up on the floor. Cradled within it, like a crustacean in a half-shell, Tony Stark lay stripped to his briefs.

"Mister Stark!"

She rushed to him and knelt down quickly, shoving aside a pile of scattered equipment. A complex of plastic tubes fed in and out of Tony's nose, arms, and legs, and into a metal plate across his stomach, all leading to ports built into the inside of the tub. Bruises covered his limbs; one knee was bent at an unnatural angle, and he seemed to be lying in a crusted puddle of dried blood. His eyes were closed.

"Tony," she said, nudging him gently. "Tony, Mister Stark! Are you alive?"

"Dormammu!" he cried.

His eyes flashed open. He lurched upward, struggling to sit up. The tubes strained to their limit, threatening to pop free. They're feeding him fluids, she realized. Keeping him alive!

"Easy!" She reached out and pressed his chest back down. "No Dormammu! Dormammu's not here! It's just me."

His head whipped around to face her. His eyes visibly dilated, then contracted. "Ms Marvel?" he gasped.

"Yeah. Don't try to move," she added quickly, as he started to rise again. "What happened here? What is all... this?" She gestured at the tub.

"This?" He tried to smile. "This is a somewhat out-of-date Heavy Lifting Unit."

"You mean..." She peered at the tub, noticing for the first time the red and gold plating along its outside surface. "...it's one of your suits of armor?"

"Ty Stone tried to steal it." He waved a hand upward, at the broken display cases along the upper wall. "Always taking my stuff. Guess I should be glad he grabbed a big one... stealth armor wouldn't have had room for all this..." He ran his fingers across a couple of the plastic tubes.

"I don't understand." She frowned, pushing aside a few more pieces of armor to clear a place to sit. "This armor was constructed with medical tubing in it?"

"No! Oh no, kid." He leaned back, closing his eyes. "I put all this together after Dormammu attacked."

She blinked. "You..."

"I was bleeding out. Ow!" He flexed his leg, stared at it, and lowered it back into the suit-shell. "Armor damaged... losing blood, losing fluids. Two choices, I told myself. Two choices, Stark. Lie down and die, or..."

"...or *invent* something," she whispered.

His eyes met hers. He laughed, then erupted into a coughing fit. She watched, grimacing, as he spat blood onto the floor.

"You need a doctor," she said.

"Yeah? Where you gonna take me, Dormammu General? I hear they got a hell of an emergency room."

She nodded. "Point taken."

"No, I got everything I need right here..." He looked past

her, at the accumulation chamber, and gave a little wave. "Hey guys!"

She turned to look. Right behind her, within the chamber, the symbiotes swirled, watching with a hundred eyes. She shivered. She'd almost forgotten about them.

"I..." Ms Marvel paused, shaking her head. "I don't understand any of this. What are these things doing here? Did they attack you? Are they... working for Dormammu?"

"No! No no no." He raised an eyebrow. "These little oily dudes, they're our friends. Well, maybe not *friends*. Any one of 'em would probably bite your face off, if they got out of that chamber."

She eyed the chamber, noticing for the first time a small vertical crack in the outer layer of plastiglass. Thankfully, the inner layer was still intact.

"OK," she said. "So why are they here?"

"They're part of the plan. Actually, they're most of the plan."

Haltingly, his voice croaking, he explained the plot to cripple Dormammu's power. Tony himself, he explained, would merge with the symbiotes, leading them into the realms beyond our own. The symbiotes would follow Venom's trail to the Dark Dimension, where Tony would set off a bomb containing a solvent so deadly it could destroy the Earth. Let loose in this other realm, the solvent would dissipate Dormammu's essence, freeing the Multiverse from his tyranny.

Ms Marvel listened in silence, eyes wide. When Tony finished, she leaned back against the chamber and sighed.

"That's the most ridiculous plan I've ever heard," she said.

"Yeah, that's kind of my specialty." He shifted his leg. "Ow."

"You..." She gestured at the chamber filled with symbiotes. "You built this all yourself?"

"I had some help." He looked away, muttered something.

She leaned in closer. "What?"

"Doc Ock, I said."

"Doc *Ock?*"

"Among others." He looked up at her, pain in his eyes. "You turned me down."

"Ow," she said. "Right to the heart, huh?"

"Sorry." He leaned back into the suit. "Another of my specialties, I'm afraid."

"I… I don't…" She paused, gathering her thoughts. "I don't even know where to start with this. What makes you think you could control the symbiotes, anyway? There must be a hundred of them in there. Eddie Brock has – had… he could barely handle *one.*"

With effort, Tony reached outside his suit-shell and grabbed hold of a piece of equipment – one of several strewn across the floor of the damaged workshop. He held it up: a shoulder-harness with a layer of transparent fabric hanging down from it, and a metallic casing of some kind on the back.

"Control unit," he explained. "The sheer-mesh fabric is a full bodysuit, and it's nano-thin; it'll allow me to meld with the symbiotes but prevent them from taking me over."

"It looks…" She ran a finger along the transparent fabric, "… flimsy."

"It'll protect me. In theory, anyway."

"Assuming that's true…" She touched the metal casing, noting the blue fluid visible through a window on its side. "What's this?"

"That, ah, that's, that right there is the bomb."

"The bomb." She looked at him. "It's *attached* to the control harness?"

"Yeah, Ock and his friends came up with that cool innovation."

"So it'll blow *you* up along with it."

"Well, maybe. Maybe not! Not if I can–"

"Never mind, never mind that for now. How exactly were you planning to open a portal to these other dimensions?"

He looked away. "Still working on that."

"Uh-huh. And is there navigation tech of some kind in this harness? Some sort of Dark Dimension GPS?"

"No, that's what the symbiotes are for. They'll home in on Venom, their brother."

"And then? How did you plan to find your way home again?"

He let out a tired noise and closed his eyes.

"What about..." She waved her hand around the room. "Won't Dormammu know you're coming? He's on to you, right? He attacked you here?"

"I've been thinking about that," he replied. "He sent a Mindless One, and he made a quick spot inspection after I was down. But the Big D..." He broke off in another coughing fit, then resumed. "I think he's distracted, ruling a billion newly conquered realms. Why else would he leave without destroying the accumulation chamber?"

She leaned back again, sighing heavily.

"So there's still a chance," he continued. "But only if we move fast."

"It doesn't matter," she said. "None of this matters. There's no way you can pull this off – no way even one single step, out of the dozen preposterous steps in this plan, can be put into action."

"Why not?"

"Because *YOU CAN'T STAND UP!*"

He blinked, staring at her. Started to rise, winced again, and slumped back down in despair.

She stood up and paced away. I should feel sorry for him, she thought. The poor guy's lying in a pile of his own blood, half dead. What's worse, he just faced off against Dormammu – or one of Dormammu's agents, anyway. And the sacrifice he was planning to make…

She glanced at the symbiotes, at their hundred glaring eyes, and shivered.

I should feel sorry for him, she thought again.

But I don't.

"You always do this," she said.

"Wh-what?"

"You really thought this would work?" She whirled back toward him, feeling the fury rise inside. "You thought you could pull it all off by yourself?"

He stared at her, silent.

"You did. You really did," she continued. "You stupid man. You came up with an incredibly risky plan, ignored all the holes in it, and hired a bunch of immoral jerks to put it into action. Did you really think a pack of *rich people* could save the world?"

"I…" He spread his arms in a helpless gesture. "The Avengers weren't…"

"You always do this," she repeated. She crouched down, glaring at him. "You play around in your lab – spend more money than my family makes in a *year* – and pat yourself on the back for your cleverness. And you make a big honking mess, and then somebody else has to clean up that mess."

"Dormammu," he said, shaking his head. "He has to be… What's going on here? Why are you so mad at me?"

She reached out and, with a fury that surprised even her, yanked the control harness out of his hand.

"Because now *I* have to do this," she said.

His eyes went wide. "No!" He struggled to rise. A fluid tube popped free of his arm, spurting some sort of saline solution into the well of the armor. "No, that's not the plan."

"The *plan*," she spat.

"I don't want this," he said, forcing himself to a sitting position. "You can't… you'll never survive. You'll die!"

"Probably."

"You're right," he said, his voice growing desperate. "You're right, I screwed up. But I can't let you pay the price… not for *my* mistakes…"

She tuned him out, studying the harness in her hands. It was true, she knew: If she took on this mission, she would die. The bomb would atomize her, reduce her to elementary particles along with Dormammu and most of his realm. If she somehow survived the detonation, her mind would be torn apart, ravaged by the raging thoughts of the symbiotes. And if she cheated *that* fate, too? She'd still wind up lost, stranded forever in a realm of madness, with no way home.

The Eye of Vouk could have guided her home – maybe. But it too was gone, destroyed by Dormammu's agents.

I will die, she thought.

Then a strange thing happened. Having articulated the thought in her mind – having made the decision – she felt an odd sense of calm. As if her life, her destiny, was now written, and all she had to do was carry it out.

Tony had subsided into a half-sleep. His eyes fluttered open and closed, his lips twitching. Forming a single word, over and over: *No. No. No.*

Ms Marvel turned to the symbiotes. They watched from the chamber with hungry, shifting eyes. "You and me, guys," she said grimly. "That's how it's gotta be."

A noise from the stairwell: footsteps. And then a helpless little moan from Tony. As his whole body shivered, Ms Marvel knelt and clasped his hand, squeezing it tight.

"Hang on. Hang on, stupid man." She glanced at the stairwell. "The Doctor is coming."

TWENTY-TWO

"Quit squirming, Stark! Your leg is fractured in three places."

"I know, Doc. That's why I need to reconfigure this cargo cart into a makeshift hoverchair. Hand me that laser wrench?"

"I'm a little busy sewing up the gaping wound in your stomach."

"Oh, that's nothing. *ARRRH!* OK, it's – *UHH!* It's something…"

Ms Marvel watched in vague fascination; she'd never seen Doctor Strange in this role before. He was one of the most powerful sorcerers on Earth, capable of bending reality, casting world-altering spells, and piercing the veils between the realms. But he was also a real doctor! His hands stretched and ripped at an Ace bandage, wrapping it expertly around the improvised splints he'd positioned up and down Tony's injured leg.

For his part, Tony couldn't seem to stop moving. He sat on a small table, goggles over his eyes, welding together a floating hoverchair while the increasingly frustrated Doctor Strange worked on his leg. Behind them, the symbiotes surged and roiled within their tank.

"*Stark.* If you don't put down those tools, I swear by the

Winds of Watoomb I will break the few intact ribs left in your body."

"I need a mode of transport, Doc. Unless you want to carry me around like a baby for the rest of the day."

"Like a baby." Strange sighed, dabbing a bit of cream onto Tony's burned face. "That's appropriate."

She'd never seen Strange like this, but then, she'd never seen two men interact the way they did either. Their personalities were miles apart; it was clear they'd never be friends. At the same time, they seemed to acknowledge each other's expertise. The barbs they threw back and forth were laced with a bizarre mixture of contempt and mutual respect.

She was thinking about this, she knew, in order to avoid thinking about something else. Most of her mind was occupied with a single thought, a voice in her head that kept repeating: *You're going to die.*

Strange stepped back to examine the bandages on Tony's ribs and stomach – just as Tony activated the hoverchair. The boot jets mounted on its underside sputtered, lifting it at an angle. The chair lurched, almost colliding with the symbiote tank.

"Whoops," Tony said. "Almost got it… whoa!" The hoverchair tipped again, threatening to spill him onto the floor. "Little help here?"

Ms Marvel reached out, elongating her arms, and took hold of the chair by both of its armrests. She twisted, leveling out the contraption in midair, just a foot or two above the table. But as soon as she let go, it started listing again.

Strange shook his head. "Another fine product of Stark Enterprises."

"I got this," Tony said, his fingers darting over a control pad.

"The jets just weren't built for this level of... Yeah, here we go. That's it."

He smiled, his face red from the burns he'd sustained in battle. He looked a bit ridiculous, Ms Marvel thought, hovering there with his right leg extended straight out in a full-length splint. His torso was bare except for the huge bandage over his stomach, the smaller splints over his ribs, and, of course, his glowing chest plate.

"So." Strange gestured at the symbiotes. "This plan of yours..."

"Yeah. Not here, maybe." Tony glanced nervously at the hole in the wall. "There might be eyes in the sky."

"I thought Mindless Ones didn't have eyes," Ms Marvel said. It wasn't much of a joke, but Doctor Strange smiled at her anyway.

"Anyway," she continued, turning to Tony. "You told me the whole plan right here, remember? A few minutes ago?"

"Um, yeah..." Tony looked away. "Guess I wasn't really thinking things through."

He can't meet my gaze, she realized. He feels guilty for what I'm about to do. And you know what? He probably should.

"Come on," Tony said, taking off at surprising speed in his chair. "I know a safe place where we can talk. Have the rest of your guys meet us?"

Strange gave Ms Marvel a tired look, then turned to follow Tony, whose chair wobbled around the room, past the hole in the wall. He paused at the open staircase, waiting.

Ms Marvel cast a quick glance at the symbiotes, muttered, "See you soon, partners," and followed them out of the room.

"Better let me go first," Tony said, his hoverchair vibrating awkwardly. "I'm still getting the hang of this thing – don't want to take anyone out by accident." He started down the maintenance staircase, wobbling from side to side. Doctor Strange levitated an inch up from the top stair and wafted down after him.

Ms Marvel followed, feeling almost numb. She felt anxious, but in a distant way. She was resigned to her fate: the world was in peril, but maybe she could save it. At the cost of her own life, of course.

Her legs, still sore from the climb to the workshop, began to ache. Ten floors down, she started stretching her limbs out to cover the distance faster. A couple floors further, the Shadow Avengers entered the stairwell from a service door: Luke Cage, Spider-Man, and the Black Panther.

"Most of the building got off light," Cage said. "A few injured on the upper floors… we got 'em stuffed into ambulances."

"Took some work," Spider-Man added. "Those Dormammu-influenced EMTs aren't exactly motivated self-starters." He turned to Ms Marvel, raising his lanky arm for an elbow bump. "Hey, kid!"

She returned the bump, forcing herself to smile. She really was glad to see them all, alive and back on Earth. But that happiness was tempered, again, by the voice in her head.

You're going to die.

Doctor Voodoo joined the group last. He hung back, conferring with Doctor Strange in low tones as they continued their descent. Wizard stuff, Ms Marvel thought. Probably comparing eyes of newt or talking about some rare breed of monster they saw in one of the other realms. Like birdwatchers, home after a walk in the woods.

Or – she chided herself – maybe they were talking about something much more important. Like saving the world.

The stairwell led to an elevator, then a heavy wooden door. Tony bumped and clanked his way through it, leading the others to a dim stone staircase, then down to the deep underground levels of the building. At last he swooped down to the bottom of the stairs, gesturing at a thick iron door with a large, old-style keyhole.

"Most secure room in the building," Tony announced. "The Iron Vault."

Spider-Man cocked his head. "Is that like a steel cage?"

"More like… ah." Tony paused in midair, patting his sides. "Left the key in my other pants. I mean, in my pants…"

"…fifty stories above our heads," T'Challa sighed.

Cage grunted, rolling up his sleeves. He stepped forward, raised one booted foot, and kicked the door down with a single, ringing blow.

"Could be more secure," he muttered, and strode inside.

Tony raised one singed eyebrow. "Noted," he said.

Kamala followed them in, examining the cramped dark space. A small table with a single chair sat before a darkened screen. A row of large, unlabeled drawers was mounted on the wall, just above eye level.

"Mister Stark." Doctor Voodoo stared at one of the drawers. "May I ask why you have a 'Rapid Flesh-Devouring Pantovirus' in this compartment?"

"What?" Strange exclaimed, rushing to his side.

"How do you know that?" Tony asked, nearly colliding with Strange's head as he maneuvered his chair in the small space. "Never mind. It was worth it to see Stephen lose it for a minute there."

T'Challa stood before an open drawer, holding up a sharp weapon crusted with an odd, green-tinged sort of rust. "This blade is eighty-five percent vibranium," he said. "Where did it come from?"

"Outer space – it's a whole thing. How did you open that drawer?"

T'Challa didn't answer. He retracted his mask long enough to throw Tony a suspicious glare. Then he placed the blade carefully on the floor, keeping a hand on its hasp.

"That, ah …" Tony gestured at the blade. "That thing's leaving with you, isn't it?"

"It was stolen from Wakanda," the Panther replied, in a voice that allowed no argument.

Tony shrugged. "Lights," he said to the air. "And get us some chairs, will you?"

As the room's lights came up, another of the wall-mounted drawers began to hum open. Kamala took a step back; she could feel the others watching in alarm. What was inside this compartment? A Kree death ray? Ultimate Nullifier? Couple of Infinity Gems, maybe?

A mechanical arm dropped down from the ceiling, reached inside the drawer… and pulled out half a dozen folding metal chairs. The whole room exhaled at once.

Tony laughed, maneuvering his hoverchair into position at the head of the table. "Lighten up, will you, guys?" he said. "It's only the fate of the world at stake here."

They settled into the chairs, facing him. Only T'Challa remained standing, the vibranium weapon propped up against the wall beside him.

"First off," Tony said, "I'm really glad you're all here."

"We noticed the smoking hole in your building," Strange said dryly, "and thought we'd drop in and see what you'd blown up this time."

"Nevertheless. As, uh, Ms Marvel will tell you..." He gestured at her, but again, didn't meet her eyes. "...I haven't had a lot of luck lining up partners lately. Even the Avengers–"

"We're the Avengers," Cage stated.

"Oh." Tony frowned, his chair listing slightly in the air. "Yeah, I mean the real–"

"The Shadow Avengers," T'Challa said. Slight tinge of menace in his voice.

"The what now?"

Kamala raised a hand to her face, hiding a smile.

Tony held up both hands in surrender, wincing as his ribs shifted. "Let me start over," he said.

And once again, he told them his plan. The whole thing: symbiotes, harness, bomb. Hammer, Stone, and Doc Ock. The Dark Dimension. The incredibly dangerous Stane Solvent, which had been stored in one of the drawers of this very room.

Kamala already knew the story, so she studied the others as they listened. Cage had a tough-guy look pasted on his face that never wavered during Tony's speech. T'Challa had donned his mask again, hiding his expression. Spider-Man kept cocking his head one way and then the other, as if struggling to take it all in.

Doctors Voodoo and Strange sat together, listening intently. Every now and then they glanced at each other with obvious concern.

Tony left out only one detail: who, exactly, was supposed to carry the bomb. He was just wrapping up, describing the passage into the Dark Dimension, when Cage cleared his throat with a loud, theatrical noise.

"That won't hunt," he said flatly. "I mean, bombs, dimensions,

Venom's even-less-civilized cousins…" He turned in his chair toward the doctors. "Don't *you guys* have a plan? A better one, maybe?"

Strange glanced at Voodoo, who grimaced back and shook his head.

"We do not," Strange said, his voice grave.

"My power is returning to me," Voodoo added. "But my ordeal has left me diminished, and Daniel is still adjusting to our new situation. I could not possibly mount a full-scale assault on Dormammu at this time."

"Looks like Big Tech wins again," Tony said. "But hey! While you *powerful* wizards are sloooowly recovering your magic and, I don't know, pulling rabbits out of hats or whatever…" Strange and Voodoo glared at him in unison. "Do you think you could manage to create an interdimensional portal? Like, inside this building?"

"I don't have the Eye anymore," Kamala said. "You, uh, you guys probably know that already."

Again, the two sorcerers exchanged a glance. This time, Voodoo nodded.

"With our combined power," Strange said, "opening a portal is feasible."

"Good! Then let's get–"

"Just a moment."

All at once, the air in the room seemed to shift. One minute, Tony was running the meeting; the next, Strange had clearly taken over. He stood up, facing Tony directly as the inventor hovered in his chair.

"As usual, Stark," Strange continued, "you've assembled an impressive array of toys. But I don't think you quite comprehend the forces you're dealing with."

"As usual, *Stephen*," Tony replied, "I have a feeling you're about to tell me."

"First off..." Strange leaned across the table. "There are *people* in the Dark Dimension. Innocent men and women, who have lived under Dormammu's thumb for far longer than you or I."

"I knew that!" Tony grimaced. "Still, uh, working on that part."

Strange actually rolled his eyes.

Doctor Voodoo reached up a hand and touched Strange's sleeve. "We can probably..." Voodoo trailed off, his hand conjuring a small mystical flash in the air.

"Yes," Strange replied. "OK, Stark... Jericho and I can probably take care of your little problem."

"Great! Go team... team..." Tony hesitated. "Sallow Avengers? Was that it?"

"On a larger scale," Strange continued, his voice rising in volume, "you need to understand what this little scheme will mean. Up to this point, we've only been... well, fleas on Dormammu's hide. As long as our acts of rebellion were confined to this realm, he had neither the urgency nor the resources to deal with us." He paused. "But the moment we set foot in the Dark Dimension... the moment we take the battle to him..."

"New ball game," Cage growled.

"He will see this," T'Challa intoned, "as an act of war."

"And he will retaliate," Strange said, nodding. "He will come for us with all the power he's got. The tiniest fraction of that power could lay waste to this city"

Tony Stark frowned. For a long moment he and Strange stared at each other. Kamala had the odd feeling they were challenging each other to come up with the next step, to solve this seemingly unsolvable problem.

"I have a question," T'Challa said. "Who is planned to undertake the mission into Dormammu's realm?"

"Ah." Again, Tony grimaced. "Originally, I was going to–"

"That's me," Ms Marvel said. "I'm doing it."

And there it is, she thought, as they all turned to stare at her. The cloud she'd been living under, the doom she couldn't escape. The words that echoed, over and over again, in her head:

I'm going to d–

"The hell you are," Spider-Man said.

She almost jumped. He'd been so quiet – uncharacteristically so – that she'd forgotten he was there. Now he stared at her, his eyes hidden behind those oversized, insect-shaped lenses.

"What?" she asked.

"I'm supposed to let a teenager make a suicide mission to Crazyland? Let a hundred symbiotes go slithering around in her head?" He leaped to his feet, jumped up to crouch on the back of his chair. "Forget it. I've got more experience, and I'm at least as strong as you."

"I can do it!" Suddenly she felt defensive. "And I don't want you to die in there. I don't want anyone to…" she trailed off.

"Listen." Spider-Man leaped down to face her directly. "I *know* the symbiotes. I was the first person on Earth to host one, remember?"

"I recall you describing that as a deeply traumatic experience," Strange ventured.

"What I'm saying is…" Spider-Man straightened up. "If anyone can pull this off, I can. I know how they think. I can keep them on a leash."

She could almost hear the words he wasn't saying: *… I hope.*

"I … I don't know what to …" She paused, looked at him with a tear in her eye. "Thank you."

Make a joke, she thought. Please! Show me this isn't a death sentence for you, that everything's going to turn out OK.

But Spider-Man just nodded. His eyes, his whole face, remained hidden behind the swirling patterns of his mask. She turned away from him, thoughts spinning. I don't have to do this, she thought. I don't have to die! That's a good thing, right?

But – but if it's such a good thing–

–then why do I feel like I'm letting everyone down? *Again?*

"The identity of the host is only one issue," Strange said, pulling her out of her reverie. "There is still the matter of Dormammu's response."

"Yeeeaaaaahhhhhhhh…" Tony swerved in midair, the jets on his chair flashing. "I might have an idea about that."

They all stood up together, turning to face him – and the energy in the room shifted again, back toward Tony. Ms Marvel stepped forward, facing him directly.

"Tell me what you need," she said.

This time, he did face her. At first, his expression showed pure, clear relief. Then, slowly, a long wide smile spread over his burn-scarred face.

"Not you, kid." Tony turned away from her. "You."

He pointed at T'Challa, who stood in the back of the room. The Wakandan monarch hesitated. Ms Marvel could almost see the frown on his face, under his mask.

"Don't worry," Tony said, gesturing at the alien blade. "You can bring the meat slicer."

TWENTY-THREE

Never in his life had Peter Parker been so glad to be wearing a mask. As he stared at the symbiotes – dozens of them, raging and surging in their confinement – he could feel his jaw clench, his lips stretch into a grimace of terror. His eyes grew wide, so wide that anyone seeing them would have rushed him to a trauma unit.

But no one could see those eyes. No one could see his face. Because of the mask.

He'd put on a good front, he knew, down in the Vault. Host a couple hundred symbiotes? No big deal – been there, done it before. I'm the original symbiote guy, the idiot that first brought one of those ugly things to Earth. I even wore the creepy thing as a costume for weeks, before I figured out it was alive!

Oh yes, he'd played it pretty cool in Tony Stark's sub-basement. But now, facing the containment chamber in the penthouse workshop, the horror of the task ahead hit him like an Oscorp tanker truck.

It had to be done, though. He couldn't let Ms Marvel take the risk, not when his strength and experience gave him a better chance to survive. A small chance, yeah, in the unknown depths of the Dark Dimension. But a better one.

And there was another reason, too: Eddie Brock. Eddie, who'd been a thorn in Peter's side for years, ever since he'd partnered with his symbiote to become the hybrid creature called Venom. Eddie, who – when faced with the threat of Dormammu – had done the right thing, helped to save the planet, and paid a terrible price for it.

I've gotta rescue him, Peter thought. I owe him that. We all do.

He pictured Eddie as a prisoner of Dormammu, writhing in pain somewhere in the Dark Dimension. His "other" raging helplessly – the same symbiote that Peter himself had once hosted. The thing that had sought Peter out, bonded with him, and lashed out murderously when he rejected it.

Don't think about it, he told himself. Push those memories down. Don't think about the way that creature felt, slithering around in your brain… filling your mind with its inhuman thoughts, its ravenous hunger… the alien rage that blotted out all rational thought–

"Uh, Spider-Man?"

He blinked. Ms Marvel stood a few feet away, around the curve of the containment chamber, surrounded by bits and scraps of Tony Stark's electronic equipment. The symbiotes watched her through the transparent wall, swirling and circling like a whirlpool made of oil. They seemed even more agitated than before.

"Yeah, kid?"

"Are you OK?"

The look of concern on her face was too much for him. He turned away, looking past her at a wall with exposed wires sticking out – was there supposed to be a big TV or something there? Below the wiring, Doctor Voodoo sat cross-legged on the floor, painstakingly drawing an elaborate mystic symbol with a stub of chalk. Every once in a while, he muttered something under his breath.

"I'm doing better than him," Spider-Man said quietly. "Imagine being stuck in that limbo dimension for all that… well, I guess 'time' isn't really the right word."

"I know." Ms Marvel walked over to join him. "Planet Dormammu's been pretty rough on all of us."

He smiled, hoping to reassure her. But she just turned away. Right, he thought, mask! Mask!

"Hey," he said, cocking his head at her. "Are *you* OK?"

"I…" She turned toward him, frowning. "I don't know. I guess I just don't feel like I'm helping this team very much."

"Are you crazy? You helped track down that planet-killer, didn't you? And we'd never have found Mister Mumbles over there" – he waved at Doctor Voodoo – "without you and your Eye."

"Yeah, but I failed at that mission. The Eye got trashed on my watch."

"That wasn't your fault. What were you gonna do, live in the bar 24/7? The wifi there is terrible."

"Yeah, but now…" She turned her back. "Now you're gonna take over my mission."

"Hey, I'm not trying to steal anybody's glory! Believe me, I got no love for these guys." He turned toward the symbiotes, then quickly looked away again.

"I know that." She grimaced. "But I know how much you *don't* want to do this."

"Aw, it's no big. One symbiote was awesome – a hundred should be a real party! You know, sometimes it feels like half my life is dealing with symbiotes. Which is actually sort of weird, for a down-to-earth costumed goofball like myself. Still, you can't always choose your friends. Am I babbling right now? I feel like maybe I'm babbling."

"A little. But thanks for the pep talk." She gave him a shy smile. "I guess I'm just glad ..."

"What?" he asked.

"I'm glad that, sometimes, you *can* choose your friends."

That would have been a nice moment, except for the dozens of alien carnivores staring at them with undisguised hunger. And the burst of mumbled cursing that erupted from the totally absorbed Doctor Voodoo. Apparently, his ritual was not going smoothly.

A chill wind blew over them. Spider-Man tensed in alarm – then realized his Spider-Sense hadn't gone off. Doctor Voodoo seemed unfazed, too.

"Come on," Ms Marvel said. She started off around the containment chamber, away from Voodoo. Spider-Man followed her, coming to a place where the wall had been ripped open during the day's attack. A curtain of energy covered the opening, shimmering with emerald runes.

As they watched, the energy rippled, shifted, and parted to make way for the graceful figure of Doctor Strange. The lights of city came into view briefly, glittering in the night, then faded away again behind the mystic shroud.

"I bring artifacts that may assist us in our task," Strange said, wafting easily into the room on his Cloak of Levitation. "Also snacks."

He tossed a bag of double-nacho chips into the air. Spider-Man was so jittery, he almost missed the catch. The symbiotes watched as he juggled the bag awkwardly, finally catching it under one elbow.

"For me, uglies," he said to the symbiotes. "Not you. Thanks, Doc – I'll pack this along with my favorite water bottle. I take it they don't have munchies in the Dark Dimension?"

"Nothing you'd want in your system," Strange replied.

"I don't think I want *those* in my system either," Ms Marvel said, frowning at the chips.

"Great! More for me," Spider-Man said. "Aren't I lucky to be going on this mission? Is it time to go? Is it briefing time? Am I *nervous*, do you think? Maybe it's all the magic that's getting to me. I'm a science guy at heart, y'know. Oh man, what am I saying? Will I ever stop talking, you think?"

Doctor Strange gave him a look that could best be describe as *patient*.

"We'll begin in a moment," Strange said. "Ms Marvel, would you do me a favor and call our friends, please? Tell them to prepare themselves."

She nodded and pulled out her Kimoyo card. Then she moved away from them, speaking in low tones into the card.

"So, uh," Spider-Man said. "The bar was trashed?"

"Only the Eye of Vquk." Strange knelt, pulling a variety of ancient-looking items out of his cloak. "By an agent of Dormammu – probably another Mindless One."

"Did you find everything you need?"

"Most of the mystic talismans I had hidden in the bar were intact. Dormammu's strike force only seemed interested in the Eye. We'll have to make do with what I found – I still cannot return home for more."

"What about that thing?" Spider-Man glanced at the shimmering mystic shield. "The shower curtain of the gods, or whatever. Will it hold?"

"The *Shield of the Seraphim* should protect us from all Earthly threats." Strange looked up, smiling coldly. "But a direct attack from Dormammu? Not a chance."

"They're in place," Ms Marvel said, stashing the communication card back in her pocket as she approached. "Everything's ready."

"Good." Strange sighed. "Then I suppose it's time to take a look at Mister Stark's... infernal device?"

Ms Marvel grimaced, nodded, and without a word crossed back around the chamber, followed as always by the restless eyes of the symbiotes. She knelt on the floor, carefully slid a few electronic components out of the way, and picked up the control harness.

"I *could* use a new backpack," Spider-Man said as she approached, "but I'd prefer something from LL Bean."

When she reached Doctor Strange, Ms Marvel held out the harness as if it would explode at any moment – which, Spider-Man realized, it just might. Strange accepted the device, turning it over in his hands to examine the straps, the sheer body covering rolled up between them, and of course the bomb casing mounted on the back.

"This," Doctor Strange intoned, "was clearly built by a pack of villains."

"Rich villains," Ms Marvel added.

"That, uh..." Spider-Man paused. "That sounds..."

"Dangerous," Ms Marvel whispered.

"Danger is my... aw, you know." Spider-Man leaned in, watching as Doctor Strange held the bomb up to the light. "So I'm supposed to take this thing straight to Dormammu and shove it down his throat. Hey, how do I find Dormammu once I'm in the Dark Dimension? The symbiotes are just gonna be looking for Eddie, right?"

"You will have no trouble locating Dormammu," Doctor Voodoo said.

Spider-Man jumped – he hadn't heard Voodoo approach. The houngan had apparently finished his work; a circle of mystic chalk marks adorned the floor on the far side of the workshop. A tiny wisp of violet smoke rose from the symbols, though there didn't seem to be a fire burning.

"My twin brother Daniel," Voodoo continued, blank eyes staring straight at Spider-Man. "He does not wish to speak directly; he still suffers great trauma from recent events. But when Dormammu took him from this plane, for a moment he passed through the evil one's realm.

"Daniel reports that, using the Tribute energy of a billion worlds, Dormammu has expanded his essence greatly. He now fills the sky of the Dark Dimension, looming over it like a true god."

Voodoo paused, as if listening to a voice inside his head. He probably is, Spider-Man realized.

"However…" Voodoo raised both hands, crackling with mystic power. "…as Stephen has said, there are also civilians living in the Dark Dimension."

"Total disregard for innocent life," Spider-Man said. "Reason number 354 why you shouldn't let villains build your tech."

"*Rich* villains," Ms Marvel repeated.

With a quick gesture, Doctor Strange flicked the harness into the air, where it hung suspended in a magical field. Voodoo stepped forward, hands flashing, conjuring dark energy that danced across the surface of the harness.

"This spell of dissimilarity should help protect the denizens of the Dark Dimension," Voodoo explained. "It will limit the bomb's effects to Dormammu himself, and anything in his immediate vicinity."

"The phrase *immediate vicinity*," Spider-Man said, "is doing some heavy lifting in that sentence."

"Indeed," Strange said. "This device was not built with the user's safety in mind, either. The bomb has a countdown period of only thirty seconds."

"I bet that was Ock's idea," Spider-Man said. "It's almost like he knew I'd be the one wearing his little deathtrap."

"Daniel and I have worked with Mister Stark," Voodoo said. "This is not atypical of his handiwork, either."

"Tony's… well, he's got some flaws," Ms Marvel said. "But he usually thinks a problem through. He was planning to wear this thing himself – why didn't he think of using magic to protect himself?"

"Stark's *flaws* tend to include a blindness to solutions outside his own skill set," Strange replied. "Magic is hardly his specialty."

"It ain't mine either," Spider-Man said. "How exactly does a spell of dissimilarity work, anyway?"

"Jericho," Strange said. "If you'll permit me…"

Strange took up position opposite Voodoo, on the other side of the hovering bomb harness. As Voodoo's hands flashed dark, white lightning began to shimmer on the ends of Strange's fingertips.

"We are dealing with the interface between science and mysticism," Strange explained, "which always presents challenges. But I believe I can 'program' the bomb to repel itself rapidly from its wearer, as soon as it's activated."

"That'll give the user…" Ms Marvel paused, eyes wide "… give Spidey, I mean, time to get away?"

Strange didn't answer immediately. His gloved hands waved like snakes, flashing through the air, conjuring energy trails that shot across the harness to meet the matching spells cast by Doctor Voodoo.

"Well," Strange said finally, almost absently. "*More* time."

That doesn't sound encouraging, Spider-Man thought. For once, though, he decided to keep the notion to himself. Ms Marvel clearly felt guilty that he was taking her place. There was no need to make her feel worse.

"*No more death,*" Voodoo said, startling Spider-Man. The mage's voice sounded different – deeper, raspier. "*No more realms burned to ash, crushed beneath his fiery heel.*"

That's not Jericho Drumm speaking, Spider-Man realized; it's his brother Daniel. Still traumatized, half broken from his ordeal at Dormammu's hands.

Strange looked over sharply at Doctor Voodoo. As Voodoo nodded in response, the mystic energy faded from both men's hands. The bomb harness lurched slightly in midair, moving first in Ms Marvel's direction, then toward the startled Spider-Man. He reached out and caught it, marveling as it settled softly into his hands.

For a moment, they all stared at him. Strange grimaced. Ms Marvel still looked guilty. Doctor Voodoo's face twitched; he seemed occupied, once again, with the trauma his twin had suffered.

"OK," Spider-Man said, taking a deep breath. "OK. Let me just make sure I got all the deets here…

"The bodysuit fits over my costume, between me and the harness. The harness lets me control the symbiotes. The portal, which you guys are about to open, shunts me into the other realms. The symbiotes will guide me through those realms to the lovely sunny climes of the Dark Dimension in which, I have just learned – to my ever-increasing terror – Dormammu basically looks like some firebug's dream of the man in the moon.

"Once I get there, I will set off the bomb, which will target Dormammu but *not* his poor innocent citizens, and which will repel me like I was a tub of spoiled guacamole. The ridiculously dangerous goop inside the bomb will liquify Dormammu, freeing the realms from having to look at his flaming face every day. If I'm lucky, I'll also find my old BFF Eddie Brock; and if I'm *super* lucky, which I'll add has never happened a single day in my life, he won't be in a mood to bite my face off."

Silence for a moment.

"Oh," Strange said. "Oh, you want an answer? Yes, that's about it."

"Just one thing," Spider-Man continued. "The symbiotes are supposed to zero in on Eddie. But how do I – we, the alien face-eaters and me – how do we find our way back through the realms, *after* the bomb goes off?"

A wide smile spread across Doctor Strange's face. He held up one finger, then swirled his Cloak of Levitation and reached inside its depths.

"You were waiting for me to ask that, weren't you?" Spider-Man said.

With a flourish, Strange whipped out… a handheld lantern, swinging on a simple metal handle. Its structure was woven of delicate iron, glowing a faint green.

"The Lantern of Morphesti," Strange said. "It's designed specifically for navigation within the realms."

He held it out to Spider-Man, who juggled the harness into

one hand to accept it. "OK," Spider-Man said. "Gizmo number two… whoops!"

He shifted, almost dropped the harness, and scrambled frantically for it. Careful, he told himself – don't break the bomb with the universal-destruction glop in it! He set the lantern down on the floor, making sure to redouble his grip on the harness.

Another frigid wind passed through the room.

"We should hurry," Doctor Voodoo said. "I can feel the evil one's eyes searching for us."

Strange nodded in response. Voodoo joined him along the wall of the room, and together they sat down cross-legged on the floor. Strange closed his eyes, and the Eye of Agamotto rose from his throat to take up position on his forehead.

Voodoo peered at the circle he'd drawn on the floor, some twenty feet in front of them along the wall. He glanced briefly at the open stairwell to his right, then behind at the shimmering Shield of the Seraphim covering the hole in the wall.

"Bit of an exposed spot for conjuring," Voodoo observed.

"Space is limited," Strange said, the Eye glowing above his brow. "And we need to remain clear of…"

He gestured toward the containment chamber. Ms Marvel stood waiting, next to a big nozzle attached to the chamber's outside wall.

Voodoo raised his staff in both hands, holding it straight out before him. Strange mimicked the gesture, summoning a flare of mystic energy that seemed to flow from one magician to the other. The two men gestured at the same time, sending the energy rolling forward in an irresistible tide, straight toward the spot where the chalk circle lay on the floor.

This is serious, Spider-Man thought, watching the power warp and shimmer in the air. This ain't some warmed-over portal left over from one of Dormammu's early sorties. This is big-time magic, wielded by two Sorcerers Supreme.

This is *Earth*, he realized. Fighting back against the invader, with everything it's got.

"Spider-Man?" Ms Marvel called. "You ready?"

He nodded, eyeing the symbiotes, and moved to stand in front of the release valve. Their eyes tracked his every movement; he could hear them bumping against the inner wall of the chamber, hungry for freedom. One of them formed a long, slavering tongue and licked dark oily lips.

"One, uh…" he began, thinking: Get ahold of yourself! "Only one symbiote at a time, remember? That's all the harness can handle. It needs time to adjust to the inputs."

"Yup, Tony told me. Before he went off to do his… important stuff." She grimaced. "I just love being the rich guy's unpaid intern."

A hissing noise made him spin around. Above the chalk circle, the tide of mystic energy had created a sort of vertical opening in the air. The barest beginning of a portal, not yet large enough for a person to pass through.

Over by the stairwell, the two Doctors sat cross-legged, pouring their shared energy across the room. Strange, Spider-Man noticed, had risen a couple of inches up into the air. Voodoo remained on the floor, the staff channeling his share of the power through its weathered wooden frame.

"Uh, Doc?" Spider-Man said.

Both mystics turned to face him. Their expressions looked strained; sweat covered their brows.

"One last thing," he continued. "The kid here doesn't have her Eye anymore. What's gonna pull me back to, well, the friendly neighborhood?"

"That would be me," Strange said.

His body glowed for a moment, flashing bright.

"Don't worry," Strange said, closing his eyes again. "I've done this before."

Spidey glanced at the expanding portal, felt the surge of power in the air. The hairs on his arms stood up straight, as if in some powerful static field. He turned, reluctantly, back toward the hungry, waiting symbiotes.

"It's not you I'm worried about," he whispered.

He hefted the harness, grimacing briefly at the bomb. With a flick of his fingers, he unrolled the bodysuit and spread the thin fabric out across his arms. He could barely see it, it was molecule-thin and nearly invisible.

He felt the symbiotes' unearthly rage as they watched him prepare for the merger. In a moment of panic, he thought, I can't do this – I can't. I swore, after the way that thing invaded my mind: never again. *Never again!*

Then he thought of Eddie Brock, and he felt ashamed. Whatever terrible fate awaited him, Eddie's was far worse. And Eddie was suffering right now, trapped in some inconceivable hell, because he'd defied Dormammu. Because he'd done the right thing.

I can't do any less, Spider-Man thought. I must do it. It's my responsibility–

A loud clicking noise made him look up. Ms Marvel stood before the chamber, backing away from the nozzle. And at the end of the nozzle… squeezing itself out like a blob of toothpaste in a tube… a dark bubble of oil was just beginning to appear.

The symbiote, he thought. She's released the first symbiote! But–

"Wait!" he cried. "I don't have the harness on yet–"

Two enormous hands slammed into him, knocking him off balance. As he fell, one of the hands reached out, snaked around, and grabbed the harness out of his grip. He caught a quick glimpse of the bodysuit, still attached to the harness, fluttering through the air.

Then he struck the floor, pain slamming through his shoulder. He rolled to a crouch, looked up, and saw–

–Ms Marvel. Retracting her hands back to normal size as she snaked her flexible form in and under the transparent body covering. Then she slipped the straps of the harness over her shoulders, positioning the bomb across her back.

"What are you doing?" he cried, rising to his feet.

She flashed him a quick, scared look. Then she turned to face the chamber. On the outside tip of the nozzle, the first symbiote was just taking form. Part of its surface resolved into a pair of glaring eyes. It looked up at Ms Marvel and snarled.

"My job," she said.

"No!" Spider-Man cried, starting toward her.

"Stay back!" she yelled, forcefully enough to stop him in his tracks. "You can't stop the process now."

The symbiote popped free of the nozzle, landing on the floor atop half-formed legs. It turned toward her, licking its lips.

"I'm not letting you down," she continued. "Any of you." She took a deep breath. "Not this time."

"Doc!" Spider-Man called. "Doctor Strange? Voodoo? Any doctor at all! You gotta stop this!"

The mystics made no move. Strange hovered several inches above the ground now, energy flaring from his hands, from the shining third eye mounted on his forehead. Voodoo's staff wavered slightly in the air. The portal before them continued to grow.

Ms Marvel reached up and flipped a switch on the harness. Lights flashed across the straps slung over her shoulders, accompanied by a low hum.

The symbiote turned in alarm.

"Come on," Ms Marvel said. "Here, boy. Here poochie poochie!"

The symbiote snarled and leaped, drawn irresistibly by the call of the harness. It slashed the air with sharp claws, with teeth, its outer surface morphing and shifting from one deadly weapon to another. Spidey flinched as it struck Ms Marvel's right harness strap–

–and all at once, it reverted to a soft blob. The teeth dissolved, the claws retracted into its shapeless body. All its hunger seemed to vanish into the air; it looked almost comical, like a balloon that someone had taped to her shoulder.

She looked at it and let out a nervous laugh. "Good boy!"

Another loud hiss. The portal expanded, smoke from the circle wreathing its oval shape. Spider-Man peered at it and found himself suddenly dizzy. Whatever was on the other side of that doorway, his mind wasn't equipped to comprehend it.

"Let's go," Ms Marvel said. "Batter two, you're up!"

She sounds like me, Spider-Man realized; chattering and quipping to keep herself from panicking. That *really* worried him.

A second symbiote burst free of the chamber, squirting straight out the nozzle and through the air. This one latched on to Ms Marvel's leg. The transparent bodysuit, wrapped over her costume, held the creature partly at bay.

"It's... working," she said. "I can feel them in my head... the hunger, oh man the hunger! But they're not in control. I am. I'm still me – *whoa!*"

The third one struck her on the side of the head. Again, the bodysuit protected her, flattening to cover the surface of her cheek where the creature had landed. One of her eyes was hidden now, covered entirely by the oil-dark substance of the symbiote's body.

Spider-Man hissed in a breath. He felt helpless, powerless – a witness to a disaster unfolding in slow motion, before him. He watched in horror as another symbiote attached itself to Ms Marvel's small form, then another and another. When one of the creatures struck the bomb strapped to her back, he flinched. But the harness absorbed the impact, as it had been designed to do.

He clenched his fists, desperate to act. But Ms Marvel was right: he couldn't interrupt this procedure. Once the harness was activated, there was no going back.

The magicians knew it, too. Their focus remained entirely on their task, energy bathing them in an all-consuming glow. The air sizzled with power, a haze of mystically charged ozone – all directed toward that ever-expanding portal.

One by one, the symbiotes squeezed free of the chamber. And one by one, the call of the harness drew them irresistibly to the young hero. They covered her like a sheath, like a coating of petroleum. They shrunk as they struck her, flowing into one another like a single organism.

Ms Marvel staggered, lurching one way and then the other as the creatures flew at her through the air. But she stayed on her feet – or at least, he *thought* she was still on her feet. Even her legs were covered now, along with the harness and the bomb. Her entire body was hidden beneath layer upon layer of symbiotic alien organisms.

Finally, the chamber stood almost empty. Only one symbiote

remained, eyeing the humans outside the transparent wall. It seemed hesitant, reluctant to leave its prison.

"Come on," Ms Marvel said, her voice muffled. "Join the party, Slimer."

With a snarl, the symbiote shot out of the nozzle, through the air, and onto Ms Marvel's form. She didn't look like a human being at all now; just a ball of shifting, swirling alien stuff.

"It's working," she said, her words barely audible. "*I can hear them! Venom. We want Venom. We will find him... our brother. Our brother Venom...*"

Can she do this? Spider-Man wondered, fear stabbing him in the heart. Can she really control the inhuman power of a hundred symbiotes? Once again, he remembered the oily feel of their touch... the terrible slithering tendrils reaching into his brain...

"No!" He took a step toward her. "I'm stopping this right now, you hear me? Strange–"

He stopped in astonishment as her *hand* – fully human, protected by a transparent layer of sheathing – poked its way out of the ball of symbiotes, barring his way. Her power, he realized. She's stretching her arm out and through the creatures, making a supreme effort to show me she's OK.

"I got this," she said, her voice still muffled. "I'm still..."

He couldn't make out the next two words. But he had a strange feeling that, in the confusion, she'd blurted out her real name.

"...I'm Ms Marvel," she continued. "And I'm a Shadow Avenger."

Then she took off, rolling and running and moving in ways he didn't have words for. As she approached the chalk circle, she rose into the air. The symbiotes cried out in protest, in hunger, in a whole spectrum of dark alien emotions.

She plunged through the portal and was gone.

Spider-Man whirled around to face the magicians. He was about to call out to Doctor Strange again – to ask what could be done, whether there was any way to help Ms Marvel, to call her back or communicate with her or even lend her some kind of moral support–

–when he saw it.

Sitting on the floor, in front of the empty chamber. Right where he'd left it.

The Lantern.

Panic seized him. In all the chaos, they'd forgotten about the Lantern... and without it, he knew, Ms Marvel would be lost. Even if she pulled off the mission – if she managed to set off the bomb, break Dormammu's grip on the realms – she'd be lost forever in limbo, fused for all time with a hundred screaming creatures... locked together with a horde of parasitic, ravenous, brain-invading –

There was no time for further thought. No time to alert the wizards, who sat together across the floor, struggling to maintain the portal's integrity. All he could do, the only thing in his power, was to act.

He sprinted across the floor and snatched up the lantern by its iron handle. Then he aimed a web-shooter at the wall, shot out a line, and swung his way up and around the shimmering energy-flow.

"Hang on, Avenger," he called. "I'm coming!"

As the portal loomed before him, he averted his eyes. His Spider-Sense screamed out a warning; every cell in his body cried out in alarm. The ozone smell intensified, mixed with a terrible unearthly burning odor. He forced himself to keep moving, reminding himself: hold onto the Lantern. Whatever you do, don't let it go!

He passed through the portal – and screamed.

A thousand realms closed in from all sides, a million realities glimpsed, burned into his brain, then passed by, gone before the onslaught of the next million. Sights, sounds, unbearably alien smells beyond anything he'd ever known before.

"Kid!" he cried. "Kid, are you there? Where are you?"

The Lantern pulsed in his grip, responding to his cries. He forced himself to search the multiscape before him, peering through the realms – desperately trying to find her. The young woman who'd taken on *his* duty, sacrificed herself for the sake of… well, everything. The brave teammate who needed his help…

He tried, but it was all too much. The sights, the smells, the tastes overwhelmed him, plunging him into a state of shock. His body shuddered; his brain overloaded. The last thing he registered was the Lantern, glowing and pulsing as it swung loose on its handle. Then his brain shut down, consciousness shattering into jagged shards of madness.

Doctor Strange's eyes snapped open. On his forehead, the amulet continued to glow, maintaining the flow of mystic energy. The portal blazed before him, a gaping hole in the air where his fellow Avengers had gone.

"Not as we planned it," he whispered. "But they're on their way…"

A hissing noise cut him off. He turned to see Doctor Voodoo, already standing, his staff clenched tight.

"I must go," Voodoo said. "You're sure you can maintain the portal alone?"

"I have an ally," Strange replied, trying not to betray the strain he felt. "Go. Go help them."

Voodoo nodded. Holding up his staff, he traced a glowing circle in the air. He stepped through it, almost casually, and was gone.

Alone now, Strange let out a long breath. He turned back toward the smoke-shrouded portal, touching the Eye of Agamotto absently. Trying, above all else, to force a single persistent thought out of his mind:

Dormammu.

Dormammu is coming!

TWENTY-FOUR

Tony Stark lifted his helmet off his head and set it down on the desk before him. When he shifted in his chair, several ribs screamed in agony. Fortunately, the Iron Man suit compensated, sensors responding to his motions to adjust his center of gravity. Slowly, the pain faded.

"Be nice," he said aloud, "if I *didn't* have to fight today." But he knew that was a vain hope.

Carefully, he raised his broken leg up onto an outstretched guest chair. Dust plumed from the furniture when he touched it. This office hadn't been used for quite some time. A faded picture hung crooked on the fake-wood wall paneling above the desk: a skull with eight octopus arms sprouting from its base, adorned with the barely legible phrase HAIL HYDRA.

He closed his eyes, shutting out the office that had once belonged to his enemies, and rubbed his temples. Faces swirled in his mind's eye, one following another in a dark spiral of fear and anxiety:

Spider-Man. He was about to embark on the most dangerous mission of his life – a mission that Tony had intended for himself.

Ms Marvel. At least, Tony thought, it's not *her* going to the

284

Dark Dimension. He couldn't bear to be the cause of that kid's death. If Dormammu were to get hold of her…

That led, inevitably, to the third face. A god made of fire, a glaring foe that Tony could barely even imagine, let alone prepare to fight.

He opened his eyes. The Iron Man helmet seemed to stare up at him from the desk, reminding him of the terrible task that he was about to undertake. "OK," he snapped at it. "I know. I'm doing it."

He sat back, hissing in another breath. Held the air in, then exhaled heavily. Again, his ribs protested, but he ignored them. He took another deep breath, then another, while his eyes slipped shut again.

Just as Doctor Voodoo had instructed.

Oxygen flooded his brain. The world faded away. Once again, he was swimming, paddling in a thick flow, a vast endless seascape inside his mind. He could already see the light ahead, feel the heat of… of…

No, he thought. Not again! *I can't do this!*

But he had to. The fate of the Earth, and countless realms beyond, rested on Tony's next actions. So, he raised one virtual arm, then the other, and paddled toward the light.

Soon he could see it clearly: the flame. The hot light shimmering in its liquid cradle, the stench so strong he could barely stand it. The endless evil fire of Dormammu himself.

Part of it will always be with you…

"That street runs both ways," he said, forcing away a wave of fear and revulsion. "I'm with *you*, too, you monster. You'll never get rid of me, you hear?"

No response. The flame burned steady, constant, untouched by the water all around.

"We'll beat you," Tony continued. "We've got a plan. You bit off a little too much when you occupied Earth, you... you... you cut-rate Thanos, you!"

Weak burn, he thought. I really am tired.

But there was no time for fatigue. The next thing – this was the tricky part. Tony had to form an image in his mind, but not a complete one. An island in the Pacific... two miles by one and a half, with the wreckage of a super-scientific citadel taking up most of its surface...

"Might as well give up now," he continued. "There's no way you can stand against us."

There! A flicker in the flame; a sickly tang in the water. He's listening, Tony thought. I've got his attention.

Dormammu. The conqueror himself.

"You're toast," Tony said. "You hear me, Matchstick?"

Now: a little more of the island. One large intact building, a former Hydra training camp, on the west side. Airstrip down the island's two-mile length, along the water. And on the other end of the island, an abandoned hangar and office building...

Well, he thought, abandoned except for me.

He let the thoughts flow out from him, not trying to hide the information from Dormammu. "We're already gathering our forces..."

The flame burned bright. A smile danced within it, a sudden glow of satisfaction.

Now to spring the trap. Tony allowed fear to rise within him – which actually wasn't hard to do, under the circumstances. At the same time, he forced down all thoughts of his *real* plan.

"Too late," said a voice that wasn't a voice.

"No," Tony said, turning to paddle furiously away. "Oh no!"

"Too late, little worm. I have you now."

Tony opened his eyes, heaved, and threw up into a small wastebasket. A sharp pain shot through his midsection – blasted ribs again!

He wiped his mouth, searching his mind for traces of Dormammu. Nothing. The flame, the scent, even the viscous sea, were gone. Voodoo's mental exercises had worked; Tony had successfully banished the "Master" from his mind, for now at least.

But not before he'd told Dormammu the location of the island.

He stood up slowly, painfully, every muscle in his body crying out in agony. He ignored the pain. There was no time to heal, no time to sit things out. Not after what he'd just set in motion.

One way or another, as Doctor Strange had said, Dormammu was about to throw all his forces against the so-called Shadow Avengers. The resulting battle, Tony knew, could devastate the Earth. But now those forces would be sent here: to this isolated island in the Pacific, one of the few places on the planet where he could reliably limit civilian casualties.

"You got me?" Tony snarled at the air. "Suck it, firebug. I got *you*."

He strode outside, his helmet floating along in the air behind him. The armor had been programmed to keep his injured leg rigid – which, he quickly discovered, made walking a very awkward process. He gave up and issued a new series of commands, jetting out onto the tarmac in little vertical hops.

"Hydra Base," Tony said, taking a deep breath of the cool, humid afternoon air, "aka Hydra Island. A cozy little getaway for the young, the young at heart, or the greatly outnumbered super group preparing to take on an army of their mesmerized friends."

Many years ago, during the Second World War, the newly formed espionage group Hydra had established its first major headquarters on this island. The airstrip, and the hangar that Tony had just exited, were the only parts of the base left from that period. Much later, Hydra had built a stunning super-scientific complex here, which had been destroyed in a mission so deeply classified, only Nick Fury seemed to know what had really happened.

Tony glanced right, using his armor's telescopic lenses to take in every detail. The airstrip stretched down the full two miles of the island, a wide strip of tar pocked and cratered by time and hurricanes, bisected by a single white line painted down the middle. Halfway down the strip, a few bits of wreckage from that long-ago Fury mission protruded onto the pavement: a chunk of an art-deco spire, the barrel of a shattered laser cannon.

At the far end of the strip stood a large, warehouse-style building – just as Tony had visualized it in his mind, moments ago. That structure, the largest one left on the island, had been used surreptitiously in recent years by Hydra as a training camp. In the time of Dormammu, Norman Osborn had taken it over, converting it into a manufacturing hub for that blasted Osdrink. A line of trucks sat parked in front of it, each one bearing the annoyingly familiar Oscorp logo.

A perimeter alert flashed on Tony's helmet display. Two figures: weaving their way around the debris on the tarmac, moving steadily toward him. The smaller of the two was a young woman wearing traditional blue-and-black Wakandan battle garb. When she reached Tony, she held up the vibranium blade from the Iron Vault, shaking it uncomfortably close to his face.

"Did you really not know this came from Wakanda?" Shuri demanded.

"I swear." He held up both gauntleted hands in surrender. "A Shi'ar thief tried to kill me with it, on one of the moons of Polaris."

Shuri peered at him skeptically. She looked much better than the last time he'd seen her, he noted with relief – back to her fierce, proud self. Only one trace of her experience with Osborn remained: a pair of tiny scars at the top of her forehead, where the dormamine implants had been.

T'Challa loped up to join them, retracting his mask to reveal his face. "I believe Mister Stark, sister," he said. "And I think you owe him a debt."

"For helping me break Dormammu's conditioning?" she snapped, turning to face her brother. "I was very close to doing that myself."

"I see." A smile tickled at T'Challa's lips. "Too many contradictions for your *scientific* mind."

"Now you are mocking me."

T'Challa turned to face Tony. "If my sister will not thank you, Tony, then I will. For bringing her back to me."

"Well, I guess I did one thing right this week," Tony replied. "Even if I was aiming for a different target – Osborn – at the time."

"And at my brother's urging, I have repaid my debt by leading you to this place," Shuri said, waving the blade in the air to indicate the entire island. "Where, I presume, we will all die."

"Well." Tony blinked. "I hope not."

"But your gambit worked?" T'Challa asked.

"I think so. We'll know soon, after Strange and Voodoo work their magic."

"I see you are wearing your classic armor," T'Challa said. "With a few extra bulges."

"Only to accommodate the splints on my ribs," Tony replied, wincing as he touched his side. "This didn't seem like the time to reinvent the… well, to re-invent."

They all turned at the sound of heavy footsteps pounding on the tarmac. Luke Cage approached from the direction of the manufacturing hub, pausing to wave away a cloud of tropical insects. "Bugs on this rock are murder," he said.

"Any trouble?" Tony asked.

"With the flies? Yeah. Oscorp workers, nah," Cage said. "I just barked out a few orders and herded them into that… what's the big building?"

"Bottling facility," Tony said. "For the green stuff."

"The workers are all Hydra agents," Shuri said. "This used to be their boot camp. All the details were in Osborn's files. I learned of this while working with him."

"Well, they're all about the green drink now," Cage replied. "I think these guys chug even more of it than the folks on the mainland… makes 'em very suggestible. I just shoved 'em all inside and locked the doors." A troubled expression crossed his face. "Not a management technique I approve of in the real world, but…"

"Again," Tony said, "Hydra agents, remember? Disciples of an evil cult, dedicated to overthrowing the legitimate governments of the world?"

"Evil or not," T'Challa said, "their lives will be in danger."

"So will ours, if they escape their prison," Shuri snapped. "Dormammu's disciples can be quite determined." She looked down, and for a moment the tough mask of her expression flickered. "I speak from experience."

"We'll just have to protect 'em the best we can," Tony said, "and hope our plan survives contact with the enemy." He paused, grimacing. "*All* the enemies."

They turned together, as if on cue, to look out over the water. Rolling clouds covered the high waves of the Pacific, slowly blotting out the sun. There was no sign, yet, of the attack to come.

A mystic circle appeared in the air, startling Tony. He stepped away, wincing at the pain in his leg. Doctor Voodoo stepped calmly out of the air, staff clasped firmly in one hand.

"The incursion has begun," Voodoo said. "I will stand with you here, while Stephen maintains the portal."

"All as planned," Tony replied. "How's Strange holding up?"

"How are any of us?"

"Yeah, fair point."

"Doc," Cage said, "where's Ms Marvel?"

Voodoo hesitated.

"What?" Tony whirled toward him. "What happened? Why isn't she with you?"

But he already knew. Before the magician could reply, Tony's intuitive mind had figured all the angles, dotted all the I's, and come to the only possible conclusion.

"She went through the portal," he whispered. "With the symbiotes."

Voodoo nodded, a barely perceptible motion.

"No." Tony lurched forward, then gasped as his stomach seized up in pain. "No, she can't. She can't do that!"

"It is done," Voodoo said.

"You don't understand." Suddenly Tony felt all the weight again: the panic, the fear, the terrible burden of guilt. *"I can't let her die for–"*

"There!" T'Challa cried, pointing out to sea.

They all turned to look. High above the water, slicing through the cloud cover, an object drew closer, approaching the island at high speed. A squat craft with a sharp nose and a single high fin, lights glimmering across its hull.

Shuri frowned, hefting the Wakandan blade. "What is that?" she asked.

The four figures lined up along the shore, staring at the sky. Cage, fists clenched and ready. T'Challa, crouched like his jungle-cat namesake; Shuri with the blade clutched tight in her hands. Doctor Voodoo, staff glowing in his grasp.

Reluctantly, Tony joined them. Be calm, he told himself. Be ready. Whatever your burden – whatever your *guilt* – it'll have to wait.

"That, I'm afraid, is the Avengers," he hissed.

"I told you," Cage rumbled, smacking a fist into his hand. "*We're* the Avengers."

Tony shot up into the sky, charging his repulsors to full power. The Quinjet drew closer, speeding up as it shot toward the island.

"Time to prove it," he said.

PART FIVE

D-DAY

TWENTY-FIVE

"So," T'Challa said, watching the approach of the Avengers' Quinjet. "Five of us against an army."

More like four and a half, Tony thought, considering my own injuries. But he kept that thought to himself.

"I don't see an army yet," Cage replied. "Just one guy. Is that Captain America?"

Hovering in place, Tony turned toward the Quinjet and zoomed in tight. Sure enough, a brightly colored figure stood astride the Quinjet, clasping a very familiar shield in his hand. Both fists clenched, eyes searching the sky ahead.

"Yep," Tony said, "that's Cap all right. Surfing on the nose of the jet, like the showoff he is."

"Some things Dormammu takes from us," Doctor Voodoo intoned, his face grim and impassive. "And some he does not."

Tony glanced sharply at the sorcerer. How, he wondered, could Voodoo and Strange possibly have allowed Ms Marvel to... to...

No, he told himself. Put those thoughts away. Deal with them later. You've got to get your head in the game!

"OK, people," he said, jetting back down to join them on the tarmac. "This is a Secure Crisis, not an Extraction Crisis. It's a waiting game. Hold the Line, not Take the Hill."

Silence. Only the sound of the Quinjet's engines, growing louder.

"What the hell are you talking about?" Cage asked.

"Don't any of you play… I mean we've got to restrict the battle to the island!" Tony exclaimed. "The more of Dormammu's forces we keep bottled up here, the less damage they'll do to the rest of the planet. We've got to buy time for… for the Dark Dimension plan to work."

"Sister," T'Challa said, "you should stay back. You may not be fully recovered from your recent ordeal."

"Ha!" Shuri pointed the blade at Tony, waving its tip perilously close to his face. "Even *un*recovered, I gave him a good run for his copious American money."

Tony jetted away from her, tracking the Quinjet with his built-in sensors. It swung upward, slowing slightly as it reached the island. As it swooped down toward the far end of the airstrip, the man with the shield tensed his legs and leaped into the air.

"All of you," Tony said, "follow the Quinjet."

"You sure?" Cage asked.

"There could be a dozen Avengers in that thing! Go…"

A few feet down the runway, Captain America crashed to the ground. He paused, dazed, his eyes an unbroken sea of Osdrink-green.

"… I've got Cap," Tony finished.

The Panther took off at a run toward the hangar, following the Quinjet as it descended. Shuri went with him, waving her blade in the air, and Cage followed. Doctor Voodoo hesitated for a moment, watching as Tony and Cap turned to face each other, then moved to join his teammates.

Cap stood very still, his legs spread in a battle crouch. His eyes blazed green, his mouth was curled into a sneer. Tony jetted over to confront him, eyeing him carefully.

"Steve Rogers," Tony said. "You're looking a little... glassy."

Once again, Tony felt a burst of rage. Dormammu, he thought, you'll pay for this. How many teammates have I lost? What scars have you inflicted on them – on all the people of Earth?

A soft growl escaped Cap's lips. Holy crap, Tony thought, he can't even speak! Dormammu's dialed up the juice on his mind-control – to get through Cap's notoriously strong will, presumably.

"So what's the play, old man?" Tony struggled to keep his voice even. "We doing the whole Civil War Two thing here? Or is it Three by now?"

Before he finished the sentence, Cap leaped into the air, shield held before him. Tony took half a step back – and winced at the pain in his injured leg. He raised one hand and fired off a medium-strength repulsor ray.

The ray sizzled onto Cap's shield, point-blank, exploding in a massive energy burst that blasted the two men into the air. As they flew off in opposite directions, Tony saw Cap tumble to the ground, landing with a hard jolt across the white line of the airstrip.

Tony struck down right at the edge of the strip, just past a huge chunk of molded plastic that protruded onto the tarmac. He toppled backward, seeking shelter behind the odd, brightly colored piece of wreckage. Part of a fallen wall, he realized, from the super-scientific Hydra base that had once dominated this island. Those ruins dated from Fury's apocalyptic battle, which had blown the entire complex to bits.

He rolled onto his back – *ow ow ow stomach wound!* – and paused to catch his breath. He could hear the sound of fighting nearby: the sizzle of force-blasts, heavy body-impacts, assorted grunts and gasps.

"Friday," he said, "talk to me. What's going on?"

"The Quinjet has landed in front of the hangar," the A.I. said in his ear. "Mister Cage and the others have engaged the Black Widow in combat."

"Natasha," Tony said. "Just her?"

"So far."

He rose to a crouch, risking a glance over the plastic wall. Captain America was dazed, rising to his feet… slowly, though. Was he fighting Dormammu's influence? Trying to reject the juice in his system?

Either way, he looked like hell. "Guess we've both seen better days, old man," Tony whispered, wincing at the pain in his side.

He risked a look in the direction of the hangar. Natasha Romanov, the Black Widow, stood with her back to the now grounded Quinjet, firing off stinger blasts at the heroes assembled against her. Like Cap, she seemed utterly possessed, her eyes a blaze of green energy.

Cage moved steadily in toward her, the blasts bouncing off his steel-hard skin. Panther and Shuri backed him up, flanking him on either side. Bright sun blazed down, glinting off the vibranium laced into Shuri's and T'Challa's outfits.

Only two Dormammu-Vengers so far, Tony thought. We can handle this. The odds are on our side–

"Stark!" Doctor Voodoo called, levitating toward him at high speed. "Above–"

A massive energy blast struck the tarmac, carving up the pavement between them. Voodoo lurched backward in the air; Tony pushed his jets to full power, speeding up and away. Another blast struck the exact spot where he'd been, a second ago. Then a third and a fourth.

He recognized those blasts – pure photonic energy. As he whirled around, he knew what he'd see: the hovering, majestic form of Carol Danvers, Captain Marvel. Her cropped blonde hair and red-and-blue uniform shone bright against the clouds.

And yes, he noticed – her eyes, too, blazed with green energy.

"So much for the odds," he whispered.

He dodged in midair as she let off another blast. The beam sizzled past him, striking the ground right next to Captain America – knocking him off his feet again.

Tony smiled grimly. "Better schedule some teamwork drills, 'Master.'"

He kept his eyes on Captain Marvel, watching as she wheeled around for another attack. Steve and Natasha were one thing, but Carol wielded a whole different level of power. The only way to deal with her was hard and fast.

"Friday," he said, "turbo mode!"

His boot jets flared, servos drawing his feet inward and mag-locking them together. Microcircuits hummed and charged, fusing the propulsion units in his jets into a single, Apollo-level jet engine.

Before Carol knew what was happening, he slammed into her with the force of a guided missile. She gasped, briefly stunned, the energy fading in her eyes.

"Brazilian jiu-jitsu!" Tony cried. "Or, uh, something."

Her eyes flashed green again. Energy sparked on the tips of her fingers. She let out a gasp, kicked him hard, and tumbled away in the sky. A stray photon-bolt sliced through the clouds.

Tony cried out in pain as the impact of her kick shot right up his spine. He flailed, waved his arms, and began to fall. With a hurried mental command, he reverted his boot jets to normal and blasted downward–

–not *quite* in time to break his fall. More Hydra rubble rushed up at him. He twisted sideways, narrowly missing a jagged support beam that could have impaled him. He landed hard on a patch of grass, just inland from the airstrip. His ribs cried out in pain; he winced, seeing stars.

A figure approached. Tony rose to his knees, holding up one repulsor-charged palm.

"Easy," Doctor Voodoo said. "I have you."

Tony lay back, exhaling heavily. Voodoo caught him as he swooned, lifting him easily and carrying him behind the rubble, out of sight.

"Your wounds have reopened," Voodoo said, setting him down on a patch of grass. "You cannot continue like this."

Tony waved a hand toward the hangar. "Others…?"

"They are holding their own. But more forces are coming." Voodoo held up one bare hand, haloed with mystic energy. "You must recuperate. I can induce a healing sleep that will–"

"No!" Tony scrambled to his feet, a sudden terrible suspicion flooding his pain-wracked brain. "What are you doing?"

Voodoo's brow narrowed. "Saving your life?"

"Really? Is that it?"

Tony held out a glove to the impassive sorcerer, repulsor glowing with deadly force.

"Or are you working with *them*?" he demanded.

TWENTY-SIX

"What are you …"

Voodoo paused, as if listening to an unseen voice. When he turned back to Tony, his blank eyes grew uncharacteristically wide with astonishment. "Dormammu?" he asked. "You believe I am working for him?"

"You've done it before. Daniel has, I mean." Tony backed away. "What did you do to that poor girl? Did you *force* her to host the symbiotes, to subject herself to…"

He stopped, unable to speak the rest aloud. He opened his helmet – he needed to see Voodoo's face clearly, unfiltered by electronic lenses. The ruins rose up several feet here; the airstrip was visible over them, but only barely. For the moment, the two of them remained hidden from view.

Doctor Voodoo glared at him for a long time, watching with blank white eyes. Eyes, Tony saw, that bore not a trace of green in them.

"That *young woman,*" Voodoo said, "is capable of far more than you know. And as for myself: you have no idea what I've been through." He paused, twitching slightly. "Either of me."

Tony paused, steadying himself. His head throbbed; his ribs

ached. And Voodoo, whichever side he was on, was right about one thing: Tony's stomach wound had opened up again. He could feel hot blood spreading across the inside of his armor.

"I understand your despair," Voodoo continued, "but this is pointless. We must work together – more enemies will be here soon."

"If you're on my side," Tony gasped, "then prove it."

"How?"

"Fix me up." Tony grabbed at his stomach, wincing at the sudden flash of pain. "Give me a boost, some kind of mystic potion. Just enough to get me through the fight."

Voodoo stepped closer, glancing quickly at the sky above. This time, Tony let him approach.

"I can temporarily seal the wound," Voodoo said, "and knit your bones together. But there is a price."

"Fine. Put it on my tab."

"I am serious." Voodoo stared at him, those blank eyes unnervingly close. "The universe demands balance. You will pay for this later, in nerve-racking agony."

"Look." Tony forced himself to stare back. "Ms Marvel might be about to die, doing *my* job. I couldn't hack it, so here we are. I've got to buy her every minute of time I can!"

"Even if it costs you your life."

"Yes," Tony said, his vision beginning to blur. "It's literally – I mean, it's the very *definition* of *the least I can do*."

Voodoo motioned for him to sit on the ground. Then, standing back, the magician leaned down and grabbed hold of Tony's armor, right where it covered his gut wound.

"Oh," Tony said. "Oh wow. Looks like the nerve-racking agony arrived a little *early*–"

Then he screamed. However much pain he'd felt before,

whatever damage he'd done to his body, it was nothing compared to this. He could feel his ribs swimming through tissue, reaching out to one another, snapping back into place... the skin over his stomach growing, regenerating, veins cutting off the flow of escaping blood...

And every move, every flash of dark magic, set a fresh burst of agony flaring through his system.

The pain seemed to last for weeks, even months. Tony leaned back against a piece of rubble, fading in and out of consciousness. Combat sounds came to him on the wind: Cage's rumbling voice, the sizzling whine of the Black Widow's wrist-stingers.

At some point the pain lessened, and he found himself staring up at Voodoo's impassive face. Tony reached down and gingerly touched his stomach; it felt tender, but the wound was closed now.

"Th-thank you," he said.

He held out a metal-gloved hand. Doctor Voodoo took it and helped him to his feet.

"I'm sorry," Tony added. "It's hard to know who to trust, these days."

"I know," Voodoo acknowledged. "And believe me: if I could possibly have stopped Ms Marvel from risking her life, I would have done it."

"Well..." Tony jetted up a few inches, marveling at the lack of pain in his stomach. "If I'd had your magic surgery a few hours ago, I might have been up for that mission myself."

"That would not have been possible," Voodoo replied. "My power was not yet–"

"*Look!*"

Tony pointed up over the water at another aircraft, just

soaring into view. No, not a craft – a living creature, with flashing teeth and sharp claws, scales gleaming a bright metallic emerald as it emerged from the clouds. It opened huge jaws and let out a roar of fire, spreading its wings wider than the length of a soccer field.

"Is that... is that a dragon?" Tony asked.

"A Shashou Dragon," Voodoo said, "from the realm of Huor."

Tony shrugged, thinking: ask an expert...

"They are normally peaceful," the sorcerer continued. "But I have never seen one with scales that color."

Tony zoomed in even closer. The dragon's scales shone bright silver, like chain mail, shifting and clinking in the wind. But a wetness glistened on its underside, lending those scales a peculiar green sheen...

"Osdrink!" Tony shook his head. "Looks like Osborn got his big other-realms export business going. I wonder if there's time to get in on the IPO?"

"Look up," Voodoo said sharply. "On the Shashou's back."

Tony willed his faceplate closed, zooming in as the dragon's enormous wings swept upward. When they flapped down again, he saw the two figures standing astride the creature's back. One was tall, dressed in red and gold, a curved gleaming sword held high in one hand. The other was pale, slim, and bone-white, glowing like a star.

"Shang-Chi and Dagger," Tony said. "Again."

"Again?" Voodoo asked.

"I, uh, kind of tried to recruit them before."

The dragon slowed as it drew close to the island. Shang-Chi's sharp eyes turned, locking for a moment with Voodoo's. Tony tensed, powering up his repulsors.

Shang-Chi flung his sword arm out to the right. The Dragon

let out a roar and moved in that direction, veering sharply toward the east side of the island. The side where the hangar stood, and where a fierce battle still raged on the airstrip.

"It appears you weren't successful," Voodoo said.

"What are they doing?" Tony asked.

He jetted up a few feet, turning to zoom in on the battle raging half an island away. Cage, Shuri, and the Panther stood back-to-back, fighting off a combined assault from the Black Widow and Captain America. Shuri was managing to keep Cap at a distance, slashing wildly with that vibranium blade.

But as he watched, Captain Marvel rejoined the fight, sending fierce photon bolts slashing into the tarmac. Cage dodged a bolt, leaping away – and wound up right in the path of the Widow's taser-like sting.

"Our friends are on the defensive," Voodoo said, as if he were narrating Tony's thoughts. "They are weary from their ordeal among the realms."

"We're all weary," Tony said.

He looked up at the dragon, watching it swoop low above the fight. Captain Marvel drifted aside in the air, making room for the massive creature's approach.

"It's gonna blast them!" Tony exclaimed.

But to his surprise, the dragon didn't stop. It turned, roaring, and climbed up into the sky. As it did, Dagger's small shining form executed a graceful dive into the air, dropping down to join the battle. Shang-Chi let out a cry, raised his sword, and leaped after her.

"That doesn't help our odds," Tony said. He powered up his jets, aiming toward the hangar–

–and then he noticed something odd. The dragon was riderless now, but it hadn't stopped. As he watched, it executed a wide U-turn in the air and soared through the sky, incredibly fast. Before he could react, it had passed clear over their heads.

"Oh no," Tony said. "*Oh* no. That thing is headed straight for–"

"–the bottling facility," Voodoo finished.

As the dragon neared the large warehouse, its jaws opened wide. Flame sparked within its maw, growing and building in intensity. Then it tilted its head sharply down – and let forth a blast of fire that incinerated the front wall of the bottling plant.

Tony stood, shocked, taking in the carnage. A few Oscorp trucks, parked before the building, burst into flame, filling the end of the runway with thick black smoke. He switched to thermal vision, zooming in on the building's wall – three-quarters of which was gone, replaced by an enormous hole dotted with green-hot heat signatures along its jagged edges. As he watched, the temperature faded rapidly from bright green to normal.

Mystic flame, he thought. Judging from the signatures, it was cooling faster than normal, regular, Earth-type fire. Must be from the realm of… oh, who could keep all those dimensions straight?

He switched to normal vision. The smoke began to clear, revealing the gaping hole in the facility's wall. And inside that hole… peering out, just beginning their cautious advance…

"Hydra agents." Voodoo's voice was grave. "Dozens of them."

One by one, and then three and four at a time, they emerged from the smoking building. All dressed in green and yellow, helmets covering their eyes, weapons gleaming on their belts. A growing swarm of possessed human insects.

"Looks like Norman let them keep their villain uniforms,"

Tony observed. "A rare concession on his part to workers' rights."

"I will remind you," Voodoo said, "that every one of those *workers* is in thrall to our enemy."

Tony glanced at Voodoo, then ran a quick survey of the island. On one end of the airstrip, Cage, Panther, and Shuri faced a powerful attack force of possessed heroes. On the other end, an army of Hydra agents advanced slowly out of their improvised prison, ready to join the battle.

"With us caught right in the middle," Tony said.

"You help Cage and the others," Voodoo said. "I will contain the Hydra agents."

Before Tony could argue, the sorcerer wafted up into the air, gripping his staff. Voodoo leaned forward and sped off toward the bottling facility.

"You look like you're riding a Segway, when you do that!" Tony called after him.

He turned and jetted off toward the hangar, zooming in to take stock. Dagger faced off against Shuri, who deflected her beams with that flashing vibranium blade. But a dark figure suddenly appeared in a cloud of energy, right behind the pale light-powered woman. Cloak, Dagger's partner, teleporting in to join her in battle.

Cage and the Panther, meanwhile, backed up slowly toward the hangar building, facing a three-way attack from Captain America, the Black Widow, and Shang-Chi. They could probably win that fight, Tony thought, especially with Cap's movements dulled by the fog of Dormammu's influence. But Captain Marvel still hovered above, firing blasts down into the tarmac – forcing T'Challa and Cage farther and farther back.

And this, he realized, is only the beginning. If Dormammu

wants, he can send every super-powered person in the world against us. Armies, too – the combined air and ground forces of every nation on Earth. Then he'll start tapping the other realms. The dragon, the Mindless Ones, the various threats the Shadow Avengers had already faced – all a tiny sample of the infinite resources at the Big D's disposal.

Once again, he thought: this is a waiting game. All that matters is that we hold the line, until the bomb can be detonated in the Dark Dimension.

"Ms Marvel," he breathed, his heart racing as he sped through the air to join the battle. "Oh, kid. Good luck in there."

TWENTY-SEVEN

"Spider-Man?"

A woman's voice: deep, concerned, firm yet fearful. A hand in his: slim, strong fingers, gripping him tight.

Spider-Man. That's me, he thought. That's my name!

It was also the only thing he could remember. The rest was a blank.

"Can you hear me?" the voice continued.

His eyes, he realized, were squeezed shut. He preferred it that way. The last time they were open, they'd seen things. Terrible, fearful things that crashed his mind and overwhelmed his senses.

But now there was the voice, and the hand. Soothing him, lending him strength. An image came to him: a woman, a brave woman who'd helped him survive in the past.

"Aunt May?" he asked.

The reply, when it came, was very different. Loud, masculine, threatening. Menacing.

"Not quite."

He opened his eyes and gasped. A horrible creature, twice the size of a man, floated in the sky before him, its shifting skin jet-black and oily. A face grinned at him from its surface, tongue lashing back and forth in a sea of teeth.

"If you're my Aunt May," he said slowly, "then we're overdue for a trip to the dermatologist."

The creature laughed. Eyes, teeth, and gaping mouths took form on its surface, then vanished again. He looked away in terror; he was floating, along with the creature, in a strange blue-and-white void. It could have been a cloudy sky, or a reflection of waves on the sea. Late afternoon in a space without time, a realm without form.

As he turned back toward the creature, his memories began to return. Venom! he thought. Is that you...?

But no. As he watched, the face flattened out, receded, and vanished into a mass of oily protoplasm. He recoiled, tried to pull away–

–but the hand held him tight. It was the only human part of the creature: small, dark, human, protruding from the mass of black goo. Three tight bracelets fastened to its wrist. He knew those bracelets – knew who they belonged to...

"Ms Marvel?" he gasped.

In response, the creature let out an odd sort of grunting noise. Its oily skin began to roil and pucker, bubbling outward. With a gasp, Ms Marvel – her head, anyway – burst out of the dark-swarming mass.

"I'm here!" she said, shaking black goo out of her hair.

He clasped her hand tight, pulling himself closer to her.

"I found you," she continued, smiling weakly at him. "I wasn't sure I could do it."

"You... found me..."

And then he remembered. Tony Stark's workshop; Ms Marvel's enlarged hands shoving him away, taking the harness in his place. The symbiotes attaching themselves, one by one, to her. Her leap through the portal ... his frantic pursuit, clutching the Lantern. The sights, the overwhelming psychic trauma of the passage through the realms ...

"I was lost," he continued. "And you found me. In this ... what is this place, anyway?"

"I'm not sure," she replied. "It's not the Dark Dimension, I know that."

"Yeah," he said, staring at the aquamarine vastness all around. "That explains the lack of, you know, Dormammu."

"I think it's a kind of limbo, between the realms. A jumping-off point, maybe."

He blinked, watching her. Her voice sounded so normal, so matter-of-fact. As if wearing a harness with an interdimensional bomb, covered by a couple dozen flesh-eating symbiotes, was just another day at school to her.

"How you doing?" he asked.

"I'm ... I'm still me. I think. But I can hear them, all the time, in my mind. It's ..." She paused, twisting her head around to stare at the symbiotes. "It's a lot."

"Is it tough to stick your head out like that?"

"I can stretch, remember? My powers." She grimaced. "Neck's a little sore, though."

"I bet it is!"

Oh, kid, he thought – why did you do this? I should have been the one hosting the symbiotes. I should be the one with the voices swirling around in my head. I should have the sore neck!

"I didn't find you, by the way," she said, eyeing the symbiotes. "*They* did. They followed you as you plummeted through the dimensions. They're drawn to you, somehow."

"Just like they're drawn to Eddie," he replied. "Because we've both hosted symbiotes in the past."

"They can feel you. Taste you, almost." She frowned. "They can taste your guilt."

On the surface of the Ms Marvel creature, one of the faces formed teeth, reached out, and snapped at Spider-Man. He flinched, but kept hold of her hand.

"They'd *like* to taste me, that's for sure."

"They can feel him, too," she said. "Eddie… Venom. He's in the Dark Dimension, with Dormammu. But they don't know how to get from here to there."

"Maybe the Lantern can…"

He stopped, suddenly panicked. The Lantern, he thought. Where is it? I've lost it. I've lost the Lantern!

That, he knew, meant they were trapped here. Even if, by some miracle, they managed to find the Dark Dimension, their link to Doctor Strange was gone. They'd never make it home again.

Strangely, Ms Marvel didn't seem concerned. She stretched her head out farther, craned her neck around, and began arguing with a half-formed symbiote face.

"Give it," she said.

The face snarled.

"I said *give it up!*"

The face stuck out its tongue, then grimaced and receded into the mass of protoplasm. With a quick sucking noise, the Lantern of Morphesti popped free of the creature and floated off into the void.

Spider-Man shot off a quick webline with his free hand, snagging the Lantern. "You found it too?"

"You were clutching it tight when we located you," she explained, smiling. "I just tucked it away for safekeeping."

He stared at the Lantern, which gave off a yellow glow at his touch. "I don't think you need my help at all," he said.

"I do. I really do." She smiled, a tear in her eye. "But you shouldn't have come – they need you back on Earth. Tony needs you."

"Nah," he said. "One friendly neighborhood Spider-Man isn't gonna make a difference against a mind-controlled army."

"Well, I'm glad you're here. Wherever 'here' is, I mean."

"*You*, on the other hand, shouldn't be here at all," he said. "Next time leave the heroics to your elders, OK?"

She made a face. "How 'bout a little less big-brother-type scolding, and a little more dimensional mapping action?"

"Yeah…" He shifted, letting her hand go, and concentrated on the Lantern. "Thing is, the Doc didn't exactly tell me how to turn this thing on – *oh*."

A dozen beams of light stabbed out, all at once, from the Lantern. He twisted it in his hand, positioning it so the beams all aimed at the sky beyond. Where they struck the cloudy substance of the void, they formed a multicolored map marked with alien symbols.

"I don't recognize that language," he said. "Are those… realms?"

"I think so." Ms Marvel's eyes went wide. "Oh. Whoa, the guys are getting wild now. Easy, boys. Easy, friendly people-eating symbiotes!"

More and more beams flashed out from the Lantern, filling the sky. In the projected map, Spider-Man could see hints and flashes of other worlds: a blazing sun, a bubbling primordial swamp. An army of one-eyed creatures marching across a burnt, cratered landscape.

He stared, mesmerized, as the map branched out into layers,

realms overlapping realms like a three-dimensional diorama. Then – in some manner he couldn't explain – the lights reached into a fourth dimension, forming yet another layer. Then a fifth, and a sixth…

He forced himself to look away. He could feel his brain overloading again, preparing to shut down. He couldn't let that happen… not again…

"Oh," Ms Marvel said. "Oh, man."

He looked over at her in alarm. The symbiotes bubbled and puckered, like pudding on a stove. Along her shoulders, the lights of the harness blinked and flashed, intermittently visible through the symbiote skin covering it. Bits of black plasm crept up and down her exposed face, threatening to pull off her mask.

"It's OK," she said. "They're talking to me. They're saying something…"

She floated past him, straying into the path of the Lantern's beams. Her hand, the one still sticking out of the mass of symbiotes, reached out and pointed at a single jagged-edged realm. A realm marked, on the map, in pure blood-red.

"There," the symbiotes said, all together, in a voice that chilled Spider-Man's blood.

They're not confused by the multiple dimensions, he realized. They can see clearly, straight to their destination. All they care about is finding their brother.

"That's the Dark Dimension?" he asked.

Ms Marvel said nothing. She simply floated in the void, pointing her shaky hand at that one spot on the map.

"Kid? Are you OK?"

"I've got it." She blinked, shook a few bits of symbiote off her face. "I know where he is."

"Eddie," he said.

"Yeah."

"Are you ..." He hesitated. "I mean, can you do this?"

She shuddered, eyes wide. For a moment, a terrible haunted expression crossed her face. Spider-Man remembered the feel of his own symbiote, crawling through his head, and wondered once again: what is she going through?

Then she shrugged. Well, it was kind of a shrug. As much of a shrug as a person could manage, with their head sticking out of a solid ball of floating symbiotes.

"I've got to," she said.

She turned away and shot off into the sky, toward the vast realm map projected from the Lantern. Her dark blob-like form began to shrink, to recede, fading slowly into the deep red spot that marked their destination.

Spider-Man felt a renewed burst of panic. Go after her, he told himself. Quick. Before it's too late. Before you lose her again!

Gripping the Lantern tight, he kicked off and followed her into the Dark Dimension.

TWENTY-EIGHT

As a young man, Jericho Drumm had been fascinated with dominoes. His teacher, Papa Jambo, used to stand them up in a long row that wound around the floor of the old man's ramshackle house. With barely a touch, Jambo would send them tumbling over, one after another, until they all lay fallen on the floor.

"Such is vudu," Papa Jambo said. "One wrong move may undo… everything."

Now Jericho stood in the hot air of a remote Pacific island, watching Hydra agents pour out of the only intact building at the end of the island's airstrip. One by one, and in groups of three or four, they popped their heads up through the hole that the dragon had blasted in the wall of the bottling factory. They crawled and tumbled and spilled out onto the tarmac, where they began a deadly march down the runway.

Like dominoes, Jericho thought, but in reverse. Rising instead of falling; an ascending army of evil.

He lunged forward, straining his power as he reached out to erect a powerful mystic shield across the hole in the building.

The Hydra agents still inside, eyes glowing Dormammu-green through their helmets, jerked in surprise as they slammed up against it. A few of them aimed their guns at the barrier, firing off bullets, miniature missiles, and particle beams.

Osborn let them keep their guns too, he thought in surprise.

No, Daniel replied, inside Jericho's mind. *Dormammu did.*

Jericho grunted, reinforcing the shield as a volley of heavy machine-gun fire struck it. The barrier was holding so far, keeping the Hydra agents penned up inside the building. But a few of them had already slipped out around the corners, squeezing their way onto the tarmac. He'd taken one out with a sleeping spell, but the other two had run off to join the battle on the other end of the runway.

A bulky Hydra agent let out a yell and charged the shield, muscles bulging, teeth gritted in Dormammu-fueled fury. In a shocking display of brute force, the agent pushed his way straight through the barrier and lunged forward, hands outstretched to grab Jericho's throat.

Jericho raised his staff on instinct, cracking the man on the head. The yellow-clad man gasped and fell to the ground.

You cannot stop this, brother, Daniel said. *You'll never defeat them all.*

Jericho swore, in a language never before heard on Earth. The Shield of the Seraphim, he knew, could have stopped the entire Hydra army cold. But that shield was being used by Doctor Strange, to safeguard both Strange's life and the mission to the Dark Dimension. As the other Sorcerer Supreme of Earth, Doctor Voodoo could not call upon it without sapping the power available to Strange.

So instead, Jericho had cobbled together a smattering of lesser spells to form his barrier. A touch of voodoo here, a bit of ancient Sumerian there. But those spells had their limits, and the strain was showing.

What had he told Tony Stark about the Shadow Avengers? *They are weary from their ordeal among the realms.* So am I, he realized. So am I.

Two more Hydra warriors pressed themselves against the barrier, battering it with the butts of their machine guns.

We cannot win, Daniel continued.

Jericho reached into his pocket and pulled out a small paper packet. He emptied a handful of dust into his palm – red brick dust, the color of blood – and blew it toward the Hydra agents. The dust struck the barrier, spreading out to shimmer across its surface – and the Hydra agents bounced back, startled, as the barrier's surface suddenly turned rock-hard.

The rest of the Hydras took a step back. They moved like a single entity – which, in a way, they were. They turned toward Jericho, studying him coldly with those glowing green eyes.

Suddenly he could tell which direction the dominoes were about to fall.

More and more Hydra agents began to gather behind the shield. Behind them, through the hole in the wall, Jericho caught a glimpse of the bottling facility. Gleaming conveyor belts, a few transparent vats filled with that blasted Osdrink. It reminded him of the high-tech ruins, the shattered Hydra facility that covered most of the island.

First Hydra, he thought grimly, and now Dormammu. All conquerors are the same in the end.

More of the Hydras are escaping, Daniel said. *Your friends are now badly outnumbered.*

Let's just see, Jericho replied.

As the Hydra agents regrouped, glaring at the shield, Jericho pulled out a tiny bottle of divination oil. When he snapped off the cap, the smell of lilacs filled the air. In three quick motions, he dabbed the thick violet oil on his left temple, forehead, and right temple. Then he closed his eyes.

The oil on his forehead flared, burning, seeking and searching like a third eye. His awareness expanded, spreading out to cover the island. All at once, like images on a split screen, he saw:

Iron Man. Swooping and flashing high above the island, trading repulsor bursts with the deadly photon beams of Captain Marvel. The dragon eyeing them both, keeping its distance, waiting for the moment to strike.

The Black Panther. Leaping and darting through and around the rubble, just inland from the airstrip. He ducked, catlike, as a barrage of Dagger's light-blades sliced over his head. Abruptly Cloak appeared; a fierce wind seemed to erupt from his dark form, threatening to pull T'Challa into the eerie void of Cloak's body. T'Challa grabbed onto a hard plastic pillar embedded into the ground, and held on.

Luke Cage. Facing off against Shang-Chi in a battle of brute strength versus lightning-fast moves. Shang-Chi landed a bone-shattering blow to Luke's stomach, staggering the big man slightly. Luke replied with a roundhouse punch. Shang-Chi avoided it easily, leaping up into the air.

Shuri. Running from Captain America and Black Widow, who advanced slowly toward her – either they didn't consider her a real threat, or else their Dormammu conditioning was weakening. Oddly, Shuri seemed to be heading for the Avengers' parked Quinjet. Did she have a plan of some kind…?

And all around them, the escaped Hydra agents were

gathering. Eyes glowing with hunger as they watched each battle, waiting for their chance to–

  Brother! Daniel cried. *Look out!*

Jericho whirled back toward the Hydra agents still trapped behind the mystic shield. As he watched, they dragged something out of the building, aiming it at the jagged hole in the wall. A thick piece of tubing – a hose of some kind, its far end anchored to some machine inside the bottling facility. They paused, turning all eyes toward Jericho–

–as a flood of green liquid came lashing out of the hose. It struck Jericho's shield with enormous force, shattering and disrupting the mystic energies. The liquid passed right through, slamming into Doctor Voodoo with the force of a thousand firehoses. Knocking him off his feet, propelling him backward, covering him head to toe with–

–with Osdrink!

Jericho hurtled backward, struggling to keep hold of his staff. His back hit the pavement, painfully, and then his neck struck something hard. He craned his head around to look: the metal guardrail at the side of the airstrip. Beyond lay a sharp drop onto jagged rocks, and then the open sea.

He turned, coughing, and spat Osdrink onto the pavement. *The shield*, he thought. *That's the important thing. Maintain the shield!*

Inside his mind, Daniel sighed. *Allow me, brother.*

Jericho shook his head, shaking the foul liquid out of his locs. He looked up to see the shield – glimmering once again, blocking the path of the startled Hydra agents. They cast aside the dripping hose, then hefted their guns once again.

Daniel, he realized – Daniel, the other half of Doctor Voodoo – had stepped in to restore the shield. *Thank you, brother,* Jericho said, wiping the last of the Osdrink off his face.

Do not thank me yet, Daniel replied. *The drink… the dormamine compound within it…*

Jericho felt a stab of panic. He rose to his feet, struggling to concentrate. Something invaded his consciousness – something dark and threatening. Something vile, evil. Something that wasn't Daniel.

… the drink is inside us now.

It was true. The Osdrink had seeped in through his pores, spreading through his body. Jericho knew its effects; he could defend against it – but that would distract him, dividing his already depleted power. Power he needed badly, to keep the remaining Hydra agents at bay while half his teammates fought to stay alive, and the other half carried out their crucial task in the Dark Dimension.

And the situation, he knew, was even worse than that. Jericho might be able to fight off the dormamine's effects – but he was only one of two personas inhabiting the shared form of Doctor Voodoo. The other one, Daniel, was already severely traumatized from the months he'd spent trapped in the void realm. And Daniel had succumbed to the lure of Dormammu once before.

I can feel him, Daniel said. *So strong… so welcoming…*

Jericho could feel his brother's pain, the need for comfort. Dormammu, he realized, offers that comfort. A life free of choice, of decision-making – of all the pain that came with free will.

He felt the Hydras' fists, too, the blows of their weapons against the mystic shield. As they sensed weakness, their eyes glowed bright, their teeth bared in otherworldly hunger. He pulled out another packet of red brick dust – his last – and blew it at the mystic shield. That strengthened it slightly... but for how long?

Brother, Jericho called. *You must resist. If Dormammu takes you, we are lost!*

Dormammu, Daniel repeated.

I just got you back, Jericho said. *I brought you home, to Earth, after an eternity away. Don't let him destroy that home, just when you've found it again!*

Dormammu, Daniel said again. *The Master...*

Jericho dropped to his knees, pouring all his remaining power into the shield. A terrible wave of sadness, of hopelessness, washed over him. He remembered his own words, spoken what seemed like an eternity ago: *Dormammu is despair.*

That thought, that terrible mantra, echoed over and over in his mind. Followed by Daniel's warning, just moments ago: *You cannot stop this.*

The Osdrink, the invader within him, cried out in triumph. The Hydras surged in response, bashing and pounding at the barrier. A few more slipped through, running off to join the battle against the beleaguered Shadow Avengers.

In desperation and fear, Jericho closed his eyes. Shutting out everything else, he latched on to the mystic link to his fellow Sorcerer Supreme and gasped out a frantic message:

Hurry, Stephen, he said. *Tell our friends to hurry!*

TWENTY-NINE

Hail Hydra!

Not long ago, that cry had echoed across every inch of the island. The soldiers of Baron Strucker had built a vast, super-scientific base from which to conquer and terrorize the world. Domed laboratories squatted amid huge flat training fields, topped with high ridged spires studded with deadly weapons. At the height of Hydra's power, those weapons had threatened all life on Earth; one particularly lurid tabloid had referred to the place as a "metropolis of evil".

Now the domes lay shattered, trees poking up through their jagged remains. The weapons were long destroyed, splintered and shattered to scrap metal. And the once-fearsome soldiers had become wage slaves, working for the tiny pensions and stingy overtime pay doled out by Norman Osborn.

T'Challa led his pursuers deeper into the ruins, leaping and racing over the fallen spires, seeking the shelter of the young trees and darting out again as soon as it was safe. All at once, he realized he was smiling.

It was an odd reaction, when he thought about it. On almost every front, the situation remained dire. Cloak and Dagger were hot on his tail, Tony and the others were badly outnumbered on the airstrip; the last time he'd looked, Doctor Voodoo's efforts to keep the Hydra agents penned up weren't going well either. And everything hinged on the Shadow Avengers' youngest member negotiating a hostile realm, where – he hated to think of it – she would probably die.

And yet: in this bizarre, apocalyptic place, pursued by powerful foes, T'Challa found himself oddly at home. His muscles flexing and stretching, the hot wind whipping through the trees, even the obstacle course formed out of Hydra wreckage – all of it made him feel very much alive. For the first time in months, he realized, *I feel like myself.*

It certainly beat giving Tribute to Dormammu.

He crouched down behind the remains of a rusted ray-cannon, propped up at an angle in the dirt. Across a clearing, in a small copse of trees, he could see Dagger approaching. Knives of light shone at her fingertips; her possessed-green eyes scanned the area, platinum hair whipping back and forth in the wind.

T'Challa shook his head. The young woman wielded significant power, but his experience and training made him a far stronger tactician. Also, Dagger had grown up in the city; she was used to fighting on narrow streets, between high buildings laid out on a regular grid. In this chaotic outdoor forest, all he had to do was wait her out.

Soon Cloak, Dagger's partner, would arrive through one of his teleportational nether-warps. Then T'Challa would outmaneuver them both, as he'd been doing for half an hour now.

He didn't fully agree with Stark's tactics. Sooner or later, Dormammu's possessed hordes would escape this island to wreak havoc elsewhere. But T'Challa's allies depended on him, so for now, he would fight this battle. If he could continue luring Cloak and Dagger further into the ruins, that would remove them as a threat to his fellow Shadow Avengers.

The ground shook briefly, a sudden vibration spreading inland from the airstrip at the edge of the island. T'Challa glanced in that direction, but he couldn't see much through the debris and the trees. Whatever his teammates were dealing with, they'd have to handle it on their own–

–because, like clockwork, there was Cloak. Twenty meters away, stepping out of a warp in the air. Glancing around, looking up...

"Tandy!" Cloak cried, pointing up. "Look!"

Tandy – Dagger's real name – looked up in surprise. T'Challa followed her gaze, watching as the Avengers' Quinjet came swooping down out of the clouds.

He tensed, waiting. Had Captain America decided to join this battle? That would tip the odds against T'Challa – and pose an ethical problem for him as well. In saner times, Captain America was a valued friend.

He shifted in place, preparing to leap. Then, to his surprise, an amplified voice rang out from the Quinjet's hidden speakers.

"Brother! *Ku'keleele!*"

Two thoughts ran, all at once, through the stunned mind of T'Challa, King of Wakanda:

Shuri. That's Shuri's voice. She's stolen the Quinjet!

And:

Ku'keleele?

The Quinjet swooped low, pulling up hard just a few meters above the ruins. "Brother!" Shuri cried again.

T'Challa shrugged, tensed his legs, and leaped. For a moment he thought he'd miss his target, but he reached out and grabbed hold of the Quinjet's large roof fin. He pulled himself up onto the hull, holding on tight with both hands.

On the ground, Dagger yelled something – he couldn't hear it over the roar of the Quinjet's engines – and fired off a trio of light-daggers. The Quinjet lurched to one side, nearly dislodging T'Challa from his perch. Then it swung upward, nose pointed to the sky, and began to climb. Another volley of light-daggers whizzed past, but Shuri veered the Quinjet from side to side to avoid them.

Soon both Dagger and her partner were lost from sight. When it was safe to move one hand, T'Challa touched a bead at his throat.

"Little sister," he said. "Don't you remember what our mother told you about stealing vehicles?"

Shuri's laugh, high and wonderful, came to him over the Kimoyo bead's hidden circuitry. "She said they do it all the time in America!"

The Quinjet climbed higher, clearing the treeline. T'Challa risked a glance down. Now he could make out the vastness of the ruins, spread out across the island. Further inland, at the exact center of the destruction, the remains of an enormous Hydra command globe lay sprawled in jagged, sharp-edged pieces. Weaponry and support beams, all forged from the same black, teardrop-shaped Hydra metal, were scattered all around the globe, pointed outward like the frozen record of an explosion.

The genius that went into building this place, he thought; *the huge sums of money that must have been required to build it. What other, better ends could those things have served?*

"Shuri," he said, "why did you call out *Ku'keleele* to me?"

"Brother," she replied, contempt dripping from her tone, "do you remember nothing of our homeland?"

"I know what the word means," he snapped. "The Ku'keleele is a Wakandan bird known for its deafeningly loud screeching noises."

"Yes!" She sounded smug. "And I believe it is time to take a lesson from the wise Ku'keleele."

Sister! he thought. Can't you ever just say what you mean?

He started to reply, then noticed something in the air ahead. He shifted position on the Quinjet's hull, peering forward as they approached… two airborne figures, sparring, high above the island: Iron Man and Captain Marvel. She seemed to have him on the run, firing photon beams in rapid-fire bursts. They struck his armor, jolting his chest and torso, shaking him one way and then the other in midair.

"Captain Marvel," T'Challa said into the Kimoyo bead. "I will take her." He tensed his muscles, preparing to leap.

"No," Shuri replied, "I've got Shiny Lady. You take Big Boy!"

T'Challa looked from side to side: what was "Big Boy"? Then a shadow fell over him, covering the entire Quinjet, blotting out the sun. He looked up and saw–

–the dragon – the one Shang-Chi had arrived on! It dipped down, riderless now, its scales glistening metallic green. As it swooped alongside Captain Marvel, Tony Stark let off a pair of repulsor blasts, momentarily stunning Carol.

But the dragon was already opening its mouth–

As T'Challa watched, a burst of flame shot out to engulf Tony. He arched his back and screamed, his armor glowing bright.

"Get me over there!" T'Challa yelled. "On top of it!"

The Quinjet veered sharply upward. Captain Marvel hadn't noticed the vehicle yet. She seemed distracted, partly by her own battle and partly, T'Challa supposed, by the dormamine coursing through her system. The dragon, though... the dragon tracked the jet's every movement with one enormous, green-glowing eye.

Shuri slowed the Quinjet as it approached the beast. Then, vertical jets blazing, it shot straight up. The dragon snapped at it with an impressive array of jagged teeth. But Shuri maintained their ascent, keeping the jet out of reach.

When the Quinjet reached the top of its climb, T'Challa leaped off. As he twisted in midair, he caught a quick glimpse of the dragon's gaping, snapping jaws. Then he reached out with all four limbs and landed on its back, hard enough to knock the breath out of him.

"*Wakanda Forever!*" he cried.

Because, why not?

The dragon twisted its neck around, searching for him. He dug his hands into those hard scales, gripping them tight, and began to crawl forward. This far back, near the creature's tail, he was vulnerable; it might be able to turn its head far enough to blast him with that fire-breath. If he could climb onto its neck, that would become impossible.

A high whine filled the air. T'Challa recognized the sound: the Quinjet's sonic cannon. He touched a bead at his throat to block the sound, then turned to see:

Iron Man hung smoking in the air. Autopilot jet circuits held him in place, but his armor was clearly damaged. Past him, the Quinjet circled around in a wide arc, basically making a gigantic U-turn in midair. Captain Marvel turned her attention to the jet, her hands pulsing with photonic power.

T'Challa tensed, ignoring the bucking muscles of the metallic dragon. "Shuri!" he cried, "get out of there!"

Shuri made no reply. The sonic cannon rose in pitch, its whine penetrating even the built-in dampeners in T'Challa's headgear. Captain Marvel winced, raising hands to her ears.

The dragon reared back. T'Challa held onto its neck, once again realizing that he was smiling. "You don't get rid of me that easily!" he cried.

The Quinjet shot straight toward Captain Marvel – who looked up in sudden alarm. Shuri's intention was clear: she planned to ram Carol head-on.

"Sister, no!" he said. "She'll kill you. You don't know how powerful she is!"

The dragon roared in reply. T'Challa rapped it hard on the neck. It snarled back at him.

"Shuri!"

At the last second, Captain Marvel raised her hands and let out a blinding flash of stellar energy. The Quinjet slammed into her, exploding in a split instant. Fire erupted, the raging flames almost lost within the unleashed light particles. T'Challa had to shield his eyes from the horror.

"*Sister!*" he cried.

The glare faded, revealing several shattered pieces of Quinjet falling rapidly toward the forest. A detached wing, still smoking, a shard of the transparent cockpit cover. An engine, spitting flame as it spiraled down.

Amid the wreckage, a single figure plummeted to Earth as well. The limp, blue-and-red form of Captain Marvel, knocked unconscious by the explosion. Her half-Kree physiology, T'Challa knew, would allow her to survive. But she'd be out of action for a while.

There was no sign of Shuri.

T'Challa sat for a moment on the dragon's back, utterly bereft. Shuri, he thought, I only just got you back. To lose you now… in this terrible place…

"You will be honored," he whispered. "Your sacrifice will be remembered forever…"

A familiar sound echoed over his Kimoyo bead: laughter.

"Shuri?" he asked in astonishment.

"I'm OK!" she replied. "I bailed out at the last minute. That was wild!"

He searched the sky. There – almost a half mile inland – he could make out a small parachute. The winds pulled it away, farther from the airstrip. Away from him.

"Sister," he said, his voice trembling. "You gave me a scare."

"I did it," she replied. "With the sonic cannon. I shrieked like the Ku'keleele bird!"

"You realize that bird screams only to protect its *children*. Its young."

"Oh, brother. Those people you hang about with… the ones in the silly costumes…"

"Yes?"

"Don't they seem like children, most of the time?"

He laughed. The dragon snarled, but otherwise ignored him. It seemed to have gotten used to having a passenger.

"I may have to miss the battle for a while!" Shuri's voice sounded fainter now.

"That would be… a relief," he admitted.

"You can still honor my sacrifice, you know," she said. "Even though I'm not dead!"

"That would be *WHOAAAHH!*"

The dragon bucked unexpectedly, taking him by surprise.

One gloved hand slipped free of its scales; he scrambled for purchase, throwing both arms around its neck. But it was no use. The creature executed a full backflip, twirling upside-down in the air. T'Challa lurched, scrabbled–

–and fell.

He was in midair for less than a second when a pair of strong metal arms grabbed hold of him. Iron Man shifted, said "Your highness," and raised one hand to fire off a blast at the dragon.

The beast growled and let out a petulant huff of flame. Then it turned, tail whipping, and wheeled away into the sun. Iron Man slowed in midair, watching it dwindle out of sight.

"It appears to be tired of us," T'Challa observed.

"I have that effect on people," Tony admitted.

T'Challa hung loose in Tony's grip, eyeing the landscape as his armored teammate put on a burst of speed. The airstrip came into view, stretching two miles down the side of the island. In front of the hangar, a mixed group of colorful figures traded blows and energy blasts. But the real trouble, he saw, was down the other end of the strip...

"Doctor Voodoo," T'Challa said. "He's down."

"Yup," Tony replied. "And that puke-green plague spreading down the middle of the runway? That's a couple of hundred Hydra agents."

T'Challa hissed in a breath. The Hydras dominated the runway now, their emerald-and-gold uniforms staining the weathered gray of the tarmac. Two hundred Hydra agents, he thought. And all of them, like Dagger and the others, mindless thralls of Dormammu.

"Drop me over by Doctor Voodoo," T'Challa said. "Perhaps I can help him."

The bottling plant, with its gaping scar in the wall, came into view. Assorted machinery spilled out of the building: racks on broken wheels, a length of conveyor belt, and an enormous hose emptying onto the runway itself. Osdrink flowed out of the hose, forming a stream of green liquid spilling down the airstrip and over the side, into the ocean.

A pack of Hydra agents paused in their sprint down the runway, pointing up at the airborne duo. One of them squeezed off a few shots from an AR-15. Tony accelerated, soaring right over their heads.

"T'Challa." Tony hesitated. "Please remember…"

"Yes?"

"We're all expendable." Tony's voice, filtered through his helmet, was grave. "If it comes to a choice between saving Voodoo or containing the threat – well, it's no choice at all."

"We are Earth's last line of defense. I understand."

"Yeah, I know you do. Just reminding myself, I guess."

T'Challa tensed as they swung low. From the air he could see the fallen form of Doctor Voodoo, crumpled at the side of the airstrip, his body partly sheltered by an Oscorp semi truck that had been toppled over in the chaos. Hydra agents swarmed past, onto the runway.

T'Challa tensed his muscles, preparing to leap.

"Ms Marvel," he said. "She can do this. If anyone can."

"It's that last part that worries me," Tony replied. "Strange has been teaching her?"

"We all have." T'Challa paused. "As she teaches us."

"That makes me feel a little better," Tony said softly.

Once more, T'Challa glanced back at the ruins spread out behind them on the island. He tried not to imagine Wakanda, his beloved homeland, cracked and shattered like the citadels of Hydra. If they failed here, on this island – if *any* of them failed to hold the line – then that fate would surely follow.

He wriggled free of Tony's grasp and dropped to the ground.

THIRTY

The fiery countenance filled the entire sky, stretching from one horizon to the other – if there had been horizons, which there weren't. Flames fanned out in all directions from the blank golden eyes, the gaping, hungry mouth. Everything about that face screamed: *This is my domain. I am your Master.*

Ms Marvel almost laughed. What had Doctor Voodoo said, back in the workshop? *You will have no trouble locating Dormammu.*

She was running on fumes – exhausted, overwhelmed, barely able to process what she saw. The symbiotes were bad enough, a constant din of primal rage-hunger echoing in her brain. But the passage through the realms had stretched her to her breaking point.

This must end, she thought. We have to finish the mission!

At least they'd reached their goal: the Dark Dimension, in all its disorienting, brain-searing glory. Grassy pathways snaked through a multicolored sky, intersecting the orbits of several hundred rocky islets spread out like breadcrumbs in a three-dimensional duck pond. And all of it laid out under the burning, watchful gaze of their supreme ruler.

No, she thought – not under… *before* his gaze. There was no "up" here, no "down". Just a dizzying expanse of rocks, paths, and the shifting, brightly colored sky. Every now and then she caught a glimpse of a monster made of crimson stone, with four arms and a single eye, peering out from behind a large asteroid. The sight made her shiver.

One of her arms was still buried under the thick layer of symbiotes. She twisted that limb around through the thick goop, feeling blindly until she located the harness. The mechanism was still intact; the bomb still hung on her back.

The bomb, she knew, that would certainly end her life.

She eyed the looming face with nervous curiosity. Dormammu didn't move, didn't speak, didn't seemed to acknowledge her presence at all. Was he just preoccupied with the affairs of a thousand realms, events beyond all human understanding? Or – the terrible thought struck her – did this godlike being know something she didn't? That, despite all the Avengers' advanced technology, magic, and meticulous planning, she really posed no threat to him at all?

"Whoa!" Spider-Man said, winking into existence behind her. "That was quite a trip. Good thing I've got my trusty Lantern."

Ms Marvel didn't answer. The symbiotes, she noticed, didn't seem to care about Dormammu any more than he cared about them. Their thoughts were all focused on one thing: Venom. Venom. *Venom…*

"So," Spider-Man continued. "I hate to bring this up, but maybe it's time for some crazy bomb action?"

She peered closer. Those rocks, she remembered, were the homes of thousands of innocent people. The people Doctor Strange had told her about. And on one of them–

"Eddie," she said, her eyes going wide. "Eddie Brock is down there."

"Oh yeah," Spider-Man replied. "Well, be careful. You know he might not be all *yeah I guess we're moving now!*"

She was already in motion, speeding down toward a virtual meteor shower of rocks. Or rather, the *symbiotes* were in motion. She probably couldn't have stopped them if she'd tried, so she just gritted her teeth and let them run the show.

"Slow down!" Spider-Man called, the Lantern swinging in his hand. "I want to find him too, you know!"

The symbiotes did not slow down. As they swung past a large rock, Ms Marvel caught sight of several dozen people in robes and gowns watching from the parapet of a medieval castle. Another rock whizzed by, this one covered entirely by a stone maze with interlocking doors.

"Shouldn't, ahh…" Spider-Man shot out a web, swinging himself around a small, boulder-sized rock in the air. "Shouldn't we be worrying about the giant burning sky face a little more?"

"It doesn't seem worried about us!" Ms Marvel yelled back.

"Still! Giant sky face – oh wait. Hold up!" He pointed. "There he is!"

She stretched her neck out, extending her head farther forward. Up ahead, on a small asteroid that was barely more than a slab, Eddie Brock lay still. His arms and legs had been lashed to the rock, a thick cable around his neck. His face was visible, but the Venom symbiote's oily substance still coated his legs and torso.

The creatures within her screamed in outrage. Who, they cried, has done this to our brother? What deadly enemy bears responsibility for this offense?

Duh, Ms Marvel thought. Look up in the sky, guys!

Spider-Man fired off a web, which struck the rock right next to Eddie's bruised, very human-looking head. Spidey yanked on the line, pulling himself in for a landing on the small boulder. He shifted the Lantern to his shoulder and crouched down to examine his one-time friend.

Ms Marvel followed, coming to a stop just above them. Or beside them, or something! In any case, there wasn't room enough for her balloon-like, symbiote-covered form on Asteroid Venom.

"Eddie," Spider-Man said, leaning down. "Oh, man, I found you. I can't believe it."

Inside Ms Marvel, an inhuman voice snarled: *WE found him.*

Eddie Brock squirmed, agitated. Bruises covered his face; one cheek was split and bloody. His lips moved slightly, but his eyes stayed closed.

The symbiotes responded, flaring with anger. They could feel Eddie's pain, his confusion. They struggled, along with him, against the bonds that held their brother–

"Easy," Spider-Man said, grabbing hold of the thick cables fastening Eddie to the rock. "Let me just get you free, and then we'll– "

"NO!"

All at once, Eddie went Full Symbiote. The plasma-stuff stretched up to cover his head, concealing his face. The wide jaws of Venom took form, sprouting a deadly array of sharp teeth. The creature's monstrous tongue lashed out, hungry and desperate.

"D-dude?" Spider-Man said, flinching away.

"No more visions, Dormammu," Venom said, flailing and struggling against his bonds. "No more demons, no more tortures!"

Ms Marvel's head exploded with anger, with violence, with thoughts born of ancient, alien hunger. The symbiotes, dozens of them, relived Eddie's ordeal – an endless parade of horrors, a subjective eternity of torment at Dormammu's hands.

And they screamed, a piercing wail that sliced through her brain. They didn't care, now, about the bomb, the plan, or the billion realms that hung in the balance. They didn't even care whether they lived or died.

All they wanted was to kill.

Through the haze of symbiote rage, she saw Spider-Man weaving, dancing, dodging to avoid the snapping jaws and lashing tentacles of his one-time friend. She knew he wanted to save Eddie Brock, just as she did, to rescue him from this terrible fate. Assuming, she thought grimly, that any of us get out of here alive!

But Eddie was lost to madness. Kamala was perilously close to losing her own mind, too. And in the sky, the eyes of a god followed their every move. The cruel fiery eyes of the Master, who'd lured them here to his realm – and who now watched with cold, distant pleasure as his enemies threatened to tear each other apart.

Doctor Strange hovered just above the floor of the workshop, legs crossed beneath him. All his energy, his focus, was directed at the shimmering portal across the room, kept open by the flow of mystic power streaming from his outstretched fingers.

He glanced briefly at the accumulation chamber, now standing empty in the center of the room. The mission had taken an unexpected turn. Ms Marvel had seized the initiative, foolishly risking her life to take on the symbiotes. And then

Spider-Man, equally foolishly, had launched himself through the portal after her.

That meant *two* Shadow Avengers would probably die, instead of one. As leader, that burden sat squarely on Strange's shoulders.

Once again, as in the early days of Dormammu's reign, he felt an enormous weight pulling him down. He had found new allies, yes, but still he held the lives of everyone on Earth in his hands. Everything depended on keeping this portal open.

Dormammu, he realized, would know that too. Which made Strange a uniquely vulnerable target. True, he had resources he hadn't yet shared with the others. But that didn't stop the cold specter of fear from creeping up his spine.

He resolved to discipline his mind, calling up meditation techniques devised by ancient Tibetan monks. Trying not to think of the risk to himself; of his friends who might be dying in a far-off dimension; or of his teammates who faced an army of mind-controlled enemies, half a world away.

But even at this desperate time, Strange was reminded that the universe has its own bizarre sense of humor. For just as he pushed all thought of Hydra Island, of Tony Stark and Ms Marvel and Doctor Voodoo, out of his mind – at the very moment he vowed to die, if necessary, to carry out his part of the mission – a desperate message reached him, borne on dark etheric winds:

Hurry, Stephen. Tell our friends to hurry!

THIRTY-ONE

Tony Stark paused in the air, watching as the Black Panther landed gracefully on the tarmac. T'Challa looked around quickly, then took hold of Doctor Voodoo by both shoulders and hoisted him to his feet. Voodoo shook his head, blinked, and allowed T'Challa to lead him behind a row of Oscorp trucks, out of sight of the oncoming Hydra horde.

They'll be back in action soon, Tony thought. *I hope.*

He turned, climbed a few feet up into the air, and shot off down the airstrip. Down the other end of the island, he knew, Luke Cage needed backup. Badly.

Hydra agents charged down the runway below, paralleling Tony's path, splashing and stomping in the flowing Osdrink. One Hydra agent dropped to his knees in a green puddle, raised his particle-beam rifle, and fired upward. Tony dodged the beam easily, then shot off a repulsor to take the man down. The other Hydras started to flee. Tony knocked a few more of them out of action, just for good measure.

He didn't want to hurt them, though. Sure, they were villains, capable of all sorts of atrocities on their own. But they *weren't* on their own, not today. Their minds were totally, utterly under Dormammu's control.

Besides, he couldn't stop them all – there were just too many. And, he thought grimly, we're running out of heroes. He'd expected to have Ms Marvel on the team, but... there was no time to think about that. What about Spider-Man? If Ms Marvel had taken his place in the Dark Dimension, then where the hell was he?

The hangar came into view at the far end of the island: a squat structure three stories high with a flat roof. The airstrip came to an abrupt end just past it, terminating at a tall, reinforced brick wall.

In front of the hangar, Luke Cage stood with legs wide and arms crossed over his chest, like some giant immovable redwood. Hydra agents assaulted him on all sides, grabbing his arms and legs, firing weapons point-blank, even bashing him with clubs. Cage remained perfectly still, his steel-hard skin protecting him from every attack. Occasionally, he reached out and flung a Hydra agent out onto the runway.

"Cage!" Tony called. "You holding up?"

"All good." Cage grimaced, pausing to break a Hydra agent's nose. "I miss the city," he added.

"I hear that–"

"Boss?" Friday cut in.

A small window appeared on his helmet's display. He blinked at it, and it expanded to show a scene some distance inland, in the wreckage of the Hydra complex. Cloak and Dagger were picking their way through the forest, heading this way. Eyes glowing green, of course.

"Hate to break this to you, Luke, but you're about to get more trouble," Tony said, swinging low. "Be there in a min*WHAAAAAT?*"

Something grabbed hold of his leg, astonishingly fast, and

swung him around midair. He caught a quick glimpse of a crimson glove, a white star on a thick blue chestplate. Then he was flying, uncontrollably, down the end of the airstrip… straight toward that brick wall.

Stupid, he thought – never let an enemy sneak up on you. Especially when the enemy is Captain America!

His armor let out a barrage of alarm klaxons – and then Tony slammed, shoulder-first, into the wall at the end of the runway. Bricks shattered, metal struts bent and snapped free, and he plunged all the way through into open air. Flailing, he fired off his boot jets, arresting his fall. Trying not to look at the rocky shoreline below, the raging sea beyond.

His body took a moment to remind him: *You are injured.* The impact had torn his stomach wound back open; hot pain coursed out from his midsection. But Doctor Voodoo's mystic "surgery" quickly reasserted itself, stanching the bleeding and dampening the pain.

Tony whirled, fired off his jets, and soared back toward the island, passing straight over the pile of bricks that had once been a wall. He flashed out over the runway, turning to assess the situation. Cage was still under assault, off to his right. Hang in there, Luke! Tony thought. I'll be there as soon as I can–

–but right now, I've got another problem.

Steve Rogers stood dead ahead, both fists clenched. Imposing as ever in that star-spangled uniform, his eyes glowing a deep, furious Dormammu-green.

"Cap!" Tony cried. "It's me, remember? Your best friend? Well, uh, sometimes?"

Cap made no reply. With lightning speed, he flung his shield through the air. It grazed Tony's armor, sending a flare of pain up from his injured ribs.

"OK," Tony gasped. "So much for friendship." He righted himself in the air and fired off both repulsors.

Cap's shield flashed back into his hands; he dropped to one knee and raised the shield to block Tony's attack. The energy flared off harmlessly into the air.

"Come on," Tony said. "We're both Avengers, remember?"

Cap rose to his feet, snarling. Green fire leaked from his eyes. He took a heavy step forward, beginning a steady march toward Tony.

Tony veered sideways and took aim again. That tin frisbee is a wonder, Tony thought. But it can only block an attack from one direction at a time.

"Strike one, friendship," he said. "Strike two, team spirit. How 'bout patriotism, Cap? What exactly is it you think you're fighting for here?"

For just a moment, Steve Rogers hesitated. The green glow faded from his eyes. Tony could almost see a skinny Depression-era kid trapped inside those eyes, crying out for help.

Then the glow surged back, and Captain America let out a howl of rage. He lunged forward, sweeping his shield wide before him. Tony jetted up in the air, barely avoiding the attack. His armor could protect itself from almost anything – but Cap's shield was made of a unique vibranium-adamantium alloy. Its strength had never been accurately measured.

Tony reared back, fired – and struck a Hydra agent, who lurched forward at the last minute to protect Captain America. Three more Hydras moved in, taking up position flanking Cap. They raised their weapons, in perfect unison, and fired them all at once.

A trio of particle beams sliced into Tony, sparking short-circuits along the joints of his armor. Small electrical shocks racked his body; he shook back and forth, his arm and leg servos failing. He dropped to the ground with a painful clatter.

When he looked up, Captain America loomed over him. The three Hydra agents stood just behind him, grim faces hidden behind those emerald masks.

"Cap," Tony croaked. "Cap, listen to me."

He checked his armor's systems: bad news. The displays all read REBOOTING. The suit was holding power, but the close-range Hydra attack had crashed all his onboard computers. It'd take at least ninety seconds for them to recover, and by that time…

Only one thing to do. It was dangerous, terrifying, and it probably wouldn't work. But this was Captain America, standing before him – his friend, his comrade, veteran of a thousand side-by-side battles. If there was the slightest chance of saving him, Tony had no choice.

Wincing, terrified, he flipped open his helmet and stared Cap in the eyes.

"Steve," he said. "Look around you."

Cap hesitated. His gaze flickered briefly to one side, then returned to Tony.

"See these guys you're fighting with? The St Patrick's Day fashion disasters with the oversized guns?" He gasped, forced himself to continue. "They're *Hydra*, Cap."

Cap's eyes went wide. The green glow faded again.

"You're fighting ALONGSIDE HYDRA!" Tony cried.

Captain America lurched upright, turned to one side – and vomited onto the pavement, narrowly missing a startled Hydra agent. A stream of green liquid poured out of his mouth, dripping down to form a sizzling pool.

The Osdrink, Tony realized. His system is purging itself of the poison!

At that moment, the lights on Tony's display all flashed green. He shot to his feet and fired off both repulsors, taking the other two Hydras out of action before they could move.

Hydra agents milled about all around them; in the distance, Tony could still hear the noise of Luke Cage's battle. But right now, all he cared about was Cap. The super soldier staggered for a minute, gasping. When his eyes turned toward Iron Man, there was not a hint of green left in them.

"You back with us?" Tony asked, jetting over to join him.

Captain America stared at him for a moment, blinking. Then he held out a hand to Tony, who clasped it firmly.

"I think I missed a few beats," Cap said, smiling wearily. "Bring me up to speed?"

Eyeing the Hydra agents all around, Tony quickly recapped the situation. He explained the island, the threat, the mission to the Dark Dimension. The attack on Stark Tower; the Hydra horde that had taken out Doctor Voodoo; the overwhelming odds Luke Cage was facing, right now.

In his shame, Tony omitted only one detail: the fact that he'd passively sent a young woman to almost certain death.

"Got it," Cap said, looking around. "So this is a Secure Crisis."

Tony grinned. "It is *so* good to have you back."

"Earth one-hundred percent conquered… Hydras all around us… an army of extra-powered people backing them up…" Cap raised an eyebrow. "Odds aren't good, are they?"

"Yeah, this is the kind of plan I come up with when I only have robots to talk to."

"At least Dormammu hasn't opened any portals," Cap said, glancing up at the sky.

The Hydra agents started gathering around them, two dozen green-glowing eyes staring at Tony and Cap. Slowly, the agents spread out on all sides, penning their enemies within a solid ring of yellow-and green-clad bodies.

"He doesn't have to," Tony replied grimly.

The wall of Hydras parted to let through a small woman in black leather. Natasha Romanoff, the Black Widow. She paused and blinked, the green energy flashing bright as she turned to stare at Captain America.

"Traitor," she hissed. "The Master will char you to–"

"Yeah, yeah, got it," Tony said, activating his repulsors. OK, Cap: back to back. I'll–"

"No," Cap said, raising his shield. "You go help Cage."

Tony eyed the Hydras as they moved closer. "But–"

"I sparred with Tasha just this morning. I know her tics, how the Osdrink has affected her fighting style." Cap turned toward the group, facing them head-on. "I got this. Go!"

Tony hesitated, then shot up into the air. He took one last look back. Cap was already wading into the sea of foes, fists and shield swinging in all directions at once. Tony felt a surge of joy at the sight: the living legend, back in action against overwhelming odds.

A quick survey of the battlefield took the steam right back out of him. Halfway down the airstrip, T'Challa and Doctor Voodoo had indeed rejoined the battle. But now they sat crouched down, back to back, protected by a thin mystic shield. As Tony watched, Voodoo gasped and the shield flickered. The Hydra agents would soon break through.

And the Hydras were *everywhere*. They covered the airstrip, swarming like a carpet of ants. Tony could barely make out the pavement beneath the flow of yellow-and-green uniforms.

As for Cage: he stood pressed up against the door of the hangar, dodging and deflecting fists, particle beams, and rifle butts. Luke had never really shown fear, at least not in Tony's experience. But the alarm in his dark eyes was clear. He knew he was losing.

We can't hold out much longer, Tony thought. But this is a brave group of heroes. It had been arrogant of Doctor Strange to appropriate the word "Avengers", but Tony had to admit: his group had more than lived up to the name today.

Cloak and Dagger emerged from the wreckage, striding out onto the airstrip. Cloak swept forward, glaring at the besieged Luke Cage. He swept his dark arm wide, and the Hydra agents paused in their assault, moving aside to make room.

Dagger stepped forward, bright eyes flashing. A cruel, alien smile crossed her face. Her hands flashed, crisscrossing the air before her, and a dozen light-daggers shot forth at once.

When they struck Luke Cage, he screamed. White-hot energy stabbed through him, spreading across his skin, bathing him in a blinding glow. He gasped and dropped to his knees.

"Luke!" Tony cried. He aimed himself at the hangar, dove low to intercept–

–then cried out, choking, as a pair of dark-clad, muscular legs locked around his throat. He flailed in midair, jets firing, servos whining to compensate for the pressure. But the attacker twisted those legs at just the right angle, sending a jolt of pain shooting through the nerves in Tony's neck.

The sky reeled, the pavement loomed closer, coming up hard and fast. Tony swore, twisting in midair, struggling to get his bearings. But even without his armor's screaming alert readouts, he knew exactly who had leaped off the roof of the hangar to intercept him in flight.

Shang-Chi!

THIRTY-TWO

They struck the ground together, but at the last second, Shang-Chi twisted his body, forcing Tony's helmet to take the brunt of the impact. Before Tony could recover, Shang-Chi chopped down with a series of karate swipes, laying him out flat on his back.

Pain, all through his body – especially those ribs, which seemed to have developed a whole new array of painful fractures. He looked up to see Shang-Chi's glowing eyes staring at him, the martial arts master's mouth twisted in unearthly hatred.

"*You,*" Shang-Chi spat.

Tony reared up, headbutting him. Shang-Chi flinched away – too late to avoid the impact of the solid metal helmet, but soon enough to minimize the blow. He fell to a crouch and raised both hands, beckoning Tony closer.

"Demon!" Shang-Chi cried. "Why do you plague me?"

"Everyone needs a hobby," Tony muttered.

Shang-Chi danced forward, drawing the long staff from a holster on his back. He jabbed and thrust, landing blow after blow on Tony's armor. Tony stepped back, firing his repulsors. The martial artist leaped and lunged, avoiding the beams. Tony couldn't get a bead on him.

Tony clenched his fists in frustration. Hydra agents surged all around, blocking his view of Cage and the others. So far, they'd kept their distance, but at any time they could decide to move in, all at once or in packs...

Shang-Chi charged, surprising Tony with an uppercut punch to his metal chin. The impact jarred Tony to the teeth; alarms rang out in his helmet. He fired off all jets, somersaulted backward, and whipped around to fire off his repulsors again. The Hydras retreated, forming a sort of open-air arena while the two heroes fought it out.

Once again, Shang-Chi dodged Tony's blasts – mostly. One burst caught the edge of his tunic, burning it away down to his skin.

Tony jetted a couple of feet up into the sky. Normally, at this point in a battle, he'd convert his armor to another Special Purpose setting – Samurai Mode, perhaps – or summon one or more remote-controlled armors to assist him. But there was no time. Shang-Chi's assault was too fast, too constant, too relentless–

"Why?" Shang-Chi gasped.

Tony turned sharply and looked down. For a moment he thought he'd actually injured the man – but no. Something in Shang-Chi's tone...

"Why do you threaten the peace I have found with Dormammu?"

All at once, Tony remembered his previous battle with Shang-Chi. The pain in the martial artist's eyes when the EgoMech had confronted him in the guise of his father. The desperate longing for what had been lost… for some kind, any kind, of inner tranquility…

This is no mere pawn of Dormammu, Tony thought. This is a good man – a man I must try to reach.

Before Shang-Chi could make another move, Tony pivoted in midair, lunged down, and grabbed hold of his throat. Lightning-fast, he knocked Shang-Chi flat and pinned him to the pavement.

"You can squirm all you want," Tony said, maintaining a firm grip. "You can jab out and find my pressure points. I bet you could cause me a bunch of pain along the way, too. But my armor still has eight to ten times your strength, and at a certain point that's all that matters."

Shang-Chi's eyes burned bright green. The pain was still there, visible somewhere behind the blazing alien rage. "Demon," he croaked. "You will pay. I vowed you would pay."

"Listen to me," Tony continued. "Just listen, right? I'm not a demon. I'm a person, like you. And I'm going to prove it."

He cast a nervous glance at the Hydras. They still hung back, as if they knew this battle was beyond their power level.

Wincing – thinking, *This is a mistake!* – Tony opened his helmet to reveal his face. Shang-Chi wriggled under his grip, trying to look away, but Tony held on tight.

"I'm not a demon," Tony repeated. "You're wrong about that. But you were right about something else you said, when we met before." He took a deep breath. "You said my armor weighs me down."

Shang-Chi said nothing.

"You were right," Tony continued. "Sometimes I get too convinced of my own cleverness, too weighed down by my gadgets. I used one of those gadgets to try and trick you, before – look how *that* worked out."

Tony could feel himself shaking. The words seemed torn from him, as if he had to make a confession. But he held on tight to Shang-Chi's throat. Was the green in those eyes fading slightly?

"You said something else," Tony continued. "You said 'The word *I* no longer exists'. For you, that's true. Your ego is completely subdued, because of him. Subdued beneath the will of Dormammu."

Shang-Chi closed his eyes, grimacing. "Dormammu," he echoed.

"As for me – I guess I've gotten a long way on ego. Even used it to snap myself out of the Dormammu haze. But now, I... aaahh, this is tough to say."

The struggles had stopped; either Shang-Chi had given up trying to break free, or else he was marshaling his strength for the future.

"An innocent young woman..." Tony paused, tears forming in his eyes. "A very brave hero may be dying right now, scared and alone, in an alien dimension. Because... because I thought I was clever." He shook his head. "Because of my ego."

Shang-Chi shook his head, as if he were trying to dislodge something. "What are you saying?"

"I'm saying, I think it's time for me to put my ego aside."

"If... if that is true..." Shang-Chi blinked, "...then why would you take *my* peace away from me? Why tear me away from Dormammu, from my father?"

"Because it's a lie!" Tony said. "Because you're a person, like me."

"Boss," Friday said, "the Hydras are getting restless."

He ignored the A.I. All that mattered, all he cared about right now, was Shang-Chi. Shang-Chi's pain, his relationship with his father, was the wedge Dormammu had used to conquer his mind. But now Tony knew it was also the key to breaking him free.

"We're all people," he continued. "We have free will – we can *think*. We can break free of the chains binding us, body and mind. If we don't… if we can't do that…"

Keeping one hand on Shang-Chi's neck, he reached up and swept his other arm in a wide arc – firing repulsors, mowing down a half-dozen approaching Hydra agents in their tracks.

"…then we're just like them."

Shang-Chi settled back peacefully onto the ground. When he looked up at Tony, there was a deep sadness in his eyes.

But no green.

"Yes," he said. "I see it now."

Slowly, keeping his eyes on Shang-Chi's face, Tony loosened his grip.

Shang-Chi sat up slowly, raising both hands. "I will not harm you," he began–

–then shrank back, lightning-fast, as a volley of light-daggers split the air between them. Tony snapped his helmet down and scurried away in the opposite direction, swearing. He recognized those gleaming knives – Dagger's weapons!

But before he could even turn to face her, a mob of Hydra agents grabbed him from behind. Tony twisted and kicked up, activating his flight circuits–

–and tilted in the air, lurching dangerously. An alert flashed on in his helmet: BOOT-JET MALFUNCTION.

The Hydras grabbed him, gloved hands pulling him down to Earth. They couldn't actually harm him, he knew – even damaged, his armor would protect him. But there were so many! He swept his arms around, scattering the nearest ones.

He didn't want to blast them unless absolutely necessary. At close range, his repulsors might kill them.

More Hydra agents closed in, circling all around, blocking his view of the airstrip. Eight of them grabbed Tony's arms and legs, forcing him down to his knees. Another man pushed through the horde, stopping right before Tony to stare down at him. Green eyes glowing through the lenses in that yellow helmet.

"Look," said the Hydra, eyes flaring. "Just look."

The mass of Hydras parted, moving in unison – an unnatural motion that reminded Tony of a sliding door opening. Tony looked up and gasped.

Cloak sat on the tarmac, legs crossed, his face obscured as always by his heavy-shadowed hood. Shang-Chi lay dazed on the ground, his head resting on Cloak's lap.

And Dagger–

Dagger knelt before Shang-Chi, tipping a bottle of Osdrink into his mouth.

"Shang-Chi!" Tony cried, eyes wide with horror.

The martial arts master blinked, wiped a trickle of green liquid from his cheek. He turned and met Tony's gaze. Once again, Tony saw the desperate pain behind his eyes.

"It's OK," Dagger said, tilting Shang-Chi's head to face her. "We're together again."

"We lend each other strength," Cloak added, his eyes flaring.

A look of terrible desperation crossed Shang-Chi's face. "Light-Child," he said softly, "and Dark-Child." Then his eyes, too, flashed green. "My family."

He took the bottle gently from Dagger's waiting hand and upended it into his mouth.

"You can't win," the lead Hydra agent said, turning again to glare at Tony. "We are too many."

Tony slumped down, the horror of the scene washing over him. It's true, he thought. Dormammu demands only one thing from his subjects: unconditional loyalty. And the world is full of people, an endless supply, who will grant that loyalty to a dictator in exchange for the smallest taste of security. For the safety of the womb, or of the grave.

And those people, in turn, can corrupt even the strongest minds. Like Cap's, or Natasha's… or Shang-Chi's.

"Boss," Friday said, "Mister Cage is down." The A.I. paused for a moment. "Doctor Voodoo and the Black Panther, too."

"Cap?" Tony whispered.

"He and the Black Widow seem to have pummeled each other into submission." Another pause. "Both down."

Tony stared at the scene before him. Shang-Chi stood up uneasily, supported by Cloak's strong arms. Dagger stood behind them, one arm around each of their shoulders. She glowed even in the hot sunlight, in the waves of heat rising up from the tarmac.

Suddenly Tony wondered: do I even have a *right* to stop this? To break up this – this twisted, makeshift family? Even if the cost is their own subjugation, their willing enslavement?

He caught a quick glimpse of flashing metal, of something like a metal hose slashing through the air. It struck Dagger on the temple, knocking her to the ground. Cloak followed, a fraction of a second later; and then Shang-Chi.

Tony struggled – and then, all at once, he was free. The Hydras released him, turned away, and took off running down the airstrip.

He barely noticed. He was too busy staring at a thick-bodied figure in green, standing triumphant over the fallen trio of mesmerized heroes. A figure wearing thick goggles, long metallic arms flashing in the air.

"Doc Ock?" Tony gasped.

Ock waved his metal arms wide, casting a quick glance around at the chaos. Almost casually, he reached out and snatched up a fleeing Hydra agent, dangling him from the edge of a single tentacle. Then, with a twitch, he flung the screaming man inland, high over the Hydra Base ruins. As he watched the Hydra agent's helpless descent into the jungle, a vicious smile tickled at Ock's thin lips.

"Surprised?" he asked.

Then he turned to face Tony directly. The smile spread into a rictus grin, an expression that chilled Tony's battered bones.

"Wait till you see what comes next," Ock said.

THIRTY-THREE

Peter Parker and Eddie Brock had been through a lot together – some of it good, a lot of it very bad. As competing journalists, they'd wound up on different sides of the infamous Sin-Eater story. As hero and villain, they'd fought each other more times than Peter could count. And after Eddie became the "Lethal Protector", they'd battled side by side against some pretty horrific threats.

Their methods differed a lot, in ways that usually made Peter uncomfortable. But something always bound them together. Maybe it was the symbiote, the other half of Eddie's Venom persona, which had also bonded with Peter at one point.

Whatever the reason, Peter's heart sank as he watched Eddie thrash and flail, held tight to the surface of his asteroid prison by the mystic bonds of Dormammu. The Venom symbiote's jaws snapped in the air, its oversized eyes glared at Peter's costumed form.

"Sssssspider-Man," Venom cried. "Not real – not reeeeeeeeeal!"

"Eddie," Spider-Man said. "Take it easy, man."

"Not real," Venom repeated. "No more. No more, Massssssster!"

Spider-Man shook his head. What tortures had Dormammu

inflicted on Venom, these past months? What terrible things had Eddie seen?

He looked up to see Ms Marvel floating in the shifting sky. The symbiotes covered her small form, giving the absurd impression that someone had covered her with balloons. Only her head was visible, along with that one hand she'd managed to free from the symbiotes. She would have looked comical – except that he, better than anyone, knew what those alien creatures were doing to her.

"They're agitated!" she said, looking nervously around at the roiling plasma covering her skin. "They're reacting to Venom's emotional state."

Spider-Man slipped the Lantern of Morphesti under his arm, keeping a tight grip on it. Then he glanced up, past Ms Marvel, into the depths of the Dark Dimension. Pathways cut through the air-like space, vanishing at angles that made his head hurt when he stared at them for too long.

But the main event was Dormammu's blazing face. It filled the sky, blank eyes staring, fiery mouth gaping wide. For a split second, Spider-Man thought he saw those eyes narrow, as if in reaction to something. Afterward, he wasn't sure if he'd imagined it.

Then some force seemed to lance right into his brain. Like a laser, or an icepick made of pure energy. He squeezed his eyes shut, unable to move, as a single unspoken word appeared in his mind:

HURRY

"Did you hear that?" Ms Marvel said.

"Not sure if 'hear' is the right word. But yeah." He opened his eyes, rubbing his head as the pain receded. "Doctor Strange, I presume."

She shook her head. "I wonder what it cost him to send that message."

"Whatever it was, we better listen."

They both turned to Eddie, who'd subsided a bit – he still writhed on the asteroid, but more quietly now. "I can hear his thoughts," Ms Marvel said, "through the symbiotes. It's all garbled, but he's calmed down since you stopped paying attention to him. If you try to free him again, he might not–"

"Leave that to me," Spider-Man said. "You just get that bomb ready."

She grimaced, nodded, and turned away. The symbiotes surged and bubbled as she reached for the bomb device on her harness.

"Eddie," Spider-Man said, crouching down on the small rock. "Man, listen to me."

"No!" The Venom tongue lashed out.

"Eddie, I don't know what you've been through," he continued. "What Dormammu has done to you. But I'm here, Eddie. It's me. I'm the real thing."

Venom seemed to grow calm again. He turned oversized, blank eyes toward Spider-Man, but made no further move to attack.

"Dormammu," Venom hissed. "He made me watch. Every conquest, every dimension. He bound me to this rock, forced me to watch him spread pain and slaughter throughout the realms. Every mass death... every shattered world..." He shook his head violently from side to side. "I saw it all!"

Once again Spider-Man was struck by the cruelty, the utter inhumanity of their enemy. Dormammu had exiled Daniel, Jericho Drumm's brother, to a limbo dimension as a trap, to lure Jericho away from Earth. But with Venom, the Big D's grudge was personal. He wanted Eddie *here*, helpless, in the very heart of Dormammu's power.

"I get it," Spidey said. "And I don't blame you for losing it. I almost went bananas just getting here."

The Venom substance seeped slowly down off the captive figure's head, revealing once again the human face of Eddie Brock. He stared up at Spider-Man, eyes wide with pain.

"It *is* you," he gasped.

"Yeah, it's me," Spider-Man said. "And I gotta say something. I was wrong about you."

"Wr-rong?"

"Real wrong. Super gigantic wrong, as wrong as a guy can be." He took a deep breath. "I owe you, Eddie. Everybody on Earth owes you, for what you did when Dormammu first attacked. You might be the bravest guy on Earth. Or, well, you're not on Earth *now*, of course. And yeah, Dormammu won anyway. But that's not on you."

Eddie frowned, a confused look crossing his face.

"Right, babbling," Spider-Man said. "I am babbling! Plenty of time for that later. You're gonna get sick of me all over again, man. I promise you."

Eddie stared at him for a moment, then turned his head to the side. "Is it him?" he asked. "I still can't... is it really him?"

The symbiote, Spider-Man realized. He's talking to the Venom symbiote!

Eddie nodded his head in response to some silent reply. The symbiote knows me, Spider-Man thought. It can sense my thoughts, nearby. It knows I'm here to save him.

"OK!" Spider-Man reached for the bonds holding Eddie's arms. "I can't get a lot of leverage on this rock, but I ought to be strong enough to—"

"NO!"

His Spider-Sense flared as Eddie's Venom persona reasserted itself. The symbiote stuff rushed up to cover Eddie's face, inhuman jaws snapping dangerously close to Spider-Man's face.

"Wh-what?" Spidey asked.

"Don't save me," Venom said, his voice distorted now by the presence of the symbiote. "Get out of here!"

"Huh?" Spider-Man blinked. "That's not how it works, Eddie. I owe you!"

"Leave me." Eddie gestured up at the hovering form of Ms Marvel. "Your friend is about to set off the bomb. There isn't time – I'd only slow you down."

"No way." Spider-Man reached, again, for the cables binding Eddie to the rock. "We came here to rescue you!"

"I won't be the cause of your death!"

Venom's tongue snaked out – vicious, lightning-fast. Spider-Man flinched, startled, and almost tumbled off the asteroid. He shot out a webline to anchor himself.

"You're saying… you'd kill me to stop me from maybe killing myself to save you from dying?" He stood up, shaking his head. "Even for you, Eddie, that's a new frontier of crazy."

"LEAVE ME!"

Eddie thrashed and writhed, the Venom symbiote madly forming teeth and claws all across his body. *I can't get near him,* Peter realized. *If I try to snap his bonds, he'll bite my hand off!*

"S-Spider-Man?"

He whirled at the voice – and once again, he felt the cold prickle of his Spider-Sense. Ms Marvel hovered closer now, her dark figure silhouetted against the blazing sky-face in the distance. But something was wrong. The symbiotes shifted and boiled, flowing in violent tides across the surface of her figure.

A few of them manifested teeth, briefly, and let out muffled snarls.

"They're furious," she gasped. "Venom... his mind is affecting theirs..."

"Kid," Spider-Man said. "Hang in there."

"It's not just the symbiotes," she continued. "Dormammu... oh no. No. I can see... things..."

"The bomb," he said. "Focus on the bomb. Get ready!"

"Can't. Can't move..."

He looked around, fighting a rising sense of panic. At his feet, Eddie snarled in fury. Above, the symbiotes raged and flailed in sympathy with their brother – paralyzing poor Ms Marvel.

And in the middle, as usual, stood your friendly neighborhood Spider-Man.

I've gotta fix this, he thought. Got to solve the problem. Otherwise, *both* parts of the plan are doomed – and everything the Shadow Avengers have fought for, all of Tony Stark's tech and the sorcerers' magic, will be for nothing.

"Help," Ms Marvel said, drifting helplessly toward the godlike face of Dormammu. "Spidey, *help me!*"

THIRTY-FOUR

Tony had fought a lot of battles, with many allies, in a variety of strange settings on Earth and beyond. But he'd never found himself in quite this position before: facing a swarm of heavily armed terrorists in the shadow of an eighty year-old airplane hangar, alongside a grim, battered Luke Cage...

...and the villainous genius, Doctor Octopus.

Tony swooped and shot through the air, picking off Hydra agents from above. Cage waded into the Hydras, slamming them with his unbreakable fists. Ock hovered just above Cage, balanced on two mechanical arms while he lashed out with the other two.

Bodies littered the tarmac – a couple dozen Hydra agents lay beaten and unconscious. Tony couldn't even see the fallen figures of Cloak, Dagger, and Shang-Chi anymore, beneath the pile of Hydras.

But no matter how many Hydras they punched, zapped, or slapped down with mechanical tentacles, more kept coming. How many of them, Tony wondered, had been working in that bottling plant, anyway? Must be a violation of labor laws...

"I can do this all day!" Cage yelled, pasting two Hydras

across their jaws with a single punch. "But I'm just saying, it feels like that's what we're gonna have to do."

Tony zapped a Hydra agent's gun, melting it to slag, then glanced quickly back at the hangar. "We could retreat inside," he said.

"Close quarters with these… these army ants?" Ock sneered, sweeping a trio of Hydras off their feet. "That's your worst plan yet, Stark. Which is saying something."

It was a cheap shot, Tony knew, but it hit home. He hadn't exactly covered himself in glory today. He fired off both repulsors, taking down three more Hydra agents.

"Why'd you even come back, Doc?" he asked.

"I have no more love for Dormammu than you do," Ock snarled.

"Still. When that Mindless One showed up, you turned tail and ran."

Ock started to answer, then looked down in disbelief. A Hydra agent was actually *climbing* one of his support tentacles, wobbling and wavering on the vibrating metal arm. Two more tentacles knocked the man free. He crashed painfully to the ground.

"Otto Octavius does not *turn tail*," Ock snapped. "I merely moved on to my next step. The next scheme, if you will."

"What scheme was that, Ock?" Cage demanded. "Hiding in a hole someplace?"

Ock turned out toward the sea and raised one metal arm to the clouds. Tony paused, rising slightly to get a better look. Something was approaching… no, some*one*. A lone figure in green and violet, surfing on a jet-propelled flier shaped like a bat.

Tony blinked, unable to believe his eye-lenses. He zoomed in to be sure.

Yup: the Green Goblin. The real one, this time.

"That job," Ock said smugly, pointing a long tentacle at Tony. "The one *he* couldn't finish."

"Norman," Tony breathed. "Norman Osborn. Is he on our side now?"

"I knew I could reach him," Ock said, sweeping his tentacles almost casually across a line of Hydras. "Norman is a conceited prig, but we speak the same language."

"Villain to – uhh! – villain," Cage said, landing another punch.

"I prefer to think of it as a frank discussion between two souls who understand the way the world works," Ock replied. "But either way."

The Goblin drew close, swooping high over the island. The Hydras noticed him, all at the same time, craning their necks to look up. They withdrew slightly in unison, their green-glowing eyes blinking in confusion.

"Under intense questioning," Ock continued, "Norman admitted he'd been chafing under Dormammu's rule. That the power he thought he had, as the dictator's pet, was essentially an illusion."

Tony shook his head, thinking: it took the EgoMech to shock an egotist out of his – out of *my* – stupor. Guess it took a madman to bring another one to his senses!

"To be fair," Ock said, "the attack on your home probably helped too. It proved to him that no one on Earth was safe from his so-called Master."

Osborn swooped down, glider sparking, and locked eyes briefly with Tony.

"You were right, Stark," he said. "It's time to fight my own battles."

"Norman," Tony said. "I'm sorry, did you just say I was *right* about something?"

Osborn ignored him, turning to reach inside the bag at his side. As he hovered in midair, Tony noticed something: the vial of Osdrink! Osborn was still wearing it around his neck.

"You've, ah…" Tony made an awkward gesture along his own throat. "You've got a little…"

Osborn's goblin-eyes narrowed. He frowned, then wrenched the vial free with a sharp snap and threw it to the ground. It shattered, the liquid flowing out to join the spill of Osdrink covering the battered tarmac.

"You know," Osborn grumbled, "I'd actually forgotten that."

Then he whipped out a large, sputtering pumpkin bomb, looked down, and let out an ear-piercing shriek. He flung the bomb into the middle of the Hydras, where it exploded in a cloud of gas. Hydra agents stumbled across the tarmac, coughing, scrambling to pull breathing masks from their packs.

The Goblin plunged into the mass of Hydras, swooping and screeching as he fired off all his weapons. Concussion grenades, smoke bombs, electrical pulses from his pointed fingertips. The Hydras shrank back, screamed, and began to retreat.

"Osborn," Tony repeated, shaking his head.

"Never thought I'd be happy to see that dude," Cage said, wiping blood from his face as Tony landed beside him. "I needed a breather."

A pair of Hydra agents flew past, slamming into the wall. As the Goblin, Tony recalled, Norman possessed enhanced strength as well as an arsenal of deadly weapons. Cage caught one of the men on the rebound, punching him one more time to knock him out.

"Don't they *work* for him?" Cage asked, gesturing at the Goblin.

"I think they work for Dormammu now," Tony replied.

"Nevertheless, Norman knows more than we do about the Hydra agents," Ock said, dipping down to the ground. "Their numbers, their weaponry, their fighting formations…"

"OK, OK," Tony grumbled. "You did it, all right? You did something I could not do. Happy?"

Again, Ock grinned. "We'll negotiate my fee later."

The Hydras scattered like a whirlpool, with the madly swooping Green Goblin at the center. He dipped and rose, lashing out with a seemingly endless supply of explosive devices. Like an engine of destruction, a Tasmanian devil with advanced weaponry.

Ock stumbled in surprise, edging sideways along the corrugated-metal wall of the hangar, as a fiery round portal appeared in the air. Doctor Voodoo strode out of it, followed by the masked form of the Black Panther. T'Challa paused to beckon into the portal, and his sister Shuri crept reluctantly out after him.

"I do not like this form of travel," Shuri said, wiping a bit of Osdrink off the tip of her blade.

Captain America chose that moment to run up, scattering Hydra agents before him with his shield. As the last obstacle fell before him, he turned to look up suspiciously at Doc Ock.

"See you're recruiting from the other side now, Tony," he said.

"I'm a free agent," Ock snapped. "Emphasis on the free."

"Good enough for now, I guess," Cap replied. "What's the sitch?"

"Well, Halloween came early," Tony said, eyeing the Goblin's spree of violence. "Thanks to the good Doctor Octavius. I think I'm now contractually obligated to point that out at every opportunity."

Ock just smiled.

"Osborn's really pounding those Hydras," Cage observed.

"With weaponry I helped design!" Shuri said. "Though I think he's almost run out of my special vibranium-enhanced pumpkin projectiles."

"Sister… " T'Challa cautioned.

"I manufactured a limited number," she snapped back, "and I did *not* give him the plans."

Cap swept his arm in a vertical motion, gathered them all together against the big hangar doors. Ock was the last to follow, a reluctant glare on his face.

"So," Cap said, "next moves?"

"Same as before," Tony said. "Hold the line."

Cap frowned. "I think we learned in Vietnam, that's not a winning strategy."

"We have larger problems than strategy," Doctor Voodoo intoned.

Tony turned to look out over the airstrip. The Hydras were mostly down; a final group of them swarmed around the furious Goblin. Osborn laughed maniacally, surfing up and down on his glider as he tossed more bombs down at his attackers. Amazingly, he'd almost neutralized the Hydra threat.

However…

A group of costumed figures strode down the runway, weaving their way around the fallen Hydra agents. The dark-clad Black Widow, her wrist-stingers blazing with electric power. The newly recovered Shang-Chi, his staff glowing bright green. Dagger, light-blades dancing on her fingertips; and Cloak, the Darkforce forming a swirling void within his imposing form.

And the one that made Tony grimace: Captain Marvel. She soared above the others, approaching the hangar at high speed. Her fists glowed white, her eyes a deep, blazing green.

"Dormammu's B team," T'Challa said, adopting a defensive stance.

"I think this is the A team," Cage said grimly.

"I have never faced the Captain," Ock observed, "but am I right in thinking that her power exceeds all of ours put together?"

"Well…" Tony began.

"She can be beaten," Captain America said, raising his shield. "Anyone can."

Black Widow reached them first, dropping into an attack crouch. Shang-Chi leaped down beside her, followed quickly by Cloak and Dagger. Captain Marvel hovered above, green-glowing eyes fixed firmly on Tony.

In the distance, the Goblin dispatched another group of Hydras with a vicious electrical bolt. He whirled toward the hangar, pausing briefly to catch his breath.

Voodoo whipped out a vial from his cloak and dabbed three dots onto his face. He stared up into the sky and blinked.

"The wind is shifting," he said. "A turning point approaches. But the war is not won yet."

Tony paused. He thought of Ms Marvel, of the terrible risk she'd assumed in his place. Of the sacrifices others had made, the blood that had been spilled in the name of freeing Earth from Dormammu's reign.

I'm not perfect, he thought. I've made mistakes, some out of hubris, some from plain stupidity. But as long as there's breath in my body – my aching, mystically sutured-up body – I'll keep fighting.

"For Earth," he said, activating his boot jets.

The Goblin swung down next to him, a pumpkin bomb in each hand. "For freedom," Osborn added.

Captain America's eyebrows shot up in surprise.

The others fell into formation behind them. And then, beneath the blazing sun, the last heroes of Earth charged forward to meet Dormammu's assault force.

THIRTY-FIVE

Doctor Strange's reserves were almost exhausted. He sat facing the portal, struggling to maintain its integrity. Had his message reached Spider-Man and Ms Marvel? He could only hope.

Behind him, along the enormous gap in the wall, the Shield of the Seraphim abruptly collapsed.

He turned his head to look, keeping both hands outstretched toward the portal. Sweat poured down his brow as he watched five hovering figures appear in the now-exposed gap, framed against the night sky. A muscular man in a full-face helmet, ray gun in hand. A green woman with a deadly sword. A fierce man holding two sharp knives, a long winding tree-creature, and a small furry creature holding a gun bigger than its head.

"Man!" Rocket Raccoon said, blowing smoke off his weapon. "Took my biggest flarkin' gun to get through that glowy rune stuff."

"Well, well," Gamora said, climbing past him into the room. "What do we have here?"

Strange hissed in a breath. In the best of times, the Guardians of the Galaxy weren't his favorite people. But this was hardly the best of times – as the glowing green of their eyes showed, all too clearly.

"Doctor Strange!" Peter Quill exclaimed, looking around at the assorted machinery. "What up, Doc? You Doctor *Science* now?"

They moved to surround him, their presence uncomfortably close in the crowded workshop. Strange ignored their chatter. He *must* keep the portal open, or else Ms Marvel and Spider-Man would be lost. Their lives depended on it.

"Dormammu sent us to destroy you," said Drax the Destroyer, his eyes flaring green. "In case that was not blindingly obvious."

"I am Groot," Groot said.

Quill frowned. "I thought you said–"

"Sort of," Groot added.

Strange grimaced, closing his eyes. The portal, he thought. The portal was all that mattered. But in order to fend off this threat, he would need assistance.

Invisibly, unnoticed by the approaching Guardians, he sent his astral self out into the air. *Help me*, he thought. *I would do anything to avoid putting you at risk – but I have no choice. As you guided me home from the outer realms, I must turn to you again.*

Please. I beg of you, in the name of all we once shared. Lend me your magic now!

The Dark Dimension teemed with life: monsters, animals, humanoids of all shapes and colors. Plants with acid-tipped leaves, flowers so beautiful they could melt the hardest heart. Old men who had lived their lives under Dormammu's thumb, and newborn babies taking their first squinting look up at the fire in the sky.

And all their futures – the fate of every life in this realm, and in a billion others as well – hinged on what Ms Marvel did next.

Which was a problem because she had an awful lot on her plate right now. First there was the Dark Dimension itself – a dizzying mélange of color and sound, a maze of disembodied pathways winding their way through an ever-changing sky. Then there were the hundred symbiote minds screaming constantly for attention, filling her mind with piercing wails of hunger.

All that, she thought, would have been more than enough to deal with. But as she floated in that dizzying sky, she could also feel the bomb mechanism heavy on her back. When she shifted from side to side, she heard the slow churning of the Stane Solution as it moved within its containment tube. The symbiotes felt it too, their minds cresting and churning with each new movement.

None of that mattered, though – because she couldn't activate the trigger mechanism. Her mind, her entire being, was focused on the godlike presence in the sky. The blazing, eternal flame of Dormammu himself, drawing her closer with every passing moment.

In that face – in the flames lapping the sky – she saw visions. Images of realms, a thousand billion worlds, all the places where Dormammu held dominion. A world of broken clocks. A jungle whose poison vines had been scorched to embers. A muffled music-realm, its crystalline voices stilled forever.

So much death. So much torture, so much destruction. She stared harder, helpless to look away, and witnessed the demise of a barren world – a distant industrial planet whose destruction had formed the first strike in Dormammu's campaign of terror. What was its name again?

Praeterus.

This, she realized dimly, was what Dormammu had forced Eddie Brock to witness. A thousand worlds gone, a million civilizations destroyed. And if it didn't stop soon – if the visions kept the same grip on her that they'd held on Venom – then she would follow Eddie right down into a spiral of madness.

Someone cried out nearby: Spider-Man. At first, she thought he was speaking to her, but then the meaning of his words became clear.

"All right, Eddie," Spidey said. "I don't care what you want. I need you."

A cry of anguish. She heard the exchange dimly, as if from a long distance away.

"Your *brothers* need you!" Spidey exclaimed.

Dormammu still hadn't spoken, hadn't acknowledged their presence at all. He's evolved, she realized. He's become something unprecedented, a form of life that's never existed before in the Multiverse. Vast emotions, thoughts so complex that they encompassed worlds, swirled around her in the ether.

She frowned, suddenly drawn to a strange… *feeling* in the air. Not quite sadness, not quite regret, but some sort of godlike cousin to those emotions. Somehow she knew it held the key to Dormammu's defeat. But as soon as she tried to grab hold of it, it vanished into the ether.

The bomb. The trigger mechanism. It was right there, at the center of the harness on her back. Her elongated arm could reach it easily, even through the thick layer of symbiotes.

But she couldn't move.

"Hey, kid?"

She whirled in surprise. Spider-Man was there, floating in the sky, his mask pulled up far enough to display an encouraging smile. And even more surprisingly, Venom floated next to him, a monstrous grin on the Lethal Protector's oil-dark face. The remains of his severed cable-bonds hung loose from his wrists and ankles.

She tried to speak, tried to smile back at them. But she couldn't move. Between the shrieking thoughts of the symbiotes and the all-consuming presence of Dormammu, she felt smothered, defeated.

"I know," Spider-Man said. "I know it's tough. But we're almost there. We got Eddie, didn't we? Now all we got to do is finish the job."

"You should have left me," Venom said, eyeing the fiery visage in the sky.

"Shut up, you," Spider-Man said pleasantly, as if he were talking to a little brother. "Ms Marvel, listen. Listen to me, OK?

"You said something, back in New York. On the *Daily Bugle* roof, remember? Man, that seems like a long time ago. I remember it, though, because it stayed with me. Later on, I think, it helped give me the strength to throw off Dormammu's control.

"You said you knew what it was like to get lost. 'So lost,' you said, 'that you aren't even yourself, just a… a wraith…'"

"A wraith among the voices," she whispered.

"Yeah! That was it." He paused, leaned in closer. "That's where *you* are now. You've got voices inside and voices outside, and you feel lost… paralyzed. You barely know where the world ends anymore, and you begin."

"Yes," she breathed. "That's exactly it."

"But you're still *you*," he continued. "And you can do this. I know you can."

"Come on, guys," Venom said, "help her out. Give her a break!"

She turned sharply, wondering: who's he talking to? Then

the voices in her mind shifted in pitch, and she realized: the symbiotes. He's talking to the symbiotes! Some silent conversation was happening among them, on a level she couldn't perceive.

And it seemed to be having an effect. The voices grew calmer, quieter. Not *very* quiet; the innate rage and hunger of a race of alien killers couldn't be cured by one peer-group pep talk. Quiet enough, though, that she could almost think clearly.

But there was still Dormammu. And that *feeling*, that strange emotion in the air, was building, growing stronger. As if something momentous was about to happen, and Dormammu knew it.

You can do this, she told herself, letting Spider-Man's words echo in her mind. Tony Stark designed this suit; a group of brilliant, though arguably evil, scientists built it. Doctors Strange and Voodoo enchanted the Stane Solution, giving you a chance to survive.

Now it's up to you. A billion billion lives depend on it.

A quick laugh escaped her lips. "No pressure!" she blurted out.

She stretched out her arm and flipped the bomb release.

Lights flashed across her back as the Stane Solution tube clicked loose. The symbiotes moved aside, parting to form a gap on her back, eager to avoid the deadly projectile. Doctor Strange's spell of dissimilarity kicked in, propelling the bomb away from her – toward the gigantic face looming in the air–

–and propelling *her* in the opposite direction. She shot through the sky for a moment, flailing, out of control. Then something grabbed hold of her one protruding arm.

She looked up to see the grinning face of Venom. "Hey, I gotta do something around here!" he said.

She started to reply, then turned as a presence touched her mind. That feeling again – what *was* it? She whirled, her body still covered with the symbiotes but less weighty, now that the bomb had been released. The bomb that, even now, was hurtling toward Dormammu… toward that gaping, inhuman mouth…

And then she knew.

The feeling – the emotion she'd felt, radiating from the godlike face filling the sky – it was weariness. Dormammu had conquered a billion realms, subjugated trillions of people, fulfilled all the dreams a twisted creature like him could possibly dream. And all it made him, in the end, was tired.

He wants this, she realized. He wants it to end.

She didn't see the bomb strike – but in an instant, the air felt different. The Stane Solvent broke loose, spreading its corrosive poison throughout Dormammu's form. The flames of his face flickered and began to strobe, flashing from crimson to white to a cool, weak yellow.

Far below, atop a castle on the largest rock in the sky, people looked up in hope.

The symbiotes seemed stunned, almost quiet now. She felt Venom tugging on her arm and turned to see Spider-Man, holding up the Lantern of Morphesti. The Lantern flashed bright again, projecting a smaller version of the multidimensional map that had brought them here.

"We gotta jet," Spidey said. "That Solution is nasty stuff. If we get even a speck of it on us…"

Venom frowned at the map. "*That's* supposed to lead us home?"

"I hope so," Spider-Man replied, "assuming Doc Strange is still waiting up for us!"

She turned once more toward Dormammu's looming face. It flickered, fading, as if its fire were simply running out of fuel. The mouth gaped open in the same silent scream as before, but the god's eyes seemed to stare directly at her now.

She couldn't be sure – afterward, she wondered if it was just a stray thought from one of the symbiotes. But she thought she heard, just at the end, two simple words emanating from Dormammu's fading form:

THANK YOU.

"Come *on!*" Spider-Man cried.

She turned, exhausted, and took hold of Venom's arm. Then, as the ruler of a billion realms dissolved into ash behind her, she relaxed and let her two fellow Shadow Avengers lead her out of the Dark Dimension.

And as she did – across the dimensions, throughout the infinite realms – on every world, real or imagined, that had ever existed–

THIRTY-SIX

–Dormammu screamed.

THIRTY-SEVEN

The death-wail of Dormammu was like nothing the Multiverse had ever known. It echoed from realm to realm, a deafening vibration piercing any and all dimensional veils. It cried out for endings, for new beginnings, and on every world, living beings gazed up at the sky and marveled at the dawn.

In a place of endless sand, tiny creatures poked their prickly heads up and shook them in wonder.

In a realm devastated by war, the survivors waved radiation-choked air from their faces and began to rebuild.

On Cinnamon World, for the first time in months, the air blew clear and sweet.

In a sky filled with clocks, ticking filled the air as Dormammu's foul essence wafted up and away, clearing the clogged machinery.

On Hala, throneworld of the mighty Kree Empire, the Supreme Intelligence felt his enormous mind clear as the dormamine drained from his tank. A Kree boy named Halla-ar blinked, looked around the stone chamber, and met the Intelligence's huge staring eyes. For the first time in months, he thought of a girl he'd known once, on a faraway planet called Earth.

And on the Earth itself, people shook their heads, feeling reason and compassion return. The past six months seemed like a dream to them, a drunken fugue they could barely recall. A lost night of vague, lingering shame.

They frowned at the DORMAMMU signs hanging from every storefront, every office building, every apartment complex. One by one, working alone and in groups, they tore down the signs. They ripped apart the Tribute Booths, using the walls and doors to build cabins, sheds, and homeless shelters.

In New York City, J. Jonah Jameson burst out of his office. "Night desk!" he cried. "Get me photos of Dormam... uhhhh..." He shook his head. "I mean, Spider-Man. Photos of *Spider-Man!*"

On the roof of the Order of the Golden Dormammu, the dark flame flashed once and winked out, the last wisps of smoke vanishing into a sky filled with stars.

And on a remote Pacific island, along a long cratered airstrip, outside the ruins of the once-vast Hydra Base:

The Black Panther and Doctor Voodoo paused their attack as Cloak and Dagger staggered, the green glow fading from their eyes. Dagger sent a random burst of light flashing up into the sky; and Cloak rushed to catch her as she fell.

Captain America grunted, locked in combat with the Black Widow – who stiffened all at once and let out a very un-Natasha sort of noise. When she pulled back, he could see that her eyes were clear.

She kicked him anyway, a powerful boot to his stomach. As he gasped for breath, Cap smiled. Things were back to normal.

Shang-Chi grunted as he sparred with Doctor Octopus – a frantic ballet of arms, legs, and metal tentacles, all at incredible speeds. As Shang-Chi felt the Osdrink flow out of his system, panic stabbed through him. *No*, he thought. *No, I don't want this. Father, I'm going to lose you again. Father!*

Then the weight lifted from him and his thoughts cleared. He leaped up and away, retreating to the safety of the Hydra wreckage. He'd have a lot of time to process his mixed emotions, the memories that Dormammu had stirred up inside him. That, he knew, would be a painful process.

"Hey!" Ock's voice, calling after him, carried a note of disappointment. "That all you've got?"

Shang-Chi ignored the taunt. *We have free will*, Tony Stark had said to him. *We can break free of the chains binding us.* It was true; with his mind newly freed, he knew it was true.

But Stark had not mentioned the price.

The Green Goblin watched, puzzled, as the remaining Hydras dropped their guns and held up their hands in surrender. He swooped down low, pointed at a toppled Oscorp truck, and turned to the nearest Hydra agent.

"That comes out of your salary," the Goblin snarled.

High above the island, Tony Stark tumbled and struggled, locked in a death-grip with the furious Captain Marvel. "Carol!" Tony gasped, pushing his jets to the max. "C-Carol – please –"

All at once she shivered and went limp. As they began to plummet toward the ground, she turned clear eyes to him and smiled.

"This one's on me," she said.

As the ground rose up toward them, she twisted in midair, positioning her own body beneath his. She struck first, taking the brunt of an impact that cracked the tarmac wide open, digging a trench several feet down into the ground.

The impact stunned them both. Tony passed out for a second, then he shook his head and crawled up out of the crater. He paused, looked back, and reached down into the hole to clasp Captain Marvel's arm.

"Thanks," he said, pulling her up onto the surface.

Slowly, in twos and threes, the various combatants converged on their position. Cap and Natasha; Voodoo and Cage. The Panther and Shuri, reunited, wide smiles on both their faces. A few ragged Hydras joined the group, shedding their weapons on the ground like discarded skins.

"Look!" Shuri cried.

Tony followed her pointing finger. All across the airstrip, the green Osdrink spattered across the tarmac rose into the air, droplets hovering briefly. Then it shimmered, dissolved into mist, and was gone.

"Is it over?" Cage asked. "Is Dormammu really toast?"

Voodoo paused, cocking his head as if listening to a silent voice in the air. "He no longer exists as such," he said. "Dormammu's essence has been scattered throughout the Dark Dimension. Whether or not this is a true death, only time will tell."

Tony approached, noting the distant tone in Voodoo's voice. "And Daniel?" he asked. "Your brother?"

"He is… relieved," Voodoo replied. "For the first time, his mind is at peace."

And then something extraordinary happened. Something Tony had never seen before.

Doctor Voodoo smiled.

Tony smiled back, then turned to look out over the ocean.

It was calm now after the dimensional storm, sun hanging low over rolling waves. No portals in the air, no Mindless Ones on the horizon. The sea itself seemed clearer, purged of the dormamine polluting its depths. Even the dragon had fled, leaving the island pocked and scarred, but at peace.

A trio of figures approached from the direction of the hangar. Cloak and Dagger, engaged in low conversation with Shang-Chi. The expression on Shang-Chi's face sent a pang of guilt through Tony.

I did something to him, Tony thought. *Perhaps more than any of us, he'd found a kind of peace with Dormammu, and I shattered that. It had to be, but that doesn't make things any easier.*

Shang-Chi paused as he caught sight of Tony. Shang-Chi raised his eyes – eyes clear, now, of Dormammu's presence – and nodded, just once.

Cap stretched his back. "I think I need a good workout," he said.

"Thought I just gave you one," Natasha replied, smiling.

Voices rose from the far side of the island. In the distance, Doctor Octopus stood on elevated tentacles, conferring with the madly swooping Green Goblin. The two of them pointed at the devastated bottling facility, gesturing wildly and miming explosions.

"That does *not* look good," Cage rumbled.

"Another storm rising," the Panther said. "Dormammu's passing opens new doors for those who crave power."

"Nature hates a vacuum," Shuri observed.

"Still," Cage said, eyeing the two villains. "It was kind of nice bein' on the same side for once."

"Doctor?" T'Challa asked. "Are you all right?"

Tony turned to look. The Panther and Shuri crossed quickly over to Doctor Voodoo, whose eyes had gone wide with alarm.

"Doctor Strange," Voodoo said stiffly. "He says… he says something is wrong."

Panic lanced through Tony. Ms Marvel, he thought. Oh no. *Ms Marvel!*

"What?" he asked. "Doc, what is it?"

"He says we must come." Voodoo turned blank eyes toward Tony. "He says *you* must come. Immediately."

A wrenching sound came from down the airstrip. Tony turned to see Doc Ock, in the distance, pulling a small glowing piece of machinery out of the wreckage. As he held it up triumphantly, the Goblin moved in to see, grinning. What, Tony thought wearily, are they up to? It could be anything – a Hydra weapon, leftover Dormammu machinery, even one of Ock's do-it-yourself death rays–

"Tony?"

He turned again, to see Captain Marvel standing with the Black Widow and Captain America. "We got this," Carol said, pointing a thumb at Ock and the Goblin.

"Whatever 'this' is," Natasha added, rolling her eyes.

Tony hesitated. Cage and T'Challa strode over to join the Avengers. Shuri followed, flashing her vibranium blade in the air.

"You deaf inside that suit?" Cage said to Tony. "Get out of here."

Captain America waved him away. "Go!"

Tony nodded, feeling a tear come to his eye. His longtime teammates, his fellow Avengers, stood by his side once again. They had his back, and together they could stop any threat that came along.

He was no longer alone.

But he couldn't think about that – not now. Not when Ms Marvel might be – might be–

"Get me to New York," he said, turning to Doctor Voodoo. *"Now!"*

THIRTY-EIGHT

The lights shone too bright. The screams seared her ears. Worst of all, though, were the thoughts. They scurried through Ms Marvel like rats, searing her nerves, filling her mind:

out out let us out won't go back no no no free must be free hunger hunger eat flesh eat creatures hunger hungry run wild run free hunt and kill hunt and feed

No, she thought, no no no, I can't do that. I can't let you go free!

But the creatures – the raging, ravenous symbiotes – wouldn't yield. Their thoughts grew louder, wilder, sending electrical impulses shooting through her brain. She screamed, retracting her head and hand back inside the symbiote shell. And still the din, the barrage of mental cries, continued:

did our job found your friend now you help us now you free us
NOW YOU LET US FEED

Tony burst through the mystic circle, boot jets firing at full power. Doctor Voodoo followed, closing the portal casually behind him.

Any other time, Tony might have noticed the Guardians of the Galaxy lined up against the empty accumulation chamber. He might have paused to exchange a few technical notes with Rocket, or lob a quick insult at the preening Peter Quill. Maybe even flirt with Gamora, at the risk of his life.

Not this time. He didn't notice the Guardians, or the anxious Spider-Man hanging from a webline attached to the ceiling. He barely even registered the still-gaping hole in the wall, the first rays of dawn just beginning to shine into the room.

All Tony cared about – all he could see – was a blob-like mass of symbiotes lying inside a transparent bubble, a sort of high-tech plastic pod mounted on the workshop floor. A thin nozzle, which he himself had designed, connected the pod to the large chamber that had once held the symbiotes. The pieces of tech didn't match up; the pod was dented and patched, with several layers of duct tape holding the nozzle onto it.

"Ms Marvel," he gasped, coming in for a landing right beside the bubble-pod. The symbiotes roiled and shifted, restless, within their transparent prison. "Is... is that her?"

"It is," Doctor Strange said gravely, wafting over on his Cloak of Levitation. "The plan worked."

"But?"

"But now she is in danger of being lost. Within the symbiotes, smothered by their powerful minds."

Tony raised his helmet, leaning forward to search the mass. He saw no hint of a human being, no trace of Ms Marvel within the creatures. Once again, guilt surged through him: *that should have been me! I could have controlled the creatures, kept them at bay. And if I couldn't... if I'd died in the process–*

–at least I would have had it coming.

"She pulled it off," Spider-Man said, his voice cracking. "But then, when the symbiotes got back here, they got one look at the accumulation chamber and ran wild. She started screaming – retracted her head and her hand, too, back into that, that horrible, horrible…"

"The wizard put her in some kind of suspension spell," Rocket said, creeping up next to Tony. "And I rigged up this spare cold-sleep pod we had in the back of our ship. We were kinda hoping the slimy blobbies would just bloop their way back into the chamber, but, ah–"

"But they won't go," Tony said, his eyes scanning the room frantically. "They won't be subjugated again."

"Would you?" asked Drax the Destroyer, a thoughtful look on his brutish face.

"She did it," Spider-Man said, dropping down next to Tony. "She saved *everything*. And now…"

"Now we have to save her," Strange said.

Tony turned to him, raising an eyebrow.

"That's your Deep And Portentous Voice," Tony said. "Normally it makes me want to punch you. But right now…"

"Right now, let's get to work," Strange said.

"Uh, Stark!" Peter Quill said, approaching with a nervous smile. "Anything I can… ah…"

"Peter," Gamora said, clamping a hand on his shoulder.

"Right." Quill turned toward the hole in the wall. "We'll just, ah, stand guard. Over here."

"Against what, exactly, are we standing guard?" Drax asked.

Shaking her head, Gamora led them both away. Groot hesitated, turning to Doctor Strange.

"I am Groot," he said.

"You're welcome," Strange replied. When Spider-Man turned to stare at him, he explained, "I freed them from Dormammu's conditioning."

"All but me!" Quill called. "I freed myself, months ago. Been working an inside job, ever since."

"Do you want to go out that hole?" Gamora asked him. "Right now?"

Tony ignored them, frowning at the pod. The symbiotes grew even more agitated, bubbling and simmering like liquid about to boil. He circled around to one side. Rocket took up position opposite him.

Doctor Strange stood at the tip of the pod, facing the big accumulation chamber. Spider-Man perched above them like a gargoyle, his feet fastened tight to the chamber's outer wall.

"OK," Tony said. "She's still wearing the harness, right?"

"Yes," Strange replied. "That's what's holding the symbiotes in place."

"For now," Rocket said. "But the way those guys are thrashin' around, all the power in your harness an' my pod, both, ain't gonna hold 'em for long."

"The accumulation chamber's circuitry is intact," Tony said, turning to study the large empty chamber. "That means it could send the symbiotes back home, through space. But they'd rather have an all-you-can-eat feast right here on Earth instead."

"Which we cannot allow," Strange said.

"There it is, Deep And Portentous again." Tony raised one arm and, with a mental command, extruded a sharp glowing point from his glove. "Atomic probe microscope," he explained. "It's beam is just a form of light – it'll pass right through the cover of your pod. So I can use it to remove the symbiotes, one by one..."

"But?" Strange prompted.

"But I need them absolutely still." Again, the panic, as he suppressed a tremble in his hand. "Otherwise, I might kill her by mistake."

"I can't get 'em no stiller than this," Rocket said. "I got the pod cranked up to maximum."

"Strange?" Tony asked.

Doctor Strange turned his head, acknowledging Doctor Voodoo, who took up position next to him. They each reached out one hand, mystic energy gathering on their fingertips.

"Spider-Man," Tony said. "You saw how the containment chamber works, right?"

"I get the basic principles, but..." Spidey hesitated. "Sort of?"

"No time for *sort of*! Get over to the control panel, far side of the chamber. There's a display you can use to activate it when the time comes."

"I'll help you, kid," Rocket said. He cast a sad glance at the churning blob in the chamber, then followed Spider-Man around the accumulation chamber, out of sight.

Tony jumped, almost burning himself with the probe microscope, as a flow of eldritch energy washed over the small pod. The symbiotes rippled, struggled briefly, then began to settle down.

"Whatever you're doing, Doc – Docs," Tony said, "it's working." He looked over at Strange – and jumped again.

Doctors Voodoo and Strange stood together, eldritch power flowing from their hands – and from one other hand, too. Between the two men, hovering slightly above the floor, stood the ghostly figure of a pale woman with short, shock-white hair.

"Clea?" Tony gasped.

Voodoo raised an eyebrow at Strange. "So, she was your mysterious ally."

"Yes," Strange replied. "Clea has been helping me all along." He flashed her a quick look, and she smiled sadly back.

Lot of history between those two, Tony thought. Clea was a powerful sorcerer, Strange's former wife, and – he couldn't remember – wasn't she Dormammu's *niece*, too? The life of a Sorcerer Supreme sounded pretty complicated...

"Stark?" Strange prompted.

Tony looked down at the pod. The symbiotes lay quietly now, barely rippling at all. He raised the microscope tool, activating it with a mental command.

"Here we go, kid," he whispered.

Without looking, he reached over and flipped a switch on the nozzle. "Spidey? Now!"

The accumulation chamber hummed to life. Tony hissed in a breath, aimed his hand down at the pod, and sent a micro-thin beam shooting clean through the transparent casement. When it struck one of the symbiotes forming the top layer, the creature began to bubble, separating from the others.

"Come on," Tony said. "Come on, Squiggy!"

With a *pop*, the symbiote snapped free and shot into the nozzle. A moment later it appeared within the large accumulation chamber, snarling and whipping around. A one-way hatch slammed shut, trapping it inside.

"Yeah!" Spider-Man called, from the other side of the room. "*Boom* goes the dynamite!"

Tony smiled grimly, aiming the microscope beam again.

"One down," he said, "a couple hundred hungry flesh-eaters to go…"

"Quickly if you please, Mister Stark?" Doctor Voodoo said. "We cannot keep the symbiotes still forever."

Another creature snapped free, then two more. They joined the first symbiote inside the chamber, massing together against the clear wall to watch Tony work.

He studied the pod. A scrap of Ms Marvel's blue tunic became visible, through the thinning mass of symbiotes. He leaned forward–

–and felt something snap. He gasped, stumbled, and almost fell.

In an instant, Spider-Man was at his side. "Tony? Man?"

Pain lanced through his side. "Rib," he gasped.

"I warned you," Doctor Voodoo said, power still flowing from his fingertips. "There is a price."

"Don't I… uh!… know it."

The Guardians took notice, moving in to help. Tony waved them all off, turning back to his work. Ignore the pain, he thought. Keep moving. He raised the glowing microscope on his glove and, with a superhuman effort, forced his hand to remain steady.

The next half hour was an exercise in agony. Every movement, every action he took, seemed to open up new frontiers of pain. His ribs cracked apart, one by one, as Doctor Voodoo's healing spell wore off. His stomach wound reopened, thick blood seeping out into the circuits of his armor.

He ignored it. He ignored it all. Because nothing was more important than Ms Marvel – than this brave young woman who'd risked her life. Who'd taken on *his* mission, using the tech *he* invented, who had suffered so much from the dice he'd thrown, the gambles he had taken – laughing, shrugging, thinking he'd always come out on top – that he'd always be, well–

–invincible.

Endorphins surged through him; stars swam before his eyes. He dropped to his knees, unable to stay on his feet. But he kept working. He would not stop, no matter what. And when her face came into view – when he first saw her eyes, squeezed shut, come clear beneath the thinning symbiotes – he gritted his teeth and choked down a tear.

"Almost there, kid," he gasped. "Almost home."

The first thing Kamala saw, when she opened her eyes, was her teammates standing over her. T'Challa, the Black Panther, his kind eyes looking down. Luke Cage, tall and proud, an unashamed smile on his face. Doctor Voodoo, his staff clasped firmly in his hand. And, of course – crouched in front of all of them, his concern obvious even through his full-face mask – the Amazing Spider-Man.

They looked so comical – the naked worry on their faces! – that she couldn't resist.

"I just had the strangest dream…" she began, "…and *none* of you were in it."

Cage and T'Challa smiled.

Spider-Man just shook his head. "I told you, kid: leave the humor to me."

I'm in Tony's workshop, she realized. Morning light streamed in through the gap in the wall. She lay in a portable hospital bed, her head propped up on a pile of soft pillows.

She felt a hand on hers and turned to look. Next to her, in a matching bed, Tony Stark smiled weakly at her. He lay stripped to the waist, bandages and splints all along his chest and neck.

Doctor Strange hovered nearby, shaking his head as he laid a bandage across Tony's stomach. "This is why I left private practice," he muttered.

"You made it," Tony said quietly, patting her hand.

"Looks like we all did," she replied.

"Is she awake?" a familiar voice said. Rocket loped over to join the group, followed by – to Ms Marvel's surprise – the rest of his team. Peter Quill in his vintage spacesuit; Gamora with her sword; Groot, on lurching bark-legs; and the lumbering form of Drax.

"Wow, you invited the space people," she said. "Is it my birthday?"

"I dunno, kid," Rocket said, "but if anybody deserves a party today, it's you."

"You mean…" Ms Marvel winced, struggling to rise. "It worked? The worlds, the realms… they're all free now?"

"Thanks to you," T'Challa said. "Even the villains of this world are back to their usual schemes."

"We just sent a couple of 'em packing, though." Cage grinned, cracking his knuckles.

"The Multiverse is in for a readjustment period," Doctor Voodoo said. "I suspect we're going to be busy for a while."

Strange looked up from his work, his eyes meeting Voodoo's. "Good thing there's two of us."

"Three," Voodoo said, tapping his forehead.

"Four. Remember?"

The woman's voice was so faint, so ethereal, that at first Ms Marvel wasn't sure she'd actually heard it. But Doctor Strange smiled sadly up into the air and whispered, "Thank you, Clea."

"Relationships! They're tough." Tony smiled and gave Strange a friendly slap across the chest. "Especially, I imagine, after you've reduced her uncle to subatomic vapor. Tell you what, Stephen, after you patch me up, how about I take you out for a good stiff soda water? Drown your troubles?"

Strange stared at him for a moment. "It's a very very sad thing," he said slowly, "but that actually sounds nice."

"Hey, where's Venom?" Ms Marvel asked.

"He split, right after we got back." Spider-Man shrugged. "He's got a lot to work out. Figured we owed him that much."

She nodded, settling back into the bed, as the others broke off into small conversations. The symbiotes, she realized, were gone. She couldn't feel them in her head, and the accumulation chamber stood empty again. Tony had sent them back into space, to whatever crazy planet they came from.

Just like me, she thought. Back from the Dark Dimension, from a realm she could barely imagine. She thought back, recalling the images – even as they began to fade from her mind.

"Kid?" Tony asked. "You all right there?"

"Dormammu," she said softly.

"He's gone," Spider-Man said. "You took him out, remember?"

"I know." She furrowed her brow, struggling to concentrate. "And I think, toward the end… right at the last minute…"

"Yeah?"

She looked up at the faces of her teammates. "I think he wanted it to end."

Silence, for a long moment, as they all took that in.

"Well," Strange said, "in my experience, the cosmic entities of the universe often manifest baffling contradictions."

"Deep," Tony said, rolling his eyes, "*and* Portentous."

"I'm just glad of one thing," Ms Marvel said.

They all turned to look at her. The Shadow Avengers, who'd been through so much with her; the Guardians of the Galaxy in their ragged spacesuits. And Tony Stark, the infuriating genius who was also – beyond the slightest doubt – her very dear friend.

"I'll never have to recite 'one nation under Dormammu' again," she said.

ABOUT THE AUTHOR

STUART MOORE is a writer, a book editor, and an award-winning comics editor. Recent novels include the *Marvel Crisis Protocol* book *Target: Kree* (Aconyte Books) and three volumes of the *New York Times* bestselling middle-grade series *The Zodiac Legacy*, cowritten with Stan Lee (Disney Press). Stuart's comics include the original series *Captain Ginger* and *Highball* (both AHOY Comics), *EGOs* (Image), and *Earthlight* (Tokyopop), as well as *Deadpool the Duck* (Marvel) and *Firestorm* (DC). His other writing includes prose and comics set in the universes of *Stargate*, *The Transformers*, and *Star Trek*.

stuartmoorewriter.com
twitter.com/stuartmoore1

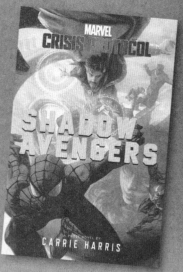

EPIC SUPER POWERS
AMAZING AVENTURES

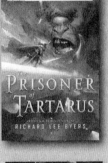

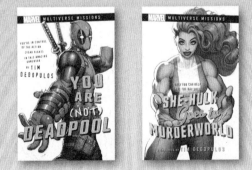